THE

CONSCRIPT;

A Tale of the Empire.

FROM THE FRENCH OF

ALEXANDRE DUMAS,

———◆———

Fredonia Books
Amsterdam, The Netherlands

The Conscript:
A Tale of the Empire

by
Alexandre Dumas

ISBN: 1-58963-753-4

Copyright © 2002 by Fredonia Books

Reprinted from the 1855 edition

Fredonia Books
Amsterdam, the Netherlands
http://www.fredoniabooks.com

In order to make original editions of historical works
available to scholars at an economical price, this
facsimile of the original edition of 1855 is
reproduced from the best available copy and has
been digitally enhanced to improve legibility, but the
text remains unaltered to retain historical
authenticity.

PREFACE.

————◆————

THIS book is a translation of *Dieu et Diable*, the last work published by A. Dumas, if we except the short story of Catharine Blum.

The author called the book "DIEU ET DIABLE: *Conscience l'innocent*," which the translator has rendered, "Conscience the Conscript," etc. to avoid trenching too familiarly on things our Protestant prejudices teach us to avoid, and because it was thought impossible to find in English a term equivalent to the French *innocent*.

Since the appearance of PICCIOLA this is one of the most chaste and at the same time most interesting stories which have been printed in the French language. It is essentially a book for the fireside circle, and as such is confidently recommended to the public attention.

Richmond, Va., July 20, 1854.

CONTENTS.

———

PART I.

Contents.

PART II.

Contents.

THE CONSCRIPT.

I.

THE TWO COTTAGES.

ON the verge of the department of Arrezes, to the
east of the little city of Villers Cotterets, lost in
the edge of that magnificent forest which covers twenty
square leagues, shaded by the most magnificent beeches
and most robust oaks of all France, is the little village
of Haramont, a perfect nest amid the moss and leaves,
the principal street of which ascends by gentle declivity
to the chateau des Fosses, in which the first years of
my childhood were passed.

As we advance in life, and in reality separate ourselves from the cradle and draw near to the tomb, invisible threads which attach man to the place of his
birth become stronger and more tenacious. The reason is, that the heart, mind and intelligence, the whole
being in fact, reacts on the spectre we call Time, which
ever forces us forward with a stronger hand and more
sensible impulse, as if our life were an inclined plane,
and as if obedient to the laws of gravity it passed
more rapidly towards the end, than at the beginning.—
Then man returns in sorrow, and cries and clings to all
that he weeps with ; and as every thing he sees has the
same proclivity, borne by the same torrent, he feels
that resistance is vain and desperate. He then reaches

5

after distant objects shining in the morning horizon, as the expiring twilight sometimes illumining on the opposite horizon the walls of some humble cot, or it may be gilding the windows of a splendid chateau.

Human life is separated into two different phases. The thirty-five first years are those of hope, the last of recollection.

Another mirage then appears in the desert we have to pass, the oases of which are rare. The reason is, that the objects which attract attention at the beginning of our career, when with brow erect and arms open, we pursue the fugitive goddess called Hope, objects, to which we scarcely paid attention, which we left unnoticed by the road-side, despised as too obscure, disdained as too humble, as soon as we have passed the intermediate sign, from the moment of the disappearance of hope, except through the medium of memory, while we yet continue on, because FORWARD is the desire of life, but with a drooping brow and hanging arms, objects we say re-appear gradually before the perceptions of the soul, and as it, the daughter of heaven appreciates them differently from the estimate placed on them by pride, their darkness becomes light, their humility greatness, so that we love what we despised and admire what we disdained.

And why instead of advancing, considering according to the caprices of my mind or the outbreaks of my imagination, looking for new types, creating new and unknown situations—why do I return sometimes in thought at least, to this home of my infancy, in which I find the marks of my shortest steps besides those of my beloved mother, which were measured by my own, from the day when my eyes were opened to that when hers were closed, leaving me sad and isolated by her absence, as young Tobias must have been, when the angel re-ascended to heaven after having guided him to the miraculous river, the name of which Moses forgot to tell us?

Well! to-day I will tell you what I saw at the commencement of that route, not far from Haramont, on the first descent of the road which led down to the little chateau of Haramont.

Two cottages, one on each side of the road, are separated by it alone, with doors and windows exactly opposite, smiling the one beneath a vine which covers it with a diadem of leaves, and the other beneath a profusion of green moss, which having decked the roof as with a cloak, adorns the walls with a robe of green.

Two families inhabited those two houses.

One of the families was composed of an old man of seventy, a woman of thirty-eight, and a lad of sixteen, grand-son of the old man.

Besides these was a large St. Bernard's dog; an ass and an ox completed the family.

These inhabited the cottage on the left of the road.

The other family had the same number of individuals but had fewer animals. It was composed of a mother, her daughter, and her son. The daughter was sixteen, and the son five years of age.

A single cow sanding in the out-house with a rack always full of fresh grass, lowed in reply, with her outstretched neck and smoking nostrils to the ox, to her neighbor, whenever it pleased the latter to bellow forth an interrogatory about news.

Perhaps the reader, if city bred, and if he has not led this patriarchal and pleasant kind of country-life, will be amused to hear me enumerate among the members of a family, a dog, an ass, an ox and a cow.

I will however say to them, my friends, you are too severe on the humbler portion of creation. I know very well that the benediction of the church does not reach them, that they have no salvation, and beyond the protection of law are pagans and impure; that the man-God did not die for them, that the church recognises no soul to them and does not permit them to pass its threshold to receive the universal benediction. Yet during the holy anniversary of Christmas our Saviour was born in a manger, the type of all humility between an ass and a sheep. Do you however remember that in the east whence we adopted this faith, animals are souls either enchanted or asleep : do you remember that India, the majestic and grave mother of our disputations west tells us of the revelation of poetry to the first poet ? As he sate pensive and alone he saw two doves fly by. He admired the grace of their flight and the ardor of their amorous pursuit. Suddenly an arrow from an unseen hand whistled through the air and killed one of the birds. Then he shed tears of pity, and his sighs measuring themselves with the pulsations of his heart, assumed a rythm. Poetry was born, and since then, verses, melodious doves flit across the earth.

Do you remember Virgil the profound and tender poet, when he deplores civil war, depopulating his paternal fields, when he pities the shepherds compelled to leave their pleasant meadows, thinks of long horned and white oxen, the race of whom has disappeared from Italy ? Hear him when he pities the sorrows of Gallus; after the gods whom he brings to console him for his fatal love, does he not point out to him his sheep which stand and sadly bleat around him, does he not cry in that melodious language which caused him to be called the

Swan of Mantua, " humble sheep; they do not disdain you.   Do not disdain them, oh Divine poet."

Passing from antiquity to the middle ages, do you remember the charming and pitiful story of Genevieve of Brabant ?   The wife denounced by a traitor, is scorned by the husband.   The child guilty of life, is repelled by his parent. A she-wolf shows the mother its cavern and suckles the child.   The animal has forgotten that pride of man has excluded them from the family of the undying and receives the wanderers.   A beast in the woods saves the innocent mother and child.   Succour comes from the humble, safety from the lowly.

Do you remember that manuscript of St. Gall which teaches us how we may lead bees when they are swarming back to the hive ?   Tell me if any more touching prayer was ever addressed to an intelligent being than to the Queen of the winged host—" I adjure thee, oh mother of the bees, by God, the King of Heaven, and by the Redeemer of the world, the Son of God, not to fly so high, but to return as soon as possible to yon tree ; there engroup yourself with your companions and with your children, and you will find a good vase prepared in which you may work for the glory of the Lord."

The peasant thinks not as you men of towns do. Animals at once take their places in the rustic family after the youngest members as in noble Saxon families servants sate at the foot of the table.   In Brittany even now they share in the joy and sadness of the family. In happiness they are crowned with flowers, in sorrow are draped in mourning.   Why then should those horses of Achilles who shed tears at their master's death, and the dog of Ulysses who expired when he saw the

1*

King of Ithica die, be deprived of the privilege of grief?

Look at the intelligent expression of some, at the dreamy air of others : do you not see there is a profound secret between them and the creator, a mystery understood perhaps to Homer when he wrote the myth of Circe. Does not the crow with melancholy cry, which lives three centuries, that is to say thrice the age of a man, speak in those sad tones of a past sad and sombre as his plumage ? Has the nightingale which comes from the south, nothing to tell us of the grand deserts untrod by the foot of man, it has flown over ? The eagle who gazes at the sun, the owl which sees by night, do not they know better than we, the one what passes by day, and the other, what takes place by night? In fine, can the great ox, who beneath the tall oaks chews the cud, love those long reveries and utter those painful sighs, if no thought crossed his mind, if he did not perhaps complain to God of man's ingratitude, of the elder brother, who contemns him ?

Oh ! the child, that flower of the human race, is not as unjust as man ; he speaks to animals as to his brothers, and in their gratitude they reply to him. Listen to a young animal and to a child. Listen to the inarticulate sounds they exchange amid their sports and their caresses, and you will be tempted to believe that the animal is learning to speak the language of the child.

Certain it is, that whatever tongue they speak, they understand and comprehend each other ; they interchange those primitive ideas, which tell us more truth perhaps about God, than ever Plato and Bossuet did.

Now let us return to those two huts, and seek to make our readers acquainted with the kind peasants by whom they are inhabited.

II.

The Cottage on the Left.

———◆———

THE cottage on the left, the one overshadowed by the vine, was inhabited by an old man of seventy, by a woman of thirty-eight, and by a young man of sixteen. It had at the door of the house a large dog which lay at full length basking in the sun, and in the stable, a neighing ass and a bellowing ox, and had for a master, although not the principal person of our story, an old man of seventy, who was the father-in-law of the woman and the grand-father of the lad.

The true name of the old man was Antoine Manscourt. He had however been a second son and from the moment of his birth, about 1740, to the day we write of, that is towards 1810, was called *Cadet ;* subsequent to his marriage and the birth of his son he had been called *Father Cadet*.

Few persons in the village recollected his original name which he had almost forgotten himself. The result was that his daughter-in-law and grand-son were called *Femme* and young Cadet.

When we come to speak of the latter we will tell how this surname, in consequence of the nick-names usual in villages, had again been changed, not like his grand-father's from the secondary position he maintained on the genealogical tree of the family, but from his inferior position according to the estimate of the other families he held in the intellectual order of nature.

Father Cadet was a true peasant, on the outside acute and shrewd as a Pacard should be, frank, loyal and honest as it becomes a native of the old territory called the isle of France. Perhaps it might be thought difficult to reconcile this frankness with loyalty, but one may remember that a veil may cover a face and yet permit it to be seen at the least effort made to penetrate its transparency. This comparison will exactly express the idea we wish to convey.

A peasant, the son and grand-son of a peasant, Father Cadet in the person of his progenitors had undergone all the changes of the soil on which he had been born, or rather from which he had sprung. As the soil had been slave, serf or free, he had been slave, serf or free.

In 1792, the soil became free, and Father Cadet became free with it.

Then he entered as a laborer, the service of the farmer, who succeeded as proprietor of Longfre, the monks who had owned the abbey of the same name.

By industry and by economy in the use of the two great necessities of country life, bread and wine, he had set aside the little sum of twelve hundred francs, with which towards 1798 he had purchased two acres of land.

Then, they said in the village as Father Cadet became a proprietor, that he had found a treasure. This was true: This treasure, received from God himself, was perseverance, sobriety and moderation.

One idea is deeply rooted in the mind of the French peasant, that of owning a portion small, so even as it may be, of the soil of France; to own a piece of land even if it be no larger than a cradle for his child or the tomb of his father, is to be not a mercenary whom Caprice fixes to-day and anger turns adrift on the next day. It is to be not a slave, serf, nor a vassal, but to be *free;* a grand and magnificent word which dilates the heart of all who utter it, which exalts man and makes him better.

About 1798 then, Father Cadet purchased two acres of ground for the sum of twelve hundred francs saved during the thirty previous years of his life.

It was not the best land of the region. Such produced three or four per cent. and was covered regularly every year with golden barley, with green clover and purple trefoil, while that acquired by Father Cadet long stood unimproved, was covered with stone, and produced almost nothing but thistles.

Then began the struggle of human labour with a barren soil. Bent over this soil from four in the morning until six in the evening, Cadet was seen pulling up thistles and heaping up the stones which he dared not throw on his neighbour's land.

Who knew but that some day his neighbour's land might become his own?

You remember the charming German ballad called Undine. It is the fable of the attraction of water on the fisherman. Amid the limpid stream he sees the face of a fair-haired nymph smiling on him and reaching forth her arms. Undine gradually approaches the surface of the lake, and her blue eye is covered only by a veil transparent as gause; her fair hair floats on the water and her coral lip breathes in the air a mingled sigh and kiss. The fisherman plunges in the water expecting to grasp the nymph, but she, on the contrary, drags him below to her grotto of sea-weed and shells, whence he never will emerge to see again his old mother who prays for him, nor his weeping children.

Well, to the peasant, the fascination of land is far greater than that water exerts over the fisherman.

If the field he owns be round, he purchases land to make it square.   More than one, alas! yields to this ambition.   He buys, and to do so borrows at six and eight per cent. on a soil which produces but two per cent.   Then a contest between usury and toil begins, and Undine with her claw-like nails often drags the peasant down not to a grotto of sea-weed, not to a palace of shells, but to the pallet of misery and to the grave of the pauper.

Fortunately for Father Cadet he was far too prudent for this, and had learned the maxim "borrow not but amass."

When the thistles were pulled up, when the stones were cleared away, when the time to till it had begun, he and his daughter each took a spade, put their breakfast and their dinner, poor they were, being composed of bread, cheese and a few fruits, in a basket.   Their drink was on the spot, from a spring which gushed from the mountain side; fresh and transparent as the sun, it wound around the field like one of the silver threads seen in autumn on a green leaf.   What else did he need? at the Sunday dinner the three drank together half a bottle, and the quantity was sufficient to remind them during the rest of the week of the flavour.

Seed time came and brought rest to poor Madeleine, Cadet's daughter-in-law.   Then she could return to her child who had while she was at work been left with her neighbour across the way.   Labour fatigued her much, but she dared not complain.   She, poor woman, had nothing but her piety and patience, and as her father-in-law fed her child and herself, she had to earn their bread.

In seed time however she was useless, for Father Ca-

det alone could do all—and be it said that whatever he could do alone the old man did.

Then came the harrowing. Father Cadet like all
industrious peasants, was something of a joiner: and
having purchased wood made a harrow. On the evening of the day of its completion, he told his step-daugh-
ter that on the next day they would harrow it.

It was necessary to cover the seed with earth, for
fear the November rains should rot it.

This was the hardest work yet. They had to harness themselves like beasts of burden to the harrow,
the weight of which was increased by a heavy stone.
To Father Cadet this was nothing, but the labor surpassed Madeleine's strength. A neighbor who owned
about thirty acres of ground, and who harrowed with
an ox and an ass, had pity on them, and gave them a day
and a half work, and the ground was harrowed.

"Thank you Matthew," said Father Cadet when all
was over, " you have done Madeleine a great favor."

"Ah! that is not worth talking of, but if you take
my advice by the next year you will buy an ass."

"There now is Pierrot," pointing to his ass; "a good
animal rising four. As I have just inherited a trifle
from my uncle at Yours, I will buy another ox, so as to
have a pair. I will let you have Pierrot for less than
his value."

Father Cadet shook his head and said:

"That is more than I can afford."

He however looked around and saw Madeleine panting
and listening to him.

He sighed.

"Exceeds your means?" said Matthew laughing, "then
it is not true that you have a secret treasure."

"Alas no! Had I a treasure, would I harness my daughter-in-law, poor William's widow, to a barrow?"

"True," said Matthew, who understood that neither the look of Madeleine, nor the tone of Cadet could be feigned, and that what he said was a sad melancholy truth. "It is true Father Cadet," said the good natured farmer, "and on that account I will sell Pierrot to you very cheap."

Cadet looked at Pierrot, who was a handsome ass with a shining coat, long ears, and a magnificent black line on his back. When he looked at him he dared not ask him the price.

Matthew saw what was passing in the old man's mind and hastened to encourage him.

"Ah!" said he, "he will not be dear and you will never have such another opportunity. You can have Pierrot for sixty francs payable in three years, twenty francs at each Martinmas—I may you see almost say that I give you Pierrot?"

This was true.

Anxious as he was to do so, Father Cadet did not beat down his price.

He looked at Madeleine who dare not meet his glance. She did not wish to impel her father-in-law to such an expense on her account.

"I must see," said Cadet.

"Look you, Father Cadet; to another the price would be eighty francs, to you it shall be sixty. I will not besides sell Pierrot without letting you know."

"Thank you," said Cadet. "You are very kind to us.'

"The reason is that you are good people and deserve the blessing of God. Therefore Pierrot shall be yours when you please. Forward Tardif."

Mounting Pierrot he rode home preceded by the ox, who aware that a sack full of fresh hay awaited him, did not need the goad, thus contradicting his name Tardif.

Father Cadet had said "I must see" not because he had not seen all the benefit he would derive from the bargain, but because he would not need Pierrot until it became necessary to work his land again, and till then there was no use in feeding him.

There was no danger that Pierrot would escape him, for Matthew had promised not to sell the ass without telling him.

Besides another thing was to precede the purchase of Pierrot. It was the erection of a stable for him.

The peasant had become a joiner to make a harrow; to build a stable he became a mason.

Fortunately he had now room enough back of the house, and there were countless stones in the fields. He had only to purchase a few sacks of plaster.

Without speaking to any one Father Cadet set to work, though the building of this stable in advance could only have the effect of making Pierrot dearer.

Matthew was a good man, but no one is so good that the devil does not get into his head at least seven times a day, and we make a low estimate, for if it be only seven times one is almost a saint.

With a calculation however which doubtless resulted from a secret ambition, he made the stable large enough for two animals.

In about three months the stable was built, plastered within and without, and a shed fixed on the outside and a rack within it.

On the day after the stable was finished Cadet heard an ass bray within it.

He arose in surprise and went to look. He saw Matthew who entered at one door as he came in the other.

Matthew waited for him and bowed to him in a mocking manner.

"Tell me," said Cadet, "did you bring Pierrot hither ?"

" Certainly I did."

" But I did not ask you, neighbour."

" No, that is true, but I saw you build the stable and I said 'Father Cadet has determined I see to buy Pierrot.' As I bought another ox yesterday and had not room in my stable for three animals, I said now is the time to fix Pierrot, and I put him in the stable.

" Still at the same price ?" asked Cadet anxiously.

"Ah! an honest man sticks to his word. Sixty francs you will owe me, twenty of which are to be paid each Martinmas for three years."

Father Cadet reflected for an instant. It was easy to see that a great idea revolved in his mind.

After a few seconds, he decided and said,

"Well for cash, would you not make some deduction ?"

"Ah ha! father Cadet, I knew you had a secret treasure."

"That is not the matter at stake. A question has been put to which you must answer like an honest man. Would you not make some deduction ?"

"Yes—I would make a deduction of six livres and pay for the bottle."

"I had rather you said ten livers and left out the bottle," said Cadet.

" Ah! true," said Matthew, "I forgot that you were a water-drinker."

" Wine does not suit me," said Cadet.

" Well give me fifty livres," said Matthew, "and I will pay for the bottle too."

"Very well," said Cadet, "wait for me at your house, whither I will bring the fifty livres."

"Yes," said Matthew, "that I may not see the hiding place whence you take them. Ah Cadet, you are fine as amber."

Matthew was as shrewd as Cadet, for he had guessed correctly.

Father Cadet deemed that to be the reason of his postponing the payment, all his protestations however did not change Matthew's opinion. He left shaking his head and muttering, "Father Cadet is fine as amber, fine as amber."

When Matthew had gone, Father Cadet shut the door behind him and went to the foot of the stairway to listen if Madeleine was in her room or not. Then approaching his bed and looking anxiously around him he took from a hiding place in the wall an iron box which he opened with a little key, tied around his neck by a leathern string, removed it carefully, as if he thought the fifteen louis d'or it contained would take wings and fly away, closed it, and replaced it, after having taken two louis, completing the sum of fifty francs with a thirty sous piece, he took from a bag and ten sous he dug from his pockets. He then sighed to see the two louis which were about to change their master, and set out for Matthew's house, passing through the yard that the sight of Pierrot might console him for the sacrifice he was about to make.

III.

FATHER CADET AND HIS FARM.

THE bargain was made, and as Mathew had promised was concluded at the cabaret of Mother Boulanger, the first hostess of Haramont.

The next year Madeleine had only to spade. This was hard for the poor woman who was not strong, and as Matthew worked his own land, he saw her, and again had compassion on her.

"Father Cadet," said he, "I have a proposition to make you."

Cadet looked anxiously at his neighbor.

"I know from M. Niguet, who is both your notary and mine, that you have purchased three-quarters of an acre of ground next to me, and paid in cash seven hundred francs in louis d'or. Well, for these three-quarters of an acre which are separated from you, I will give you an acre and a half which adjoin you. The land is not so good, but an acre and a half is double three quarters of an acre."

Father Cadet scratched his ear the offer was acceptable.

"Dame, I must see," said he

This we know was his word.

"Accept quickly," said Matthew, "for this will suit my arrangements, and as an evidence that I desire the thing to be, I wish to make a proposition which I know will suit Madeleine."

"Father Cadet," said she, "is master."

"Explain yourself," said Cadet.

"Well. Do you pull up your thistles and carry the stones away, and in the meantime, I will work not only your three-quarters of an acre but the acre and a half; as the latter is not very fertile, I will give you a load of manure in addition. What say you to that?"

"You must give something more," said Cadet.

"Hark you, Cadet, you are an old beggar, but that matters not, for I love Madeleine who was a friend of my dead wife. It breaks my heart to see her toil thus. I make her, mark you, her, a present of Tardif, who is too small for his yoke-fellow and not strong enough for the work he has to do."

"Tardif is old," said Cadet, who spoke at random, not having the slightest idea of the animal's age.

"Bah" said Matthew, "old! he is five years old and if I wished to kill him, the butcher would give me eighty francs. I have, however, had the poor animal three years and would not like anything to happen to him. For that reason I give him to Madeleine, who I am sure will never send him to the shambles."

"No, certainly not."

"You talk, Madeleine, as if the bargain was made," said Cadet.

"I was wrong, Father," said the meek-minded woman, "and I ask your pardon."

"You ask my pardon. You ask my pardon. I do not see why. Matthew is right. The bargain may be made. Yes, it may be made."

"Yes! it will be made. It is too much to your interest not to."

"Well!" said Cadet, "if it be not also to your interest, why do you propose it?"

Matthew looked at him in a mocking tone and said, "Why do I propose it? Because I wish to be useful to you, because I love Madeleine with all my heart, and because, if she had chosen, she never told you of it, she might three years ago have been Madame Matthew. She did not choose, though, but resolved to be faithful to poor William. One should not pout however for that, you understand, for she is an excellent woman, and therefore I propose to you a bargain so advantageous that you have accepted it, and would hang yourself if I were to retract my word."

"Yes, but," said Cadet, without making a direct answer to the question, "who will pay the expenses of the contract?"

"Well, is that what wounds you?"

"It will cost from thirty-five to forty livres, you see."

"There is a way to arrange all that. Niguet made a contract for you yesterday which has not yet been registered. My name will be substituted for yours, and to the same contract will be made an act of transmission of the land I convey to you. We will then each pay our half of the expenses."

"Hum!" said Cadet, glancing at the piece of ground offered, as if to see how it would look if it were added to his own.

"Well!"

"But if between now and the time you are to deliver me, Tardif the ox die?"

"If Tardif die! Is he likely to do so?"

"It is possible. The almanac says there will be a great mortality of horned cattle."

"Father Cadet, you are a man of precaution."

"Certainly: it is my character."

"Well; if Tardif die as I told you, he was worth

one hundred and eighty livres, I will not contradict my word and will pay you the money. Have you any other observation to make?"

" Have you any old ploughshare that you do not use, by chance?"

" We will find one."

" And if we happen not to harrow at the same time will you not lend me Tardif?"

" He will be lent to you."

" Well; then I ask nothing better. I come to terms at once."

Offering his hand to Matthew he said,

" *Tope*."

" *Tope*," replied the other, tapping his palm.

" Thus it is. I have given my word and I never back out from it."

" I think not," said Matthew, looking at him rather discontentedly.

" Never, never!" said Cadet.

Madeleine thanked her kind neighbor with a look, for she saw that for her sake he had made these sacrifices.

From that time Madeleine was excused from plough-ing and harrowing and would devote herself to house-hold cares entirely.

Father Cadet from this time really became a proprie-tor, for to the house he already owned he had added a field, an ox, and an ass: also a harrow and a plough.

The field fructified. From two acres it had become eight, and Father Cadet often said, like the Seigneur of Boursonne and the rich farmer of Lurgny, " My land."

If he had owned one half as much as they, he would have said, " My lands."

He had often thought of purchasing this pleasure for himself. But often as this idea returned to him, his self reply, a perfect revelation of his ambition. was heard saying " No; it is better to make it compact."

We repeat that by virtue of this axiom, Father Cadet had rounded and gradually and slowly by annual purchase had passed from two to eight acres.

He loved his land more passionately than he ever had his wife, than he had Madeleine whom we see he had nearly sacrificed to his land—yet he loved Madeleine.

He was on his land every day; and the soil is grateful. The more care one takes of it, the more fruitful it is. He thought of it every day from morning until evening; he dreamed of it at night. When his eyes were shut he saw the spots where the clover was thickest and the grain most abundant. This was in summer. In winter he saw any forgotten stone, any tuft of parasitic grass and said to himself, to-morrow I will throw that stone from the field or I will pluck up that tuft. Thus it was every day and every night.

Sunday, the day so longed for by the workmen of cities came; the day when God himself the source of all goodness as well as of all power, assumed fatigue in order that men might have a day of rest. Father Cadet would then say after supper,

" On my word, Madeleine, I will rest well to-morrow.

Madeleine with a smile would say,

" You will be right to do so."

The next day came, and the bells rang and said:

" This is the day of rest, the Lord's day. Rejoice poor disinherited children of society. Forget the fatigue of yesterday, forget what awaits you to-morrow, deck yourselves in your best and breathe freely between two days of toil."

At the sound of the bell, while Madeleine with her prayer-book in her hand, went to the church where her son served the mass. Father Cadet put on his best coat, it was brown, and his wedding coat, put on his dress breeches, his cotton stockings in summer, and grey woolen ones in winter. He then sate awhile on the threshold of his door uncertain what he would do. The passers by would say :

"Father Cadet, come play with us a match at this and that game—Father Cadet, drink a cup with us."

To each of these propositions, the one more attractive than the other, Cadet shook his head and replied,

"I have not the time."

And why?

Because on Sunday, the day of rest, Father Cadet had a walk to make a visit . . . .

To his mistress, his land

On this day he did not, it is true, go directly to it as on other days, but took a street which lengthened the way by two hundred paces. He sometimes went out of the other extremity of the village, and passed around it. Then he was a quarter of an hour longer.

The real object of the walk, however, was always the same. It was then in vain that Cadet said,

"I will not go to the farm to-day. God knows I go often enough in the week."

Yes, Father Cadet, and because you go thither every day in the week, is the reason why you will go to-day.

In fact, without knowing how, when, or why he had come, Father Cadet always found himself opposite his farm.

Be at ease, however—it is Sunday, and he will not work. He will not even touch it with his feet, as he may not touch it with his hands.

Ah! here though is the stone of which he has

2

dreamed. It is a troublesome stone, and he will be rid of it.

And he saw that very tuft of grass in his dreams. He will pluck the troublesome thing up by the roots.

Thus for one, two and three hours he looks on, growing momentarily more impatient. He hears the bell ring for twelve. It is dinner time on week days, but on Holydays it is an hour later.

He must go, or he will keep Madeleine waiting. For if he consumed half an hour in coming, he will need an hour to tear himself away.

It is not an easy thing, however, for Father Cadet to tear himself away. Before he has gone ten paces, he faces about, crosses his arms and looks.

At first he smiles. Then he becomes serious, and looks sadly for a long time at this insignificant piece of ground, so small in comparison to larger properties, which yet absorbs his whole existence.

The clock strikes the half hour and he must return. Having gone thirty paces, however, he faces about again, looks at his ground with a more sad and sombre air, at the same time more passionate than lover ever cast on his bride.

He then sets off with a sigh, as if he were not sure that he would find on the next day, his beloved land where he had left it.

Thus it was always one, or a quarter after one o'clock, when Father Cadet was in sight of the two cottages.

Not however to the cottage on the left, as one might think, but to that on the right did he look.

In fact, at the threshold of the cottage on the left, almost always awaiting his return, stood grouped two women, a young girl, a lad, a child, and a dog.

All this group awaited Father Cadet, for as soon as he appeared, all said, "There he is."

The two women stood on the threshold, the three young people stood on a bench, and the dog sate on his haunches, sweeping the ground with his lion-like tail.

Without going to the cottage on the right side of the road, Father Cadet paused, and taking his hat in his hand, said,

"Your servant, Dame Marie.   Good day, Mariette. Good day, Pierre.   Well Madeleine, come."

Then bowing, he replaced his three-cornered hat on his bald head, and went to the cottage which was on the opposite side of the road.

Then Madeleine said to the elder of the boys, "Come, Conscience."

"Come, Bernard," said the boy thus addressed, to the dog.

Madeleine then followed Father Cadet—Conscience Madeleine—and Bernard Conscience.

When at the door of the cottage on the left, all turned to smile once more on the woman, the girl, and the boy, and from every mouth came the words,

"This evening we will meet again."

We now know Father Cadet perfectly, and almost know Madeleine.   Let us now describe Dame Marie, Mariette. Conscience, little Pierre and Bernard.

IV.

IN WHICH THE READER IS TOLD ABOUT DAME MARIE, MARI-
ETTE, PIERRE, CONSCIENCE, BERNARD, AND SOME-
THING OF THE BLACK COW.

———◆———

DAME Marie was the wife of the schoolmaster, and
lived opposite Father Cadet.

One day with her daughter just three weeks old in
her arms, she entered the cottage of Madeleine, whom
she found dressed in mourning and weeping over the
cradle of her son, a babe five months old.

"My poor neighbour," said she, "they tell me your
milk is all dried up. Is it true?"

"Yes, Dame Marie, it is too true. Do you not hear
my poor Jean weeping for hunger?"

"Well, Madeline, do not suffer that to make you uneasy, for luckily the Lord has given me enough for two,
and my Mariette will be glad to share with Jean."

Without regard to what Madeleine said she took Jean
from his cradle, and with a child on each knee, with the
sublime disregard of appearances of mothers, aware that
public veneration protects them, uncovered the two
globes of her bosom and placed a child at each.

Then Madeleine fell on her knees and clasping her
hands wept.

"What are you doing, Madeleine?" asked Marie.

I adore one of the great Christian virtues, charity.

Jean drank until he was satisfied of this great cup of

28

life, the only one with a rim of honey and with no dregs
of bitterness.

When he was done, Dame Marie said:

"I will return thrice a day to give your child as much,
and if in the meantime he cries, call me. I will not be
far, and will have the bottle."

She then gave the child to his mother, who after
clasping him to her bosom, replaced him in the cradle.

Alas! poor Madeleine thought she was become less
the mother of the child since another nursed him.

Why did the poor woman dressed in mourning weep?
Why had her milk so suddenly dried up?

William, her husband, a soldier of 1792, after having
passed a fortnight with her, while on his way from La
Vendee to Italy had been killed at Monte-Notte.

She had learned the news three days before by a letter which William, when in the agony of death, had
caused a comrade to write to his wife, and the shock
was so violent that her milk had dried up.

She had noticed it on the previous evening, and at
first could not realize this new misfortune. She could
not believe that a mother's bosom would be exhausted
of milk as long as her veins contained blood. Her
child's cries, however, had most unwillingly convinced
her.

She wept with grief, as Jean did from hunger—
but Dame Marie, with Mariette in her arms, at once
relieved the child's hunger and thirst.

Now why did they call her simply Madeleine and
Marie, Dame Marie?

Not because the latter, poor woman, was either
proud or wealthy. She was in fact almost as poor as
the humblest in the village. She was the wife of the
village schoolmaster—and as in the eyes of children he

is a great character, they called him Monsieur Pierre, and his wife Dame Marie.

Both husband and wife for a time had been thought rich; this was true when France, France regenerated, popular France, declared by the voice of the Convention, that the teacher was sacerdotal in character, and that the schoolmaster who instructs the mind was the equal of the priest who purifies the soul; it was when, during the terrible famine of 1795, it voted 11 Brumaire, Year 9, at the instance of Lackanas, fifty-four millions for primary instruction. The austere and bloody matron lost her honor. The Directory succeeded her, and what mattered it to the Directory, that schoolmasters died of hunger, and those the people paid the least were exactly its teachers—that is to say, those who contributed most to its intelligence and liberty?

Thus Dame Marie became Jean's second mother.

He grew up half on her knee and half on his mother's. On the other hand, Madeleine loved Mariette as if she were her daughter, and often carried her in her arms, while Dame Marie held Jean. One sometimes carried both. There was an exchange of love between the two women, though neither had ever calculated which was in advance, and which in arrears, on the mutual account of charity.

Mariette grew like a field flower, like a violet amid the grass, like a daisy in the grain. She called Jean her brother, and Jean called her sister.

Jean did not grow in the same manner. He did not speak as Mariette did, and did not seem to live in the same manner. Jean lived a strange, interior, almost vegetative life. Jean was not a child of this world, for what delighted and amused him, did not delight and amuse other beings.

His poor mother, who sometimes looked at him and shook her head, often in tears, attributed this phenomenon to the following circumstance.

When William, on his march through France, had left her, after his fortnight's visit to join his regiment, a deep feeling of sadness seized the poor woman, as if she was aware that she would see her husband no more, and that William had left her for ever. Sadness in pure hearts is the sister of religion, and always pious, Madeleine gave up to prayer, and passed in church every moment she could spare from her labor.

Now in the church was a large painting which had been presented to it by a rich Abbe named Conseil, who lived in the neighborhood. The picture represented Christ among the children, one of the most touching parables of the Testament.

The children seemed to bend their knees, and to kiss the hands of Christ. One only stood in the back ground with a large dog.

This one represented a parable not less full of piety than the others.

Christ reached forth his hand more kindly to him than to the others, and seemed to make a sign for him too to come. A jealous woman, however, said,

" Let him be, Lord, for he is a simple, and poor of spirit.

Jesus answered :

" Blessed are the poor of spirit, for of such is the kingdom of heaven."

This child playing alone with his dog, the simple, innocent and poor of spirit, whom a jealous woman sought to remove from the holy communion of love

preached by Jesus, had always engrossed poor Madeleine. She pitied the poor deserted one, and when she
knelt in prayer before the picture, she always looked
at the child called by Christ, to see if it would not
leave its place with the dog for whom it prayed, to
come with the other children to receive the blessing of
the Man-God.

Every day she said, as she left him thus isolated and
far from the Lord,

"To-morrow I will find him close to his side."

Her first glance, however, the next day, told her that
the position of the child was unchanged, and she murmured,

"Poor child! happy are you that the Lord has said,
'Blessed are the poor in spirit, for of such is the kingdom of heaven.'"

Let science, as it will, explain the phenomenon so
well explained by faith, but when Madeleine gave birth
to Jean, she said, looking at the child,

"Lord God, have you blessed or chastised me—for
my child has all the features of the poor innocent you
have called to you?"

Then she added, with a mother's holy faith,

"Ah! do not fear, for he will go whither you guide
him."

Jean really was like the innocent in the picture; his
fair hair, his great blue eyes, which seemed to observe
nothing that passed around him—as if a veil hung between earth and his understanding.

The resemblance was so striking, that all recognised
it in the child when his mother took him out in her
arms, and the women of the village, ever ready with
their pity, often more painful than their indifference,
exclaimed as they saw him,

"Jesus God! Poor little thing. It is the very fac-simile of the innocent in the picture."

Madeleine smiled, for in her eyes Jean was the most beautiful of children, and she would not own that even Mariette was so handsome.

Her anxiety, however, was very great. When one year old Jean had never spoken a word, and she feared the child would be dumb.

One day, however, she was at once delighted and surprised. As she ever said, "My God, enable my child to speak—let him not be dumb," the child remembered the word he had so often heard, and said,

"God—"

Madeleine fell on her knees and said,

"Lord, I thank you not only for what you have granted me, but that the first word uttered by my child was your holy name."

From that moment Jean began to speak, but not as other children did. Other children have, so to say, two tongues, that of childhood, and afterwards a serious language. He however at once began with the serious tongue. He however spoke but little, uttering only two or three words, and completing his sentence by a smile, a gesture or a glance.

Mariette was his only companion, and he was never seen with the other children of the village.

Besides Jean did not play—he dreamed.

He loved Dame Marie and his mother almost equal-ly. He loved Father Cadet with all his heart, and little Pierre when the latter was born. The rest of the vil-lage, however, we will not call stranger, but unknown to Jean.

He loved animals, and they loved him. What was there about the child to induce such animals to love

2*

and follow him? The obstinate Pierrot, who would often obstinately refuse to cross a rivulet or a ditch for Father Cadet, as soon as Jean either took the bridle or mounted him, became docile as a lamb, and obedient as a dog.

Tardif, who by his laziness often deserved his name, saw the child far off, and lowed as he drew near. True, the child never entered the stable without bringing his little arms-full of fresh grass and tender flowers, and Tardif then ruminated so voluptuously that one might have thought he had possession of the secret as to what grasses and flowers Tardif preferred.

The black cow was doubly productive to Dame Marie. Every year she bore a calf, and gave milk every day and thanks to Jean, who had taught Mariette to select the most savorous grass; the milk of the black cow was famous in all the environs. It often happened that when the calf was sold the poor mother became sad, and refused to let down her milk to those, who, to enjoy it wholly themselves, had killed her offspring. Then Jean would go into the stable, take the black cow by the muzzle, raise her head as high as his face, and look the dark-eyed animal directly in the orbits and would talk to her—what was his language? the Lord only knows, but the animal would low two or three times, and Jean would call Dame Marie. He would keep his hand on the animal, who submissive, if not consoled, would suffer the white cream it sometimes had retained three days to stream down.

With wild animals, however, the theory is very different. As Jean had never done an injury to any living creature, all except those the instinct of which leads them to do injury, loved him. One might have said " they fancied the child to be an angel passing over earth with a tongue speaking all languages in the name of the Lord." In fact, from the dreamy manner in which Jean lay on the moss or leaned against a tree listening to the singing birds, one might think from his silent attention, that he understood their song, and could have translated and explained it.

Mariette, who understood nothing of that tongue, would ask Jean:

"What bird is that singing?"

Jean would say:

"It is a nightingale, a jay, or a redthroat," for he needed not to see the bird to recognise it.

As he listened, Mariette would say:

"What does it sing about?"

Jean answered,

"It thanks God for having spared it a long flight hence to the pool, and for having deposited a drop of dew in that leaf."

Or else:

"It thanks God for having permitted the thorn by the wayside to pluck wool from the sheep, for the brood time is come, and with that wool the female will make her nest."

Or yet:

"It complains that some village child has robbed her nest, without knowing with what seed to feed her young, so that they will die of hunger."

So too, it was with the plants, grass, and flowers. Jean had never uselessly trampled a plant beneath his feet, cut the grass with his reaping hook, or torn up any flower; if by mistake he had trodden down any twig or any branch on which he had trodden, he carefully lifted it up, and said if he had done it,

"I did not see you; forgive me."

If another had done it, he said:

"Be not angry with him who has crushed you thus, for he knew not that you live and suffer and weep as we do. He has broken your stem, but your roots remain, and from them a new twig will put forth, which will be more fortunate, will grow and will spread its seed around you, so that next year, instead of being alone and isolated, you will have a family around you."

Thus it was when he cut grasss for Tardif or for the black cow or when he pulled a flower for the girdle or hair of Mariette.

If he cut grass before he touched it with the reaping-hook, he said:

"Not to injure you do I cut you; for it does not injure you to do so for a good purpose, but to feed the ox and Dame Marie's cow who famish."

The result of this faculty with which he seemed to have been endowed by God, was that he heard and understood all creation, that he was happier with the trees, plants, flowers and birds, in the air and rain of heaven, than in contact with man; thus while in their language, trees, plants, birds, the air of heaven, rain and sun, said as they sheltered, amused, and caressed him, "he is an angel" the villagers looked sadly and silently at him, and at the age, when children are play-ful and turbulent, shrugged their shoulders, or in the air of mockery said:

"He is an idiot."

Yet as he answered the questions put to him cor-rectly, as he never told an untruth; as he told the truth whether it was pleasant or not, they called him Con-science, instead of Jean.

The result was that after a while Mariette, Marie, Father Cadet and Madeleine herself adopted the name Jean bore in the village, and like other people called him Conscience.

I am thinking that it was a good name, a name after God's own heart. The lad gradually became unfamiliar with any address but Conscience.

V.

How Bernard and Little Pierre Completed the one, Father Cadet's Family, and the other Dame Marie's. How the Latter became a Widow.

<hr />

IN 1805 Conscience was ten years old, and I, the author, scarcely five. In 1805 my father left the Chateau des Fosses, about a quarter of a league from Father Cadet's cottage, for another chateau three leagues distant called Antilly.

After the campaign of the Alps, my father brought from St. Bernard a couple of those magnificent dogs which the monks of the Convent preserve pure with such care. These dogs were of magnificent size and looked like two year old lions. When we were about to leave Fosses for Antilly, the female gave birth to five pups, two of which had been given away, two left, and the fifth with the cruelty habitual to vulgar men, had been thrown out of the gate by my father's game-keeper, the name of whom was Mocquet.

Conscience, who was always wandering about, chanced to pass in that direction, and having heard the cries of the whelp, picked it up and carried it not to the cottage of Father Cadet, for he was not sure of his generosity, and feared lest having Pierrot and Tardif, he might not wish a new guest, but to Dame Marie's stable.

As long as Bernard, thus by abbreviation Conscience

called the dog, fed on milk, there was no difficulty, for the black cow was there, and the two children could always obtain from Dame Marie, the soul of humanity, whatever it required. But when grown or growing, Bernard with his colossal form and corresponding appetite would become a heavy tax on any household.

Conscience however resolved to run the risk of Bernard's introduction into his paternal home.

Consequently he took advantage of an opportunity when it was empty to introduce Bernard, and consequently to protect him from Father Cadet's first emotion stood before the animal.

But not Father Cadet, but Madeleine was the first to enter.

When Madeleine saw Conscience standing with a dog by his side, she uttered an exclamation of surprise.

Nothing but the likeness of the dog had been wanting to complete the realization of the picture in the church.

Madeleine was a devout believer, and saw the hand of Providence everywhere. She saw that not in vain, the dog had chanced to fall in the pathway of her child, and that it would be almost sacrilege to separate those who had been joined in the picture.

Father Cadet however, remained, and it would not be easy to induce him to adopt the dog. Father Cadet not only disdained, but hated useless things, so that they feared he would drive away Bernard who would have to be introduced either as an object of luxury or of sentiment.

Fortunately at that time there was a talk of robberies in the neighborhood, and two or three nights before Father Cadet thought he heard some one in his yard. Bernard was presented to him as a guardian and

defender, and having been besought to his own satisfaction, much to the delight of Madeleine, Conscience,
and Mariette, consented to his remaining.

It really would have been a pity to separate the boy
and his dog, for a wonderful friendship existed between
them. Bernard exhibited an attachment to Conscience
which would really lead us to believe in a sentiment, we
almost uttered at the commencement of this book, that
animals have a soul. The soul of Bernard was grateful
to him who saved his life; this gratitude was translated
by an obedience which seemed almost fabulous. At a
simple gesture of the boy, the dog would cross water or
fire; his eyes never strayed from his, and if closed in
sleep, they always re-opened in the direction of Conscience. They were always together walking side by
side. Conscience let his hand towards the dog hang,
and the animal licked it as he walked by his side.

It was well that Bernard was so gentle and obedient
to the child, for he was of colossal power and would
have been dangerous had not a word or glance made
him powerless as the strongest steel muzzle.

Next to Conscience the person Bernard loved best
was little Mariette, then Madeleine, then Dame Marie.
As for the heads of the families, the schoolmaster and
Father Cadet, Bernard exhibited the most marked indifference to them.

As we have mentioned the schoolmaster, let us pause
a while on the good man, who having for a moment
hoped that the Convention would add something to the
three hundred francs, he received from the commune as
instructor and chanter, had been forced to relinquish
the hope, a mortification which increased as he saw his
family increased by a boy, who was consigned by him
to the especial care of the Prince of the apostles, and

been called Peter or Pierre, his father's name, to distinguish him from whom, he was called in the Picard *patois*, QUIET Pierre or little Pierre.

To complete his misfortune, not long after his son's birth, the schoolmaster became sick and died, so that the two women were reduced to a pension of a hundred francs which the commune granted them, and to what they could earn by their hands.

This took place about 1810 : Mariette was then about fifteen, and could understand the irreparable loss. As was the case in all important events, the two houses became one, and Madeliene and Conscience shared the grief of their neighbors, as if they could thus relieve it.

But while he wept with the mother and daughter, Conscience had words of consolation for them which seemed wonderfully inspired, so that the two women would often lift up their tearful eyes to see if it was really Conscience the poor innocent who was talking to them.

Thanks to this voice which seemed to come from above, their grief without disappearing entirely, lost its bitterness, and at the end of six months their hearts like their apparel, without being entirely out of mourning, no longer bore that dark tint by which Hamlet characterises mortal grief.

A merciful providence watches over the poor ; when misfortune strikes us, we think not only that our strength will not suffice to bear it, but also, that it is really insupportable. We examine the resources left us, and as we reckon them up shudder and ask whither they will conduct us. Life then seems reduced to impossible conditions, and we tremble to enter into a new life which seems ready to close around us, and to finally stifle us : then days roll by and months follow, while from the bosom of misery seem to spring blessed in-

spirations : we lift our brows to heaven and there catch
a glimpse of God.   Then the afflicted, miserable as he
may be, is like a criminal, who, while being led to the
scaffold, meets a king.   He sees that he will not die.

After having as well as he could, and without sus-
pecting that he had the power, consoled, Conscience saw
that he ought to aid the two women.   Considered even
by Father Cadet, a being apart from the rest of the
world, Conscience was almost master of his own time.
He could then employ it in their service.   At first, he
suggested to Mariette, the idea of selling in the city,
not only the milk of the black cow, but that of the cows
of Longpre.   It was arranged between her and the
owner, a young woman left a widow, with a child five
or six months old, and unable to give her personal attention to all the details, that Mariette should have one
measure of the milk out of every four she sold, and then
as Mariette could not without Conscience's assistance
take twelve measures of milk to the city, and as Father
Cadet needed Pierrot, and also was not a willing lender,
Conscience, with two old wheels, made a kind of hand-
cart, to which he harnessed Bernard without difficulty.   Thus accoutred, he willingly enough drew his
liquid load to Vitters-Cotereto.   When there, Mariette,
who had the address of the principal houses of the
town, and especially of the Inspector of Forests, offered
them her services, saying that if her milk was liked,
she would every day deliver to each of her customers
the quantity they wished.   Mariette was pretty, graceful, and had a good voice.   Her mourning made her
interesting, and on the very first day she fixed herself
well enough.

Every measure she sold for eight sous : she got eight
measures from the mistress of Longpre, for selling

which she received sixteen sous. The black cow also gave two measures, which paid sixteen sous in addition, which belonged to Mariette and her mother alone.— This was thirty two sous a day, or almost forty-eight francs a month.

This, with the hundred francs given to Dame Marie by the commune, amounted to nearly six hundred francs a year, and assured the poor household at least twice what they had during the life of the schoolmaster.

Every morning at six o'clock, Conscience, Mariette, and Bernard, set out with the little car. In three quarters of an hour they reached the city, and Mariette entering the various houses, measured out milk to each one, while Conscience and the dog waited, the latter looking and asking if they were satisfied with him.

Mariette measured her milk so gracefully, and received her money so thankfully; there was something too so novel in the attendance of the dog and idiot, for in the city as in the village the poor lad was so esteemed that had the mistress of Longpre owned ten cows instead of four, and if Bernard's car had been four times as large, and contained four times as much milk, Mariette would never have brought a drop to Haramont.

On her return Mariette arranged the empty vessels so as to allow herself a place, got in, and Bernard drew her back without fatigue, Conscience walking beside her.

At nine o'clock, they were generally on their return.

The result was, that Mariette could assist her mother all day, either with her needle or in taking care of her little brother.

When the season of the *faine** came, the aid which God himself has extended to the poor people who in· habit the forests, as of yore he gave manna to the He- brews in the desert, Conscience again assisted Mariette in gathering the precious fruit; instead of permitting the young girl to gather the faines, grain by grain, kneeling on the ground, instead of himself gathering it in this way, he put a broom and a fan in Bernard's car and went into the depths of the forest.

When there he picked out a tree well loaded with fruit, and ascended it with an agility almost equal to that of the squirrel, and shook down the faine on the green carpet below. When the grass was thus hidden beneath the fruit, he descended and making a heap of it with his broom, in a half-an-hour fanned out all the faine he had collected.

The faine being fanned, that is, seperated from the dry leaves, sticks, pieces of wood and empty hulls, was put in the car, covered by twigs and carried home.

The first year Conscience adopted this plan, Dame Marie made and sold one hundred and fifty francs worth of oil, which made her income amount to seven hundred and fifty francs, that is to say more than Ca- det's, though the latter at that time owned six acres of land which thanks to the manure of Pierrot, Tardif and the black cow, yielded to him in exchange for Con- science's services, had become much improved and among the best in the region.

Conscience had yet dreamed of another thing; he had dreamed of endowing the house, into which God's bless-

* Faine is the fruit of the beech, and contains an oil infinitely better than that of the walnut. When fresh, it is almost as pure as that of the olive.

ing seemed to have entered with him, with a swarm of bees. This was since he had discovered in a hollow trunk a whole family of these laborious animals. The consequence was, that by the advice of the fan-maker, he made an excellent hive, covered it with golden straw, and waited until the bees swarmed.

He followed them to the tree on which they were about to settle, and as he long had known them, spoke to them as he did to other animals. When the time was come for them to leave he opened his bosom to them without the least idea that any of his little friends would injure him, received a portion of the swarm with the Queen-bee, and followed by the others who playfully hovered around him, he passed through the whole village which looked with amazement at the winged swarm, and reached the new hive, which the Queen entered first followed by her subjects as if into a palace worthy of it.

From the next year Dame Marie and Mariette had the best honey in the village to eat at breakfast with their milk.

But what was especially wondered at, for man wonders at all he cannot understand, was that as soon as Conscience appeared in the garden, the whole swarm flew to him and settled on his hands and neck, buzzing about the flowers he held in his hands, and which he brought to the Queen, as if in adoration of her majesty.

The Queen would gravely fly to his finger, shake her diaphanous wings, and rub her legs covered with the pollen of flowers together.

VI.

What happened at Haramont between 1810 and 1813.

———

IN the early part of 1810 a great event took place; a villager returned from the army with the cross of the legion of honor, and having lost two fingers of his right hand.

He was young, being scarcely twenty-five; he had his furlough, two hundred and fifty francs, his cross, and a pension for three years.

He was a handsome fellow, with a round joyous face, had red hair and moustaches, the latter of which was always waxed and pointed.

He had served in the Hussars, and when he returned to the village with his blood-colored pelisse, with yellow lace, his blue dolman, his furred colbach, from from which hung a blue tassel, and his pantaloons with yellow buttons, his appearance produced a double sensation, in the first place, as a child of the country whom fathers and mothers were glad to see, and then as a young man agreeable to the village maids.

He had been enrolled when seventeen, about 1803. He had participated in the campaigns of Austerlitz and of Jena, and in that last brilliant campaign closed by the battles of Esling and Wagram.

In this last battle while charging a regiment of infantry, with his squadron, he received a ball which broke the index and medium fingers of the right hand, which it had been necessary to amputate, and his colonel, who had already remarked him, once or twice when under fire, asked and obtained for the brave lad, three well-deserved favors, his cross, his pension, and his discharge.   Though regretting him as a brave soldier, his inferior officers did not lament him as a comrade.   The fact is, Bastien, so he was called, after two glasses of wine became quarrelsome, and it often happened, that after having entered a cabaret, arm-in-arm with a comrade, he left before long, to find some hedge behind which he could fight with and cut his throat.

Bastien was himself aware of his unfortunate character, but as he thought it would be too difficult to correct, he preferred to cultivate carte and tierce with assiduity, so that he had become an excellent swordsman. The consequence was, that scars on the arms and face, always common in regiments that use the curved sabre, were especially so in Bastien's regiment.

The majority of these scars had been given by Bastien.

For this reason, though regretted as a soldier, Bastien was not much mourned as a comrade.

This did not prevent his comrades giving him a grand entertainment on the day of his discharge.   Perhaps the festival was especially cordial and brilliant because he was about to leave them.

When about to separate for ever we forget many things, and they had been able to see, much to the honor of the French soldier, that those who were the most scarred were kindest to Bastien.

Bastien therefore left Vienna, where this farewell dinner took place, crossed a part of Tyrol and Switzerland, whence he entered France, and appeared at Haramont a very impersonation of the god of war.

We have told the effect he had produced.

Alas! amid this generous sensation Bastien sought in vain for the gentle caresses without which there is no real happiness in this world, the embrace of a father and a mother's kiss.

Bastien, an orphan from his childhood, had never known this great happiness, and his determination to enlist doubtless arose from his isolation.

In other respects, as may be seen, Bastien had not lost his time. He returned relatively rich, for he had five hundred and fifty livres secured him for his life.

He could therefore either live and do nothing, or add to his possessions by every trifle he earned.

Bastien, however, while in his regiment had never worked, so that he adopted no business, but went into the house of Matthew, who continued to add to his possessions, and took special charge of his horses.

This occupation suited Bastien the Hussar as he was called: it reminded him of his squadron, and Bastien fancied he was conclusive when closing his teeth and extending the lower jaw, he said, seeing the letter R,

" Ah! the Regiment! so it was there—it was pleasant."

The phrase did not seem to convey much to others, but it was not so to Bastien, to whom it recalled a series of duels, love scrapes, and good dinners and battles. He even recollected his unhappy hours—for, it is not the memory of them that we are most unwilling to relinquish.

Those who heard him make this exclamation looked at him with surprise and amazement.

"Ah!" said he, "you *Pekins* cannot understand this."

This the Pekins never could, unless Bastien deigned to enlighten them—a thing he never did, so that Haramont never knew what was the pleasure Bastien so piteously lamented.

Bastien, we have said, produced a profound impression on the women of Haramont. Bastien was young, rich, and handsome, and wore the Cross when that decoration was not so prodigally bestowed. This was more than enough to turn the heads of the village girls. Yet Bastien was far from having exhibited all his attractions. He had not yet exhibited his dancing.

On the Sunday after his return Bastien made this great choreographic display. The arts touch and unite —the great swordsman could not but be a great dancer.

They danced about five hundred paces from the village, on the edge of the forest, beneath a circle of hock beeches, on a place carefully beaten by the village master of ceremonies, who levied on each man a *sou* a contra-dance in return for his weekly labor.

When on the Sunday after his return he was seen advancing towards the *dancing hall*, clad in his brilliant costume, with his spurs and well blacked boots, his hair hanging on each side of his face, and with a superbly *dandinant* gait, every eye was turned towards him, and awaited him with curiosity.

A decided opinion in relation to Bastien had not yet been expressed by the young girls, who wished to see if he danced as well as he did every thing else.

Every one too was anxious to see whom Bastien would ask first.

3

Bastien approached a dark-eyed girl with arched brows, named Catharine, who had, they said, been to the great city.

Catharine in fact had entered the service of a noble lady of the vicinity, had gone to Paris with her, and had in about a year returned pale and thin, but with about an hundred louis, which she had put out on a first mortgage in Master Niguet's office, and which brought her about one hundred and twenty livres a year.

Whence came those louis?

Catharine gave this explanation. Her mistress had a dangerous illness, during which Catharine had attended her with such devotion, that on her recovery she had been presented with an hundred louis.

Unfortunately for Catharine, all the world did not believe this very ingenious history. One single objection made a breach in it.

They asked Catharine why she had left so kind and grateful a mistress.

To which Catharine could only reply, that she suffered from ennui and had returned to the village.

Many doubted if this was the source of Catharine's little fortune.

Some even went farther, and assigned another origin at Catharine's little fortune.

They said that not the mistress, but the maid, had been ill, as was proven by her pallor and emaciation.

They added that the hundred louis Master Niguet had invested were derived not from the benevolence of the Baronne, but from the liberality of the Baron.

We must say that this tradition, malevolent as it was, explained the return of Catharine more clearly than the other, and was more generally believed.

Consequently, in spite of Catharine's brilliant beauty —in spite of the hundred louis securely placed, no villager had yet been found willing to marry Catharine.

Many however had paid court to her.

Catharine however had declared that she was an honest girl, and that she would listen to none who did not appear with the marriage pen in his hand.

This caused the miller of Wealu, a rather rough growler, to say that the egg of the goose who was to produce that pen, was not yet laid.

Bastien approached Catharine with his leg thrown forward, his arms loose, and presented her his chamois-gloved hand.

Catharine accepted it with a glance of triumph, and took her place in the circle with Bastien.

During the ritornella Bastien took off his belt, and gave his sabre and sabretasch into the hands of the son of the master of ceremonies, (who collected the toll between the dances,) with as much grace and dignity as Mars when about to dance with Venus would have deposited his buckler and shield in the hands of Amor.

Much was expected from Bastien, but we must say he surpassed all anticipations.   Bastien had a step for each of the four figures which complete the contradance. Things were done that the Haramontese believed impossible.   All crowded around to see Bastien dance, so that he himself, in spite of this triumph of his self-love was obliged to ask his compatriots, if they wished to see him dance to allow him a little more room.

All recognised this request to be just, and complied with it, and Bastien concluded his last figure with two or three entrechats which were so perfect that all the spectators applauded loudly and long.

Bastien took his partner proudly to her place, and

looked around to see whom he would next honor with his hand.

At the foot of the dancing place, not mingling with the dancers, and attracted by curiosity alone, were Dame Marie and Mariette. Bastien saw her sweet pure face, and without noticing the color of her dress, said to her, in his most flowery style,

"Mademoiselle, will you honor me with your hand at the next contradance?"

Mariette blushed, for the eyes of all had followed Bastien, and were directed on her.

"Thank you, M. Bastien, but you see, I am in mourning for my poor father."

"Ah!" said Bastien. "You see when I saw you approach the dance, I fancied."

"You are right," said Mariette. "I was wrong to come with a sad heart, and in mourning, where people are amusing themselves. Will you go, mother?"

She hurried Dame Marie away by the road which led by the edge of the forest.

"Oh, ho!" said Bastien, "little Mariette seems while I have been absent, to have changed her name. She mnst be Mlle. Pincee.

Mariette did not hear what Bastien said, but others, among whom was Conscience, did.

Conscience had paid so little attention to the dance, that he lay stretched out on the other side of the bank, and his great dog served him, as he usually did, on such occasions, as a pillow.

He looked at Mariette through the dancers, and he forgot all this as he saw them moving in time to the music, and the violin players beating time.

Like every one else he had for a moment looked at Bastien and pitied him sincerely, for being forced to dance in so fatiguing a manner. He could not comprehend a man moving his legs so violently, and giving himself such fatigue, unless constrained to do so, by some law or obligation.

When he saw Bastien leave the circle, and advance towards the young girl, he suspected his intention, and would have been sorry to see Mariette make herself a spectacle by dancing with a young man who moved so differently from the other villagers.

Distant as he was from the group, the faculty he enjoyed of hearing the most distant sounds enabled him to hear the question and the answer. He thought Mariette had replied correctly, and that Bastien was rather impertinent. He however thought a man who who had taken such violent exercise might very well be a little put out.

He pitied him therefore, instead of blaming him, and with Bernard followed Mariette. This he did naturally as the satellite follows a star.

VII.

SEQUEL OF WHAT HAPPENED AT HARAMONT BE-
TWEEN 1810 AND 1813.

FROM this moment a position was definitely assigned to Bastien the Hussar. The women looked on him as the paragon of perfection and of good manners; men esteemed him the most disagreeable person they had ever seen.

The only persons who had escaped the sympathy and antipathy were Conscience and Mariette.

Mariette was indifferent.

Conscience pitied him.

Conscience would have agreed with the Dey of Algiers, when present at a magnificent ball, the giver of which danced and waltzed like one of his guests, sent for him, and said with an expression of great simplicity and good humor:

"Monsieur, why is it that being as rich as you are, you take the trouble to dance yourself?"

The result was, that the men whom Bastien took good care not to give the least idea of turning in, three times left the field of the waltz free to Bastien, who like an Eastern Pacha had but to throw down his handkerchief without any fear of difficulty.

The peasants had wished to protest, but at the first rumor, Bastien had faced about and twined his moustache like a cork-screw around his finger, saying in the peculiar manner of his regiment of Hussars, "If you please?" All was then submitted to at once.

Not as a dancer alone had Bastien gained the admiration of the Haramontese, but also as a rider : Bastien sate his horse like an Hussar of Guard, that is to say, with a rare perfection. As he had especial care of horses, he did not fail to mount Matthew's colts and ride them bare-backed, through the environs, chosing those roads which took him through the village both going and coming.

Strange though to say, though sought after by the handsomest girls of the village, better received than the other young men by Catharine, who seemed disposed for his sake to renounce the matrimonial rigorism she affected to others, all seemed indifferent to him so long as he could not see Mariette following him as he caracolled through the street.

Therefore the more restive and evil disposed the horse he rode, the more inclined he was to go to Dame Marie's side of the village, so that Mariette might be obliged to see him a modern Alexander display his skill in breaking a new Bucephalus.

Sometimes his attention was half rewarded, for Mariette looked at him from curiosity, and Conscience because Mariette did, asking himself sometimes why instead of using the spur and whack to subdue the restive animal, he did not use the simple means of speech, with which, in the course of a few moments, Conscience subdued the most restive animals brought him.

Bastien either because he saw that Conscience's heart was filled with love for Mariette, and that Mariette had a great tenderness for Conscience, did not like him. Let us at once say that this feeling of aversion did not amount to hatred. Conscience was so good and quiet that none could hate him, but he was unpleasant to Bastien, as any thing that annoys us, and is in our way, always is.

Bastien therefore never lost an opportunity to mock Conscience and his angelic sweetness of disposition, which to Rastien seemed pusillanimity—that was his principal theme.

Conscience was not a dancer, nor a rider, nor a swordsman; he was ignorant of the three arts in which Bastien excelled.

Bastien therefore laughed at Conscience not only for what he was, but for what he was not.

We need not say that Conscience listened to all this ridicule with calm indifference.

A thing however happened one day which made Bastien reflect.

As he had in the whole neighborhood, great reputation as a horse-breaker, the farmers and proprietors who had bad-tempered colts or restive horses, sent for Bastien, who after two or three trials, reduced the rebels as Baucher or Franconi would have done.

One day Bastien was sent for to ride a horse purchased by a farmer in the neighborhood named M Detournelles. As it was Sunday, Bastien naturally vain-glorious, resolved to make a public display of his equitation, and chose the village square, and the hour when the people would leave mass, as the scene and time.

Just when the first young girls, and it is always they who are most anxious to regain the light and liberty they have lost during divine service, appeared at the

church-door, Bastien appeared on his horse at exactly
the opposite side of the square where a street ended.

The horse had consumed an hour in coming from
the farm to the village, the distance being half a league,
and had been restrained by his rider, anxious to arrive
neither too early nor too late.

The consequence was, that the horse was white
with foam, his eyes blood-shot, and his nostrils smoking
with rage.

When on the square, that is to say, on a fitting
arena, the exercises began.

Victory at first seemed about to declare itself in favor
of the man, but either because the horse was sensible
of the instinctive dignity, of which Buffon speaks, or
that he had during the previous hour borne all Bastien's affronts to gather up strength to inflict signal
vengeance, when he saw himself in front of the crowded steps of the church, as if of a circus, the windows
filled with faces, like the boxes of a theatre, began a series of jumps and rearings, terminated by so
unexpected a leap, that good a rider as Bastien was,
he was thrown in the dust ten paces from the spot
where his horse had stood.

As soon as the horse was rid of his rider, with his
head and tail erect, he galloped back to the farm.

This fall was much laughed at by the young peasants, who totally eclipsed and constantly laughed at
and supplanted by Bastien, did not very closely sym-
pathise with him; when, however, they saw Bastien,
instead of rising at once, as one does under such circumstances, remain motionless in the place where he
had fallen, they saw that his head having struck the
ground, he must certainly have been stunned. They
hurried therefore to his assistance.

3*

They were not wrong—for Bastien was completely stunned.

They lifted him up, gave him a glass of brandy, fanned his face, and Bastien at once opened his eyes and his mouth.

His eyes, he rolled wildly about, as if to search for his horse.

His mouth, to swear and blaspheme, thus informing the peasants of Haramont how much richer the language of camps is than that of villages.

All at once his eyes paused and his mouth closed, as if he had seen the head of Medusa.

He had seen something more terrible to him.

Conscience was bringing the restive horse back again —having mounted him and found him gentle as that animal on which the Lord made his entrance into Jerusalem. As he held a green bough in his hand, he recalled Palm-Sunday, which, his feet hanging out of the stirrups, his kind eyes, sweet smile, and the separation of the crowd before him, presented as accurate a resemblance to God as a poor mortal could.

For a moment Bastien fancied himself in dreamland; he rubbed his eyes, muttered indistinctly, but saw that positive real thing draw near as a fantastic vision might have done.

" M. Bastien," said Conscience calmly, " I was on the road to Longpre, and saw this horse running away, and was afraid you would be uneasy, and brought it back."

All laughed except Bastien, and Conscience looked at the crowd with astonishment, not understanding why they laughed.

He blushed, dismounted, and handed Bastien the bridle. Then placing his hand on Bernard's head, he set out to follow Dame Marie and Mariette, who being among the last to leave the church, had no very distinct idea of what all this was about.

Bastien forgot to thank Conscience, and anxious for his revenge, sprang again on the back of the horse.— One might almost think, however, that the devil which a quarter of an hour before possessed the animal, had been exorcised by Conscience. The horse submitted to his rider without a curvet or a start.

Bastien took back M. Destournelles' animal completely broken.

We need not say that the hussar was careful not to tell how this had been accomplished, and received the greatest credit for it from the farmer.

As, however, he never could account for the means adopted by Conscience to subdue an animal which had unseated him, and as he, Bastien, was too proud to ask Conscience for his secret, which the latter would have found much difficulty in explaining, the result was evident, but the cause remained obscure.

Another circumstance also happened, which much to Bastien's distaste, left him under obligations to Conscience.

Besides dancing, fencing and riding, Bastien was very fond of the chase. Before he enlisted in the army Bastien had been one of the most expert poachers alive ; on his return, thanks to his Cross of the Legion of Honor, a decoration at that time much respected, he hunted where he pleased on the estates of Haramont, Longpre and Largny.

At first there had been one difficulty : the amputation Bastien had undergone of the index and medium fingers of the right hand, made the management of the gun impossible at first. Instead, however, of persisting in firing from the right shoulder, Bastien learned to use the left. For a month he missed all that he fired at—then three out of four—then half, until finally he became as skilful with the left as he had been with the right—that is to say, he became one of the best shots in the canton.

One of the favorite hunting fields of Bastien, because it is usually the fullest of game, was the marsh.

The marsh he visited most frequently, because it was, but half an hour distant from Haramont or Longpre, was that of Wualn.

There lived another famous sportsman, the malicious miller who ventured on the jest about Catharine's matrimonial pen.

Bastien had heard of this, but instead of being angry had more than once laughed over the matter with the miller, a thing that proved, the matrimonial pen, so much coveted, would not be presented by him.

The miller and Bastien then were the best friends in the world, and when the season came, shot three or four times a week—sometimes together and sometimes alone.

One day, then, when Bastien was hunting alone in an immense pond extending from the north to the south of the valley, overlooked by a dam on which stands a mill, a snipe arose, which with his usual skill Bastien knocked over.

The snipe fell in the pool.

All know how a sportsman dislikes to lose his game —and Bastien being more unwilling even than the majority are to do so, resolved to have his bird at all risks.

For this purpose he laid his gun on the grass, so as

to be able to use both his hands, and began to advance with care along the trembling bank of the pool.

When as far as he could get, Bastien was yet eight or ten feet from the bird.

Bastien, though a good shot, rider, dancer and sportsman, yet had a defective education—he was unable to swim.

Bastien could only reach the bird by swimming—a thing he would have undertaken had he been but a swimmer of the third order.

Just at this moment Bastien would willingly have exchanged either of his other talents to be able to swim.

He would not however relinquish the snipe.

Fortunately there was no current in the pool, and the bird remained stationary.

Bastien looked around him and saw a willow, to which he went, and having broken off the longest branch, returned to the extremity of the trembling promontory.

By the addition of the length of his arm to that of the willow, he was able to reach the bird.

But the pliant extremity of the twig was not sufficiently strong to draw the bird to him.

By a miracle of balancing he gained six inches more space.

He bent further forward and described a semicircle.

Bastien made a greater effort yet, and fell in.

He saw the consequences at once.

The chances were ten to one that he would be drowned.

Short, then, as the time was, he uttered a cry of distress, for he was in a truly lamentable situation

Fortunately Conscience, returning from Vanciennes,

crossed the dam of the pond, in company with his faithful Bernard. He heard the cry and hurried to the place whence it seemed to come.

There was a pathway through the rushes which Conscience followed, and thus reached the extremity of the promontory whence Bastien had fallen.

He saw the water bubbling as if air was rising to the surface.

Amid all this, he saw two hands attempting convulsively to grasp something.

He needed no more to tell him that a man was being drowned, and without looking to see who it was, called to Bernard, who sprang into the water, beneath which he disappeared.

Five seconds afterwards he rose to the surface holding Bastien by the collar of his coat, and swam to the shore, where Conscience pulled the half-drowned hussar from the water.

Then the two recognised each other: Conscience was really glad that he had been able to extricate Bastien from danger, and the latter somewhat ashamed at having received such a favor from Conscience.

As, however, in the main, Bastien was a good enough fellow, and as his fear of death had made him estimate the value of life, he began by thanking Conscience from the bottom of his heart. As Bernard also had powerfully contributed to his preservation, he preferred to owe something to a dog than to a man, and contrived that the greater part of the glory should accrue to Bernard.

Thus whenever Bastien saw Bernard he exhibited an excess of gratitude to him, which was but ingratitude to Conscience.

Conscience, however, did not remark this bearing

which would have been painful to another with a less christian heart, and as often as the matter was alluded to, Bastien said with forced gaiety :

"On my word, I was in a bad way, and but for Bernard there, would now have been food for the pikes of Father Charpentier, would I not, Conscience?"

Conscience would simply say, "Bernard is a good dog."

Days, months, years thus passed with such simple events, and such as we have recorded, almost reflect the life they led, as a mirror would.

VIII.

CONTINUATION OF WHAT HAPPENED AT HARAMONT BETWEEN 1810 AND 1813.

THUS they reached the end of October 1813, and on his return from his farm one day about noon, Father Cadet found Dame Marie, Madeleine, Mariette, Conscience and Bernard, grouped on the threshold of the cottage on the right, and thence, as we have already said he usually did, proceeded to the right.

That evening the Veillee began. On that day with Mariette having served the milk in the city, Conscience had returned through that part of the forest called " the chesnut grove," and had gathered a large bag of nuts which Bernard brought back in the car.

These chesnuts, with a few bottles of sweet cider, were to be the repast of the evening, at this village rout, as most luxurious food is at city entertainments.

The veillee took place in an immense cave, into which every girl took her spinning wheel; a lamp hung from the roof lighted with its quivering blaze every face. It was dim, to be sure, but gas light was not needed to manage the wheel, and in this half darkness labor lost little, and love gained much.

As may be presumed, as soon as the young men were admitted. Bastien, who was also admitted with,

and would have been to the exclusion of the others,
was the principal ornament.

Bastien, for Sunday evenings, invented many games,
which in spite of the imagination displayed, had little
chance of being adopted. Some submitted to the mothers, and to the most prudent of the girls, were pronounced too hussarish not to receive corrections.

Mariette, like the other young girls, attended these
veillees. Not to have done so would have attracted
attention, and it would have been thought contemptu-
ous in Haramont, to remain out of the circle of young
girls of her age.

Mariette, however, rarely sang, danced, or joined in
the little games in which Mme. Longueville used to join,
under the pretext that she was not fond of innocent re-
creations.

Mariette, therefore, usually sat in a corner occupying
the least possible place, and having Conscience before
her, either erect or on the ground, with Bernard at his
feet. He seemed to look at the young girl's beautiful
face, not only with his eyes, but with every aspiration
of his body.

From custom, no one disputed this place to Conscience. Had any one wished to affront him, all the
village would have risen en mass, for they adored the
poor idiot as he was called, to avenge the affront. They
objected, however, to Bernard, a mere quadruped, and
who took in the dances and games but a secondary interest, but who, occupping much room, added nothing to
the pleasure of the company.

On this occasion an exception had been made in his
favor, in consideration of his having pulled the chesnuts from the neighborhood of Villers-Cotterets to Haramont.

The weather without, was cold, sombre and dark, but the cave being close and well heated, the young people heard the wind whistle through the branches, from which it tore the dry leaves which whirled in the night like a flock of owls.

All the world resumed the state of things of the previous year. Those of the women who like Mariette expected to be mere spectators, and there were two or three, had taken the precaution to bring their wheel and distaff and span.

The veillies always began with songs, which sometimes are naifly simple; it is well known that the modesty of young villagers is not easily roused as that of city-bred young women is, and that what makes the latter blush and look aside, the former receive with a merry laugh.

They draw by lot the name of the person who is to begin. As they knew Mariette declined taking an active part, her name was not placed with the rest.

The others were thrown into a hat which was placed before Conscience, who put in his hand and drew out Catharine's name.

All were delighted when Catharine sang, for she not only knew the best songs, but executed them with an air and style, they said she had acquired at the Parisian spectacles, when she had accompanied her kind mistress to the great city.

Catharine did not wait to be besought. She called nine young girls to her, and then the ten seizing hold of each other's hands, received each a name which occurred in the ronde.

They balanced their hands backward and forward, and the slightly metallic voice of Catherine began a song in

the Picard patois which, we are sorry we cannot repro-
duce in a suitable form to please our readers.

The Rondo of Catharine had great success with the
young men and women, but did not suit Bernard who
as if he wished to protest against its volubility of the
two last verses, lifted up his head, looked towards the
door, and howled.

We need not say that this protest was not well received by the company, and that the dog was told to be
silent. The company unanimously asked for a second
song.

The names were again put in a hat and handed to
Conscience, who seemed engrossed by Bernard's howl·
He took out Bastien's name.

Bastien was not likely to be frightened by a song, for
he had a full repertory. It was however of a peculiar
kind, and not calculated even to suit the least shame-
faced young women.

"Ah ha!" said he, twisting his moustache, "so it is
my turn to sing."

"Yes," said the girls, "a good song."

"How good! I never sing any others."

A murmur of incredulity pervaded the room.

Almost immediately, as if to reassure the company
Bastien thundered out the following song.

> Les hussards en campagne,
> Rintintin !
> Les hussards en campagne,
> Rintintin !
> Un pied chaussé et l'autre nu,
> Pauvre hussard ! d'ou reviens-tu?
> Rintintin !*

> * The Hussars in campaign,
> Tira la Tirala !
> The Hussars in campaign,
> With one leg booted, and the other bare,
> Tell me, hussar, what you are,
> What you are, etc.

But here there was an outbreak of opposition which was apparent at the first verse.

"Ah! Monseieur Bastien," said the young girls clasping their hands, "another!"

"Why another?"

"Because," said the young men, "we know that. You have already sung it ten times."

Bastien frowned on the young men and said, "Suppose I have, and choose to sing it eleven."

"You can sing as you please, Bastien, but we are not bound to listen."

Two or three started to leave.

Bernard was of the opinion of those who protested, for he arose a second time, and uttered a second howl, yet more lugubrious than the first.

All trembled.

"My God!" said Mariette, "some one is dying."

"Will you make that dog hush?"

"I can," said Conscience, "tell Bernard to pull Bastien out of the water when Bastien is drowning, but I cannot make him hush when he wishes to speak."

'You can not? Then if he howls again, I will make him."

"Bastien," said Conscience, in a persuasive voice, "let me advise you not to quarrel with Bernard."

"Why not?" said Bastien.

"Because Bernard wishes you to do so."

"Bernard does? and why?"

"You do not like me, Bastien, and Bernard does not like those who hate me."

All, even Bastien, were mute at this melancholy answer.

"What folly! I do not hate you," said he. "Far the contrary."

He offered Conscience his hand.

Conscience smiled, and gave him his.

Bernard arose, put out his tongue and licked their united hands.

" You see he does not hate me," continued Bastien, who persisted in pronouncing the word *hate* in his peculiar manner.

" Because you are good enough in the main," said Conscience, " and sometimes say to yourself that your ill-feeling towards me is unjust."

The opinion Conscience uttered accorded so exactly with what passed in Bastien's mind, that the latter could not reply, and changed the subject of conversation.

" Well!" said he, "do you wish another song ?"

" Yes !" said all.

" Well, I will sing you one in the Bressan patois; but you must dress me for that."

" What ?" said the young men, " dress you ?"

" Yes, the ladies with their white hands must dress me as an old woman, else no song."

" What do you want, then ?"

" Oh! a cap, a cape, and an apron will do ; give me a wheel, and a distaff too, and you had as well give me a little tow. However, as we said at the Regiment, one cannot make an omelette without cracking the eggs."

As what Bastien asked for was easily to be procured, he was soon transformed into an old woman, and to tell the truth, with a cape modestly pinned on, with spectacles on his nose, as he put the distaff in his waist, and turned the wheel with his left foot, the triumph he desired was complete, that all, even Mariette, clapped their hands and applauded him.

Bernard, however, seemed uneasy.

Conscience alone however, attended to this, and he began to think the dog was not uneasy without a cause. Without noticing it or paying any attention to him, Bastien began this song with an accompaniment on the wheel.

> " Ah quy fait donc bon,
> Quy fait donc bon
> Garder les vaches
> Au pasquier des boeufs
> Quand on est deux !
> Quand on est quatre on s'embarrasse;
> Quand on est deux
> Quand on est deux
> Ca va bien mieux.
> Zon, zon, zon.

We need not say that the syllable twice or thrice repeated translates the round of the wheel. Unfortunately we cannot preserve on paper, Bastien's accent and grimace, or we would exert on our reader that produced on the company by Bastien. We would make him laugh.

Thus encouraged, Bastien resumed, and sung a dozen such couplets, not models either of good taste, style, or propriety.

Scarcely had Bastien concluded, amid universal applause of the young men and girls, than Bernard, as if he waited an opportunity, took up the phrase where Bastien had dropped it, and gradually rising from base to the highest notes, filled the whole cave with one of the saddest sounds ever heard.

Even Bastien had not courage to menace Bernard.

The howl was succeeded by a yet more melancholy silence, until at last Conscience arose and pronounced the word,

" Fire !"

At that moment the church bell rang the alarm.

The cry fire aroused the whole population of the village.

IX.

SEQUEL OF WHAT HAPPENED IN THE VILLAGE OF HARAMONT BETWEEN 1810 AND 1813.

———◆———

THE most terrible cry to which human terror gives utterance, beyond doubt, is *fire*.

Especially when this cry accompanied by the bell is is heard during a dark and stormy night.

At this cry, the young people of each sex rushed from the cave into the street, and followed the current which rolled towards the northwest.

Above the houses of the village, a great light was seen to diffuse itself over the heaven, increasing from moment to moment, and diffusing itself in sparks, which the wind bore amid volumes of smoke.

As soon as the young men and girls had reached the last of the village houses, there being no other obstacle, they were able to realise the extent of the disaster.

The farm of Longpre was in a blaze.

Mariette saw Father Cadet standing with his arms folded, on a stone, looking at the conflagration, and rendering no assistance, doubtless from the certainty that such aid as a frail old man like himself could yield was an useless aid.

" My God ! Father Cadet," said Mariette, " what is the matter ?"

" You see, my child," said the old man.

" But why ?"

71

"Because, in spite of what I said, that obstinate Julienne would store her hay before it was cured, and it has itself taken fire."

"Poor Julienne!" said Mariette.

Julienne was the woman who every day gave Mariette eight measures of milk to carry to Villers-Cotterets.

Then the peasants, overcome with stupor, stood still as if they were petrified.

"You that are men," said Mariette, turning to Bastien, Conscience, and the others, "fly to her and at once."

This appeal of Mariette, was electrical: except Father Cadet and three or four old men, who stood motionless at the entrance of the village, each one hurried to the fire.

In general, fire is one of the accidents, in relation to which it is least necessary to take trouble to excite attention: one might say, that during a fire each one fears for himself, and that all by the risk of some personal danger, are impelled by fire to extinguish it.

The little farm now burning, was on the other side of a ravine, scarcely five hundred paces distant, had one been able to reach it in a right line. It was, however, necessary to ascend and descend the declivity, a thing which doubled the distance.

As they approached they could distinguish by the light of the flames those who had come first, and who hovered around the volcano, extending a useless aid.

As Father Cadet said, the barns were burning first, but from them the fire soon spread to the main buildings.

A few minutes sufficed for Mariette, Bastien, and Conscience to reach the scene.

They were followed by those who had left the veillee with them.

Those who came first were obliged to beat in the door. Julienne had doubtless gone to pass the evening in the neighborhood. The plough-boys were at the cabaret, and the maids with their beaux.

On entering the yard, the cries of the cattle were heard. All know the effect produced by fire on domestic animals. Usually, nothing can induce them to leave the place in which they are; horses remain in the stable, oxen in their stalls, sheep in the fold, until death overtakes them.

The first comers had used every means to save horses, cows, and sheep, who with their usual obstinacy, had resisted, and poor Julienne seemed likely, not only to have her house burned, but in the conflagration to be entirely ruined by the loss of all her stock.

The strange power, however, which Conscience possessed over animals was then displayed ; in their fright they had broken their halters, and stood in a group, of which their heads formed the center, and assailed any who dared to approach them with kicks. When, however, they heard Conscience's voice, they neighed and lifted up their heads, suffering the young man to approach them through the wreaths of smoke which gushed through the open places of the floor of planks above. He mounted one of them, directed it without difficulty towards the door, and rode out, followed by all the others ; then as they ran wildly off, he whistled to them with a peculiar modulation, and all came to rejoin the one Conseience rode in a corner. Lest they should again become frightened, he ordered Bernard to watch them, a command the dog instantly obeyed.

Then he entered the cow-house, as he had the stable.

4

Two or three men, who had already sought to do so, had been thrown down and trampled on, and all had ceased to attempt to subdue these furious animals. Conscience, however, advanced directly to a bull, who was scattering the straw of his litter wildly around. He seized him by his smoking nostrils, and led the animal, which became completely submissive. As soon as they saw the bull walking in obedience, the cows followed in an instant; cows and bull under the care of Bernard as the horses did, sank on their trembling legs, and slept by the side of the ruins.

The sheep remained: it was not necessary for Conscience himself to enter the fold, which already was almost destroyed. He called to them from the door as the shepherds call, and at his voice they rushed forth like an avalanche, with bounds and bleatings which at once testified the terror they had felt, and joy at their rescue.

The peasants had seen Conscience accomplish this triple rescue, deemed impossible, with a mingled feeling of astonishment and veneration. Bastien especially, who had narrowly escaped being trampled beneath the feet of the horses and oxen. Bastien, who, in order to save a single sheep, had been forced to carry it out on his shoulders, was tempted to look on Conscience as a village sorcerer, to whom countless miracles, each more singular than the other, were attributed. Only the miracles attributed to the sorcerers none ever saw them perform, while Conscience, in the presence of all, with his ordinary simplicity, had accomplished things reputed impossible.

The peasants then collected around him, as if the simple young man was about to become to them, a sublime inspiration, before which fire was extinguished, when all at once, terrible cries were heard in the distance, from towards the tower of Vez, gradually, however, growing more and more distinct. These cries were the sad, heart-rending exclamations of a woman, amid which could be distinguished only the words:

" My child! my child! save my child!"

Julienne rushed up panting, with her hair loose and her arms extended. Her child, scarcely three months old, had been left by her in charge of one of the maids, who had shut it up in the chamber, and passed the evening in the village of Bonneil, knowing that Julienne had gone to her father's house at Vez, and would remain there all night.

From Vez, however, Julienne had seen the conflagration, and knew it was her farm. She had returned, and on the way had seen another woman hurrying forward also.

This was the unfortunate maid, who at once saw how imprudent she had been, and what might result from her conduct. On that account she hurried forward if possible to save the child.

When she saw her alone, the poor mother at once understood all, and far outstripping the hireling, with the force, courage, and fury of a mother, had, uttering the cries heard at such a distance, hurried on.

All had shuddered at her cry, " my child! my child! save my child!"

They had been busy in saving horses, cows, sheep, and had suffered the fire to extend to the house which was thought empty. Julienne's fortune had been saved, while they suffered her life to be devoured.

All removed from the path of the woman, who rushed against the kitchen door with such violence, that it was broken; when, however, the air penetrated within, the fire burst forth on all sides.

They could go up stairs to the room in which the child was, only by a wooden stairway.

It was on fire.

Julienne rushed towards the flames, but was seized from behind, and pulled back into the room.

Her cries, however, increased, and with hands out-stretched towards the windows, through which the fire shone, as the glasses cracked in the heat, she could utter but one cry, but one exclamation,

" My child! my child! my child!"

Mariette looked around and saw consternation in the face of every man.

They looked for Conscience, he had disappeared.

" Bastien! Bastien!" said she, " do you hear that poor mother?"

" Oh, Monsieur Bastien," said Julienne, " you are a soldier and are afraid of nothing."

" Mon Dieu," said Bastien, " it is just as if one said, ' Bastien, throw yourself from the tower of Haramont,' I would have as much chance of escape. I will try, however."

He rushed into the interior, accompanied by cries of " courage! Bastien! courage!"

These cries came from every lip, or rather sprang from every heart.

In spite, however, of this encouragement, Bastien could ascend the staircase but half-way, and soon ap-peared walking backwards, and seeming to fight with the flames.

His hair and moustaches were burned.

" Bastien, my preserver Bastien!—one more effort."

Bastien obeyed and disappeared amid the smoke—

but the burning staircase gave way beneath his feet, and he fell amid the wreck.

Hope, however, though lost by all others, never leaves a mother's heart.

"The window! the window!" cried Julienne.— "There is a ladder—there must be one. My God! if I had that ladder I would go for my child myself."

"The ladder! the ladder!" exclaimed Bastien, "and no one shall go for the child but myself."

They looked for the ladder in vain, and the mother wrung her hands in despair.

Just then a gentle voice, as if from heaven, was heard above.

"Room! room!" it said, "here is the child."

They looked up, and amid the smoke and flames saw Conscience, with the child in his arms, draw near to the window.

He had taken the ladder, come through the garden, and having entered the house through a window, had reached the cradle of the child, whom he found half stifled.

He had then sought to retrace his steps, but the fall of the staircase had made the flames more intense, and the way by which he might have returned, was cut off! . . .

For that reason it was that he now came to the window with the child in his arms.

"Get a sheet or coverlet ready to catch the child."

Two or three persons rushed into the house, for the poor mother stood motionless, with her arms extended, muttering inarticulate sounds.

Those who had gone into the house returned with a coverlet, which they stretched out, holding tightly to the corners, beneath the window.

It was time: as if furious at seeing its prey borne from it, the flames appeared on every side, and surrounded Conscience with a circle of fire.

As soon therefore as the coverlet was within reach, he let the child fall. It was uninjured, and the mother rushed wildly across the fields with it.

Three hundred paces from the house, she sank completely exhausted on the ground.

What cared she for her burning house? What cared she for the destruction of her harvests? Had she not saved the only thing she lived for—her child?

In the sublimity of ingratitude, she had forgotten even Conscience.

The window was twenty feet from the ground.

Having thrown the child out, Conscience lifted his meek eyes to heaven, folded his arms on his bosom, muttered a few brief words, and leaped out.

Though he fell on his feet, the violence of the concussion was so great, that he trembled, uttered a painful cry, and fainted.

When he regained consciousness, he was lying on some bundles of fresh straw in the yard.

Bernard whined by his side, licked his right hand, and from time to time smelt his face, to ascertain if he was dead.

Fortunately the two mothers, Dame Marie and Madeleine, knew nothing of all this.

When he opened his eyes, Conscience saw Mariette.

He smiled, and made an effort to place his face close to hers.

Mariette forgot all: she uttered a cry of joy, and pressed her lips to the young man's.

Since their childish caresses, it was the first time their lips had ever touched.

The two then for the first time perceived a thing which they had not suspected.

They had ceased to love each other as brother and sister, and had begun to love as lover and mistress.

They arose, holding by each other's hand, and followed by Bernard, proceeded on their journey homeward in silence.

When two thirds of the way home, they met their mothers, who had come to meet them.

They had already learned the service Conscience had rendered to poor Julienne; the two mothers, like her, had not thought of the horses, cattle and sheep—but they said,

" My child, so you saved the little one !"

Conscience smiled and was silent, but Mariette told what he had done during this terrible night—and the story which escaped from her heart, was bathed in tears of love. It exhibited Conscience as he really had been—an intermediate between Providence and misfortune.

The two mothers listened in amazement to Mariette's story; they had never seen her so much excited and so full of fervor. They had never seen Conscience so calm.

At last, though it was not said, they saw that the prayer of their hearts had been granted. Dame Marie put Mariette in Madeleine's arms, while she herself embraced Conscience.

Then from the lips of the two children escaped the murmurs,

" Dame Marie, I love Mariette."

" Dame Madeleine, I love Conscience."

" Well," said both mothers, sighing with joy—

"there is no harm in that, and we will talk to Father Cadet about it."

Father Cadet, it will be understood, was the supreme arbiter of the destiny of the two cottages.

The next day overtures were made by Madeleine to Father Cadet.

Father Cadet listened gravely to what Madeleine had to say, and when she had done, said :

"Hm !—we will see."

Now as this was the ordinary answer of Father Cadet when he was disposed to yield, the two families looked on it as a consent, and joy, the benediction from heaven, descended on the two families.

Alas !

X.

What passed in Europe from 1810 to 1814.

━━━━◆━━━━

FROM the very moment when the eyes of Conscience
opened and met those of Mariette fixed on him—
from the moment when the chaste lips of the two children met, that is to say from about ten o'clock in the
evening of the 9th of November, 1813, the centre gate
of the Tuilleries was swung open before three post carriages, one of which had six horses. The three drove
rapidly across the court-yard, and paused, the first
under the gateway, and the others just in front of it.

Footmen in a livery of green and gold, rushed to the
door. The steps were put down, and a man in a grey
frock-coat over a green uniform, with white breeches
and top boots, wearing a little cocked hat that has become a type, got quickly out and looked up the staircase, where stood a blonde and delicate woman, dressed
in red velvet, with a fair rosy child in her arms. The
man ascended the staircase amid a crowd of courtiers,
on whom he did not deign even to look, embraced the
woman and child, and hurried them into a boudoir hung
with green cashmere, and closed the door behind him.

"Ah! It will be time enough to play the Emperor

to-morrow.   To-night let me be a father, a husband, a man! My good Louise! My poor child! We are once more united."

Five minutes after, the grand Chamberlain appeared in the saloon and said,

" Gentlemen, his majesty the Emperor thanks you for your zeal, but is fatigued, and will receive no one until to-morrow."

The embroidered crowd bowed submission, and respected the fatigue of their master.

For the man before whom the gate of the Tuilleries opened—the man who wished to be a man, a husband and father, that night, and who postponed the Emperor until to-morrow, was Napoleon.

Alas! great changes had been effected in three years in the fortune of that man.

If human creature had ever been ordained by heaven for a providential mission, it was the Conqueror of Marengo, and he who was defeated at Leipsic.

Until 1810, that is to say, as long as he represented the popular interests of France, he had succeeded in everything.

In 1810 he repudiated Josephine, and married Marie Louise.

All then began to re-act.

It is true, till then, nothing had resisted him.

Portugal placed herself in communication with the English, and he occupied Portugal.

Godoy exhibited animosity by arming, and he forced Charles IV. to abdicate.

Pius VII. made Rome the general rendezvous of the agents of England, and treating the Pope as a temporal Prince, he deposed him.

Nature had refused him children by Josephine, and

forgetting the companion of his youth, the angel of his first wars and glories, he repudiated his wife.

Holland, in spite of its promises, had become a depot for English manufactures, and he deposed his brother Louis, and united his kingdom to France.

Then the French Empire, reviving the Roman world of Augustus and the Frankish Empire of Charlemagne, had one hundred departments.

It extended from the Breton Ocean to the Grecian seas, from the Tagus to the Elbe.

A hundred and twenty millions of men then obeyed one will; subjected to one power, and led in one way, they cried "Vive Napoleon" in eight different languages.

On the 20th of March 1811, a hundred and twenty guns announced to the universe that an heir to the master of the world had been born.

It was the last favor fortune had to bestow on him.

Thus it is that human pity veils the eyes of a man she guides to death.

"Sire, there are limits to human prosperity. You have rushed to the south, to the burning sands which are a pathless Ocean, and you have been forced to retrace your steps. Sire, you now hurry to the north, to those polar ices which will repel you more mutilated than did the southern sands."

It matters not, Providence impels him forward.

Besides this man who warred on all Europe, has now, with the exception of Russia, which he is about to invade, all Europe on his side.

Does not Austria, which he defeated at Austerlitz, furnish him thirty thousand men?

Does not Prussia, defeated at Jena, furnish him twenty thousand?

Does not the confederation of the Rhine, of which he

has declared himself Protector, furnish him eighty thousand?

Does not Italy, of which he has declared himself king, furnish him twenty-five thousand?

In fine, did not the Senatus-Consultum divide the National Guard into three bands for internal service, and besides the huge army which marches towards the Niemen, has he not at his disposition, one hundred cohorts, each a thousand strong?

Thus, on the 22nd of March, 1812, burst forth that proclamation addressed to six hundred thousand men. That is to say, the most magnificent army, which ever, since the time of Attila, obeyed the orders of a single chief.

"Soldiers, Russia swore an eternal alliance to France, and war on England. It violates its oaths, and now will give no explanation of its conduct, unless the French eagles recross the Rhine, and thus leave our allies at its mercy. Does it deem us so degenerate? Are we no longer the soldiers of Austerlitz? It offers us between dishonor or war, and the choice we will make will not be doubtful. Let us march onward, cross the Niemen, and carry the war into Russia. It will be glorious to the French arms, and the peace we shall conclude will put an end to the unhappy influence, the Muscovite cabinet has for fifty years exercised in European affairs."

Yet when he reached the banks of the river, where three years before, Alexandre had sworn him eternal friendship, and where he had dreamed of the conquest of India, and the annihilation of English power, he paused.

Passing his hand across his brow, he said:

"Fate overwhelms Russia, let its behest be fulfilled."

His fate was about to be accomplished.

It took three days for this immense army to cross the Niemen.

Soon he began to read the manner that the Russians opened their campaign as an open book. They were not the three words of flame on the walls of a festal hall, but the open menace of the future.

The Russians retired before him and as they did so, destroyed everything, harvests, castles and hovels; six hundred thousand men advanced into the same deserts which a hundred years, before had been unable to feed Charles XII. and his twenty thousand Swedes. From the Niemen to Wittepsk they marched by the light of a perpetual conflagration, and met neither soldiers, Generals, nor army. Terrible was the war in which they looked in vain for men to fight with, and where ruin and devastation alone were to be found.

Having thus arrived at Wittepsk, not understanding a war where vacuity alone met him, he threw himself into an arm-chair, and sending for Count Dorn, he said:

" I will remain here. I wish to reconnoitre, to rally, and to rest my army. I wish to re-organise Poland The campaign of 1812 is done; that of 1813 will accomplish the rest. You, sir, contrive to sustain us here, for we will not re-enact Charles XII."

Turning to Murat.

" Let us plant our eagles here, 1813 will see us at Moscow, 1814 at St. Petersburg. The Russian is a three years' war."

His ancient genius, the genius of the Pyramids, of Arcola, of Marengo, called forth these words. To induce him to break this resolution, which disturbs Alexandre, the latter has only to show him the soldiers he has hitherto concealed. Like a gamester who has sunken to sleep, but who revives at the first sound of gold, at the first shots, Napoleon awakes, and rushes in pursuit of soldiers, the existence of which he had begun to doubt. On the 14th of August he overtook and defeated them at Kramoi; on the 18th he drove them from Smolensk, which he left in flames; on the 30th he took possession of Viazma, the magazines of which he found destroyed. At last, when he could return, and while this magnificent army might escape the destruction Moscow prepared for it, he was informed as by a cartel, that the Russian army commanded by the Conqueror of the Turks, awaited him at Borodino, on the banks of the Kalouga.

The cartel was accepted, and on the 6th of September, at three o'clock in the morning, the two armies stood face to face.

But God continued to withdraw his hand from him. In vain as a gentle and charming presage, the portrait of his son by Girard was brought to him with letters from Marie Louise. Having placed it for a few moments in front of his tent to be admired by those Kings, Dukes, Princes and marshals, who served under his orders, he was seized by one of those melancholy dreams such as Cæsar and Charlemagne knew, and with a motion of his hand, he said:

"Take the picture of that child within. It is too young as yet to be introduced on a field of battle."

He was right, for never was a battle more violent nor more undecided, never was *te Deum* more dearly purchased.

Eleven generals died on that field, to which the sword was as unimpressible as to the plough.

From that moment he was lost; like a vessel in the Polar seas; the ice which is to envelope already floats around him.

Then he enters Moscow, the Capital he was not to have occupied until the next year. He discounts time.

But Moscow is not like other capitals. Though he has conquered it, he is not master of Russia.

From the evening of his entrance into the city, Moscow revealed itself to him only by conflagrations.

Then doubt seizes him, apprehension takes possession of him. Fatal doubt, terrible apprehension, of which he was not guilty on the 18th Brumaire, and which he will again exhibit in 1814 at Fontainebleau, and in 1815 at the Elysee.

Then instead of deciding, on either marching to Saint Petersburg or returning to Paris, instead of pitching his winter quarters in the heart of Russia as Cæsar had done in Gaul, he entered into negociation with Alexandre, who kept him undecided at Moscow.

Precious months, irreparable months, had been suffered to glide by between the conflagration of Moscow and the winter.

At last, on the 22d of October, Napoleon leaves Moscow: it is his first step on retreat.

On the 23d the Kremlin is blown up.

For about eleven days, the retreat was effected without too great disasters. All at once, however, on the 7th of November, the thermometer sank to 18° below freezing point.

God will at least leave this consolation to human pride. That army was not conquered by man, but by the elements.

What a defeat though was that!

It was a disaster which equaled that of the greatest

victories : it was Cambyses enwrapped in the sands of
Ammon, Xerxes in a single ship recrossing the Helles-
pont : it was Varro leading the wrecks of his army from
Cannæ to Rome.

Twenty days, twenty mortal days, pass beneath a sky
of snow, on an earth of snow, like a double pall above
and below our heads and our feet.

During these twenty days the army strewed on the
roadside two hundred thousand men and five hundred
pieces of artillery.   It rushed to the Beresina like a torrent to a Gulf.

On the 5th of December, Napoleon got into a sleigh
and left Smorgons; at evening on the 8th he reached the
Tuilleries.

On the next day but one, the great bodies of the state
congratulated him on his return.

On the 12th of January 1813, a Senatus-Consultum
placed at the disposal of the minister of war 350,000
conscripts.

On the 10th of March, he heard of the defection of
Prussia.

For four months France seemed transformed into one
immense camp.

The 350,000 conscripts were formed into regiments.

Mothers wept.   They discovered that the sonorous
words of which proclamations were formed, were a poor
balm for deep wounds.

On the 1st of May, Napoleon was at Lutzen ready to
attack the Russo-Prussian army with two hundred and
fifty thousand men, of whom two hundred thousand had
been furnished by almost exhausting France, and fifty
thousand by the Saxons, Westphalians, Wurtemburgers,
Bavarians and the Grand Dutchy of Berg.

The Giant they fancied overthrown was again arisen, not only was ready to sustain, but to resume the contest.

Anteus had touched the generous and fruitful mother, called the soil of France.

After the victories of Lutzen, Bautzen and Wagram, according to dates, comes Leipsic of fearful memory.

Leipsic, in which the French alone fired one hundred and seventeen shots, that is to say, eleven thousand less than at Malplaquet.

Every French shot cost ten louis: who can tell how many tears every Russian, Prussian or Saxon shot cost us?

Charlemagne another one of your peers sleeps at this new Roncevalles —Pomatowski who was drowned in the Elster.

On its reaching Erfurth on the 23d of September, the French army was reduced to 80,000 men.

On the 30th it met the Bavaro-Austrian army drawn up in front of Hanau, and intercepting the road to Frankfort.

It cut its way through, killing six thousand men, and on the 6th and 7th of November, recrossed the Rhine.

On the 9th of November, as we have told at the commencement of this chapter, at the moment when Conscience, reopening his eyes, Mariettte, at the moment when their lips met in the first chaste kiss, Napoleon returned to the Tuilleries.

Perhaps it may be asked what connexion existed between the new Hannibal, the modern Cæsar, and the children whose story we write, and how the terrible events we have recorded can influence the humble lot of two poor peasants of Haramont.

We will explain without trouble.

On the tenth of September, Napoleon said to the Senate:

"All Europe in one year will march against us. I want soldiers."

A levy of three hundred thousand men was at once ordered.

In this levy the only sons of widows from eighteen to to twenty-five were included.

Conscience was eighteen, and was a widow's only son.

Do we not know that the thunder-bolts of God sometimes strike the humblest creatures.

XI.

The Impost of Blood.

———◆———

IT is true they were far—those two children whom
love had united with its golden ring—from appre-
hending the danger which menaced them. During the
eight days which had passed since they knew they
loved, they had forgotten all the rest of the world, and
were so occupied with each other that they scarcely
knew what occurred in the village.

Poor innocent souls, they did not occupy themselves
with the great society which boils in cities; not taking
notice of it, asking nothing of it, they fancied it was as
neglectful of them, and continued to live in their pleasant hopes and in their holy faith.

One Sunday, as they came from Mass, the peasants
of Haramont saw at the corner of the street a printed
paper recently put up.

They read it.

It was an order from the prefect appointing the next
Sunday, October 26, as the day for drawing lots for
conscription, in the Department of Ariege.

From the canton of Villers-Cotterets alone, there
were required one hundred and two men.

None except the infirm, therefore, had any chance of escape.

The Maire had caused the order to be put up during Mass, that the mothers seeing it first when they came from church, where they had been praying God, might be better able to bear the news.

From the sobs that were heard on all sides after reading the notice, one might have concluded that the divine consolation was powerless.

The two children had come side by side from the church, without seeing or hearing anything that passed around them.   They had gone into the cottage of Dame Marie, where they preferred to be, for Father Cadet sometimes got angry at their loves.

Besides he had said—We must see.

But he had not said—Yes.

They sate side by side, holding each other's hands—they had not heard the rumors current in the city—they had not heard the thunder rolling above their heads; yet they spoke in such a low tone, that if any one had been at the other end of the room, he could with difficulty have distinguished the words exchanged in so low a tone from two mere aspirations of inarticulate breaths.

All at once Madeleine appeared in tears, and said, embracing him,

" My child, my poor child !"

He opened his great blue eyes; his mother had snatched him from poor Mariette, and pressing him to her bosom, kissed him.

" Mother," said he, " what misfortune has happened that you weep for me thus ?"

" The greatest possible misfortune to a poor mother," said the unfortunate woman.

Conscience looked at her with surprise.

Mariette trembled and foresaw some catastrophe.

" Do you not know, Mariette ? They will take him, and he will be killed like William. Is it not sacrilege to take the child, when the father has aldreay been taken ? My poor William ! my poor Conscience !"

Mariette began to understand, and growing pale, could only murmur with her trembling lips, the holy name of God—that name, which springs from our lips at every grief, because it is the spring of all consolation.

" Oh !" said Conscience, who had divined all, " when, dear mother ?"

" Next Sunday. I had supposed they would at least have left poor widows their last consolation and support. Oh ! he has no pity on mothers—he will be punished in his son."

At the same hour, alas ! a similar cry was heard throughout France—echoing the lamentation and the malediction we have heard.

My God ! did this Cæsar, Emperor, this demi-God, not fall because you had not heard this universal curse ?

Time rolled by, and the grief was equally profound, though not so loud, in each of the cottages. Dame Marie wept for both Conscience and Mariette. Father Cadet, who heard the news as he returned from his vineyard, seemed to become at once an octogenarian.

From time to time, however, a ray of hope descended on this silent sorrow, as a warm sun-ray penetrates into a dark and icy cavern. About ten of the numbers the highest would be good : perhaps it was possible Conscience wou!d draw one of them.

The two mothers parted : Mariette made a vow to

go on a pilgrimage with Conscience to Notre Dame de Liesse, if heaven granted Conscience a good number.

Father Cadet did, what all thought him incapable of doing; he said,

"Mon Dieu, I would give a hundred crowns if Conscience got a good number."

Conscience consoled every body—even little Pierre, who wept because he saw others weep.

"Mother," said he, "be calm. You know that God loves me. My father too died, and our debt was thus paid. All do not remain on the battle-field as he did, for Bastien has come back. I will return, mother, perhaps with a pension . . . perhaps with a Cross. I will return, Dame Marie. Be at ease—Mariette will pray for me, and God's angels will hover over her head to gather her prayers."

Madeleine said, "You talk thus, my child, to console me. Have such one, and such one, come back? Does any one know where they are? No! They have disappeared and left no trace—"

The poor mother repeated the names of villagers who had gone as William had—as Conscience would—who had never returned, and whose mothers yet wept for them.

From time to time Bastien came also; he knew that his presence was a consolation, because he was a hope. As his sympathy, however, was expressed with oaths, it became more energetic as the women became moved. Their religious susceptibility made them fear the guardian angel of their cottages would be offended at the soldier's words.

For eight days, except the trips of the children and Bernard, at the village all was confusion.

The two mothers who had deplored so much the

losses of Julienne, who had her buildings and her harvest burned, wished that like her their houses might be
burned, so that they might retain their child in their
arms, at the age when the child escapes from human
laws and holds only from God.

Father Cadet neglected his farm, and walked up and
down before the door of his empty cottage, for the mothers and their children preferred to sit in the cottage
of Dame Marie : from time to time he looked to heaven, but sometimes seizing with his hand the stock of
the vine which grew before his house, he would stand
longer than he knew of, taciturn, sad and motionless,
looking at the ground as if he looked at a tomb.

The animals, themselves, shared this sadness.   Pierrot pushed forth his long curious head, with its outstretched ears, from the window of the stable; Tardif
and Noire exchanged long lowings : Bernard stuck
more closely than ever to Conscience, one might have
said that the poor animal, knowing that he was about
to be separated from his master, was unwilling to lose
a single one of the moments he could pass with him.

The fatal Sunday came.

On the previous night no one in the two cottages,
except Father Cadet and little Pierrot, the old man and
the child, the two frail creatures which need sleep,
because the latter yet lingers in the night of the past,
and the former is about to enter into that of the future.

When the *Angelus* rang, the two mothers arose, and
went to pray at the church.   Dame Marie, at the high
altar, and Madeleine before the picture, which was the
object of her veneration.

Alas, what at another time had been an object of
veneration, now became a terror.

The beckoning of Jesus, for the child to come

to him, signified that the death of Conscience would be premature. Was not to go to Jesus, to ascend to heaven?

During this time the children had remained together.

"If you be unfortunate, and have a bad number, Conscience, will there be no means to escape this trouble?"

"Mariette, there is always one way to avoid trouble, it is to bear it. You love me, Mariette?"

"Ah! yes."

"You think that I too, love you."

"I am sure of it, Conscience."

"Well, my dear Mariette, everything is in those two words, you see: they can take me from you, and dress me up as a soldier, send me to the wars, and even kill me. They cannot, however, when I am gone fighting or dying, keep me from thinking of you."

"Dying," said Mariette in tears. "Do you think then of dying?"

The poor child raised her clasped hands to heaven, and then threw her arms around Conscience's neck.

"Die, die," said she.

"Alas! to die," said Conscience, "I know is only to part for a time; but Mariette, it is not to forget. Nothing but forgetfulness is a total separation. Look at my mother. My father has been dead nineteen years, yet not a day has ever passed without her speaking of him, not an hour without her thinking of him. My father, too, sees and thinks of her; smiles at her sacred fidelity. He reaches forth invisible arms, which she will not see nor perceive until the moment of death. For that reason, Mariette, the dying smile while the lookers on weep, the dying see what is hidden from the living."

"My God! Conscience, who told you all these sad, yet beautiful things?"

"Mariette, you know that I was one of the children of the choir."

"Well!"

"Well, I used to attend the Cure when he administered the extreme unction."

"Yes! just as the other children did; why though do not the other children talk of life and death, say such beautiful things as you do, which beautiful as they are, make me shed tears?"

"Mariette, I see things that others do not. You know very well Mariette, that I am an innocent," said Conscience, naively.

"Yes, they say so," said Mariette.

Conscience smiled, and with a fixed eye shook his head, as if he was gifted with second sight.

"Well: I told you when I accompanied the Curate to attend on the dying, I saw one thing that even his reverence did not."

"What did you see, Conscience? You terrify me. My God, did you see death?"

"No, Mariette, but I saw life, life eternal. Do you see, Mariette," (the young girl approached him trembling,) "there is always a moment, just before he closes them forever, that the dying man keeps his eyes fixed and motionless. He moves his whole body, as if to rush forward, and his lips quiver, as if to say, 'Lord, I come.' That, Mariette is the passing moment between this world and the other, the line which separates space from the infinite, time from eternity, night from day. Look, Mariette, it is what now passes in heaven, light striving with darkness, the sun revealing itself by its first ray. Oh! that look of the dying, their eyes rolling

5

in the void, as ours just now did in the night, then fixing themselves on the sun of the unknown world, as ours now do on the real world; Mariette, that glance says, 'My God, the hope of my whole life has not been deceived! My God, you are then behind the veil of life, as day is behind the veil of night. Lord, here I am, ready to enter your bosom whence I came, and to restore the immortal soul you lent me.'"

"Oh, Conscience, why did you not say that to the dying? How you would have consoled them!"

"It was not necessary, Mariette, for what I thought, they saw."

"Alas!" said Mariette weeping, "all this is very beautiful, yet it will not console me: for if you are drawn and leave, you will not be here to tell me."

"Let us hope," said Conscience, clasping Mariette's hand. "See our mothers come from prayers."

XII.

THE MAIRE, THE DOCTOR, AND THE INSPECTOR OF FORESTS OF VILLERS-COTTERETS.

WE have already said the drawing took place at the city.

Every morning it is well known Mariette, Conscience and Bernard took their milk thither.

So great was the simplicity of life of these people, that sad as the day must be to them, it began like all others, entering into the same details, and into the total of the good and bad days the Lord granted them.— Only, as the two children were much beloved, and as they were always seen together, without any one ever having doubted in the least the purity of their love, and as it was known that the drawing was to take place on that day, all looked at them with mingled sympathy and interest.

The Maire, a good-humored magistrate, first made them come in, and sought to inspire Conscience with hope, by jesting about the way to get a good number. Conscience smiled sadly, and Mariette wept at this.

When he saw the effect of his jests, the Maire stopped; he was a kind and an excellent man.

"But," said he, "are you not an innocent? Do not get angry, for I speak for your own good."

Conscience smiled.

The Maire continued—

" As you are an innocent, perhaps you are mistaken. Dame, if by chance you were a year younger, a means would be contrived to postpone you to the next year, and then to the year after." The Maire hummed the first bar of a little song. " Between now and next year much water will pass under the bridge—"

Conscience shook his head.

" That is true, M. Mussart. The name of the Maire of Villers-Cotterets was Nicholas Brice-Mussart. " It is true I am an innocent, but I know my age. I was born on the 10th of March, 1796, and this is the 26th of November, 1813. Consequently I am now eighteen years and eight months old, and am therefore liable to the law."

" The law ! the law !" murmured the kind Maire,— " as if there was any law to authorize the taking of children from their mothers, and sending them to be butchered—especially when like you, they are only children and innocents. Conscience, my lad, God is up there to correct the laws of men, and when the latter are too cruel, to reverse human wills."

" I know that, Sir," said Conscience, " and I am glad that you do also. It proves that you walk in the way of the Lord."

" How !" said the Maire as he heard him speak thus, " he must have learned that from the Cure of his village."

" Toinette," said the Maire, " have breakfast at nine, as the drawing takes place at eleven. Go tell Heraux to come and eat an *omelette au lard* with me."

Going back into his office, he said,

"Did you hear how that lad talked? Parole d'honneur, the Abbe Gregoire could not have replied better!"

Conscience and Mariette continued their rounds, and having been to several other places, reached the house of the physician of the place.

The Doctor's wife wished to see them.

"Well, my children," said she, "the great day of suffering is come at last."

Mariette began to weep.

"Fortunately, Madame Lacosse, your children are yet young," said Conscience.

"Yes, certainly: one is ten and the other eight—but you see, this year they are taken at eighteen, and next year he will want them at sixteen. Perhaps, so many of the poor creatures are killed, he may want them the year after at fourteen. You see that in three or four years, my poor Conscience, I shall be unhappy as your mother is."

Madame Lacosse wiped from the corner of her eye a tear, which was at once sympathetic and selfish.

"Madame," said Mariette, encouraged, "cannot Conscience speak to M. Lacosse?"

"Yes, my child—why?"

"Madame, M. Lacosse is a physician."

"Ah! I see—you wish to know if there be no way to save the boy. Yes, he can speak to him."

Then calling:

"Lacosse! Lacosse!" or rather said she to Mariette "let him go into his Cabinet. They can say there, where there are none but men, things they cannot talk of before women."

Mariette opened her great blue eyes with surprise.

She did not understand that there were any things that could not be talked of before all the world.

Madame Lacosse pushed open the door of the room, and Conscience was in the presence of the Doctor, who from having heard this conversation, was informed of the object of his visit.

" Well! so it is your turn now, my poor innocent.— Let us see. Perhaps there may be a way, for they tell me you are simple."

" Yes, sir," said Conscience naively, " so they tell me."

" Is it true—"

" Dame! they say so, and it must be true—"

" What do you think? I do not ask you the question as I would a philosopher, a poet, or a statesman, but—" the Doctor smiled—" what do you think about it?"

" Doctor," said Conscience without any hesitation— " if you speak of my intelligence, I think God has classed me amid the humbler portions of creation."

" Indeed! do you think so?" said the Doctor, surprised at the distinctness of the reply, both in thought and form. " You think so—and who taught you? Why?"

" It is easy enough, Doctor. Besides the society of my mother, of Mariette's mother, of Marietta, and little Pierre her brother—apart I mean from my family, I prefer the company of animals to men."

" Ah! ha!" murmured the Doctor. " You are right, my child, and that is perhaps a proof of innocence, but not of idiocy. Why do you prefer the society of animals to that of men?"

" Because it seems to me that they walk more directly in the paths of nature; because they act in obedience to their organization; because all they do is the result of their instinct, and that all the animals which God has given to man to be useful to him, are so naturally and simply, some at the expense of their liberty—as the horse, the ass, and the dog—others of their lives, as the ox, the sheep, and fowls; because I, that know what they say, being a poor creature like them, understand them when they complain, as they do sometimes; they never curse."

The Doctor heard Conscience with astonishment.

"And who do you think," asked he, "has taught the animals to act thus?"

"God."

"And then, thanks to your simplicity, do you also talk with God as you do with the animals?"

"No, for I cannot see God as I see them. God is not a visible nor a material thing."

"What then is God?"

"The Universal soul diffused through nature, of which this soul we have in us, is but an atom, a parcel, a breath which yet suffices to animate us. One does not see God, Doctor. One feels him."

The amazement of the kind Doctor almost amounted to stupefaction.

"Who," asked he, "taught you thus?"

"Long nights passed in reveries in the forests, the murmur of winds beneath the great trees, the song of the rivulets in the meadows, and the flowers in the gardens."

"Was it not the Cure?"

"The Cure never talks of these things. Once I wished to speak of them, but he shrugged his shoulders, and said, 'yes, yes.' Then he left me, full of compassion, and as he went, murmured 'Poor innocent.'"

" Then you have never talked of them."

" Yes, Doctor."

" With whom ?"

" With the things that speak of them; with night, with the wind, with the stream and the flowers."

"Then, were the Council of Revision to talk to you of such things, would you answer thus ?"

" Certainly, Doctor."

" You could not answer and say simply, ' I do not know,' or ' I do not understand.' "

" Yes! if I did not know, and if I could not under stand."

" But if you did know, and understood ?"

" To do so would be to lie."

" You would not lie, then, to avoid being a soldier."

" No Sir."

" Even if your mother and Mariette begged you ?"

" Oh ! they would not do so. If I did, I would not be an innocent as you call me ; I would do as men do, not as animals."

He shook his head.

" No," continued he ; " and even if Mariette, and my mother asked me, I would not."

" Parbleu !" said the Doctor. " This is a strange innocent. I never saw one like him."

Then, seized with great pity for the poor lad.

" Let me see your body, as nothing is to be hoped for from the mind."

He made Conscience undress.

Conscience had no idea of modesty as society understands it ; modesty, to him, did not consist in showing a greater or a less part of the body naked. Did not the animals, trees, and flowers show themselves entirely to him? His modesty consisted in not deceiving, not lying, not committing a guilty action.

At the intimation of the Doctor he then took off all his clothes.

Poor Conscience. He had nothing to hope for there.

His body was handsome and pure as his soul was: he might be called a living model of Ganymede or Apollo.

The Doctor shook his head, and said:

"You have nothing to hope for in that respect. Dress yourself, my child. Ah; your sight."

Then beckoning Conscience to him, he said,

"Let me see your eyes."

Conscience approached him.

"Odd;" said the Doctor. You are a nyctalop." —

"I do not understand."

"It means that you see by night as well as by day."

"True. I see better. The objects though are all of the same color, of a rich blue, more or less deep accordingly as it is more or less dark."

"Do you see far?"

"Very far, Doctor."

"It matters not. All kinds of phenomena have been seen."

The Doctor took a pair of spectacles with green glasses and put them over Conscience's eyes."

"Well?" asked he.

"Doctor," said Conscience, "take away these spectacles, they blind me."

"Then you do not see?"

"I am in a cloud."

"What color is it?"

"Grey."

5*

"Yes! in the dark," said the Doctor, "deep red becomes grey. Well! there is no means of passing you for near-sighted."

And he took off the spectacles.

"The cloth was red," said Conscience. "I was deceived."

"No, my friend, you were not deceived. Nature never deceives, but your senses were veiled by the interposition of art. Conscience, commend yourself to God, for nothing but chance now can save you."

"Thanks, Doctor," said Conscience, "for I feared as much. As it would please Mariette, though, I consulted you as she desired."

"So, my child! I am sorry to say, that I can do nothing for you."

"I am not the less grateful, however," said Conscience in his mildest voice.

He rejoined Mariette, and continued his rounds with her.

After visiting two or three houses, they came to that of the Inspector of Forests.

The latter had just reviewed his Guards, whom he had been ordered to place on a war establishment.

His son for whom he had already purchased two substitutes, had been forced to leave as a guard of honor.

"Ah! is it you, Conscience? You have to draw to-day?"

"Alas, yes, M. Inspector."

"Then, my dear boy, I advise you to draw number one at once, in order that the brigands may not make you languish after all."

"To me, M. Inspector, it would be all the same, but for my mother's sake, Marie and Mariette,

my departure will be a matter of much sorrow and perhaps of importance."

"As for the sorrow, I can understand it, for I have
already much to console at home, and cannot undertake
three other women. I cannot however understand,"—
and he looked at Conscience with something of an expression of pity, "what use a poor innocent like you can
be. But your departure need not prevent Mariette
from bringing us milk. And as for your two mothers,
I will attend to their winter supply of wood, so that
they shall never have been so well warmed."

Conscience was deeply touched at this offer of the inspector, M. Deviolaine—this was his name—who had
a hard face which was but a mask to cover up a kind
and excellent heart.

"M. L'Inspecteur, I thank you from the bottom of
my heart for this, in the first place on my own behalf,
and then for Mariette, who is weeping too much to do
so; also for my two mothers."

In fact Mariette had again began to weep.

"Come!" said the inspector. "For some time we have
had tears enough here without yours; go, for if my wife
and daughters were here, and chanced to see your
tears, they would begin again, and water enough would
fall to beat down all the crops in St. Remy. Go, my
lad, go!"

Tapping Conscience on the shoulder, he kindly put
him out of doors.

Conscience knew that he could rely on the noble offer
of the inspector, and, that if any trouble supervened
while he was gone, at least the houses of his two mothers would be warm.

XIII.

THE DRAWING.

IT was half-after-ten, and at eleven the drawing was to begin. As however the villages of the Canton of Villers Cotterets, and the city itself would follow in alphabetical order, Haramont was the third or fourth.

Haramont would not draw until half-after twelve or one o'clock.

This enabled Conscience to take Mariette to Haramont.

Alas! the poor children felt that they had so little time to pass together, that they were unwilling to lose a moment.

Conscience also fancied that he had not warmly embraced his mother, and he wished to do so again.

They then walked side by side across the park.

In the Inspector's garden, there was a gate which opened into this park, and made it unnecessary for them to pass through the city.

They were on foot. Bernard who knew the way better than the postman, walked before them and looked back from time to time, not to see if the children followed him, for his instinct taught him better than his eyes could, that they did.

Bernard for eight days had known perfectly well that one of the two houses was in great trouble. We will not dare to say that he knew which, but during that time he had become more affectionate to Conscience, who was exposed to danger, the danger of being separated from him.

When he had now reached a place in the park called the Pheasantry, where two roads met, each of which led to Haramont, called the one the high-road, and the other the by-path, Bernard, contrary to custom, appeared to turn aside from the latter, and take the path.

Conscience recalled him, to go as he usually did with Mariette and himself, but the dog shook his head and went on.

Conscience, now about twenty paces distant, called him back again, but instead of obeying, Bernard sate down, and looked at the two children.

Mariette wished to call to him again, but Conscience checked her.

"Bernard is not mistaken, Mariette. He has something to say to me."

Approaching the dog—

"Well!" said he, half talking, half scolding, "what is the matter, Bernard?"

Bernard whined in a low tone, without any expression of sadness, and lifted up his paw towards the forest.

"Yes, Bernard," said Conscience, "you are right. You are an animal, and instinct does not deceive you."

"Well," said Mariette, who had rejoined Conscience, "what does Bernard say?"

"Look," said he.

Extending his right hand towards the forest, he pointed out, debouching from the shade and approaching them, an old man riding on an ass, and followed by two women dressed in black, who leaned on each other.

A child's hand was held by one of the women, and the lad—as children will do—suffered himself to be half dragged.

The man and ass were Father Cadet and Pierrot.

The women were Madeleine and Dame Marie; the child was little Pierre.

As if to sustain in the isolation which awaited them, the Lord had permitted them to receive the baptismal names of two holy women.

The two groups advanced until they met, and then mingled together.

The poor family had been unable in their sorrow to await so long, the decision of the drawing, and Father Cadet, who two years ago by means of a mortgage on his land, had contrived to add three new acres to it, was on his way to take to Master Niguet, the notary, the first instalment of its price—that is to say, eight hundred francs.

The harvest had been good, and Father Cadet saw with satisfaction from the weight of the sack he carried in the pocket of his chestnut-colored coat, which he had tied up so tightly with a string, that the rattling of the money did not betoken its presence—Father Cadet, we say, saw with satisfaction, that the harvest of each year sufficed, with the addition of two or three hundred francs, to pay for the land in three years.

We do not mean to say that amid the trouble which had befallen the poor family, Father Cadet was preoccupied only by his land, for this would be an insult to the old man's heart, but we will say that as wine and idleness equally delighted Figaro's heart, the land and his grandson shared that of Father Cadet.

He therefore took occasion to hurry his visit to Villers-Cotterets, and consented to part with his dear money, though the date of payment was a week distant.

The consequence was, that all were journeying towards Villers-Cotterets.

It was after eleven when they reached it. The whole population was collected before the Maire's house, that is to say around the church and the castle square. The Maire's house was next to the church, and overlooked the square.

There, in groups mournful as those in which the Israelites wept on the banks of the Euphrates, were mothers, sisters, fathers and young men who were to draw for the conscription ; among these groups were young people who had barely left their childhood, and who were remarkable for their paleness and debility, and especially by their tears.

These groups did not mingle. Each was composed of the inhabitants of one village, and each looked at the others with hatred, asking that the heaviest portion of the impost of blood might not fall on them.

Some had sought for consolation in intoxication— and their intoxication, the cause of which was apparent, was perhaps more distressing than the tears of others.

They awaited the conclusion of Mass to commence the drawing of lots.

The people came out sadly and in tears. The church was so full, that people on their knees were seen as far as the middle of the street; sorrowful days are always those of piety.

The rolling of the wheel echoed sadly in every heart. It was a kind of premature summons. The sound of the drum for three or four years, had been sad indeed to mothers' hearts.

The Maire, wearing his scarf, accompanied by his two adjuncts, and followed by a corporal and four gens d'armes, appeared.

As he passed, all saluted him most respectfully.— Those who had the honor of his acquaintance, called him by name, to which he replied by a protecting motion of the hand.

They wished to win the Maire's favor. It seemed to all these poor creatures in their distress, that they should procure friends from all directions, and that the Maire was a powerful one, even against Providence and chance.

After the Maire, there entered the hall where the drawing was to take place, all that the room could contain, enclosed by barriers, like those around a theatre door.

The name of the first village in alphabetical order was called.

It was Boursonne.

Then began a doubly painful spectacle, the joy of some enhancing the grief of others, which not unfrequently enhanced the delight of the fortunate.

Those who rejoiced did so because they had drawn a number high enough to have some chance of remaining, and the drawing of each high number lessened that of those not yet called to the wheel.

What caused the joy of some caused sadness to others.

An inferior number increased the sadness of those who had drawn it, and the joy of those who remained, since by condemning the drawer, it left some chance to those who had not yet drawn.

This joy and sadness soon extended from the room to the crowd without.

The Conscript having drawn his number, which was proclaimed by the Maire and registered, if the number was good rushed forth with open arms, looking delightedly to heaven, and at the very door shouted out his own joy and that of his family, bearing triumphantly the saving number aloft.

If on the other hand, his lot was bad, the Conscript appeared at the door, sad, with hanging arms, and shaking his head, caring little for the fatal number which proclaimed by the Maire, was inscribed by the clerk on the register, and yet more deeply recorded on the heart of the young man, by despair.

This scene was renewed every minute. Of, however, one hundred and twenty numbers which had been deposited in the urn, thirty or forty only, were reputed as good, the alternative of sadness was far more frequent than that of joy, and there was far more sorrow than pleasure in the sad precinct.

This grief was the more profound as each village had seen some of its children set out on the two terrible campaigns of 1812 and 1813, of whom none had returned, except some poor mutilated individuals, so that mothers in their tears pressed their children to their bosoms, and as they felt their mutilated limbs, murmured,

"Balls! bullets! My God, My God! can it be with your consent that man thus treats your flesh and blood?"

Three villages came before Haramont. These were Boursonne, already named, Corcy and Damplieux.

Two of the villages seemed manifestly protected by God. These were Boursonne, and Damplieux. In all probability, of the thirty Conscripts, they were to furnish six or eight. Almost all the good numbers were in their hands.

Corcy, none knew why, was to be crushed.

In all cases, such strange and unaccountable whims of fortune are observed.

After Damplieux came Haramont.

Conscience left his two mothers, Mariette and little Pierre, with many kisses.

Bernard wished to follow him, but dogs were pitilessly proscribed from the interior, and Bernard then returned and sate at Mariette's feet.

Father Cadet was gone to the notary's to avoid the fatal explosion if such should be.

Conscience, surnamed Jean Manscourt, came out fifth.

The two first who left the room, appeared sad and downcast. They had drawn bad numbers. The third had a doubtful number in his hand. The fourth was joyful, having drawn 164.

The poor mothers, Mariette and little Pierre, knew that Conscience came fifth.

What grief and anguish passed through the hearts of the three poor women in that moment of expectation, God knows! God alone counted the hasty beating of their pulses. God only knew how pale they were.

At the moment Conscience put his hand into the urn, they had calculated it before hand; at that very moment the dog slowly lifted his head, and howled sadly The women trembled.

The howl was not finished, when Conscience appeared sad but resigned at the door, his usual melancholy smile yet lingering on his lips, with the usual melancholy expression on his brow.

The three women shrieked, for they saw that their misfortune was complete.

He approached slowly, embracing the three at once, as it were, to assume the three-fold grief.

He then, in a tone, the sadness of which it is impossible to describe, said,

"Nineteen, just the number of my age."

"My God, my God;" said the two women falling from his arms on their knees, "have we been proven sufficiently?"

Mariette stood erect, and consequently was alone in Conscience's arms; he pressed her to his bosom, and murmured:

"Dead or alive, you know I am yours."

For some seconds he pressed her lips.

At that moment, Cadet returned from the notary's, and appeared at the corner of the church, leading his ass by the bridle.

He saw the women kneeling, with uplifted hands; he saw Mariette weeping in Conscience's arms, and understood all.

"Ah!" murmured he, "so Conscience is to be treated as my poor William was."

With an effort over himself, he added:

"I would have given five hundred francs to ensure him a good number. On my word I would."

XIV.

IN WHICH THOSE WHO HAVE FORMED A BAD OPINION OF CA-
DET AND BASTIEN WILL PERHAPS CHANGE THEIR MINDS.

NAPOLEON was anxious to get his three hundred
thousand Conscripts, and therefore the Council of
Revision sate on the next Sunday.

It was the last ray of hope left to Cadet and Mariette. It seemed to them that the poor innocent must
be refused, though in her maternal pride, Madeleine
shook her head, and said :

"They will never refuse him ; he is too handsome."

Since his conversation with Doctor Lacosse, Conscience knew perfectly well what he had to expect.

Then, though the women continued to hope, he
smiled sadly, and said nothing, for a falsehood would
have been needed to console his mother.

The road from Villers-Cotterets to Haramont presented a sad spectacle. Haramont furnished nine
young men. Of the nine, the village furnished five, so
it had not, it will be seen, been badly treated.

The four who had escaped, or thought so, for at
that sad epoch, nothing was sure, returned with their
numbers on their hats, surrounded by triumphant ribbands and were dancing, shouting and filling the woods
with their joy.

Of the five others, two had sought for consolation in drunkenness, and shouted and sang as the others did, but so sadly, convulsively, and painfully, that they seemed phantoms wrested from the tomb and forced to share for a moment in the unknown or forgotten joy of the living.

The others who had preserved their sang froid, and among them was Conscience, returned without noise, without ribbands, without eclat, humble, modest, and Christian-like in their sorrow.

Those who had drawn good numbers reached home first, and brought the news of their own joy, and of others' distress. We must say there was general grief at Conscience having been drawn.

Conscience was so good, so gentle, so inoffensive, that all loved him.

Bastien was in the cabaret when he heard the news. As was sometimes the case, he had drunken more than he should, and with flashing eyes and voluble tongue, was fighting his campaigns over again, drinking from time to time to the conqueror of Austerlitz and Wagram. He was placing the glass to his lips for the fifth or sixth toast, when he heard:

" Conscience has been drawn."

Though the glass touched the Hussar's lips, we must say, that he did not taste the wine.

" What is that you say ?" asked he.

One of the Conscripts entered the cabaret, with his head all decked with ribands, and said :

" We say Conscience has been drawn. That is all."

" That is all ?" said he, placing the glass on the table, " that is enough, I think; it is too much, for it makes two families unhappy."

He added sadly:

"Poor Mariette! how she will weep!"

Rising without touching his half emptied glass, without looking at his bottle, he left the cabaret, asking as he did so, of those who had been fortunate,

"Where is poor Conscience?"

"Behind us."

"Did he come by the high road, or by the pathway?"

"The pathway."

"Very well; if possible I will console him."

He went towards the pathway.

More than a hundred persons were waiting this sad cortege, which was seen through the trees slowly approaching.

Conscience and his mother came first. His heart, so perfectly correct in its appreciation of sentiment, had understood that at such a time all was due to his mother.

Next came Mariette and Marie.

Then came Cadet and Pierre riding the ass,—as both were silent, the child understood neither the cause nor the import of this sorrow.

All who awaited advanced to meet them as soon as they were visible. Bastien was the first. It seemed to him that he had countless reasons to satisfy Conscience, a thousand horizons to open to him, so that after ten minutes' conversation he must infallibly be convinced. When he saw him, however, his tongue seemed paralyzed, and slackening his pace, he suffered himself to be gradually come up with and passed, by the first, the mass, and the last of the cortege. When he saw the deep distress of the families, he shook his head and said,

"I was wrong—God only can console those poor people."

All, it seems, were of Bastien's opinion, for none hazarded a word of consolation, and nothing but sobs and ' alas !' were heard.

Bastien was no longer even on the road ; he had stood aside to allow them to pass, being determined not even to notify Conscience of his existence, for he was aware of some·little wrongs he had done, if Conscience did not notice him. Nothing however escaped Conscience's great round blue eyes, and he saw Bastien ;— he who could read hearts sought so deep compassion in that of the Hussar, that he left his mother's side and advanced directly towards Bastien.

Bastien saw him approach, and cast a look to the right and to the left, to ascertain if Conscience was coming to see him. As no one else was near, there could be no doubt.

He then with outstretched arms advanced to Conscience.

At the same moment a sentiment with which he had hitherto been unacquainted, took possession of Bastien, and completely shook his heart.

" Ah ! poor Conscience ! poor Conscience !" said he, embracing him, " so you are about to go. The lot has then fallen on you ? Just God knows. A brave boy like you . . . the pearl of good sons—who saved my life . . . yes, my life . . . I, Bastien, say so," continued the Hussar, speaking to the peasants, who saw this expansion of sensibility with amazement, for it was in him a novel thing. " My life—Yes ! I said, true enough, that it was Bernard who pulled me out of the water ; but had Bernard been alone he would not have come to me—he would not have wet his paws, he does not like me well enough. No, it was kind Conscience who sent him to my aid. It was he. Listen—on the

evening of the fire at Julienne's . . . I made many
boasts and brags about that evening.   Well! on that
evening Conscience did every thing; he saved the
horses, oxen and sheep : well, Conscience went to rescue the child amid the flames—Conscience is a lad
none should interfere with—well ! I look on him as the
bravest and most courageous of us all.   Go, Conscience, for your mother calls you.   You have in Bastien a friend for life and death, and when Bastien says
that, it is true, and he will prove it any way he can
contrive to.   Go, Conscience, go—"

He pushed the young man back to his mother's side.
She, poor woman, received him, all grateful to Bastien
for what he had done, for she saw that his conduct
was prompted by his inmost heart.

The two families, as they were wont to do, with the
exception of Cadet, went into the cottage of Dame
Marie, and left the door open, that all sympathy might
reach him who was the object.

All at once, amid the crowd of friends who pressed
around the desolate family, a woman appeared : 'twas
Julienne, the mistress of Longpre.   She had her child
in her arms, and went directly to Conscience, who sate
by his mother on a bench, and placed the child at his
feet.

"Conscience," said she, "truly as you saved the
life of this child, I wish he were old enough to go in
your place : Conscience, truly as you saved his life, he
should go, and you should remain with your mother
and Mariette."

The poor mother pronounced these words with such
gratitude, that all sobbed aloud, and Mariette threw
herself in her arms.

Bastien was without, leaning on Catharine's arm—

he had seen through the door what had passed, and heard what had been said.

He put his hand on the round and dimpled arm of Catharine, and said—in reply to a thought which Julienne's words had awakened in his mind—

" Listen ! that is an idea."

"What ?" asked Catharine.

"Nothing, my beautiful—unless as you probably will not die of sorrow at losing me, as this poor woman will do at separation from her child, I do not risk your health by telling you that I am about to take a short journey."

" And whither ?" asked Catharine.

" Be easy. Not far—to Soissons, sub-prefecture of Aisne, and as I presume Matthew will not refuse me a horse, thanks to the quadruped, I will be back to-morrow evening, or the next day at farthest."

" To remain here, Bastien ?"

" Who knows ?"

Disengaging himself from Catharine's arm, he said,

" Come, my love, kiss me and wish me a pleasant journey.   Let me go, for the sooner I do, the sooner I shall return."

Catharine knew Bastien : she was aware that when there was an idea in his mind, it was not easy to rid him of it.   Besides Bastien had told her so often of his great acquaintances in regiments and in office, that she fancied he had some such at Soissons, to whom he wished to speak of Conscience.

As she was a good girl enough in the main, she, confiding in his speedy return, opposed no difficulty to his departure.

Bastien did not fail at once to do what he had re-

6

solved on, and readily obtained what he wanted from Matthew.

Father Cadet too had gone into his house, after having put Pierrot in his stable. He then turned his empty sack wrong side out, to see if some crown did not stick at the bottom, and seeing that it was really empty, he had returned to sit in his great wooden chair whence through the open door he could see all that took place in Dame Marie's house.

What he saw really distracted him.

Father Cadet loved as all old men love—selfishly. The misfortune of others was not a direct sorrow to him, but one which recoiled on him. In fact, he was not aware of the absolute necessity to him of seeing Conscience and his dog every day, and treated them both as idlers. Had Conscience been about to leave for three, four, six months, or a year, leaving in the cottage however the certainty of his return, Father Cadet would have bid adieu to him without too much emotion. This was not the case, though. Conscience was going away, one did not know whither—or rather, one did know, to be butchered. He was about to leave despairing hearts, tearful eyes, and sobbing voices. All this deranged Cadet's old habits, for on his return from the field the old man loved to see smiling faces and to find his supper ready. His life was to be changed, and he had reached the age when all change is painful. In seventy years Cadet had been able to reach that point.

Besides, in spite of what socialists say, the idea of inheritance is a great stimulant to man. To amass for the purpose of leaving to a child, who in his turn, will amass and bequeath to his twice what he received; to sleep the eternal sleep in the belief that a field of three, four or five acres, to become the ball of snow, to be the germ of an estate in the hands of a son and a domain to a grandson, and a fief in a degree yet farther removed, is one of those dreams of pride, which greatly soothes us in the passage from this world to the next. Father Cadet looked at his nine acres, on which he owed sixteen hundred francs, a sum he could easily pay in two years' increase in Conscience's like a cloth of gold, ever increasing, and grown in the hands of his descendants large enough to cover all the plain of Largny.

If, however, Conscience left and were killed, and Father Cadet died, what would become of the nine arpents so hugely extended in imagination? To Madeleine, who would die without children, and would bequeath it not augmented? For how could a lone woman add to it? Besides, what would her augmentations amount to, as it would have passsed out of the family?

In the course of his life, too, Cadet had some qualms of doubts about what he was pleased to call Conscience's sluggishness. Father Cadet was not satisfied that this sluggishness with which he charged the young man, was not more productive during the three or four hours he suffered the lad to have his own way, than was Father Cadet's whole day. He had seen, on certain days, when he was forced to go to Villers-Cotterets or to the market at Crespy and Compiegne, to buy or to sell, when Conscience went in his place with Pierrot and Tardif, to plough or to harrow, the next day he observed such progress that he could not realise that not one, but that two days' toil had been done. Father Cadet, then, astonished and surprised, had questioned his grand-son about the mattter, and had been told— "I sang to the animals, Father Cadet, and they worked well;" as Cadet did not comprehend this answer,

though he reflected long on it, one day when he was
about to plough, he took Conscience with him. When
he reached the plough, and the ass and ox were harnessed to the plough, he sate down at one end of the
field, and said to Conscience, "Sing to the animals, to
enable me to see how you manage them." Conscience
at once put Tardif and Pierrot on the line he wished
them to travel over, and he planted at the extremity of
that line, as guide to them rather than him, a thorn
wand, he sate quietly on the plough-beam, with his feet
resting on the sock, pressing the instrument with all
his weight, instead of all his power, being far less fatiguing. He then began a song, or rather a monotonous and gentle air, which seemed to Father Cadet, in
the double character of both Tardif and Pierrot, for
they, when they heard the air had not the least need
of the goad, but did just twice as much work as when
they were guided by Father Cadet, who reflected so
much on the matter, that the next day, the old man,
who, on the evening before, thought no one could tell
him anything about agriculture, seeing the result,
was pleased to abandon the Cadet mode for that of
Conscience. Consequently, he had harnessed Pierrot
and Tardif to the plough, planted the same wand at the
end of the furrow, and had sate on the beam as Con-
sience had done, trying to sing the same air. Whether
though, from the harnessing, from the manner Father
Cadet sate, or probably because of the song which Con-
sctence sang, something was wanting, for it was in vain
that Father Cadet sate on his beam, and sang like a
Roman Conqueror on his car. He was forced to interrupt his song by dialogue and oaths, for neither Pierrot nor Tardif moved, and Cadet, having lost an

hour in vain efforts, was forced to return to the old way or Cadet mode, being forced to own that in this manner he was inferior to Conscience.

Father Cadet, thinking then that if Conscience, instead of going remained, if Conscience lived instead of dying, that instead of leaving all to Madeleine, he found a natural heir in Conscience, in spite of the slothfulness, of which Cadet sometimes complained, all would prosper in his hands, for Conscience really seemed to be favored by Providence.

Father Cadet then resolved to make a momentary sacrifice for the purpose of keeping Conscience near him, thinking that he would be easily rewarded by the application of Conscience' faculties to the cultivation of the field.

The result was that the next day, having passed the night listening to Madeleine's sobs, Father Cadet rose early; and even before Conscience and Mariette, faithful to their old habits, had set out with Bernard, he took Pierrot from the stable, and putting the pad on his back, set out himself for the city.

Thus Villers-Cotterets was pompously called at the city.

Now, what was Father Cadet about to do at Villers-Cotterets? What had also taken Bastien to the city of Soissons?

It is probable that we shall find out in the course of the next chapter.

XV.

WHAT TOOK FATHER CADET TO VILLERS-COTTERETS.

THOUGH Cadet set out last, as he had the shortest journey to accomplish, and consequently will be the first back, we will now follow him, and find out what he is about to do almost secretly at Villers-Cotterets.

Father Cadet and Pierrot reached Villers-Cotterets at about seven o'clock in the morning. They came down the street on which the church was, to the great square, turned into the Soissons road, and stopped at the corner of the street near the smaller thoroughfare at Pleux.

They were at the door of M. Niguet's office.

Father Cadet sate on the ass as women do, with both feet on one side, as our old Picard peasants always do, being satisfied that women would not sit thus, if it were not the most comfortable way. Father Cadet slid to the ground, tied the ass to M. Niguet's shutter, and tapped at the door.

Madame Niguet opened the door and recognised the old man.

"Ah! is it you, Father Cadet?" said she. "What

brings you here at such an hour? Did you make a mistake in your count yesterday? Did you give my husband a crown too much?"

"No, Madame Niguet. I always count twice, and never give a crown either too much or too little. It is a safe precaution, for one cannot be mistaken more than once. No, I do not come for that. I wish to speak on business to M. Niguet."

"Is your business so pressing though, that you come at seven o'clock?"

"Very pressing, Madame and I hope you will at once let me into the study."

"But Father Cadet, as yet there is no one in the study, not even the runner."

"I do not wish, Madame, to see the runner, but to speak to M. Niguet."

"The fire is not yet made, and you will freeze."

"I am not cold."

"Why not come in here, until M. Niguet gets up?"

"O! you see Mariette brings you milk here, Mme. Niguet, does she not?"

"Yes, Mariette is a charming girl."

"I think when she brings you milk, Conscience accompanies her?"

"Yes—your grand-son—a fine lad : unfortunately—"

Madame Niguet paused, lest she should distress Cadet.

"Unfortunately," continued he, "a poor idiot—that is what you mean, Madame Niguet?"

"Father Cadet, I am not the first person, I hope, who has told you so."

"No, certainly. Madame Niguet, I do not wish Conscience to see me here."

" Ah !"

" No !"

" Pierrot is at the door, and he will see Pierrot."

" There is a yard ! is there not ?"

" Yes."

" Well, let me put Pierrot in it, and if the door is shut, he will not see him."

" Well ! I will make M. Niguet lead Pierrot down Pleux street, and there you will find the court-yard open.   Then I will lead you into the study."

" Very well, Mme. Niguet, very well."

Father Cadet took Pierrot by the bridle, turned down Pleux street, entered the open court-yard, and was then shown into the study, where he found M. Niguet wrapped in a woollen robe de chambre, a cotton night-cap tied on by a Pompadour riband, his feet in a pair of slippers embroidered by Madame Niguet twenty or twenty-five years before.

What was beneath this costume is indescribable, and we will not attempt to portray it.

M. Niguet was altogether different from certain persons who are ill-tempered when they are awakened; he was in a good humor when his wife roused him, for he knew she never did so for nothing.

He was therefore very gracious to his early visiter.

" Ah ! Father Cadet," said he joyously ; " sit down, Father Cadet, and let us talk."

" M. Niguet and *the company*," said Cadet, " my respects."

M. Niguet looked around to see what was the company Father Cadet spoke of ; it was, however, an idea of Father Cadet, that any person he spoke of never was alone, but always had company.

He thought it was more polite than to say Monsieur only.

"Sit down! sit down!"

"I thank you, M. Niguet, I am not weary."

Father Cadet however sate down, for it was a part of his system to say he was not tired.

"Well, Father Cadet," said M. Niguet, as soon as the old man had fixed himself, "so you are at Villers, Cotterets?"

"Yes, M. Niguet."

"On business?"

"Yes, on business."

Father Cadet sighed.

'Ah!" said M. Niguet laughing, "do you mean to buy the whole of Largny?"

Father Cadet sighed, and let his head sink slowly.

"No, M. Niguet—quite the contrary."

"Do you wish to sell?"

"Perhaps I may be compelled. I do not however wish to sell."

"What then do you wish?" said the notary, seeing that the old man wished to come to the point.

"Then I said—But you know M. Niguet yesterday was the conscription?"

"Yes, and your grand-son was unlucky."

"Yes, M. Niguet."

"It gave me much distress, I assure you," said the notary.

"You are very kind, M. Niguet and *company*," said Father Cadet. "Yes, the poor child was drawn."

"No. 19, I think?"

"No. 19—yes. But I said on the day of the drawing, I would give a hundred crowns if Conscience got a good number."

6*

"Ah! you said so—"

"Yes, on my word I did—so that yesterday when it fell to him, I must own that it gave me much trouble, and I said I would give five hundred francs if poor Conscience had not been drawn."

"Diable! then you are very fond of your grandson!"

"I love him much, M. Niguet. Ah, I love him as much as—"

"Although?"

M. Niguet understanding that he had begun a phrase which might be disagreeable to Cadet, paused, but the old man quietly abandoned the phrase M. Niguet had begun.

"Though he is an idiot. Yes, M. Niguet."

"You said so, Father Cadet—"

"I do not know if it is right, but so it is. Well, M. Niguet, this is the state of things. As an honest man sticks to his word, even when the promise is made only to himself, this morning I arose at day and said, 'Well, I will take Pierrot, and go to see M. Niguet,' and here I am."

"And what then?" asked the notary, who had become anxious to hear the promised question.

"What then? why this—I said, M. Niguet, that I would give a hundred crowns if Conscience did not go?"

"Well?" repeated M. Niguet with increased anxiety.

"Well," said Father Cadet, "the money is ready—"

M. Niguet began to understand.

"Ah ha! That is to say you are unwilling for Conscience to go."

"I will give five hundred francs sooner."

"Ah! I understand. Five hundred francs will not be enough."

"You think so?"

"Certainly."

"I thought of that," said Father Cadet with a sigh, "and I made up my mind. I had rather be quits with my five hundred francs, but if it be absolutely . . ."

"Well," said the notary, who was watching the internal contest between avarice and paternity of which the old man's mind was the scene.

"Well! If I must, I would go as far as a thousand."

M. Niguet shook his head.

Father Cadet observed the motion.

"Heh!" said he.

"Father Cadet, you must think no more about it. Leave the matter to God, for richer men than you have been forced to abandon this idea. You have done what you should have done, and even more. You know the will is reputed for the deed. Then be at peace with yourself."

"Yes—you say it is too dear?"

"And that I must not think of it?"

"No."

Father Cadet arose.

"Thanks, M. Niguet. You see I come to you as to a confessor. But if it be too much for my poor purse?"

"It is, Father Cadet."

"Let us talk no more of it. Adieu, M. Niguet."

Father Cadet walked slowly to the door, and when his hand was on the knob, he turned, scratched his head, and said,

"Perhaps fifteen hundred francs . . ."

The notary took one of his hands in both of his, and said,

"It would be far more than that."

"The fact is," said Cadet, "that I know fifteen hundred francs is a large sum—but you see if one can buy back the life of an only son for fifteen hundred francs, and at the same time keep his mother, poor Madeleine, from dying of tears, well! I would say, 'As you please' It is fifteen hundred francs lost— but in the end, do you understand, M. Niguet? the land is to be his, and he would, if he worked, win back the fifteen hundred francs. But if it be more—if it be more than fifteen hundred francs?"

"It would be more than all your land would sell for, my poor Cadet."

The old man was overpowered.

"How! You do not say so? My whole field which for fifteen years I have ploughed and harrowed myself —my whole field would not be enough?"

"No, my friend, so think no more of it."

"M. Niguet, must my poor boy then go?"

"Yes, if the Council of War think so."

"The Council of War will think so."

"Probably. Why not? They do not look for intelligence, but health and strength. To learn to make a half face to the right, to load in twelve times, does not require a man of genius like Racine, or of penetration like Demoustier. You must then expect Conscience to go, Father Cadet."

"*Dame*," said the old man with glassy eyes and with difficult breath, as if he were stifling, "I must, if it seems the sale of my field will not suffice to keep him at home—"

He stood motionless, as if he were about to faint.

"Well, Father Cadet," said the notary—"what next?"

"Oh, M. Niguet," said the old man, shaking his head sadly, "do you know what you have done?"

"No, my friend."

"You have given the death-blow to Madeleine and to myself."

"Father Cadet!"

"Yes. For the poor lad Conscience, you see, will be killed as William was. How can a poor innocent like him defend himself? Conscience dead, Madeleine will die. Madeleine dead, what will you that I shall do in the world? Besides, I will soon die, and my field will belong, to whom? To the Manscourt of Pisseleu or Vivieres, far-off cousins. That is the reason I asked you if I could not save the poor lad, if I sold the field. Well," continued Cadet with the most painful sigh he had yet uttered, "perhaps it would be best to sell. Adieu, M. Niguet and *company*. I am very grateful to you, although . . . I do not know what I say, and cannot find the door. My God! M. Niguet, every thing turns, and it seems to me that I am about to die. Adieu, M. Niguet and *company*, a—di—eu."

Father Cadet here staggered a step or two, fell under the weight of his emotion in the arms of M. Niguet —who placed him in an arm chair, and called for his wife to assist him, just as the latter said to Conscience,

"My lad, are you sure of Cadet's good feeling to you?"

"Why, madame?"

"Because I think he is about to disinherit you."

Conscience shook his head gently, and went away without any anxiety on that score.

He had just closed the door behind Mariette and himself when Madame Niguet heard her husband.

What originated this idea in the mind of Mme. Niguet, was the precaution Father Cadet had taken to conceal his presence at the notary's, from his grandson, and his anxiety to put Pierrot in the yard.

She then ran to her husband, saying the while to herself, "Whatever poor Conscience may think, there is something in this."

There was this in it. Father Cadet had been seized with an attack of apoplexy, which would certainly have been mortal, if they had not sent at once for the good Doctor Lacosse, who fortunately arrived in time to bleed the old man. Bleeding at that day, when Homœopathy was not invented, presented itself as the only remedy against apoplexy.

XVI.

Why Bastien Went to Soissons.

———◆———

BASTIEN, as we have said, had borrowed a horse from Matthew, sprung on it, and set out for Soissons at full trot.

Though but two hours and a half in passing over the seven leagues that separated him from the old Merovingian city, he did not reach it till night, and till the offices were closed.

He had decided and stopped at the inn of the *trois Pucelles*, and waited until the next day.

On the next day, when the offices were opened, he presented himself at the sub-prefecture, and managed so well that he saw the Sub-Prefect himself.

The sub-prefecture was one of those providers of human blood, for one to whom no other name but that of CORSICAN OGRE could be given.

Every man who appeared before the functionary appeared as a person, subject either now or in future, to the recruiting law, and consequently as a thing belonging to him to be disposed of for the purposes of the government.

In this respect, there was, in 1814 and 1815, much emulation among the sub-prefects. Their duty was to furnish the men demanded of them, and some even wished to see which could exceed the number.

Our Sub-Prefect was very anxious to be a Prefect.

As soon, therefore, as Bastien had been announced as anxious to see him on recruiting business, instead of refusing to receive him, he ordered him to be introduced at once.

Bastien entered with his arms loose, with his colbach on one ear, his dolman over his shoulder, and the cross on his breast, making his spurs ring in testimony of his importance.

The sub-prefect stood in front of the fire place with one hand in the arm-hole of his waist-coat, with his arm thrown forward, and his nose up in the air.

This was known to be the usual mode of Napoleon's receptions ; all the world, especially the estimable class of functionaries, a peculiarly independent class at that time, modelled themselves after him.

He examined Bastien with a rapid and knowing glance, saw in him a man of twenty-eight or thirty, small but compact, and fit for service in three or four different arms.

In this matter, however, Bastien seemed to be decided, since he appeared before the sub-prefect as an hussar.

" M. Sub-Prefect," said Bastien, toying with the tassel of his colbach, " I have troubled you, for the purpose of saying . . . . . . "

" Yes, my friend, I see.   That you find yourself subject to a recall, and that you wish to rejoin your regiment.   Is it not so ?"

" No, Monsieur, you are mistaken."

" Your *route* will be given you.   That is not my business, but you were right to come to me.   Your

Majesty and King has need of men, and it is our duty to facilitate the wishes of every soldier to resume his service.'

"Excuse me, M. Sub-Prefect, no, I am not come about that. I have a leave of absence, and a retired pay, besides this cross which you may observe; consequently, I have a right to cross my legs on the fire-irons. Here is a ticket in perfect order, adorned with a turkey-cock, and I am come to see you, wearing the uniform, which suits my general appearance."

"What then, do you want? tell me."

"I was about, M. Sub-Prefect, to do so, when you interrupted me,—by cutting off my sentence so shortly and inappropriately."

"How, inappropriately," said the Sub-Prefect with a frown.

"Excuse me, M. Sub-Prefect, it is the word we used in the Regiment to express when a thing is done without reason, wrongly, in fine inappropriately."

"Then explain yourself! What were you about to say, if I had not interrupted you inappropriately, as you said in the Regiment?"

Bastien looked in the white of the Sub-Prefect's eyes to see if some insult was not concealed in the words of the functionary.

"Yes," said he, "so we used to say in the Regiment."

"I am waiting," said the Sub-Prefect, "for you to be pleased to tell me for what purpose, you did me the honor to ask for me."

"If you had let me tell you, you would already have heard. I wished to tell you I come from the village of Haramont."

"Where is the village of Haramont?"

" What ? you do not know where the village of Haramont is ? And you the Sub-Prefect of the Department
of Aisne ! You are a droll Sub-Prefect."

The Sub-Prefect was disposed to ring for two gens
d'armes to put Bastien out. But Bastien had a sword
by his side, and a cross on his breast. The age was
one when sabres were drawn in serious battles, and
crosses enough to fill a page of the *Moniteur* were not
rained down every morning—even in the presence of so
important a personage as Sub-Prefect of a Sub-Prefecture, it was something to wear a cross and sabre.

Instead of engaging in hostilities with Bastien, the
Sub-Prefect went to a map on the wall, and looking
over it carefully, said :

" Heu ! Haramont, that is it. Canton of Villers-Cotterets, sixty six fire places—four hundred souls—levy
of 1814, nine Conscripts."

" Good," said Bastien, "you know now what Haramont is. We can talk."

" Nine Conscripts," repeated the Sub-Prefect.
" Well, has it furnished them ?"

" My village has furnished what it owes," said Bastien, piqued at the Sub-Prefect's manner. "The proof
of it is that the village drew yesterday."

" Why then, are you come ?"

" Why, I tell you that is the reason why."

" Why ?"

" Why, on account of the Conscription."

" Well ; you are not a Conscript. You have your
leave."

" Take care, my dear Sub-Prefect. You are too
quick, as we said in the Regiment."

The Sub-Prefect made an impatient gesture.

" Be calm ! be calm !" said Bastien. " When I say

that I come for that, I mean that I come to replace one who has been drawn."

"Then come to the point. You wish to replace one of those who have been drawn?"

"Yes."

"Then you sell yourself?"

"No, M. Sub-Prefect, I give myself."

"What! Give yourself?" said the Sub-Prefect, with amazement.

"Can I or not?"

"Certainly, but—"

"If I can, there is no but about it. You understand I give myself, on the express condition, you understand, that the one for whom I give myself is left."

"That is just. You go in his place?"

"Exactly. Then enroll me, and let me go—the sooner the better, since you say the little smooth-face wants men, he must not be kept waiting."

"How! the little smooth-face."

"Thus we called him in the Regiment. It may be he is called so now! It may be that he is prouder now than he used to be, and that when met, he is called your majesty. We are slow though in the campaign; let us come to business, if you please."

"Ah! then," asked the Sub-Prefect, "it is a relation, your nephew or brother, whom you wish to replace?"

"Not at all."

"Do you make such a sacrifice for a stranger?"

"No: Conscience is not a stranger—no."

"His name is Conscience?"

"Yes, does that surprise you?"

"Why, peasants have such strange names."

"Do they not? You never hear of Conscience in cities."

" You are decided then to go for Conscience ?"

" Very decided."

" You have thought well of it ?"

" Certainly."

" Very well. A note to the Doctor will be given you, that he may ascertain that you have no disease."

" Ah ! M. Sub-Prefect."

" Well ?"

" I do not think I look sick."

" It matters not.   It is a formality."

" Ah ! if so, nothing is to be said but to submit to it."

Bastien waited quietly until the Sub-Prefect had written.

" Now," said the Sub-Prefect when he had written, folded and sealed the letter, " take this to the Doctor. What have you in your hand though ?"

" Never mind that," said Bastien, putting his left hand out for the letter, and keeping the right behind him.

" Not that hand," said the Prefect.   " The other, it seems to me, wants two fingers."

" Well, what of it ? You certainly would not have them cut off and be there still !"

" Ah ! but if you have lost two fingers, you are maimed."

" How ?   Maimed !"

" Certainly, you are aware that his majesty, Emperor and king, wants complete men ?"

" You are very particular, M. Sub-Prefect, I think."

" If you had been drawn yourself, my fine fellow, perhaps they would not be too particular. As, however, you wish to go for another who perhaps has all his members, we cannot reasonably accept you."

" Heh ! then you refuse me ?"

" I say you are unfit for military service."

"And when men built like me come to you, you bargain with and depreciate them, do you?"

"My friend, you should have begun by showing me your hand, and then I could not have bargained with, but would have told you plainly, 'It may not be,' and all would have been over."

"So you will not take me in Conscience's place?"

"Sorry to say anything disagreeable, but my friend it is impossible."

"So poor Conscience must go?"

"Unless he, like you be deficient, he must probably go."

"You do not know, this will make a whole family unhappy."

"Peuh!"

"His mother will die."

"Bah! if all the mothers were dead, one would not see so many women in mourning."

Bastien was terrified at this cynical reply.

"It is well," said he, with a dignity of which one might have thought him incapable. "God is my witness, I did this to protect those poor people from despair, and you have wished to make them unhappy. God will judge us according to our deserts. Adieu, M. Sub-Prefect."

He left.

"Ah!" said the Sub-Prefect as he left. "That fellow does not know that in three months he will have to rejoin his regiment, and that if I accepted him, I would rob the Government of a man."

XVII.

Understandings.

———◆———

FATHER Cadet was led mounted on his ass to Haramont by the Runner of M. Niguet.

This new sorrow was a relief almost to the afflicted family.

Doctor Lacosse had sent with him a prescription which was to be taken with the greatest punctuality.

In spite of the promptness and efficaciousness of the attendance, as the blood had been extracted from the right side, the left was menaced with complete paralysis, and the tongue was palsied that it could scarcely articulate.

Doctor Lacosse, however, promised that he would be better, though he did not guarantee a complete cure. It was, however, evident, that Cadet was become unable to cultivate his farm just at the moment that Conscience was called away. With a paralyzed arm, of course he could not work.

This however was a future misfortune, and no one perhaps in the whole house, except Father Cadet, thought of anything except present trouble.

Bastien returned to the village two hours after the return of Father Cadet. The accident which had befallen the poor man was the talk of all Haramont. It was the first thing he heard.

"Well!" said he, "that alone was wanting."

He went to the cottage to ask about Father Cadet's health, and did not say a word either of his journey to Soissons or of the cause.

From time to time, however—before, it had always been with pride—he looked at his mutilated hand with pain, and exclamations of discontent

On the next day Mariette and Conscience, as usual, took their milk to the city, and returned at the usual hour.

When they did so, Conscience, without seeming to notice either his mother, Dame Marie, Mariette, nor Catharine, who were present, went directly to the old man's bed and knelt by it, aiding Father Cadet in the effort he made to place the hands on the head.

"Father," said he, "I ask your pardon for being the cause of the terrible accident which happened to you, and the Lord alone can know how grateful I am to you."

The two mothers listened to Conscience with amazement.

Mariette, however, said to them in a low tone,

"Father Cadet tried to sell the field to procure a substitute for Conscience: M. Niguet told us."

The women clapped their hands, and knelt by the bed of the old man.

The field of Father Cadet was his heart, and more than his heart.

The old man wished to give more than his heart for Conscience.

This spectacle seemed to surpass Catharine's imagination. for all at once she exclaimed,

"On my word! and he is not the only one."

"What do you mean, my child?" asked Madeleine.

"I wished to say, that people who are not relations even, were willing to do as much as Father Cadet, who is his grandfather, and who having no land to offer, offered themselves."

Madeleine, Dame Marie, and Mariette looked at Catharine with amazement.

Conscience, with his head hanging over the old man, seemed to pray.

"Yes," said Catharine, "I can mention a brave lad who is not far from here, who went to Soissons to offer himself in Conscience's place—and if the Sub-Prefect had not excused him on account of his hand, at this time you need only to have been anxious about that old man."

"Bastien!" exclaimed all.

"Hem! What is the matter? Who called Bastien?"

"Bastien!" exclaimed Dame Marie, Mariette, and Madeleine, "did you do that?"

They all burst into sobs.

"Well," said Bastien, "Catharine has been talking. That is the way with these damned women; they never can hold their tongues."

"Well," said Catharine, "I could not, and told why you had gone to Soissons."

"Not true—"

"That you saw the Sub-Prefect?"

"Not true—"

"That he refused you on account of your hand?"

"Not true! not true!"

Madeleine seized the mutilated hand and kissed it—

Dame Marie put the other on her heart, and Mariette gliding between the two women, presented the other brow to the Hussar to kiss.

"What is all this?" said Bastien in surprise.

"Do you not see?" said Catharine. "You fool, Mariette presents her brow to you to kiss. Ah! I see you are not used to kiss the brow."

"Mariette," said Bastien, "you too!'

"Bastien," said Mariette, "did you do that?"

"It is not tr . . . It is strange, Mariette, that I cannot lie to you. I can lie well enough to Catharine."

"Just hear!" said Catharine.

"Well! it would be no great matter if it were true. Did not Conscience save my life? Was it not my life he saved? Does it not therefore belong to him? Or was it after all any great matter for me to go back to fire? I am used to it. For seven or eight years I ate it morning and evening every day, and not unfrequently during the night. But then they refused me. It is not my fault, but that of my hand. Let us say no more. Come, Catharine. You were wrong to talk of this before the women—or rather, you were right, as it procured me the honor of a kiss from Mariette."

"Just listen to the mad Hussar!" said Catharine.

"Come, come, I feel that I am giving way, and I always look like a fool when I weep. Come, Catharine, come."

He hurried Catharine out of the cottage, but at the door he met Conscience.

"Ah! you are waiting for me," said Bastien. "It is your turn now."

"No," said Conscience. "I know what you have done, and I wished to speak to you."

"To me?"

7

"To you—"

"Alone?"

"Alone."

"Now?"

"No—to-morrow, while Mariette is at the city, and when Doctor Lacosse is with my grand-father."

"Very well, when I take Matthew's horses to water I will wait for you at the three oaks behind the house."

"Thanks, Bastien."

"Ah," said Catharine, "he is not wise."

"Catharine," said Bastien, "that may be the case, but in two cases he has taught me that those who make the most noise do not do the most work."

The family passed the day in the usual mode, except that additional cares and tears were produced by the illness of old Cadet. As Conscience understood the language of animals, it seemed that heaven had given him the power of comprehending the mutterings of his grandfather. As soon as Father Cadet wished for any thing, it was given him : as soon as his glassy eye was looking at any object, Conscience had it in his hands, and used it as the old man wished he should.

The next day, Conscience, instead of going with Mariette to Villers-Cotterets, told her to go alone, and begin with the house of Doctor Lacosse, and to ask him, if he were not already gone, to come as soon as possible to Haramont.

Mariette never asked Conscience for his reasons ; she knew that by means of that internal illumination, the rays of which animated his glance, Conscience had a reason for what he did. She therefore set out with Bernard, whom Conscience's thrice reiterated orders could scarcely induce to set out with Mariette.

It usually was nine o'clock in the morning when Bastien took Matthew's horses to water. On this occasion, however, in his anxiety to comply with Conscience's wishes, he had set out at ten minutes before nine, and was almost immediately at the three oaks.

Conscience sate at the foot of one of them.

When he saw Bastien, he arose.

Bastien pushed forward his horses, and when at the three oaks, sprang on the ground, and sought to tie his horses to the branch of a tree.

"It is not worth while," said Conscience, "I have but one thing to say to you."

"More than that, my dear boy. It has been so long since I could talk to you."

He moved towards his horses.

"I wished you to tell me what took place between you and the Sub-Prefect."

"Ah, did you stop me for that? On my word, it was not worth while."

"Yes," said Conscience, "it is, for I wish to know all that passed."

Conscience spoke so gravely, that Bastien found himself overpowered by the gentle and firm voice, which at at the same time besought and commanded.

"Indeed, you wish to know?"

"Yes, Bastien."

"Well—you understand—I ask your pardon, I saw you had no great vocation for the military profession."

"That is true!" said Conscience.

"Though I declare, for I have seen you act, that in the whole army, not even among the old growlers, is there a braver man than yourself."

"It is not bravery, Bastien, but the confidence I put in God."

"Well, be that as it may, seeing, I say, that you had little vocation for the profession of arms, I conceived, from what I heard Julienne say, when she placed her child at your feet, and when I saw the tears of everybody, the idea of going in your place."

"Kind Bastien!"

"Yes, I argued thus. I like the military profession, and am fit for nothing else. Besides you see the profession is not always unpleasant. There are some good days, and some nights that are not bad. You know nothing of that though, and have no vocation for the profession. I said plainly to the Sub-Prefect, 'You see we should help each other in this world. Conscience has been drawn, he does not wish to go, and here I am in his place.'"

"Give me your hand, Bastien."

"Yes, this cursed hand has spoiled all. All had been arranged; he had written a letter for the Doctor, he handed it to me, and I was about to receive it, when he asked me, 'what is the matter with your hand?' You see, I could not deny it, so I said, 'ah, a trifle, a scratch, two fingers shot off by an Austrian ball at Wagram! That is nothing, though—give me the letter.' 'No, no!' said he, ' the loss of one finger is a case of maim, and two lost, in a yet greater degree. His Majesty the Emperor and King wants no crippled soldiers.'"

"And why," said Conscience, " is the loss of a finger so important?"

"The loss of a finger," said Bastien with an important air, " is to be considered, because you see, if you be in the foot, you cannot lose your gun. If the index be gone, you cannot fire, because you have lost the trigger finger; on the other hand if you have lost the same finger, and go into the cavalry, the Hussars, for instance, and I think if you were permitted to choose your corps, you would go nowhere else, the loss of that finger would prevent your using your sword properly. That is the reason why the loss of a finger is so important."

"Thank you, Bastien, that is what I wished to know."

"Is that all?"

"Yes."

"Because you see, if you need any other information, with the same pleasure . . . . "

"Now, your hand, Bastien."

"With pleasure.   But you are not going at once."

"No."

"We will meet again?"

"Certainly."

Bastien untied his horses and mounted one of them.

"But," said he, putting his hand over his eyes, "·who is that riding from Villers-Cotterets?   Oh! Doctor Lacosse."

"Yes," said Conscience. "It is he.   He promised to visit Father Cadet, and he is come.   Go water your horses, Bastien."

Conscience spoke so seriously that Bastien looked at him with surprise: he said with uneasiness,

"What are you thinking of, Conscience?"

"That perhaps there is a way to keep Madeleine from dying of grief, and Father Cadet of hunger."

Bastien reflected for an instant.   But seeing that he could not penetrate into Conscience's thought, he said:

"One should never despair.   Forward Squadron. Ah! at the Regiment, it was pleasant to hear that."

He rode at full trot towards the village square, where the water-box was. Conscience returned slowly, by the back door to Cadet's cottage.

XVIII.

The Finger.

———

DOCTOR Lacosse had ridden his mare to visit
Father Cadet at Haramont. He had not seen the
old man for twenty-four hours.

The Doctor was awaited with great impatience by
all the family. The patient had passed a bad night, and at
seven o'clock on the previous evening, the fever had
increased, and scarcely had left the old man, who laid
in an alcove, which the daylight scarcely penetrated.

The Doctor had a lamp lighted that he might examine him with more ease. His patient was pale, his eyes
were sunken, and his pulse, it was true, was a little high,
but his trembling tongue uttered but indistinct sounds,
and could scarcely be put from the mouth. The patient could scarcely move the left arm, and the left leg
was powerless.

In spite of all this however, he was much better: as
on the previous day he had taken from him nearly six
ounces of blood, a second venesection, the Doctor
thought dangerous, especially to a peasant, the blood
of whom is always thin, in consequence of insufficient
food. He therefore recommended Mustard Cataplasms,
and for the head, which was to be kept high, Compres-

151

ses steeped in spring water, renewed freqently enough
to be always fresh and cool.

Cadet's life was saved, but it was probable that he
would never be able to use his arm, and that he would
walk with difficulty.

Yet even this was much to the unfortunate family,
of which Conscience was the soul, but Cadet the head,
to know, that weakened as it was, it yet would be preserved to it.

The Doctor, therefore, left the house with the blessings of the women. Pierre held his mare by the bridle,
and having mounted her, he began to go towards Villers-Cotterets.

About a hundred yards off, he saw Conscience.

The young man was very pale, and had his right
hand wrapped in a blood-stained cloth.

"My God!" said Doctor Lacosse stopping his horse,
"what is the matter?"

"Doctor," said Conscience, with a mild but calm
voice, "I have met with a great misfortune."

"What, my child?"

"While cutting wood in Father Cadet's yard, I cut
off the finger of my right hand."

As he spoke, Conscience unfolded the cloth, and
showed the Doctor his mutilated hand."

The index was cut off below the second joint, and
the flow of blood was so great as to induce apprehen-
sions of a hemorhage of the little artery.

"How long since this happened?" asked the Doctor.

"About ten minutes."

"And why did you not come to me at once?"

"I feared lest I should frighten Mariette and my
mother too much, so I waited for you here."

"But do you know I have a very painful operation to perform on you?"

"Yes, Doctor," said Conscience calmly.

The Doctor looked at the injury carefully, and as if he would test Conscience's courage, said:

"Do you know, I will have to dearticulate the finger?"

"Do so, Doctor," said Conscience, as if he had not heard, or did not understand the terrible signification of the term.

"Where?" asked the Doctor.

"How, where?" said Conscience.

"Where shall I perform the operation?"

"Under these trees. Can you not?"

The Doctor looked at the young man in amazement.

"Well, who will aid me?"

"I will, Doctor," said Conscience.

"You?"

"Yes!"

"And if your strength gives way—if you faint?"

"There is no danger, Doctor, of that."

"There must be some one, if not for you, Conscience, for me. I shall have the digital artery to take up, and while I do so, a strong man must press on the palmar arch. Wait here, and press your thumb thus in the hollow of your hand, so as to lose as little blood as possible, while I go to the village to find some one."

The Doctor did set out, at a trot.

"Doctor, you need not go," said Conscience, "here is exactly the man we need."

He nodded towards Bastien who was rapidly riding back the horses, a little delayed by the fact that he had stopped to drink himself.

"Ah, yes!" said the Doctor. "Bastien, an old soldier —he is just the man we need."

He called to him—

Bastien stopped his 'Bivouac of the Hussars,' a song he was thundering, and soon galloped to the place where Conscience and the Doctor were.

"Heh! what is this," said he, as he saw the bloody napkin on the ground, and Conscience compressing his hand.

"The Doctor, my dear Bastien, wishes you to aid him in an operation."

The eyes of Bastien and Conscience met; at this moment, the latter remembered the conversation he had previously held with Conscience.

"Poor fellow!" murmured he.

"Well, Bastien," said the Doctor, "you will aid us? There is no time to be lost."

Bastien sprang to the ground, tied his horses to one of the three oaks, while the Doctor let his mare, a very gentle animal, browse in the tufts of grass on the ditchside.

"Oh!" said Bastien, approaching the Doctor, who had opened his instrument case, and chosen his best vistory, while Conscience looked on—"the case is serious?"

"A surgical operation always is, my dear Bastien; this, though, you can understand, having undergone one like it yourself."

"Yes, yes, I know."

"And being a soldier, you must have witnessed many others."

"Certainly I have. So Doctor, I am now at your service, and will not budge. Conscience, my friend, take courage. Come, come."

It was easy enough to see that Bastien, who was very sensitive, was seeking himself to acquire the courage he recommended to Conscience. The latter smiled with his usual gentleness, and said—

"I am ready."

One might have fancied that his serene soul soared above the things of this world, and that pain did not affect him.

Fearing however that Conscience's strength would give way during the operation, the Doctor told Bastien to hold the hand on which he was about to operate, and to compress the artery, as Conscience did.

The Doctor had his vistory, and had prepared his bands. All was ready.

He approached the patient.

"Come, my lad," said he, "sit down on the back of this ditch."

"Why so, doctor?" said Conscience, "it seems to me, you will be more at ease if I stand."

"True—but you have not strength to keep yourself erect."

"I told you to be at ease, Doctor."

"Well, at least rest against this tree."

"Oh! willingly."

"True!" said Bastien, "that will be more convenient for me also."

Conscience leaned against the trunk, and Bastien put his left arm around it, while with the right he sustained that of the patient.

"Come, Doctor, go on," said Conscience.

"It is an affair of two minutes," said the Doctor.

"And two minutes soon pass," said Conscience.

The Doctor took off his coat, folded up his sleeves, and with a steadiness of hand which denoted the old

Regimental Surgeon, made first a single circular inci-
sion a few lines above the palmar articulation, drew the
skin towards the wrist to make the muscle prominent,
and then with the same steadiness, divided the flesh, the
ligaments and the synovial membrane, Conscience all
the while not moving or complaining.

The poor lad seemed supported by some superhuman
power.

We must say, however, that in spite of the promises
he had made, Bastien, who, as he said, had seen arms
and legs cut off in battle, coughed, uttered exclamations, and in fine, Bastien held Conscience's hand with
convulsive force, which resulted less from muscular ten-
sion than nervous excitement.

About the end of the second minute and when the
joint was about to be dearticulated, Bastien's power
was gone, he grew very pale, muttered a few indistinct
words, and sliding from the tree, sank on the ground.

" Doctor, Doctor !" said Conscience. " I believe poor
Bastien has fainted."

" Let him faint," said the Doctor, " and mind our
own business. Seize your hand as he did, and do not
move. . . all is over."

" So soon ?" said Conscience, compressing the artery
again as he had done ; " it was not long."

" Indeed," muttered the Doctor, as he finished the
operation, " if I had not talked with this lad as I did
yesterday, I should think his idiotcy amounted to insen-
sibility."

" Is it over, Doctor ?" asked Bastien, recovering.

" Yes—in a second."

Having done cutting, the Doctor had replaced the
flesh, and having closed it was occupied in making

bandages of sticking plaster, which he took care should not be too slight, and create inflammation.

This was the state of things when Bastien opened his eyes.

The Doctor seemed excited, but Conscience was calm and looked up. He seemed to behold things invisible to common eyes, and to derive from them the supernatural power he had exhibited.

While the Doctor was finishing with the bandages of the right hand, Conscience gave the left to Bastien, who, though yet weak, stood up.

"Ah!" said he, "you do not need me any more, Doctor."

"No, my friend. I will even go so far as to say that if I ever need any aid again in any similar operation, I will not come to you for it."

"You are right, Doctor," said Bastien, "especially if Conscience be the patient."

"Why so? It seems to me that Conscience has supported this operation most stoically."

"That is exactly the reason. When on the field of battle and in the ambulance, I have seen legs and arms arms amputated, the sufferers howled, cried, and cursed—so that one could say, 'Shut up! you robber!' Conscience though, you see, with his gentle glance and his eternal smile, overcame me, my head swam, and—good night. . . . Now though it is over, I will take back Matthew's horses."

He remounted, and left at a long trot, saying,

"It is all the same. I like people to hallo, though in the Regiment it was the case . . ."

"Kind Bastien," said Conscience as he saw him go.

Bastien had not gone fifty paces, when a piteous cry was heard from Cadet's cottage.

"What is that?" said the Doctor, trembling involuntarily.

"Nothing," said Conscience; "but Bernard, who is back from the city with Mariette, and knowing that I have met with an accident, he pities me."

"What! He know that you have met with an accident?" said Doctor Lacosse, as the last bandage was put around the wrist. "How does he know?"

"Ah, you ask a question I cannot answer. I only know that he knows, and here is proof—"

A second and more piteous cry than the first was heard.

"Why, then," said the Doctor, "does he not come?"
Conscience smiled.

"Be easy, he will come as soon as he is untied. I am afraid, though, that he will bring my mother with him. Did I not say so?"

At that very moment Bernard appeared at the corner of Cadet's cottage, and without either smelling or taking the direction, he rushed directly to the three oaks.

"Wonderful!" said Doctor Lacosse, looking with curiosity at the dog's rapid approach.

The eye of Conscience did not move. It was plain that he expected some one.

Almost immediately Madeleine and Mariette appeared at the door of the cottage.

"You see, Doctor," said Conscience, "that I was not deceived."

"Will you tell me how you knew?"

"Nothing is plainer. My mother, as usual, thought I had gone to Villers-Cotterets with Mariette. Seeing her return alone, she became uneasy. Then the dog knew an accident had befallen me. He howled first—

that aroused my mother: he howled again, and my mother said 'He has come back without Conscience.' Then when unharnessed from the cart, Bernard howled again and came towards me, followed by Mariette and my mother."

While Conscience was giving this explanation, Bernard had joined him, and sprang up—half-delighted, half sad—feeling for his right hand to lick it gently; while he had raised his left above his head, and waved it gently to tranquilize his mother and Mariette.

In spite of these signs, the poor mother approached pale and languid, for she saw the bloody bandages, and on the reverse of the ditch the instrument case of the Doctor was still open.

The Doctor advanced some twenty paces towards her.

"My God! my God! Doctor," said she, "what has happened to poor Conscience?"

Mariette, who did not speak, looked anxiously around her.

"Nothing," said the Doctor, "or rather an accident of no importance."

"An accident? Conscience, Conscience—"

"Mother, it is nothing. You see here I am."

"An accident, my God!" exclaimed the poor woman—"an accident!"

And she sought to see the hand which Conscience kept behind his back.

Mariette saw what Madeleine could not.

"Mother, Conscience has but four fingers on his hand."

"And that is a great blessing," said Doctor Lacosse, "for thanks to it—and it is not dangerous—Conscience is sure to be refused."

"You understand, mother, I will not leave you—I will not leave Mariette."

Madeleine fell on her knees, and lifting her hands to heaven, clasped them and said,

"My God, thy will be done. Hallowed be thy name on earth as it is in heaven."

"Conscience," said Mariette, "was it to do this, that you sent me alone to the city?"

"Be silent," said the young man.

Just then Bastien was seen behind a little eminence. He had taken his horses to the stable and had returned to meet his friend.

"Come," said Doctor Lacosse, mounting his mare—"be calm; I will return to-morrow, and as you are all good people, I hope that all will be for the best."

XIX.

The Revision.

<hr/>

ALL was going on for the better. As is almost always the case in paralytic attacks, the mind of Cadet for a few days was beclouded, so that it was impossible to explain to him the accident Conscience had met with. He did not even perceive it.

Doctor Lacosse returned the next day, as he had promised. The two patients were doing well. Conscience suffered much and had a violent fever, but bore his suffering with so much tranquility, and but for his eyes, which shone with unaccustomed lustre, it was impossible to see that he was ill.

Amid all this misfortune, however, had risen the hope awakened by a word of the Doctor, that become unfit for military service, Conscience would be rejected by the Council of Revision.

The meeting of the Council was fixed for the next Sunday, the fifth day after the accident.

The Sub-Prefecture was seven leagues from Haramont. All the other Conscripts to be at Soissons at ten o'clock in the morning, had set out at night. Though Conscience, however, said he was well enough to walk as his comrades did, at the instance of Doctor

161

Lacosse, Bastien would not hear of it, but at six in the morning came to the door of the cottage of Cadet, with a carriole borrowed from Father Matthew.

The women were unwilling to leave Conscience. In the first place, Mariette had her milk to carry to Villers-Cotterets : this was an opportunity to travel a league and to remain an hour longer with her lover; then Madeleine as a mother, asked leave to take advantage of the opportunity ; Dame Marie, being last of kin, and only a foster-mother, remained alone with Cadet.

Bernard with the little carriage, was to follow the equipage.

As he suffered himself to be harnessed, Bernard opposed great objections. He understood that a journey without him was projected, and experience having taught him that when he left his master for merely two hours misfortune had befallen him, he doubtless feared that if he left him for a longer time a greater misfortune would occur.

Father Cadet saw all the preparations with an unobservant eye, as men see in sleep, that is, without lucidness or sleep. They told him Conscience was about to leave for a short time, and that sufficed.

The two women having kissed Dame Marie, got into the carriole. Conscience sate on the second seat. Bastien by his side, whipped up the horse, and they set out.

Bernard with a long, sad howl acccompanied them.

The village on that day had arisen at an earlier hour than usual. The Conscripts who had to walk seven leagues to reach Soissons by nine o'clock, had set out at three o'clock in the morning, and as if to make the grief which had entered every household apparent, the doors had remained opened, and the can-

dles lighted. Through the open doors, and by the can-
dles was seen either an isolated mother, motionless, and
wiping away her silent tears, or some group weeping,
united by sorrow.

Had death even, entered every door, they could not
be more melancholy or sad.

Those who drawn high numbers were ordered up
as the others were, for though there had been great
difficulties thrown in the way of escaping, it was still
necessary to reject those not tall enough, or whom any
infirmity made unfit for military service. Every rejec-
tion consequently increased the number of bad chances
by one.

By day they had reached Villers-Cotterets. It was
then seven o'clock; at ten they had to be at Soissons.
They had to go six leagues, and could spare no time.

Bastien, in order to allow a few moments more to
his poor friend, did not stop until he had reached the
Soissons road at the end of the city. There they had
to post.

It was the first separation, for never during his life
had Conscience left his mother for a day.

Who knew for what time, he was now to leave her?

The hope with which they had lived, that they had
nourished and fed so long as the day of separation was
not come, the hope they had looked on as a reality,
now when they invoked and called on it, escaped from
the arms which wished to seize it, like a vapor, a cloud,
a chimera.

The embraces were long and painful. Conscience
could not embrace Mariette as he did his mother:
therefore clasping Madeleine to his bosom with his mutilated hand, he gave the other to Mariette, who leaned
over it and bedewed it with her tears.

As if he comprehended his humility, Bernard, with his eye fixed on the desolate group, did not seem even to solicit attention; but it was easy to see how deep his grief was.

Half-after seven struck, and they had but two hours and a half to travel six leagues. Wiping away a tear with the corner of his cuff, Bastien began to crack his whip in order to tell his sad companions that the parting hour was come. Then the silent tears became sobs—broken words escaped amid kisses from the lips, and even while saying to Bastien, "a few minutes more, before we separate," they separated.

A cry, however, which seemed the expression of human grief, struck Conscience's ear as he prepared to get into the carriole again.

"Oh! Bastien," said he, "I forgot poor Bernard."

He ran towards Bernard, who had modestly remained twenty paces in the rear, and who saw that Conscience remembered him, and came to him—and the dog approached so rapidly that he spilled half of the milk from the tin vessels in which it was.

Let none laugh at what we say. The parting of the dog and his master was tender. Conscience said in a low tone a few words, to which the dog replied by barkings which were unintelligible to all others : a promise, however, was exchanged between the two friends—Conscience gave Bernard to Mariette as long as he should be absent, and Bernard promised to serve and protect her.

A last kiss, rapid as a spring breeze, bedewed by tears, was deposited on Madeleine's cheek, and Mariette's whole face. Then Conscience was again called by Bastien into the carriole.

It was driven on, but by leaning back Conscience

could still with his hand and head reply to signs made by his mother and Mariette, and not till the road turned did they disappear.

Then Madeleine sate on the back of a ditch and suffered her head to sink in her hands. Mariette looked long at her as she sate with drooping head, tearful eyes, and hanging arms. Then in respect for the great grief of a mother, which compared with others always seems an abyss, she went into the city with Bernard, being confident that on her return she would find Mariette where she left her.

Bastien and Conscience advanced rapidly towards Soissons.

At ten o'clock precisely, it stopped at the door of the Sub-Prefecture. As the revision as well as the drawing was by the alphabetical order of the places, the canton of Villers-Cotterets would not be called until about four o'clock.

Conscience would therefore have been able to pass at least five hours with Madeleine and Mariette, which he whiled away on the door-steps with Bastien.

Slow as they seemed, the hours were buried one after the other in that abyss of time we call the past. The turn of Haramont came, and the five young men who had been drawn were introduced, followed by four others, who hoped in consequence of high numbers, to escape.

The room presented a stern aspect enough. On an elevation sat the Sub-Prefect, the Maire, and the municipal authorities. Two physicians of the city, and two army surgeons, stood in a kind of semicircle in which the Conscripts were introduced. A dozen gens-d'armes stood against the wall.

The order of revision observed for the city was inverted for the villages. The young men were collected in a large hall, whence they were called according to their number—that is to say, he who had drawn one was called first, and so on, until the whole contingent was supplied.

Conscience was then to appear before them, the nineteenth, that being his number.

Those who were rejected, were permitted to leave and return home at once. Those who were thought good were sent into another room, enrolled, and assigned to a regiment. Thence they proceeded to a barrack, and in two or three days marched for their respective regiments.

Of the first eighteen, three only were rejected by the board—one because he was not tall enough; another because he had broken his knee in a fall from a roof—he was a thatcher, and limped—and the third because he was far gone in a phthisis.

Then came Conscience's turn.

His name was called, the door opened, and he appeared.

It was about to be closed when Bastien's head appeared.

The gen-d'armes wished to make the head disappear; but seeing a soldier, and a soldier with a cross, he treated him more respectfully than he would another.

"Comrade," said he, "the orders are positively no admission except to the constituted authorities, physicians, surgeons, conscripts or gens-d'armes."

"Diable! so those are the orders?"

"You know I would not speak falsely to an old soldier," said the gen-d'armes.

"Then I cannot enter?"

"You cannot."

"It will not even permit me to put my head, thus, in the door?"

"Not even that."

The gen-d'armes was about to close the door.

"Wait a moment," said Bastien, "if I cannot enter or put my head in . . .

"You cannot."

"Well . . . it does not prevent, that by mistake, and from inattention, to do a favor to an old soldier, you can leave the door pushed to, thus . . so that I can alternately apply my eye and ear, as I would look or listen . . You see, gen-d'armes, I am anxious to see and hear particularly, all that relates to the lad now being examined."

The gen-d'arme looked at his companion, and said,

"Comrade, do you hear?"

"Yes, well?"

"What think you?"

"That it will be no great crime to do what he wishes."

"Very well, comrade," said the gen-d'armes to Bastien, "we are not Turks."

"Thank you."

"Look, hear, but do not say a word, else I will catch either your ear or your nose in the door."

"Be at ease, for," said Bastien, "I will be quiet."

"Oh—The authorities speak . . hush," said the gen-d'armes.

"True," said Bastien.

He listened—

During this dialogue, Conscience had been called in front of the gallery on which the Sub-Prefect sate. His name and surname were asked, as also the reasons why he wished to be exempt.

He took his mutilated hand from the handkerchief which supported it.

Two surgeons approached, and having removed the bandages, laid bare the wound which had already be-gun to cicatrise.

At the sight of the wound, which was so peculiar, the surgeons glanced at the · Sub-Prefect, and then exchanged smiles.

" My lad," said one of the medical men, in a slightly discontented air, " when did this accident, on account of which you expect to be rejected, happen ?"

" On last Tuesday, sir," said Conscience.

" Two days after the drawing ?"

" Yes, sir."

" Well ?" asked the Sub-Prefect.

" M. Sub-Prefect," said the surgeon who had spoken, " this is not a new case : the Romans sometimes acted as this boy has done, except that as the gun was not invented in their time, they cut off the thumb.   *Pollex truncatus* was a common enough term with them, and expressed what we call a Poltroon."

Having given this proof of erudition, the Doctor bowed gracefully to the Sub-Prefect, who with equal politeness returned his salute.

" The devil !" said Bastien.   " This looks badly."

" Silence !" said both gens-d'armes.

" You hear, young man, what the Doctor says ?" asked the Sub-Prefect.

" Yes sir," said Conscience naifly, " but I do not understand."

" You do not understand that you are a poltroon ?"

" I think, Monsieur Sub-Prefect," said Conscience, with the same calmness, " you are wrong, I am not a poltroon."

" Why then, did you cut off not the thumb but your

finger? For you cut it off yourself, and did so intentionally, beyond doubt."

"Yes sir, I did cut it off myself, and purposely, as you say."

"He does not lie, at least," said the Sub-Prefect.

"I never lie," said Conscience: "why should I, for God would not be deceived though you were."

"Why then did you cut off your finger? As you never lie, tell us that."

"In order that I might be rejected."

The officials were in a good humor just then, and laughed.

"This looks badly. This looks badly:" said Bastien shaking his head. "The fool! Could he not say, it was an accident? I would blarney them, if I were in his place."

"Silence!" said the gens-d'armes, "or we will close the door."

"Yes, gens-d'armes. You are right. I will hush."

"Then," said the Sub-Prefect, "you were unwilling to go?"

"I wished not to."

"And not from poltroonery."

"No sir."

"Why then?"

"Because if I go," said Conscience, in his calm and mild voice, "I have an old grandfather, who will be in danger of death from hunger, and a weeping mother in danger of dying of grief."

The accent of Conscience, as he spoke thus was so touching, that the officials stopped laughing.

"Ah!" murmured Bastien. "A good answer."

"Will you hush?" muttered the gens-d'armes.

8

"I? I did not speak," said Bastien.

The municipal officers exchanged glances.

The Sub-Prefect continued his questions, which had assumed the form of an interrogation.

"And who inspired you with the idea of thus cutting off your finger?"

"You did, M. Sub-Prefect," said Conscience.

"What! I? Why, I never saw you before in my life," said the magistrate.

"True. But one of my friends came to Soissons last Monday, and had the honor to see you."

"Me? One of your friends?"

Bastien pushed his head through the folding door.

"It was I," said he, "do you not remember me, M. Sub-Prefect?"

The two gens-d'armes at once seized Bastien by the neck.

"Ah!" said Bastien, "mind what you are about, or you will strangle me."

Opening the door with violence, he pushed the gens-d'armes aside, and entered the room.

The first idea of the Sub-Prefect was to have Bastien put out. His uniform and decoration, however, had their effect. With a nod the public functionary intimated permission for him to remain.

Bastien understood this as an intimation that he might speak and make the desired explanation.

Conscience turned towards him, and smiled gratefully.

Bastien felt the influence of the smile, and was encouraged.

"Thus it is, M. Sub-Prefect. I came as you know from the name and place of Conscience."

"Yes, I remember you."

" Whether you did or not, it would be not the less
true, because you refused me in consequence of the loss
of two fingers. You see, gentlemen,' said he, lifting up
his hand, " the fingers are gone."

" Well ! what has this coincidence to do with the
Conscript ?"

" Co-in-ci-dence," said Bastien, evidently offended
at the word. " It matters not, though. This is the
coincidence. Conscience you see, heard from a woman—women, M. Sub-Prefect, you know, have always
found it absolutely impossible to hold their tongues—
he heard from a woman Catherine, daughter of
Father Pinot, the sabot-maker, he heard why I went
to Soissons, I was stupid enough to tell her I had gone
to Soissons, had seen you, and offered to go in Conscience's place, and that you had told me, ' My dear
M. Bastien, I am sorry to refuse you, but you cannot
replace Conscience, because you have lost two fingers.
You even added, you remember, M. Sub-Prefect, that
' one would be too great a loss.' "

" Certainly, I said so."

" Well ! that was a great piece of imprudence. As
I had the honor to tell you, Conscience became aware
of it. On Tuesday morning, just as I was taking my
horses to water, he began to question, to pull worms
out of my nose, as the proverb says. I suspected
something, but he had such an innocent air, that joker
there, that the devil himself would be deceived. I told
him that the Emperor wanted men who had lost neither
two nor one finger. He said ' Adieu ! thank you, Bastien,' without any more excitement than I show now—
and having gone home, cut off his finger. Is not that
Conscience, exactly the way the thing happened ?"

" Exactly so," said Conscience.

"A quarter of an hour after, I saw him, and the amputation was made. I am ashamed to say so, as an old soldier, but truth before all things, as Conscience says, I grew sick. Up to that time I had thought I was a man—I was mistaken, I was but a child, a puling girl . . . a . . I do not know what. It is however true, that if there be any fault, either you or I must take it on ourselves. Come, Conscience, M. the Sub-Prefect sees his error. Let us go home, for the Emperor wishes no crippled soldiers. M. Sub-Prefect, your servant"—

"One moment," said the magistrate, extending his hand.

"How, why?"

"Gen-d'armes, keep silence."

"But—" said Bastien.

"Silence," said the gen-d'armes, drawing Bastien back.

Bastien in a moment saw he was hurting Conscience's case and was silent.

"Conscript," said the Sub-Prefect, "what you have done, is an offence against the military law, according to which you might be punished. This would not be severity, but justice."

"How so, how so?" said Bastien, "since Conscience—"

"Silence there!" said the two gens-d'armes.

"But since," said the Sub-Prefect, "the simplicity of your avowal disarms your judges . . your surgeons declare in what arm, in spite of his mutilation, the Conscript can serve."

"In what arm?" said Bastien. "In none I hope; if so, I will go for him."

"Put that Hussar out," said the Sub-Prefect with impatience.

"Not a bit of it, M. Sub-Prefect—on my word, I will not open my lips; just let me remain."

The surgeons said after an examination, "the Conscript, in spite of his mutilation, will make an excellent pioneer or artillery-man."

"Very well! pass him to the right, and have him enrolled in the train of the army."

At this decision, Conscience grew very pale, for he thought of the grief of his two mothers and his betrothed.

He was not the less obedient, casting on Bastien a look of farewell and of thanks.

"Ah! my poor Conscience," said Bastien, reaching forth his arms, and bathing his face in tears—"Buried in the Royal Wagon train, as they said at the Regiment . . . What a humiliation!"

He left in despair, not because Conscience had not been sent home, but because he had been put in the train.

PART SECOND.

I.

What Passed in France from Nov. 10, 1813, to Jan. 25, 1814.

IT was not without reason that the Sub-Prefect of Soissons, desiring to become Prefect, was so anxious to obtain soldiers for Napoleon: Napoleon was really in want of them.

There was no exaggeration in the words he had uttered in the Senate Nov. 10, 1813—

"A year ago, all Europe was with us; now, all Europe is against us."

He should have said,

"A year ago, all Europe was with *me*; now, all Europe is against me."

The slight substitution of a personal for a collective pronoun would have much cleared up and explained the question.

For the second time Europe was mistaken about France: the first time was in 1792, when instead of suffering the revolution to be concentrated in the great centre called Paris, it forced Paris to diffuse through the world the revolutionary lava which had embraced it.

The second time was in 1813, when instead of granting Napoleon the peace he desired, or confining him in our ancient limits, it reduced him like a wild boar to stand at bay, put him on the island of Elba, and enabled him to effect the most brilliant return, illumining history with a blaze of fire, and by crucifying him at St. Helena, terminated his life by a magnificent Calvary, and made him a god, not only to France, but to the whole world.

In fine, as we must be just even to men of genius—an example we give, and would like to see followed by our cotemporaries—we will confess that he could not accept the peace offered to him.

On the fifth of November, the Prince Regent of England declared to Parliament that it was neither the intention of England nor of the Allied Powers, to demand any sacrifice of France incompatible with her honor or her just rights.

This was perfectly played, for if war continued after such a declaration it could only be attributed to persistence in the bloody passion for destruction of the Emperor.

We repeat that England plays perfectly well, only that she is sometimes tricky.

On the 14th of November M. de Saint-Aignan came to Paris.

M. de Saint-Aignan was a man of wealth and in high favor with Napoleon, which he had won by an admirable *apropos* of flattery.

When he was Prefect at the Upper Alps, the Emperor one day visited his department, and in a brusque and dry manner questioned him.

Bonaparte loved quick answers. It was necessary to answer quickly and to stammer to him.

Many questions had been put to M. de St. Argnan, each of which had been answered instantly.

"How many men, Prefect?"

"So many, sire."

"How many arpents of forest?"

"So many."

"How much land?"

"So much."

"What birds of passage?"

"But one, sire—the eagle."

The Emperor annoyed at last by the quick replies he usally loved so much, wished to embarrass M. de Saint Aignan who had replied by this splendid flattery.

Napoleon looked on himself as beaten, and rewarded his victor by making him a member of the privy council, appointing him his Equerry, and finally by sending him to Wemar, as his minister resident.

The occupation of Germany forced M. de Saint Aignan to return to France. M. Metternich resolved to take advantage of the circumstance to transmit new propositions to the Emperor.

On the 9th November, on the very day of the return of Napoleon to the Tuilleries, so fatal to kings, and when we left him asking for three hundred thousand Conscripts, of whom poor Conscience was to be one, M. de Saint Aignan at Frankfort received from Mde. Metternich, M. de Nesselrode the Russian, and from Lord Aberdeen the English Ambassador, the following ultimatum.

"The allies offer peace on condition that France will

relinquish Holland, Spain, Germany, and Italy, retiring behind its natural frontiers, the Alps, Pyranees, and the Rhine.

" A city on the banks of the Rhine, will be selected for the Congress : the negociations will however in no manner interrupt military operations."

The conditions were hard, especially to a man accustomed to impose instead of submitting to conditions.

The abandonment of Germany was necessary as the allies already had possession of it.

To abandon Spain he was already determined on. The obstinate resistance of the Spaniards sustained by the gold and steel of England, had wearied Napoleon.

To abandon Holland, entirely ours, so rich in resources to France, and menaces to England; to abandon Italy untouched, and occupied by Murat and Eugene, were terrible sacrifices to be made only for a prompt peace, and in the hope of an absolute cure.

Besides nothing was positive, inasmuch as in spite of negociation military operations were to continue.

These unacceptable overtures were not however absolutely rejected. Napoleon, however, resolved to push matters to extremities, and to make his fortune, the fortune of France.

This accounts for the rigorous orders given to the Sub-Prefects about Conscription.

Every preparation was made to repel the war of invasion, with which France was menaced, and which was far more threatening than in 1792.

In 1792, the struggle was for liberty, in 1813 it was to maintain despotism.

In 1792 the question was, " To be or not to be." In 1813 it was simply, should Napoleon remain or not

The question had therefore diminished from the fate of a nation to that of a man.

Instead of national enthusiam, individual genius was the inspiring principle.

In a few words, let us see what genius abandoned to its own resources, exhausted by the blood it has lost in victory or defeat, is about to accomplish.

Alas! we repeat for the second time, the history of the great of this world is so mingled with that of the lowly, that we are forced to busy ourselves with the lofty, when we would attend to the humble.

The propositions sent on by M. de Saint Aignan had been communicated to the Corps Legislative, Napoleon declaring himself ready, disagreeable as they were, to accept them if they would restore peace.

Unfortunately, Napoleon consulted the *Corps Legislatif* when it was in a bad humor. Napoleon had, during his last visit to Paris, imposed a President on it, who had not been nominated as a candidate.

We do not profess any profound admiration for M. Baour-Dormian, yet as we pride ourselves in our impartiality, we will confess that in his tragedy of Mahomet there are two very fine verses.

He speaks of the Janizaries, a corps much despised by the Sultans:

Qu'il nous fort payer, cher les mepris, qu'ils endurent,
Si le trone chancelle a l'instant ils murmurent,

says Mahomet II.

The corps legislatif was like the Janizaries, it murmured.

A committee of five, composed of M. M. Laine, Gallois, Flangergues, Reynouard, and Maine de Biran, all hostile to the Imperial system, was appointed, and drew up an address, in which timidly glided the word liberty, which for some years had been forgotten.

Small as the place the poor word occupied in the address was, Napoleon observed it. To him, the word liberty was Medusa's head. He tore up the address, and adjourned the corps legislatif.

On the 2nd of December, the Duc de Vecence, who replaced the Duc de Bassano in Foreign affairs wrote to Monsieur de Metternich that Napoleon consented to the two general bases proposed by Monsieur de Saint Aignan.

December 10th they received from M. de Metternich the unexpected news, that the allies could come to no definative conclusion without the consent of England; having written to the Cabinet of St. James, awaited its answer.

All hope of a frank and honest peace then had disappeared, and Napoleon, as a last means of safety, prepared for war.

During all these illusory propositions, the allies had continued their march, and now appeared on the North, South and East.

The English have passed the Bidasoo and are about to ascend the Pyrannees.

Swartzemburg, with the grand army of a hundred and fifty thousand men, is about to violate the neutrality of Switzerland.

Blucher, another violation, has entered Frankfort with a hundred and thirty thousand Prussians.

Bernadotte occupies Holland, with a hundred thousand Swedes and Saxons.

Seven hundred thousand men, educated by their defeat in the great school of Napoleonic war, prepared to cross the frontiers of France, neglecting all the strong places and answering each other by the words "Paris, Paris, Paris."

December 21, the allied sovereigns published to the world the proclamations which were a signal for hostilities.

Henceforth France can only be saved by submission, or by energy.

Napoleon, in favor of energy, and for that reason, the corps legislatif advocates submission. Having adjourned, Napoleon dissolves it.

Coups d'etat signalise the commencement and point out the end of monarchical powers.

The news seems each day more disastrous.

On the 28th December, General Bubna occupies Geneva.

On the 30th, Swartzemburg directs his columns on Epinal, Vesoul and Besançon.

On the 14th of January, the enemy enters Vesoul.

On the 9th, Besançon is invested.

That is the condition of the grand army, composed of Austrians, Bavarians and Wurtemburgers, with which is the Russian Imperial Guard.

Blucher having paused for some time on the Rhine, as if from an irresistible dread of touching the soil of France, at last, on the night of the 1st of January, crosses the river at three different points.

In the centre, the corps of General d'York and of Langeron cross at Caul.

On the right wing, the army of Saint Priest crossed at Neuwied, where we had ourselves crossed twice or thrice in the days of the old French Victories.

The left wing under Sacken and de Kleist crossed at Manheim.

We have already mentioned the Anglo-Spanish army commanded by Wellington.

There will however be a halt for a moment.

The Duc de Bellune evacuates Strasburg, with an army of not more than ten thousand men. He, however, receives an order from Napoleon to dispute the passage of the Vosges, foot by foot. The Duc de Trevise comes by the road to Langres, with a division of the guard to sustain him.

The Duc de Ragusa, with twenty thousand men, compelled to defend his retreat, will take advantage as much as possible of the glaces of the numerous fortresses of Lorraine.

The Duc de Castiglione will defend Lyons, whither he hurries in all haste, to organize the resistance of the second city of the kingdom. He will be aided by General Deschamps who provides for the safety of Chamberg and by General Derais who organizes the levy en masse of Danphiny.

The Duc of Tarante is at Liege, providing for the safety of the places on the Rhine, and Meuse with orders to re-enter old France through the forest of Ardennes.

The Duc of Dalmatia after a battle of four days, in spite of the desertion of the German troops, who, on the evening of the 11th of December, passed over to the Spanish camp in one mass, halted on the glacis of Bayonne.

The Duc of Albufera, who retreated from the heart of Spain, halted at the Llobnegat, and fixed his head-quarters in Catalvonia.

Eugene, in Italy, defends the passage of the Adige so well that the Austrians could not force it.

This halt commanded by Napoleon, was executed in

an instant on all the line which surrounded France between the mouth of the Eschelles and the Garonne.

A moment, brief as the time, was allowed Napoleon to look over his chess-board.

The enemy advances with seven hundred thousand men it is true, but the enemy which in three months will have five hundred thousand men in the heart of France, will be able to commence operations only with two hundred and fifty thousand.

He can also hope, that the enemy will amuse himself by blockading strong places, and that by this blockade his armies will be much diminished.

Napoleon can yet rely on two hundred and fifty thousand men, but this force, which, if united, would make him master of events, is thus divided.

Fifty thousand are on the Elbe.

A hundred thousand at the foot of the Pyranees.

An hundred and fifty thousand beyond the Alps.

The other fifty thousand are in the hands of Kaguse, Caslighore and Tarante, not in his own.

In reality then, only on fifty thousand of his old troops and his new levies can he rely.

Let his activity too, be ever so great, he cannot begin the campaign before the end of January.

This delay will also give him time to draw troops from his army in Spain and in Italy.

To do that, he is about to sacrifice the claims which for four years have been the cause of his quarrel with Spain and Rome.

Early in December, Prince Ferchmond of Spain was set at liberty, and on the 11th, a treaty was signed with him.

On the 15th of the same month, the Pope was restored to Italy, and early in January, set out to re-ascend the throne of Rome.

His return to the eternal city—Napoleon hopes so at least—will protect Italy from Austrian occupation, and the restoration of Ferdinand will destroy Wellington's influence at Madrid.

But this halt, which enabled Napoleon to restore his plan of campaign, had been short. All of our lines of defence, which were too feeble to resist, were forced.

Bubna intercepted the Limpton road, and the Valais was torn from France.

Swartzemburgh forced the Vosges. Blucher is in the heart of Loraine, and Yorck before Metez.

Since January 13th, France, the France of Louis XIV, has been occupied.

On the 14th, the Prince of the Maskiva evacuated Nancy.

On the 16th, the Duc de Trevise left Langres.

On the 19th the Duc of Raguse retreated on Verdun.

Napoleon has not a moment to lose.

Since the commencement of the month, he had commissaries in the provinces with extraordinary powers, charged with the levying of men and with provisions for defence.

"Frenchmen," said he, in the proclamation, "they love—one last if I call on the people of Paris, of Bretagne, of Normandy, Champagne, Burgundy, or in the other departments to succor their brethren in Lorraine and Alsace. When all of them are in arms, the stranger will fly or make peace."

At the same time, all the troops received orders to retreat on Champaigne. On Champaigne they were to march both troops from the frontier and the last conscription.

January 20th, the Prince of Neuchatel left Paris, and informed the troops of the speedy arrival of the Emperor.

On the 23d, the Emperor signed letters patent, making Marie Louise Regent.

On the 24th, he made his brother Joseph a participant in the regency, with the title of Lieutenant-General of the Empire.

On the 25th, at two in the morning, he burned his private papers; at three, he kissed his wife and son, and ten minutes after, with Count Bertrand, got into his carriage.

Let us now see what became of Conscience, a poor atom lost in the convulsion which agitated the world.

II.

Before the Battle.

———◆———

WHILE Bastien bore to Haramont the news which was to fill the hearts of three unfortunate women with despair, Conscience, attached to the artillery of the Young Guard, was sent to Fesnes, where a considerable park taken from the arsenal of La Fere and the city of Soissons had been collected.

The military education of Conscience was effected with the rapidity peculiar to an age when practice was altogether paramount to theory. Eight hours' drill a day taught him in less than a month his double duty as conductor and defender of the caisson to which he was attached. His instructor was an old soldier, who suffering none either of the good or bad qualities of his pupils to escape him, did not fail to perceive the affinity between the mind of the Conscript and the animals with whom he had to do.

To Conscience then was assigned the special direction of the horses of the battery, who soon discovered him to be a friend to whom they were an object of care, and who, in gratitude for this amelioration of their lot, redoubled their vigor and docility.

Not only among animals, however, did Conscience acquire friends. His companions were young men like himself, with sad hearts and tearful eyes, who had come from all parts of France, and who had little enthusiasm for the profession they had been snatched from their mothers' arms to embrace : in spite of eight hours' drill a day, they made by no means a satisfactory progress.

Conscience became their consoler ; he sustained, he encouraged them, and after a month's association, just as his influence had been felt by the animals, the vigor of which it had doubled, it was felt by men who derived resignation if not courage from it.

On the 20th of January, the Prince of Neuchatel passed, and ordered all the forces to be concentrated at Chalons.

Two hours after, the battery to which Conscience belonged set out. The same evening it halted at Reims, and at night, after four hours' rest, set out for Chalons, where it arrived on the evening of the 21st.

There the approach of the evening was perceptible, and the spectacle of the horrors of an invasion for the first time struck the eyes of Conscience. Poor peasants from the environs of Bar-le-Duc, Vissy, and Saint Didier, were seen, some with all their movables in cars and wagons, drawn either by their own arms or by oxen and asses. Sometimes on the top of one of these wagons, a mother sate on a bed, bending forward as if to protect the better a child she nursed, singing it asleep in so sad and monotonous a voice, that it seemed rather a lamentation than a song. This mournful procession, which went it knew not whither, which fled for flight's sake, stopped in the public square—it was too poor to visit an inn. It lived there on public charity, on wine brought to its kind-hearted women, on bread which the soldiers gave, on alms from the charitable, who said, " May God guide you."

Conscience, who ate little, and who yet suffered with his wound, gave away all his wine and three quarters of his bread, and as the recipients clasped their hands and blessed him, said,

" If you owe me thanks, make your children pray for three pious women, Madeleine, Marie, and Mariette : the Lord knows them, I trust, and will know you pray for them."

If asked why he wished children to pray for the three women, he would say,

" Because the prayers of children are purer and more agreeable to the Lord."

Then he thought with terror that if the enemy continued to advance, and if Napoleon, of whom he heard much, but whom he had not seen, did not contrive to check him, the time might come when the three women of his heart would fly in a car drawn by Pierrot, like those unfortunates with whom he had shared his bread and wine ; he then hoped that others like him would on the journey supply them with bread and wine.

The fugitives became more numerous every hour,— for every hour the enemy drew nearer.

The enemy was but fifteen leagues distant. His outposts had been seen from Bar-le-Duc.

On the 22d he was ten leagues. Russian and Prussian parties had been seen at Vitry-la-Français.

This was the great Russian, Austrian and Bavarian army commanded by Swartzenburg. The Prussians under Blucher were also advancing.

The first had descended the Vosges by many routes, and directed the strongest of its columns on Troyes.

The Old Guard, commanded by the Duc de Trevise, is thrown forward to meet it, and though disputing every foot of ground, its retreat begins to encumber the streets of Vitry le Francais, and to fill with its first waves the Faubourgs of Chalons.

The second has passed Loraine, and occupied Saint Dizier. It advances diagonally on the Aube.

If Napoleon does not arrive in two days, his troops at Chalons, having no orders, will be obliged to fall back on Paris.

On the 25th, the fugitives began to appear in the streets of Chalons, rolling forward before them a crowd of peasants, who left their houses on fire, and who, seeing that God, in spite of their prayers, has not come to their aid, invoke Napoleon, who has for twelve years seemed to them another God.

In the very streets, however, the fugitives mingle with the first columns of troops that come from Paris, and announce the Emperor. Three days before, they had passed in review in the court-yard of the Tuilleries, and Napoleon had said, " Go ! I follow you."

At last, about five o'clock in the afternoon, while the sound of approaching cannon is listened to with anxiety, cries of *Vive l'Empereur* are heard in the Faubourg towards Paris. Five carriages, the first of which has six and the other four horses, cross the city, and stop at the door of the Prefecture. Napoleon gets out first.

He is calm and cold as usual, that marble man ; his brow though is slightly contracted, and his head hangs not on his shoulders, like that of Alexander, but on his breast, like that of Frederic, as if indicating that the weight of the globe he bears fatigued his shoulders.

In one second an immense acclamation bursts from

the whole city. One might say that the swift-winged Eagle had itself diffused the news of his arrival.

He leaves the coach, and with a gesture replies to the countless repetitions of *Vive l'Empereur*, ascends the steps of the Palace of the Prefecture, and enters the room previously prepared for him.

"Send," said he, "for the Prince of Neuchatel, the duc of Valmy, and the duc of Reggio."

He threw himself into an arm-chair, and awaited the coming of the men with the sonorous titles he had sent for.

The Prince of Neuchatel came first. He came from the advanced posts, and has had four days to acquire information.

The Duc de Bellune and the Prince of the Moskwa having evacuated Nancy, have retired by Vard, Ligny, and Bar on Vitry le Français. The Duc de Ruguse is behind the Meuse, between St. Michel and Troyes, disputing every inch of ground with the enemy, stopping him when pressed too closely. The cannon heard two evenings before was his, and his are now heard. He has been heard all day. These two fiery halts will be called the battles of Columber-les-deux-Eglises and Bar-sur-l'Aube. History will tell that the Old Guard there preserved the glory of its reputation.

The Duc de Valmy is announced.

"Come, come, Kellerman," said Napoleon, "twenty years ago you gained the title by which you were announced in the very plains in which we are about to drill our Prussians. You know what is to be done to conquer them, and will aid me with your advice."

Kellerman bowed, but did not answer.

What could he have said?

"True, sire, twenty years ago I defeated the Prussians, but then under my simple name Kellerman I represented revolutionary France. Now as Duke of Valmy I am but the representative of a man commanding France, exhausted of blood and enthusiasm, asking for repose, calmness and peace, even at the price of shame."

Turning to Oudinot, Napoleon said—

"Are you there? I waited impatiently for you.— You are of this country, are you not?"

"I am from Bar sur Ornain, Sire."

"Very well. We will study out the map for our evening's work."

Turning to his orderly officers Gourgaud and Mortemont, he said,

"Admit all those who can give me any information."

During the whole evening Napoleon leaned over a map of the departments of Aube, Marne, and Upper Marne, marked with red-headed pins, the probable positions of the enemy, whom he hoped to surprise by the rapidity of his course and the vigor of his movements.

During this time, by the light of a fire in the public place, about twenty paces from a park of artillery guarded from this fire by numerous sentinels, a young man in the artillery uniform, wrote on his knees with a pencil the following letter :

"My good and dear Mother—

"You must have received my letter from Fismes, where I was in depot. We were but sixteen leagues apart, yet except in heart were separated as completely as if you were on one side of the world and I on another.

"You have suffered much, my good Mother; you have wept—but I hope that the receipt of the first letter I wrote you, which I did as soon as my hand permitted me, God gave you strength not only to bear your own troubles, but to console others.

"I write now from Chalons, which is eighteen leagues farther. I write by the bivouac fire, just as the clock of a little church which recalls that of Haramont, strikes ten, and when all in the village sleep, except you, who watch under the care of the Lord, at the foot of my grandfather's bed. He grows better, does he not? absorbed by the recollection of your son, who watches and prays for you.

"Far different from Haramont, every door is open here, every house is lighted up, all are awake, for the Emperor arrived at five o'clock.

"I have, my good and kind Mother, seen this man who separates us, and who has cost us so many tears. I would have expected him to have had a stern and repulsive face. Alas! he has a sad, melancholy face like other men, and they say here, what none at Haramont I think, or at any other place will believe, that he regrets to make war, and did not leave Paris until he had exhausted every means to obtain peace.

"When he came, the cry of *Vive l'Empereur* was loud. Was it though because of love of him, or of hatred of the Russians and Prussians? The Lord, from whom nothing is hidden, will easily distinguish.

"I write you a long letter, not knowing whence and how I may write you again, for to night we will doubtless advance either towards Saint Merchand or Vitry-de Français. The Emperor with his marshals decides that. From where I sit, I can, by lifting up my head, see the windows of the Prefecture light as if it were on fire, and from time to time his shadow is seen on the curtains. He does not sleep, you see, and is like his army, which has not slept for a week.

"It seems we are to go to Vitry, for an orderly officer from the door of the Prefecture has just ordered the Emperor's personal baggage to go to Vitry, followed by the Imperial Guard. If we follow them, there will be six more leagues interposed between us, my kind and dear Mother.

"Tell Bastien, if he be yet at Haramont, which I doubt—for I think from the last accounts, that the soldiers on leave, must either have joined their regiments, or been incorporated with others of the same arm—that I thank him for all his kindness. I am growing used to the service of the train, and do not think it disagreeable as he said. I have made two good friends, whom I rarely leave—the horses that draw my caisson.— Though we have been but a fortnight together, we understand each other almost as well as Pierrot and Tardif, who two, ten years old friends whom I have not forgotten, and the black cow, who though old, yet gives good milk, I hope.

"My kind and good mother, tell Mariette that next to you, I regret her more than anything in the world, and that next to you I respect Dame Marie most. Tell Mariette that while at Fismes, I was not more than twelve leagues from our Lady of Liesse, who is more famous than she is in our part of the country. I know the poor child made a vow to go thither if I was not drawn; I wished to go thither in her name to accomplish her vow, and to ask the good Virgin to make Mariette always love me. If, God grant it, though I return we will go thither to give thanks not only for this last favor bestowed on us, but for all I have received since my birth, and being an object of love to three as holy women as you are.

"Adieu, my dear mother, we have but this moment received the order to march, and aides-de-camp have been sent to announce the arrival of Napoleon to the Duc de Trevise, and to tell him to keep before the enemy. We are then about to meet what is called the grand army, and I will with my own eyes see that terrible thing called War.

"A child of ten or twelve years of age who escaped from his village, and whom I found weeping for his parents whom he had lost, promises to put this letter in the office, which I have not time to do myself, as I am just ready to mount. I have given him half of my ration of bread for his service.

"Remember to pray to God that the morsel I have given this child may last him till he finds his parents.

"I embrace you tenderly and respectfully, my dear mother, and also Dame Marie and Mariette.

"Your son,

"CONSCIENCE.

"My respects to grandfather, who must be very unhappy at not seeing his farm."

In fact, as the young soldier was giving his letter, from want of time unsealed to the child, the trumpet sounded FORWARD. Conscience, a feeble unity of the force of fifty thousand men, with which Napoleon marched to oppose the Austrian, Russian, Bavarian and Prussian masses took—he was on the second one, his caisson filled with powder, the road to Vitry-le-Français.

III.

THE VILLAGE.

————

WE need not, our characters being so well known, to attempt to describe the grief that awaited the return of Bastien, bringing the bad news that Conscience, in spite of the accident which had befallen him, was judged fit for military service. The humiliating arm in which he was to serve, was not, as was the case with Bastien, what distressed the poor family. So long as Conscience left the village, what mattered it what arm he served in? As soon as he became a soldier, all arms, during the period of destruction, were equally dangerous.

Strange thing! Madeleine the poor creature to whom the blow was most cruel, was sustained by another misfortune. She felt that he did not belong entirely to herself, but also to the poor grand-father, whom the blow had stricken so severely.

What especially tormented Father Cadet, was, as Conscience said, the idea that he would be forced to give up his favorite field. Bastien, who had much spare time, placed himself at Father Cadet's disposal, but he was a poor agriculturalist, and he would not trust his beloved land in such inexperienced hands. The field, too, was so well drained and cared for, that it would itself perceive the difference between his rude touch, and the gentle hand which had hitherto managed it.

Fortunately, Matthew was there. Father Matthew, cultivating on a large scale, one hundred and fifty acres, certainly, had not the delicacy of touch, and the little personal cares of Father Cadet. But he knew his business. He was a rude antagonist, who had more than once encountered intractable land, which by strong will, by force, we may almost say, he had subdued.

For this year, what the land of Father Cadet did not yield to persuasion, would be wrested by force, and he need be under no anxiety except that of sorrow, at the idea of its being brutally treated.

In the meantime days had rolled by, and the mutilated hand of Conscience, had, as he had stated, been able to write a letter at Fismes, which had been received. Madeleine not having heard from her child, fancied he was already dead, was rejoiced when his letter came. Then, as if she understood that Conscience's love for her was so great that it overflowed on others, and that she had no right to keep it to herself—before she unsealed the letter—having informed Father Cadet —from the door of the cottage she called to Marie, and Mariette, holding up the letter that they might understand why they were convoked.

They came, followed by Bernard, who seemed to understand that he had been consigned to Mariette, and to know that he, too, had a right to participate in the news of his old master.

From the second letter which we have communicated

to the reader, it may nearly be understood what was the tenor of the first.

They sent for Bastien, who knew everything, and asked if he knew where Fismes was. They wished to form some idea of the region in which Conscience was living.

The geographical knowledge of the three women on the west extended no farther than the farm of Vez; on the east than Villers-Cotterets; on the north than Taille-fontaine, and on the south that of Boursonne.

Unfortunately, Bastien did not know where Fismes was.

True, when he heard Fismes was but eighteen leagues from Haramont, he offered to go at once to enquire after Conscience, so as on his return to be able to describe the city to the three women.

We need not say that this very kind offer was refused. They knew that Conscience was alive; had heard in what city he was, that he was well, and was mindful of them; at that time, they dared to ask nothing more of God.

Besides, as Conscience had foreseen, Bastien, one fine morning, received his *route*, all military leaves of absence being recalled, except those which were on account of infirmities which had rendered their holders utterly unfitted for military service.

On the day after the departure of Bastien, Madeleine received the letter Conscience had written from Chalons.

On this occasion joy was mingled with something of terror. Conscience was well, but had been forced to employ another to mail his letter, on the eve of his own departure for battle. At the time they received the letter, the battle was over, yet none could know what had happened.

They determined to answer his letter, and to tell him of everybody. It was, however, a most important matter to write.

Father Cadet had never been able to do more than sign his name. Dame Marie and Madeleine always made their marks, and Mariette alone, as a schoolmaster's daughter, while a child had known how to write.

She, however, from want of practice, had almost forgotten how.

It was, however, decided, that she should be secretary.

They had to write at once, and hoped that by directing to Vitry-le-Francais, Conscience might yet receive it.

They had received his.

Mariette went to the grocer's for some letter-paper ink and a ready-made pen.

She found Catharine making exactly the same purchase.

"For Bastien?" asked Mariette.

"For Conscience?" asked Catharine.

And each answered yes.

When Mariette returned, she found the table prepared at the foot of Father Cadet's bed. The two mothers sate, the one spinning, and the other knitting. Pierre was playing in the corner, and Bernard sate with his head resting on a chair, as if to keep his place.

It was the seat of Father Cadet, which it was thought, would be more comfortable for her as she wrote.

As soon as she sat down, Pierre left his place of play, to see what his sister was about to do, the occupation being altogether novel and curious.

"Oh! Pierre," said Mariette, "take care not to shake the table. I will have difficulty enough in writing, without your annoying me, the while."

"I do not annoy, but only look at, you," said Pierre.

"Well; I beg you," said Mariette, as she dipped her pen in the ink, after having moistened it with her lips, in order that it might take the ink better, " to look at me from a greater distance."

As he drew back, however, doubtless in a bad humor at his exile, Pierre gave the table so severe a shock that a large drop of ink fell in the midst of the sheet.

" There," said Mariette, " see what you did !"

" Bad boy !" said Marie. " Will you never do as your sister bids you ?"

Pierre pouted, shrugged his shoulders, and left.

Mariette sought to adopt the manner usual in such emergencies. She sought to wipe up the ink with her tongue, but the effect of this manœuvre was to substitute a spot of grey for one of ink—the former was larger than the ink spot had been.

Fortunately Mariette had foreseen the possible emergency, and had purchased, not one sheet, but a quire.

She gave the spoiled sheet to Pierre, who took a match, dipped it in ink, and going to a stool, began also to write, or rather to pretend to write.

Notwithstanding what had been spilled on the sheet given to little Pierre, enough ink was left in Mariette's pen for her to begin to write, a fact which distinctly proves that the whole fault was not Petit Pierre's.

" Now," said she, " how must I begin the letter ?"

" What do you think, Father ?"

Father Cadet was improving, and had begun to speak again, though his tongue was yet very thick.

Said Father Cadet, " Begin by saying we are all in good health—that is the way letters always begin."

" But, grandfather," said Mariette, " how can I tell

him we are all in good health, when you are yet con-
fined to your bed, and though you tried to get up yesterday, could not do so?"

"You are right," said the old man sighing. "Well,
tell him you are all well except me, but that I will never get up again."

"Grand-papa," said Mariette, "why begin the letter
by a thing that will give him pain?"

"True," said Madeleine. "The poor boy already
has trouble enough, without adding to his burden."

"Well! with all your talk," said Pierre, "you have
not begun, while I am half down the page."

Dipping his match in the ink again, he pointed to his
paper, which was well marked over.

"You are right, Pierre," said Mariette. "Let us
now begin."

"Well," said his grandfather, "first write his name
at the top of the sheet."

"'Conscience?'"

"Yes," said the old man.

"What! just Conscience?" asked the young girl.

"You are right," said Madeleine. "Conscience is
cold, very cold. Say rather, 'My dear child! my beloved son.'"

Mariette made a face at this suggestion, by which
Madeleine appropriated the letter to herself, for she saw
that she could not call Conscience her child or her beloved son.

Dame Marie understood her, and said,

"Suppose we put "Dear Friend.""

Madeleine again objected. "That," said she, "is
the way one writes to a stranger."

"Yes," said Mariette. "Suppose instead of that we
write "Dear Conscience.""

" Do so," said in chorus, the grandfather and the two mothers.

" I wrote ' Dear Conscience,' said Pierre, showing his sheet filled with hieroglyphics.

" Now," said Mariette, " keep back a little from the table, and keep Pierre out of the way, that he may not push me."

She wrote in a trembling but yet legible hand, "Dear Conscience."

" Now—" said she.

All looked at each other; their hearts were full.— Had Conscience been there, the angels would have smiled with joy at what the three would have said. Writing, however, was not an outpouring of the heart, but an exertion of mind.

The grandfather spoke first.

"Write that you take your pen in hand to ask after his health."

" As I write, he will know that I take the pen in hand, for I do not write like Pierre with a stick. His health, thank God, we know is good, since we reply to a letter which assured us it was so."

" Then write as you please," said Cadet, visibly humbled at having given two pieces of advice, each of which had been rejected.

" I think," said Madeleine, whose mother's heart confided in that of the young girl, " that you can do better by yourself."

" Do you think so ?" said Mariette, delighted and pleased that they had come to this conclusion.

" Yes," said all the members of the epistolary council at once.

" Then I will go home to write, that I may not disturb you, as I know I will here. When the letter is done, I will come hither, and add or take away what you please."

"Go," said all.

Mariette, accompanied by Bernard, went to the room of the cottage on the right, whither she took pen, ink, and paper. She shut the door.

After half an hour, she came back with four pages covered. It is true this great extension of thought was due somewhat to the size of certain letters, to the wideness of the lines, and the uncertainty of their progress from left to right, which increased as they advanced.

When she appeared, all arose, and all exclaimed at once, "let us see."

Mariette began to read in trembling voice, like that of an author doubtful of success.

"Dear Conscience—We were happy to receive your letter."

"So was I," said Cadet. "Was not I happy too? And you say no more about me than if I was dead already."

"True, grandfather, but that is a mistake easily corrected. Pierre, go home and bring the pen and ink."

The child at once crossed the street, and soon returned with the articles asked for.

Mariette took the pen, and soon corrected the phrase *

"Dear Conscience—We were happy to receive your letter; in the first place because it told us you were in good health, and in the second, that you loved us, as we do you. It was the second letter we received, but

---

* Mariette uses the word *heureuses* (happy) feminine plural, instead of the masculine plural *heureux*, which would have expressed both sexes. The first evidently excluded Father Cadet.

as none in the house can write—except myself, and you
see how badly—we did not dare to answer the first.—
To day, as you know that we did not reply, from indifference, I write as well as I can, dear Conscience, to
say that we love you with all our hearts."

Mariette paused, deeply moved.

" Is that right ?" said she.

" Yes, yes," said all.

Pierre clapped his hands; he thought it beautiful.

" Then," said Mariette, encouraged, " I continue—

" You are right, dear Conscience, in thinking that we
have suffered and wept much. As, however, you tell
us to confide in a good God, we will try to think only
of the happy moment of your return.

" As you thought, Bastien left yesterday for Chalons.
Had we known you were in that city, we would have
given him a letter for you, or at least sent you messa-
ges. We did not, however, know that city even by
name : could he have found you among so many thou-
sands ?

" You have seen the Emperor Napoleon, and say he
is like other men. Our good mothers cannot realize
that one can be like a man, who has separated so many
parents and children, so many husbands from wives.—
They think he must be like that Demon beneath the
feet of St. Michael on the left hand side of the church
of Villers-Cotterets.

" I am glad that you did not go to Notre Dame de
Liesse alone; it now seems to me for it to be impossi-
ble for us to visit the good Virgin except together.—
We will go immediately on your happy return.

" As for what you say about praying her to grant
that I may love you for ever, that, dear Conscience, is
useless. as I will do so without that."

Mariette paused a second time, and did not dare to look up, for she thought what she had just read was very bold.

She might, if she had pleased, for none present could read, have skipped over this paragraph as if it had never existed, but the poor child was incapable of such falsehood.

All in the two cottages, however, loved Conscience, and none were surprised at Mariette's speaking thus of an endless love.

All applauded, therefore, the expressions of the second part of the letter as they had done those of the first.

Mariette continued:

"The end of your letter, you may well imagine, distresses us much, dear Conscience, inasmuch as it tells us you too are about to fight. When, therefore, I went for pen and ink, I went to the Sacristan, and without telling either of our mothers, ordered a mass for to-morrow."

"Dear Mariette," said the two mothers, opening their arms to her.

"Oh my God!" said she, "and I told Conscience that I had not mentioned it."

"It matters not; you have," said Madeleine, "done what I intended to do."

"And I also," said Dame Marie.

Mariette continued:

"We hope, however, that all will be well with you. We have, however, heard from Bastien, that the soldiers of the train are not so much esteemed as the Grenadiers and Hussars, who decide all the victories. He added that they were less esteemed in the army than the Grenadiers, and especially the Hussars. All this, however, dear Conscience, is unimportant, provided you return safe and sound.

"This wish we form in the bottom of our hearts, as we bid you adieu—or rather, as we assure you of our wish to meet again.

"For grandfather, our mothers, and little Pierre.

"Your loving

"MARIETTE."

"My God!" said Marie in tears, "where did she get all that?"

"Ah!" said Madeleine, putting her hand on her heart, "I know."

"Listen!" said Mariette. "There are a few lines more."

"What are they?" said all.

"Bernard is well, and lifts his head and wags his tail whenever your name is pronounced—a proof that he knows you are spoken of.

"Pierrot and Tardif seem surprised not to see you, and to have no one to talk to. The one brays, and the other lows so sadly sometimes, that it almost breaks my heart.

"The black cow has had a spotted calf, which has been sold to M. Maupriver, the butcher from Villers-Cotterets, for thirty francs. For about six weeks, therefore, I have been unable to serve more than half of my customers. Those, however, whom I could not supply, promise to take it again as soon as we have it, for they say it is the best milk to be had.

"To-morrow, when I go to Villers-Cotterets, I will post this letter.

" Again, dear Conscience, may God watch over you till we meet again."

" *Amen*," repeated the voices of Father Cadet, Madeleine, Marie, and little Pierre.

IV.

The Invasion.

———•———

WHILE Mariette's letter mailed the day after it was written was being sent to Conscience, whom it was not to meet, Napoleon at day-break reached Vitry-le-Français, and began a battle between Saint Dizier and that place, drove the enemy for three leagues before him, and at ten in the morning, occupied Saint Dizier which for two hours had been in possession of the enemy.

The astonishment of the inhabitants was extreme; for two days had they heard the Russians say in our language that " Napoleon was lost," and that " in a week the allied armies would be under the walls of Paris," that " France would be, like England of old, into Saxon and Norman, divided," when all at once, amid the fugitives, whose flight they did not understand, in a cloud of smoke torn aside by the blaze of artillery, and the rattle of musketry, calm and motionless on his white horse, like the corse of the Cid pursuing these routed Moors, they saw him whom they had believed a prisoner, conquered, dead, exhibiting no emotion whatever.

"Be calm, my children," said he, "I am here."

Then from the wearied, crushed, and trampled on population, which had been driven like herds before the Kossack lances, arose not only exclamations of joy, but cries of enthusiasm.

Then Conscience, who followed the Saviour, alas, the false Christ was so called, then Conscience himself, great as was the purity of his mind, felt the influence of that admiration which forced even the enemies of the man to humble themselves before him.

Between Vitry-le-Francais, and Saint Didier, Conscience first heard the whistling of the balls. At the first burst of the iron storm, he had made a sign of the cross, and uttered a prayer, two things which excited the mirth of his companion, who was mounted on one of the leading horses of the caisson. While he laughed however, a bullet had cut him in two, and another soldier who saw him fall, took his place. He had no disposition to laugh.

Conscience merely said, "My God, take his soul."

Similar accidents soon initiated Conscience into military life, and were so rapid and numerous that he had time to say nothing, and looked at the fall of the dead and wounded with a kind of stupor so great that it did not seem to him even likely that such an accident might befall him.

What, however, he first owed to stupor, he subsequently owed to his courage, or rather to his confidence in God.

In the meantime, the whole day was passed by Napoleon in gathering more precise information than he could at Chalons. The corps of the enemy he had met belonged to the Prussian army commanded by Blucher. The Russians who had preceded it, must at that time have been at Brienne, and marching on Troyes to sustain the Austrians.

Napoleon began to distrust fortune, and to have no faith in his own genius. He took refuge in fatalism.

The name of Brienne, had a promising sound in his ears : there his youth had passed unnoticed, and there he had commenced his studies. Whence the eglet had winged its flight, the eagle was about to fall. After so many reverses destiny owed him revenge. He will date from Brienne the first victory of the campaign of 1814.

Napoleon ordered a march on Brienne, through the forest of Montier en Der.

He hoped to surprise the enemy at Brienne.

Unfortunately an officer Napoleon sent to Marshal Mortier, to order him to approach, falls into the hands of the Prussians, and his dispatches announce Napoleon's arrival to Blucher.

The enemy he expected to surprise, faces about, and awaits him. The battle lasts two days, the first of which put to rest three thousand men of each army. On the second day Napoleon is obliged to retreat, leaving four thousand more on the plain which was the horizon of his youth, and on which deceived by fatality, as he had been been by fortune and genius, he abandoned three thousand prisoners, and fifty-four guns.

Thanks, however, to the influence our young soldier had acquired over his horses, those Conscience drove were indefatigable, and the battery to which he belonged was one of those which accompanied the retreat to Troyes.

Then Conscience entered the whirlpool which bears him along. From time to time Napoleon disappears and seems lost, then, all at once in some unexpected direction, the roar of artillery, and the cry of victory is heard.

At Champaubert, Montmirail, Chateau, Thierry, Monlereau, in ten days Napoleon slew ninety thousand of the enemy.

Where ever though, Napoleon is absent, fortune fails, the enemy forms behind him, and though beaten, advances. The English have entered Bourdeaux; the Austrians occupy Lyons, the wrecks of the armies he has defeated re-unite, and thrice as numerous as his own. His Marshals, and in a bad humor, sluggish, fatigued, decked with orders, overwhelmed with titles, gorged with gold, are unwilling to fight. Thrice the Prussians, whom he fancied he held in his hand, are permitted to escape, first along the left bank of the Marrie, by a sudden freeze, which congeals the mud in which they were sinking, the second time by Aisne, by the surrender of Soissons, which opens them a passage at the moment he thought them pursued to its walls, the third time at Monterau by the delay of Victor, who is by an hour too late, and suffers them to seize a bridge, he should have occupied. All of these presages do not escape Napoleon. He feels that is spite of his efforts France glides from beneath his hands. Entertaining no hope to preserve his throne, he yet hopes to find a tomb. At Montereau, he becomes a simple artillery-man, points the pieces, remains among the whistling balls, and hopes, but in vain, that there will be one for him as there had been for Lannes, Duroc, and Bessieres. At Arcis-sur-l'Aube a shell fell at his feet, he forces his quivering horse above it; the shell bursts, disembowels his horse, but does not injure him. At last at Laon, where with thirty-threee thousand men he attacks an army a hundred thousand strong, he

advances within half point blank of the enemy's guns
with a light battery, and as he moves to speak to a
young soldier, whom he has before seen calm and smiling
amid danger, a shell falls into the caisson the young man
had just opened, and sets fire to it. It explodes, and
enwraps Napoleon and his horse in a crater of flame and
smoke, which devours all that surrounds him, except
himself.

Death wishes to have nothing to do with him.

The most minute details of this campaign are known,
which is always read with the strange hope that history
may, by Divine permission, change the denouement.

Finally, having, by lion-like bounds sprang from the
banks of the Seine, to Craone, to Rheims, to Saint Didier,
he hears at Troyes, whither he has pursued Winzinge-
rode, that the Russians and Prussians no longer paying
any attention to him march in close columns on Paris.

He sets out, and on the 1st of April he arrives at
Fontainebleau, hurries on, and while relaying at Fro-
menteau, hears that during the morning, the enemy occupied the capital.

He had his choice of three expedients.

He yet had fifty thousand of the bravest soldiers of
the universe closely collected around him. To enable
their courage and devotion to have its effects, it was necessary to replace the old generals, who had all to lose,
or had not all to gain. At his yet powerful voice, the
population would rise. But then Paris was sacrificed,
for the allies, in all probability, would, on retiring, burn
Paris, the great centre of intelligence, light and civiliza-
tion. This would be to decapitate France, to throw
Europe into darkness, like that of an eclipse, and who
knew, short as that eclipse was, what might happen.

Only the Russian people could be saved by such a remedy. Moscow had been burned without inconvenience, for what was Moscow but wood and stones?

The second was, with the fifty thousand men he yet possessed to reach Italy, the land of the old Republican victories, rallying beneath his flag, Angerean's twenty five thousand men, the eighteen thousand of Grenier, the fifteen thousand of Suchet and the eighty thousand of Soult. There he would find Eugene at the head of fifty thousand men. Napoleon yet commanded two hundred thousand men. During that time France would be oc. cupied, new interests would be created, old ones would disappear—it was equal to three months' work, and he had no more time to effect this almost conquest.

Perhaps too, he feared that the famous battle-fields of Lodi, Arcola and Rivoli would, as he passed, cry aloud for vengeance for the Republic he had murdered on the 18th Brumaire.

He would retreat behind the Loire, and wage a partisan war, like Charrette, Stoffler and La Rochejaquelein; an imperial la Vendee.

This seemed a poor sequel to the campaigns in Prussia and Austria.

The declaration of the allies appeared, announcing that the Emperor Napoleon was the only obstacle to peace.

This declaration left the man at whom it was directed, but two resources.

To act as Hannibal did.

To descend the throne as Sylla did.

He decided on the first.

The poison of Cabanis was powerless. This was the last treachery he was the victim of. Death betrayed him as one of his diplomates or marshals might have done.

Then he had recourse to the second, and on a scrap of paper, now lost, he wrote the following lines, the most important perhaps ever traced by hand of man.

"The allied powers having proclaimed, that, the Emperor Napoleon was the only obstacle to the peace of Europe, the Emperor Napoleon, faithful to his oath, declares, that for himself and his heirs, he renounces the throne of France and Italy, because there is no personal sacrifice, even of life, he is unwilling to make to France."

There was much grandeur in this renunciation—it may be there was merely fatigue.

The rumor of all these events which had real importance to the inhabitants of the two cottages, merely from the influence they might exert on Conscience, reached them, weakened by distance, and disfigured by transmission. On one occasion, however, they heard the guns at Neuilly-Saint-Frout, and afterwards, at Chateau Thierry and Ferte-Sous-Jonarre. Lastly, they heard them at Meux as the enemy drew nearer to Paris.

Each of the reports found an echo in their hearts, for each one might be the death-knell of their beloved Conscience.

Once, they saw the routed army of the Duc of Trevise pass by.

They heard that the marshal had suffered his park of artillery to be taken at Villers-Cotterets.

His park of artillery—perhaps Conscience had been for a moment only a league from Haramont. Perhaps he had fallen in the hands of the enemy.

They had received news twice from Conscience. Once after the battle of Montereau. He had been one of the intrepid artillerists, who had served the pieces, with which the Emperor, returning in person to his original arm of service, had crushed the Wurtemburgers at the bridge, and in the streets of Monterau.

There he had himself heard the great Captain mutter the characteristic words, as he pointed the guns, whose shot destroyed the enemy,

"Come Bonaparte, save Napoleon."

But Bonaparte, who could save France in 1796, was powerless for Napoleon in 1814.

Another letter had reached them from Chateau Thierry. Conscience had by a miracle so far been preserved. All his companions had been killed and wounded; three horses had fallen under him. Napoleon had observed him, and said,

"Twice I have seen you under fire, calm and tranquil as a veteran. The third time we meet, remind me that I owe you the Cross."

This was a great promise, and Conscience was proud of it. That night he had written, and had transmitted it to his two parents. All in the two cottages rejoiced at the idea that Conscience might return with the Cross if he met the Emperor again. Madeleine's maternal heart, however, was filled with presentiments, and shaking her head, sighed,

"Alas! amid those balls and battles, what may happen before they meet a third time?"

Since then, they had not heard of Conscience.

But, three days after the letter dated Chateau Thierry received by Madeleine—for Conscience always wrote to his mother—Catharine had heard from Bastien, (the letter was written by a comrade, for under the pretext of the loss of his fingers, Bastien never wrote himself, though if one believed him, he wrote after Wagram beautifully,) not only to Maitre Pierre, the schoolmaster at Haramont, but to M. Oblet, at the time schoolmaster of Villers-Cotterets.

Bastien had met Conscience twice; once at Troyes in Champagne, and again at Craone. The two friends had embraced with tenderness, but as the Hussars and the Artillery rarely marched together, they had to separate.

They expected, however, on the next day, to be together on the battle-field of Laon.

The letter of Bastien was dated evening of the 7th of March.

Since then, nothing had been heard either of Conscience or of Bastien.

They had intended to write a second letter to Conscience, but he had probably not received that addressed to him at Vitry-le-Français, and their great labor of heart and mind they looked on as thrown away.

Then, as we have said, they had heard from the artillery nearer Paris.

They had seen all the corps d'armee of Marshal Mortier pass Villers-Cotterets perfectly routed.

Then they had seen strange uniforms, and heard foreign tongues.

Once they heard artillery to the west.

The next day, with a joyful tone, the enemy shouted "Paris! Paris! Paris!"

Then the papers announced that the Corsican Ogre had been precipitated from the throne, that his name never had been Napoleon, but was Nicolas, and that as a special favor the little island of Elba in the Mediterranean was assigned him as a residence.

The Bourbons succeeded him on the throne. and our

good friends, the Russians, Prussians, Saxons, Austrians, and Wurtemburgers, remained three months in France. That is as long as was thought necessary to give strength to the new, or rather to the old throne.

V.

What happened when Conscience met the Emperor the third time.

ALL we have told was vague enough to the inhabitants of the two cottages.

They did not care whether the Emperor's name had been Napoleon or Nicolas, the Lion of the Desert or the Conqueror of Nations

They did not even know what Elba was.

Nor even, what the Bourbons were.

Father Cadet, however, knew the Russians had encamped on his land, which had been so well fenced in, and planted and harrowed by Matthew, and that he could not rely on the produce of the growing crop, which was crushed by the horses' feet.

Madeleine, Dame Marie, and Mariette knew they had received no letters from Conscience, and that he had not written for a month.

Bastien too was silent.

The post also had been interrupted for a fortnight, and had just begun to pass again. The roads, every where crowded by the hostile army, gradually began to admit of free circulation. The tranquility of Paris, the establishment of the new government, made this amelioration every day more apparent.

Mariette, however, had not yet dared to resume the daily service of her customers at Villers-Cotterets. It was not proper for a young and pretty girl like her to venture amid the bivouacs which covered the plain, and a garrison which filled the city. Yet the most severe orders had been issued by General Sacken, who commanded the immense army of Russians, extending from Laon to the extremity of the department of l'Aisne.

In Bernard they had remarked one thing: during the morning of the 8th of March he had been most uneasy. About one o'clock he seemed to scent something on the wind, had turned to the east, and uttered three howls, which had recalled to the poor mother his terrible cry when Conscience had cut off his fingers.

Tardif, Pierrot, and the black cow, had each echoed the cry in their peculiar manner and tongue.

All day they were very uneasy; Bernard during that and the following days had been sad but calm.— From time to time, however, he complained, as if he replied to some one far away.

Madeleine shook her head sadly.

"Something," said she, "has happened to Conscience. Hear Bernard complaining."

The two women sought to soothe her, but their consolations were the less efficacious because of the doubts that lingered in the bottom of their hearts.

On the morning of the 3d of May, Mariette stood pensively at the door, when almost at the extremity of the village she saw the letter-carrier advancing toward the two cottages.

Was he coming to the cottages, or to the Chateau des Fosses?

The heart of the young girl beat violently.

10

Her doubt was however soon removed, for the carrier saw her, and raised a letter in the air.

Mariette uttered a joyful cry, which was heard in Madeleine's cottage, and she rushed to see the carrier.

The carrier also doubled his pace.

In a second, Mariette reached him.

" A letter? It is from Conscience, is it not ?"

" I do not know if it be from Conscience, but it is from Laon," said he.

" Give it me."

Mariette searched her pockets, and pulled out ten sous, which the carrier said was the charge.

She looked at the address, which was in an unknown hand.

As, however, this letter contained another, and as the young girl alone knew how to read, and probably would have to read it, she broke the seal.

The first letter contained another, with the super scription " For Mariette only."

These three words were in Conscience's hand,—but they were strangely put together, and so crooked that instead of calming, they frightened Mariette.

Just then Madeleine appeared at the door.

" A letter? a letter ?" said the poor mother.

Mariette hid the piece of paper intended for her in her bosom, and drew near, trembling at the idea of being thus isolated from the family, by the one she loved.

" Yes," said she, " but I do not know if it be from Conscience."

" Is it sealed with black ?" asked she

" No—with red," said Mariette.

" Thank heaven !" said Madeleine, " for then it does not say that my son is dead."

She went into the cottage, and found her father had leaned so far out of bed that he had nearly fallen.

He also said, " A letter? a letter?"

Dame Marie also had heard in the garden, where she was gathering vegetables—and she with little Pierre, then came; all the family was collected to hear the letter read.

Mariette began—" Very dear and honored mother."

" Why," said she, " as it is from him, why did he not write himself?"

" We will learn," said Mariette.

She read again—" Very dear and honored mother."

" Do not be too anxious when you first see this letter, which though not in my writing is from myself. I borrow the hand of a friend to give you news of myself and to say, that at the battle of Laon, while recognising me, and doubtless at the moment that the Emperor was about to fulfil the promise he made me when he met me the third time, a shell blew up the caisson I served, enwrapped me in a cloud of flame and smoke, and stunned me as completely as if I were dead. At once I lost consciousness, and saw and heard nothing."

" My God! my God! my God!" murmured Madeleine.

" Poor Conscience!" said Mariette, wiping away the tears which blinded her eyes.

" Go on," said Father Cadet.

Mariette resumed—

" The freshness of evening revived me. They were burying the dead, and carrying away the wounded. By my complaints they saw that I was not dead, and took me to the hospital. There, only, I discovered that the action of fire had robbed me of my sight, and that I am in danger of being blind."

"Blind ! my poor child !" said Madeleine.

"Wait a moment, you hear that he does not say that he is, but is in danger of being blind."

"You are right. Read on," said Madeleine, "read on."

"Since that time my eyes have been bandaged, the surgeon of the hospital saying that it is necessary for my cure. In spite, however, of his encouragements I fear I will never see as I did."

"Blind, blind, my poor child blind !" said Madeleine, wringing her hands.

"For the love of God, Mother Madeleine, take courage," said Mariette. "You hear he says that he will never see as he did, but he does not say blind."

While thus trying to console Madeleine, Mariette herself burst into sobs.

Dame Marie had sunken back in her chair, and Little Pierre who had slowly approached her, said :

"Mother, if Conscience be blind, he will be like the poor man who asks alms at the church door."

Mariette continued :

"Yet my dear and honored mother, do not despair, for it seems to me I get better, and thanks to your prayers, those of Mother Marie and of Mariette, if it please God, I will recover.

"I wish I could tell you good news of Bastien, but those which have reached me are sad. An Hussar who is in the hospital with me, and who belonged to his regiment, saw him fall during a charge, having received a sabre-cut on the head. From the quantity of blood which ran from his forehead, they fear his skull has been cut through.

"I have not seen him since, and none know what is become of him.

" If dead, there is a brave soldier, and an honest fellow gone, and as he has done us real services, I trust, dear mother, you will not forget him in your prayers.

" Adieu, my dear and honored mother, and make Mariette write to me at the Hospital of Laon. The letter there will reach me, and will delight me in spite of my distress at being unable to read it.

" I embrace you tenderly and respectfully, and beg you to embrace for me Dame Marie, Mariette and little Pierre, and to ask grand-father to grant me his blessing.

" Your son,
" CONSCIENCE."

After the name of the young man, evidently written by himself, came two lines in the hand-writing of the rest of the letter.

" You see, my dear and honored mother, that as I can sign my name, my sight is not altogether gone."

The letter began in apprehension, and ended in tears. The three women wept, the child did so, at the sight of their tears. The old man sank back in his bed.

She who wept most painfully, though by a greater effort she repressed her tears, was Mariette; she thought with terror of the second letter she had concealed, against which her heart beat, and which contained in all probability, the truth Conscience had not dared to tell her mother.

She hastened to find out that truth, whatever it might be.

" Come, mother," said she to Madeleine, " take courage. Since Conscience signed his name, he is evidently not totally blind, and as he is not, he will not

be. I," added she, with a forced smile, "have hopes
and prove them."

She sought a pretext to leave, and seeing the reapers'
hook hang on the wall, said :

"Now, to show it, instead of being distressed, as you
are, I will cut some grass for the poor black cow, which
used to give us such good milk when Conscience went
with me to Villers-Cotterets. Do you pray for him
while I work, for the Cure says work is prayer."

Affecting a gayety, she was far from feeling, Mariette
took the reap-hook from its nail, kissed the two women
and went to the nearest part of the forest, where she
was in the habit of cutting grass, pushing her barrow
before her with a vigor to be attributed to nervous excitement.

Scarcely had she passed the village, and gotten
among the trees, than she sate on her barrow, took the
letter with a trembling hand from beneath her cape, and
read as follows :

"I wished to write this letter entirely with my
hand, my dear Mariette, painful as it might be for you
to read it, for there are things I have to tell you, which
should not pass through the pen of another."

These few lines were almost illegible, the lines running into each other, and mingling in the strangest
manner.

"Poor Conscience !" said Mariette, who, at the sight
of this disorder, divined all.

Sighing, she read on :

"Mariette, I dared not write to my mother, and tell
her the too frightful fact that I am blind."

Mariette uttered a cry, tears burst from her eyes, and

though she wiped them away with a mad resolution to reach the end, they flowed so abundantly that the poor girl could not read amid the humid veil, which perpetually renewed itself before her eyes.

Thanks, however, to the power of her will, she was able, if not to dry, at least to restrain her tears, and continued :

" Mariette, the explosion has burned my eyes : I am blind for life; I shall never again see you with the corporeal eye, nor my mother, nor Dame Marie, nor my grand-father, nor the child, nor any who love me.

" Mariette, Mariette, I shall certainly die."

Mariette did not know that she was reading aloud and sobbing audibly.

"In vain do I seek to recall the resignation I expected to find in my soul, in great misfortunes. It is impossible—I repeat ceaselessly, ' Wretched man, you are blind, and never will see HER again—never, never.' "

" Do not think, however, from what I have said, that I am selfish enough to think that you will yet consider yourself bound to me. No, Mariette, Spring is returning, though I do not see the young leaves on the trees, the light, rose-hued clouds of heaven. I feel that the wind is milder, that the air is soft and perfumed, and sometimes comes to me laden with the odors of the fields as it used to, when you approached me with a boquet from the meadows or woodland.

" With the young leaves, roseate clouds with the milder wind, our village festivals return—the festivals of Longpre, Taille-Fontaine, Largny and Vivieres. Mariette, they yet await you, and you will yet dance joyfully at them. You will go to them, Mariette, and will take advantage of your youth, for were you to suffer and rob yourself on my account, I would prefer a ball had stretched me in that great ditch in which, as I lay half-conscious, I heard so many of my comrades thrown.

"But Mariette I have a request to make you, and on that account principally, and not to give you pain, do I write; Mariette, prepare my poor mother gradually for what has befallen me, and watch my beloved Mariette, lest she sink into despair.

"Your poor

"CONSCIENCE,

"Who restores you your love, but will preserve his till death.

"P. S.   If you can send me Bernard, he will be very useful to me when I begin to go out."

"My God! this is too much," said the young girl— "Lord have pity on us."

She tried to fall on her knees, but her strength failed her, and with her arms dropping over the barrow, she sank on the ground.

She remained for an instant unconscious, and then fainted away.

The warm and caressing air of Spring, the rays of a morning sun, revived her. The blood again circulated in her veins, she lifted up her head, sought to collect her ideas, recollected her horrible misfortune, picked up the letter which had fallen near her, folded it up, and having kissed it, replaced it in her bosom. Then rising as if by force, she took the reaping hook, and in less than ten minutes, had filled the barrow with grass.

She then returned home rapidly. Her eye was fixed, her brow half-bent and her lips half-opened. She divided the grass into two rations, throwing one into the rack of the black cow, and going around Cadet's house, gave the other to Tardif.

Then she entered the cottage on the left through the door of the yard.

All sate exactly where she had left them, except little Pierre, who had already forgotten the sorrows of others and of himself in some more childish game.

"Mother," said Mariette, as she entered, "to-morrow I set out to join Conscience,"

Dame Marie trembled.

"What do you say, my child?" asked Madeleine, who feared she had heard indistinctly.

Father Cadet appeared beside himself.

"I say, mother," resumed Mariette, with firmness, "that to-morrow morning, I will set out to go to Conscience."

"But my child he is very far: he is at Laon, which, they say, is the other side of the department."

"Mother, if it were on the other side of the world."

"But you do not know the way."

"I will tell any one I meet on the road, that 'I am going to the hospital of Laon, to see a poor blind soldier: tell the way;' and they will do so."

"Is he then blind?" asked Madeleine in despair.

"Yes," said Mariette, almost beside herself, "he is."

Madeleine knelt before the young girl and clasping her hands said,

"Mariette, if you do so, for my child's sake, I will remember you on my death-bed.

"If I do so," said Mariette. "If I do so, I swear before God I will, and I will bring him back, or die."

"And you will bear him my blessing, which the good

lad asked for," said Cadet, extending his arms towards
Mariette.

It was the first time since he had been stricken with
paralysis, that the left arm of Father Cadet had regained life and motion.

VI.

The Pass.

THE journey of Mariette being decided on—and it was—the first thing to be obtained was a Russian Pass.

The roads were filled with allied soldiers, and even with a Pass, a girl young and beautiful, as Marie was, ran great danger.

True, she had with her a defender who would suffer no one to touch her with even the end of the finger.

This was Bernard.

But Bernard, who could do much against one or even two men on a high road, in a by-path, against a sentinel, against the orders at the door of a city, against walls, or against a regiment in battle array, was powerless.

What could overcome such obstacles was, as we say, a Russian Pass.

Fortunately Sacken, the Russian General-in-Chief, was at Villers-Cotterets, where a great review had taken place, and was at the house of the Inspector of Forests, one of Mariette's best customers.

At four o'clock in the afternoon, Mariette bid Bernard follow her, and set out for Villers-Cotterets.

Three quarters of an hour afterwards, Mariette rang the bell of the Inspector's door.

All knew and loved the pretty milkmaid, and as they had not seen her for more than a month, she and her dog were kindly received.

Having however replied to all civilities by a sad smile, and by shaking her head, Mariette expressed her wish to speak to the Russian General-in-Chief.

The thing seemed so strange, that the servants looked at each other and began to laugh, asking her what she could have to say to the Russian General.

"Something on which my life depends," said Mariette in so sad a tone that all laughter ceased, and one of the servants said,

"Well, I will speak to Madame—"

"But," said the cook, "she is at table with the Russian General and with the general staff, and she certainly will not leave the table to speak to the young lady."

The cook was in a bad humor. She had been reproached by a servant who waited at table, with having sent up a stewed hare with a very bad sauce.

"Yes," said the servant, "Madame will leave the table when told that she is asked for. She is very fond of her pretty milkmaid, and yesterday asked about her."

"Then I beg you, sir," said Mariette.

"I will do so, my child. It shall not be said that for fear of a rebuff I dared not say that a pretty mouth uttered a generous sentiment."

"Flatterer!" said the cook, turning on her heel to watch an omelette soufflee.

Without paying any attention to the apostrophe, the servant went into the dining room, and whispered to the lady of the house, who arose and left the table.

"What!" said she to Mariette, "is it you?" as she saw the young girl; "for a month you have forgotten us."

"You see, Madame, that I have not forgotten you—far otherwise, for in our great sorrow I come to you."

"What great sorrow is this?"

"Madame, it would be long to tell, for I must set out this evening on a journey to the other end of the department. If, however, you would enable me to speak to the Russian General, as I shall be forced to tell him all, having a favor to ask him, you will learn how unhappy we are . . . "

"You speak to the Russian General, my child!" said the lady with surprise.

"Yes, Madame," said Mariette, "and if I cannot speak to him now, permit me to wait in the kitchen, the yard, or at the gate, until I can."

"No, my child," said the wife of the Inspector, surprised at Mariette's sadness; "if the affair of which you wish to speak is so important, do so at once."

"Madame, you are very kind, and I thank you," said Mariette, following closely in the lady's steps.

The latter advanced and opened a door of a room in which perhaps ten foreign officers sate at a table.

Mariette followed her: devotion had conquered timidity.

"General," said the mistress of the house to the officer who sate at the centre of the table, "permit me to recommend this young girl, who has a favor to ask, to your Excellency."

"Recommended by you," said the officer spoken to, with the slight accent which marks a Russian's French, "she is welcome."

Then seating himself in his chair, he turned it so as to isolate himself from his neighbors.

"Come hither, my child," said he.

Mariette drew near with downcast eyes, excited at the idea of appearing before one who to her was Providence, as he could enable her to speak with Conscience.

"I am here, sir," said she.

"Your name?"

"Mariette, sir."

"Really, this is charming," said the General, caressing her cheek.

Mariette with incredible dignity, took the too familiar hand in her own, and kissed it respectfully, as an humble girl, resolved to be such, kisses, the hand of powerful man.

The General perceived her meaning, and withdrew his hand.

"Mademoiselle," said he, "what do you wish?"

"A Pass, sir, to Laone."

"What, alone?"

"No, sir, not entirely—Bernard will go with me."

"What is this Bernard?" asked the General.

At that moment Bernard, who had respectfully stopped outside the door, hearing his name repeated twice in rapid succession, thought it would not be indiscreet in him to appear—and throwing his weight against the door, pushed it open, and drew up beside Mariette.

"That is what Bernard is," said Mariette.

The General looked at the magnificent animal, who fixed his burning eyes on him, as if at a word from his mistress he were ready to spring in a second over all intermediate shades of emotion between gentleness and wrath.

"Peste!" said he, "a good companion. But why do you go to Laon?"

"To find a poor soldier who is in the hospital."

"Wounded in battle?

"Blinded by the explosion of a caisson."

"This soldier is your brother or cousin—"

"This soldier is Conscience."

"Ah! Conscience is your lover, as he is neither brother nor cousin, but simply Conscience."

"This soldier is one I love, and am to marry."

"What! you so young and pretty, marry a blind, infirm and disabled soldier? Do not do so."

"I thought, however, I said that I loved him."

"Yes, but that was before his accident."

"Monsieur, since that, I love him still more."

"Really," said the General, half-laughing, half-sympathetically, "this is interesting as an edyl of Kirloff. I have a mind to give this pretty girl not only a Pass, but my carriage and an escort of Kossacks."

"Monsieur," said Mariette, "do not laugh at me. I spoke to you in the name of the Lord, who bade me leave my village and my mother to find Conscience. I do not need a carriage, for I walk well and do not need an escort, for Bernard is with me. I only need a Pass, that none I meet may molest or impede me."

"Very well, my child," said the General, moved by her simplicity "I will not take a particle of merit from your devotion; I will therefore do neither more nor less than you ask."

Then turning to a young man who was his aid, he said:

"Elim, prepare a Pass for this girl in three languages, Russian, German and French; affix my seal, and bring it to me to sign."

"Thanks, sir; I trust God will reward you for your kindness," said Mariette, drawing back to the wall, to await the return of the aide-de-camp.

After the lapse of five minutes, he returned with the Pass written, and with a pen ready dipped in ink, so that General Sacken had only to affix his name.

Sacken took the pen in his right hand, and the paper in his left, and read—

"Russian, Prussian, and French officers, soldiers, and the civil authorities, are ordered to permit the bearer, a young girl, to pass freely throughout the extent of the department of Aisne, and also, if necessary, to aid and protect her."

Having signed it, the General nodded in approbation and wrote beneath the triglott Pass,

"The General commanding in chief the department of l'Aisne,

"SACKEN."

Then he handed the young girl the paper.

She wished to kiss his hand again, but rising and drawing her to him, the Russian General paternally kissed her brow.

"Go," said he, "my child—Saint Alexander Newski protect you."

Mariette blushed, though she understood the purity of the kiss she had received.

Then Mariette seized the hand of the Inspector's lady, and kissed it, in spite of her exertions.

"Madame, Madame," said she, "I thank you from the bottom of my heart."

She rushed from the room.

The guests resumed their seats, the conversation until the conclusion of dinner, being engrossed by the explanations made by the lady of the house about Conscience, Mariette, Cadet and the rest of the family, so vivid was the impression Mariette had made on the Russian General and his officers.

Three-quarters of an hour after, preceded by Bernard who announced her triumphal return, Mariette entered the cottage on the left, with her passport in her hand.

There was no farther obstacle in the way of her departure.

Father Cadet turned over and took the leathern bag from its hiding-place.

Alas! it contained but a single gold coin.

"Here, my child," said he, "take this, and bring Conscience back with you."

Mariette was not unaware of the difficulty in which Father Cadet had fallen, since his own illness and Conscience's departure, shook her head and said, "No, grand-father, keep the money."

Turning to Mother Marie, she continued in a low tone,

"As I pass through Villers-Cotterets to-morrow, may I not get the thirty francs which the butcher owes for the calf we sold two months ago?"

"Do what you wish, my daughter," said Dame Marie, "for the Lord inspires you. To oppose you would displease God."

VII.

THE DRIVER AND HIS CAR.

———◆———

ON the next day at dawn, Mariette having taken leave of all, sad and rejoicing at once, began her journey.

She was sad on account of Conscience's misfortune.

She rejoiced because she was about to see him.

The sky was clearly bright, and promised a fair day.

The last stars sparkled in the west, and seemed brighter than ever amid the darkness around them. On the other extremity of the horizon, the firmament began to take the colors of the sun's first rays, and to pass from the palest tints of rose to the richest purple. The lark rose vertically, for the birds awake with the day, towards the sky, welcoming the morning rays with his clear and joyful song. The grasshoppers were in the turf, and the red-throats warbled in the bushes; the squirrel hung on the branches of the trees, and only a few tardy bats protested, having taken refuge in the darkest recesses of the forest, against the invasion of light, and progress of clearness.

It was evident that one of the first days of spring, which, with its feet bathed in dew, coming from the mountain tops, advances to awaken Nature by blowing on it with its warm and perfumed breath.

Mariette, though used to cross the forest at dawn, was not insensible to the changes being wrought around her. The young girl had, on this occasion, a lighter heart than usual, and therefore remarked all these outbursts of Nature : doubtless the good action she was about to accomplish at once made her mind and brow more serene.

Her heart was light, and her little feet yet lighter. In less than a quarter of an hour she crossed the forest, entered the park, and paused no longer in the city than was necessary to get from the butcher the thirty francs which were to suffice for her journey, and took the Soissons road.

In two days she expected to reach Laon : she had ascertained that she had fourteen or fifteen leagues to travel, which would give her seven leagues a-day. She had settled things so completely that she did not doubt but that on reaching Laon in the evening, she would not be able to see Conscience until the next day, and that it would be better to sleep in the neighborhood than in the city itself.

She could not go wrong, as the road from Villers-Cotterets was a highway.

At about seven o'clock Mariette left Villers-Cotterets by Soissons street. The Spring sun of the previous days had dried the ground and she walked on the lower side of the road, where there was a pathway like that of a park, prepared for pedestrians. Bernard bounded before her, and returned from time to time, like a scout, the duty of whom it was to visit every tree and rock.

From his joy and activity, one might have fancied that he knew the young girl was on the way to see Conscience. Perhaps he did, or he would not have been so joyous.

Mariette had not progressed more than half a league, and nothing seemed easier than to walk thus, when a voice behind her exclaimed,

"Eh! Mariette."

She turned around and saw a car, the wheels of which had for some time been rolling behind her. It was the voice of the driver of the car, who at the day when diligences were rare, travelled between Villers-Cotterets and Soissons.

"Ah! is it you, M. Martineau?" said Mariette.

"Yes—it is I, and whither go you, my child?"

Mariette approached the car, and put her hand on the side, telling the driver and his four passengers why she was thus *en route*.

At first they listened with impatience to the young girl who had interrupted their journey, but by degrees interest gave place to impatience.

Besides, Martineau on his box was as absolute as a captain on his quarter deck: it was of no use for them to murmur, for Martineau travelled at his horse's gait, allowing the animal to halt to rest when he pleased, and consumed four hours in travelling the six leagues between Villers-Cotterets and Soissons.

The story of Mariette was, it seems, more interesting to the driver than to the passengers, for, as soon as she had done, he said :

"Well, it is vain to fatigue yourself as you do, by walking."

"But M. Martineau," said Mariette, with a smile, "I must walk, as I have no way to ride."

"Pardon—you have a way."

"What?"

"My car—"

Mariette drew back. "M. Martineau," said she,

"you laugh at me, for you know perfectly well, that I am not rich enough to travel thus. You charge forty sous a seat, and I have but thirty francs to go with to find Conscience and to bring him home. He will prob-ably need a conveyance more than I do. Besides, your car is full."

"Who said anything about money to you, my lass? Thank God, that is not the question, and if there be a trouble about room, you must sit closer together. Be-sides there is nothing disagreeable in being squeezed by a pretty woman."

"Thank you, M. Martineau," said Mariette, drawing back.

"Come get in. You wish to see Conscience as soon as possible?"

"Yes," said the young girl.

"Well, thanks to the car, you will reach Soissons at eleven o'clock at farthest, and will not be fatigued. You can stop a while at Soissons, and having eaten a morsel with me, who knows? you may sleep at Chavignon, or even at Etonville, so that to-morrow morning, you will see your friend instead of the day after. What say you to that?"

"Accept," said the travellers, half from interest in her story, and half because when Mariette was once seated, the car would probably continue its journey.

"On my word, M. Martineau," said Mariette, "your offer is very tempting, and I have a great disposition to accede to it."

"Very well!" said the driver, taking hold of her hand. "Houp—here you are," and in spite of a brief resistance he pulled her up on the seat.

"Now on you sluggard," said Martineau to his horse, whom he whipped up.

As the programme announced, he was at the gates of Soissons, at eleven. Russian soldiers were on guard, but Martineau, as an authorised carrier, had a pass, perfectly in form, and Mariette had not to show hers.

The poor child had never seen so large a city. The closed gates, the hanging portcullis, the guns on the ramparts, the sentinels, all at first terrified her. She thought how difficult it would have been for her to experience all these difficulties alone, and rejoiced at having accepted M. Martineau's offer.

The driver stopped at the *trois pucelles* The hour of his arrival, which was never later than half-after eleven, was known, and his breakfast was ready.

An old gastronomic proverb, which, however, is contradicted by true gastronomers, says :

'That enough for one, suffices for two.'

The driver was so well provided for at the inn, that his breakfast sufficed for two, and even for three. He led Mariette, who at first refused to accept this second offer, to the table. Finally, however, she sate down, and ate heartily, as also did Bernard, to his praise be it said.

When breakfast was over, the driver said,

" Wait here, my child, I am going to see after your affairs "

With a nod he left.

What was he about to do ? Mariette did not know herself.

A quarter of an hour after she did.

Martienau came back delighted.

" Come," said he, " the matter is settled, and you will see Conscience to-morrow."

" How so ?" said Mariette, joyous.

" Simply enough. I met with a friend of mine, a wagoner from Chavignon, come to sell his vegetables at the

Soissons market, and going back empty. He will put two or three trusses of straw in to make a seat, and will take you with him. At three o'clock, you will be at Chavignon, and will sleep in a good bed, which his wife will give you, so that you will be able to start bright and early at dawn to-morrow. So that out of fifteen leagues, you will have to walk but four or five."

"Ah! M. Martineau," said Mariette, "how grateful I am."

There were tears in her eyes.

"Bah," said the good man. "There is nothing to cry for. If there be no God for good folk like you, for whom is there one?"

"And when do we start?" asked she.

"At once. He is not ten paces from us, at the *Boule-rouge*, where he is having hay put in his carriage, to enable you, as I said, to travel more conveniently."

"Let us go, then," said Mariette.

With Bernard before them, they set out. The dog had rested, and seemed fully prepared to resume the journey.

Martineau's friend was a fat dealer in artichokes in summer, and in cabbages and carrots in winter.

He received Mariette, as if he expected her, and was as anxious to get home as she was to go four or five leagues farther.

The drivers exchanged a few words, and then the market-man, who was called Round Charles from the shape of his cheeks, asked Mariette to get in, as Javotte was waiting for him, and he would not keep her waiting for the handsomest girl in the country.

Mariette did not wait to be asked twice, but gave her hand to Martineau, and sprang lightly into the car, while Bernard drew up beside, and looked in to see if his mistress was comfortable.

He seemed satisfied, for getting down again he barked joyfully.

"On my word, you have a travelling companion that would be difficult to manage if you were spoken rudely to."

"Bah! Who would insult a poor girl like me?"

"Hm!" said the market-man, looking at her. "Yet one should not be too bold on the high road, crowded as it is with people from every land."

"Think you, M. Charles, we have any thing to fear?"

"No. Because we will get in early. But at night, in the evening, and very early in the morning, I would not be too confident."

"But," said Mariette, "I have a Pass in three languages, French, German and Russian, given me by the Russian General at Villers-Cotterets."

"That," said Charles with a laugh, "is very good, for those who know how to read; what though for those who cannot?"

"Really, you terrify me," said Mariette

"Bah! I did but laugh. Come. Adieu, Martineau. I thank you for the pleasant companion you have given me. Are you comfortable, my lass?"

"Yes, M. Charles."

"Well! Get up, Blucher."

This was the baptismal name of the horse.

It was a profession of the political faith of the owner, who thus manifested his aversion to the condition of things around him.

The words 'Get up, Blucher,' were accompanied by two sound whacks, which the robust and patriotic

Charles would have given Blucher himself, had he found him anywhere alone, without any other witness than the winds and clouds.

At the gate they opposed the same difficulties to Charles' exit they had to Martineau's entrance, but he took from his pocket book a paper slightly soiled, on which were written a few lines above a seal, which removed all obstacles. Ten minutes afterwards she left the Boule-Rouge, and as the Cathedral clock struck one, Mariette was outside of Soissons, borne onward at a gait which was a credit to Blucher's legs, and a proof of Fat Charles' fondness for Javotte.

11

VIII.

CHARLES AND HIS WIFE.

————◆————

DURING the whole journey, Charles entertained Mariette with his conjugal happiness.

Before they reached three quarters of a league from Soissons, Mariette knew that two years before Charles had married Javotte, and had three children—a thing that proved they had lost no time, and that the children were two boys and a girl.

In her own mind Mariette did not see how one woman in two years could have three children—but her womanly instinct taught her not to probe the matter too closely with questions.

She knew that Javotte was short, fat, blonde, and jealous; that her hand was quick, and that when in a bad humor, she thought no more of striking her husband than she did of whacking Blucher.

When about half a league from Chavignon, Charles had already pointed out to Mariette the roof and smoke of his house, and the roofs and smokes of all the other houses of the village.

Mariette listened with apparent attention to Charles, though in fact she was thinking of other matters. She thought that Laon was but four leagues from Champignon, and that in the same day, almost without fatigue, and without expense, she had come twelve leagues.

She also said that as Blucher shared Charles' impatience, and had come the distance home in two hours, it might happen that by seven or eight o'clock the next day, she would be at Laon.

It must be confessed that this idea took such possession of her, that it completely engrossed her, when Charles, by a concerto on the whip, announced his arrival, and pulled up at the door.

At the noise Javotte appeared at the door with the second child in her arms, followed by the eldest. The youngest was asleep.

Of all that Charles had said of his wife's qualities, as he drove home, his comments on her jealousy seemed most true.

" Ah ha !" said she, " please to tell me where you fished up that young girl ?"

The reception was not grateful, and Mariette blushed. Charles, however, touched her with his knee and bade her listen.

" Where did I fish her up ? I will tell you, Madame Javotte, as soon as you let me get out and kiss you."

" We have always time enough to kiss."

" Not so," said Charles—" not half enough."

Springing down, he advanced with open arms to Javotte, who gently pulled him in doors, while Mariette sate in the car caressing Bernard's black muzzle, which was pressed between the spokes of the wheel close to her.

It seems that Round Charles' reasons satisfied Javotte, for in about ten minutes she re-appeared, and said—

" Come, my lass, get out, you are welcome."

Now as there was no mistaking Javotte's benevolence, Mariette did not wait to be asked twice, but got out smiling.

" Ah," said Round Charles, re-appearing and winking, "you see my mode of contriving to have my own way. Well! we will put the General-in-chief in his stable, and dine, for I am fearfully hungry. Come, Blucher, come, my fine fellow."

Swinging open the great gate, he took the horse and wagon into the yard, and left Javotte and Mariette to mature the acquaintance they had begun.

This was not difficult, for Javotte was a kind enough woman in the main, and at once comprehended Mariette's devotion, and as the matter she was engaged in reflected honor on the whole sex, Javotte was glad to participate in it, even in the smallest way.

True, Mariette in the kindness of her heart had already taken possession of one of the children, while Bernard lay at the feet of the other, suffering his ears to be pulled, and his throat to be searched by the child's hand, like a good dog as he was.

Taking advantage of this relief, Javotte had gone into the cellar, and returned with a bottle in each hand— a thing that seemed to delight Round Charles, who just then re-appeared at the yard door.

In five minutes they were at the table, and Charles proved that he had not exaggerated when he said he was fearfully hungry.

It was so serious, that he was long in satisfying it.

Mariette had dined at noon with M. Martineau, and did not eat, thinking the while of how she should approach the question on her at once continuing her journey.

A good angel, however, really seemed to watch over her, and inspired all she met.

Towards the end of dinner, Charles winked to Mariette, as if to say that she would hear something worthy of her attention.

Javotte caught him.

"Well!" said she.

"By and by? Well—I wished to know what ass that is I found in the stable, eating up all the leavings of the General-in-chief."

"What! did you not know it, you fool?"

"Yes," said Round Charles, "and that is exactly why I ask. It is the ass of mother Sabot."

"She is not—"

"Do not mind her: we call her mother Sabot," said Charles to Mariette, "because she is the wife of William the sabot-maker. Now though we have to do neither with William nor with his wife, but with their ass. How came it here, Javotte?"

"Because mother Sabot lent it to the nurse who lives at Pargny, that her milk should not be heated by too long a journey. She passed to-day with the child, and left the ass here, saying that it was arranged between mother Sabot and herself that it should be sent back by the first opportunity."

"Very well," said Charles. "I knew . . ."

"That you recognised the animal?"

"I knew that our guest would find a way to continue her journey without fatiguing her little feet. Did you ever see such feet, Javotte? To say that she has thus far come thirteen leagues without doing so, is to say a great deal."

"Very well, very well!" said Javotte, who did not

like to hear her husband so expansive about the attractions of other women. "What then?"

"Well then, you have already found an opportunity; for to-morrow morning, we will put the child on the ass of mother Sabot, turn its head towards Chroy, say Hu! and it will go straight thither without stopping until it reaches the door, as Blucher came without being flogged to mine."

"Well!" said Javotte, "that is really an idea; you are not such a fool, my good man, as you seem to be."

A glance of Javotte's eye told Charles, there were moments when she did not think him a fool at all.

During this spoken and pantomimic dialogue, the imagination of poor Mariette yet reached the end of her journey.

"My God, Madame Charles," said she timidly, "a thing occurs to me."

"What is it, my child?"

"That it is not now later than four o'clock; and that we have still three hours and a half of daylight, so that if the ass of mother Sabot be not too weary, instead of taking it back to morrow, I will do so this evening."

"This evening, you are very anxious to leave us, my child?"

"Not at all, M. Charles, but quite the contrary. When, however, I think of the poor blind one, grateful as I am to you, I am anxious to rejoin him."

"That is natural enough," said Javotte.

"There is danger," said Charles.

"Danger?"

"Yes, for a girl."

"What?"

"In crossing the wood of Etonvelles, where one might meet with an accident."

"Ah," said Mariette, "there is no danger. Who would injure a poor girl?"

"Ah!" said Round Charles, with his jovial laugh, "I did not say any one would injure you."

"Will you hush?" said Javotte.

"I will, wife, I will. Own though, that I was not very wrong."

"The fact is," said Javotte, "that it would be better to wait till to-morrow."

"Possibly," said Mariette, "but I would lose two hours, if it were convenient for me to go this evening."

"Well! I tell you it is," said Charles.

"Madame Charles," said Mariette, clasping her hands, "think of the poor blind one; remember that hours to him are centuries, and that by going this evening, I shall at least be two hours nearer him to-morrow."

"Well," said Javotte, "if you think of that, you must make up your mind at once."

"Madame Charles, if you excuse me, it is already made up, and if it depends on me . . . . "

"Go, Charles," said Javotte, "and put the pad on the ass: the poor child is dying to be at Laon."

"It is not the less true that I had rather she should not cross the wood of Etonvelles until to-morrow."

"Why?" said Javotte, "you will go with her as far as Chivy. You are, perhaps, too delicate to take so long a walk."

"No," said Charles, taking Javotte in his arms, "I am not, and the proof of it is, I will run all the way back, so as to be sooner with you. Ah! you are a good woman, though you do not look like it."

Charles folded Javotte in his arms, kissed her twice, and rushed into the yard.

" Madame Charles," said Mariette, " you seem to me very happy."

" Yes," said she, re-adjusting the economy of her toilette, which was somewhat deranged by her husband's fervor, " God has ordained that we love each other."

Mariette said " that is the greatest favor he could bestow."

Two large tears streamed down her cheeks, for she thought of Conscience, and that their love would be as true, though not so boisterous as that of these good people.

Madame Charles read what was passing in her mind, and with a delicacy of feeling of which she might have been thought incapable, kissed her.

" Bah !" said she.   " God is great : confide in him."

" Hear me, my child," said she, " when at Laon you will be but a few leagues from our Lady of Liesse ; she is a Holy Virgin, and very miraculous. Every day invalids who have been cured come this way. Once there, who knows what may happen ?"

" Oh !" said Mariette, " I have thought of it, for by doing so, I will fulfil a promise."

" Good," said Madame Charles.   Then all will be well."

Her husband appeared at the door leading the ass. She then kissed the young girl, and wished her a pleasant journey.

Mariette then left not on foot but riding ; Bernard ran before, while Charles walked by her side.   Thus the procession left the house, at the door of which stood Javotte, making gestures of farewell until disappearing at the extremity of the village, it advanced towards Chivy, and consequently Laon.

IX.

———

THE ass travelled neither as fast as the norse of Martineau, nor of Round Charles, and Margot, such was the animal's name, was two and a half good hours in crossing the famous wood of Etonville, of which her host was so much afraid.

Let us say that this danger had been much over-estimated by the honest market-man. He wished to complete his good action by accompanying Mariette as far as possible, but dared not do so without Javotte's permission, to obtain which, he had either created a danger which did not exist, or had made a slight one seem more redoubtable.

As Mariette had the inestimable privilege of attracting hearts to her, Javotte had even gone farther than her husband wished.

The wood of Etonvelles might have excited some apprehension in Mariette's mind, had she passed it alone. She met a kind of Kossack patrol there, composed of eight men, who terrified her much by their Russian beards, long lances, pistols in their belts, and rope stirrups; then she met soldiers isolated and in groups; one of the latter just as the little caravan was leaving the

11*   249

wood, so arranged the three men that composed it, as
to close the road.   They had doubtless prepared to do
so, but Bernard also halted and growled so angrily,
showing his lion teeth, and Charles at the same moment
executed so superb a flourish with his iron-shod staff,
that the two demonstrations, sustained by the appearance of a young officer, who came from the wood,
whence he had seen all, fastened their menacers to the
ground.

At the sight of their superior the three Russian Grenadiers stood motionless as ancient statues, with the little
finger of the left hand on the seams of their pantaloons,
and the right as high as the gold band of their caps.

Not only was this officer young, but he was almost a
child, for this other Emperor—he of the North—who
had come to oppress us, had been forced to strip his
sterile and icy realm of men.   Yet the young officer,
blonde as was his hair, rosy his complexion, youthful his
face, had in his manner something of a varnish of bar-
barism, which made him more terrible than any virile
or rude face Mariette had seen since she commenced
her journey.

He made a gesture with his hand to the young girl,
who seeing that he wished to speak to her, checked the
ass.

Charles was not satisfied, but Mariette with a smile,
pointed to Bernard, who advanced towards the young
man.

The latter advanced and said in a half-familiar, half-
polite manner,

"Well! my child; what is the matter."

Mariette trembling, replied, "Nothing, Mr. Officer,
but I am afraid."

" Of what ?"

" Of those three soldiers who seem disposed to stop me."

" Of them ?" said the young man, with an expression of menace and contempt which nothing can give an idea of.

" But," said Charles, executing another flourish, "we were ready."

" You," said the officer, with an expression like the first.

" Especially," said Mariette, " as I have a Pass from the General-in-chief."

" Ah !" said the young Russian.

She gave him the paper.

He unfolded it slowly, keeping his eye fixed on the three men, who were motionless, as if they had been made of stone, and with some surprise read the orders of his General.

Taking it in his left hand, he read it to the three soldiers, giving each of them a violent blow with the right, from which they did not swerve their Sclavic faces.— Then coming to Mariette,

" Mademoiselle," said he, " whither do you go ?"

" To-day, sir, I go as far as Chivy, which is nearly a league distant."

" Very well," said the officer, restoring the Pass, " you can not only continue your journey, but will do so under an escort."

Turning to the soldiers, he gave them in a clear and distinct tone, in the Russian tongue, an order, which though Mariette and Charles did not understand a word of, they saw obeyed.

Having returned the officer's salute and made the ass resume its pace, Mariette and Charles saw the Russian

Grenadiers face about, and follow them at the distance of twenty paces like automata, the left hand being close to the seams of their pantaloons, and the right as high as the cap.

Thus they marched a league, and returned to the quarters of the young officer, until the hour when he chanced to return, under the penalty of twenty stripes each.

The young officer quietly returned to Etonvelles bidding Mariette adieu.

He was sure his order would be obeyed to the letter.

Mariette's heart was distressed at the blows inflicted on the three men. On the other hand, however, we must say that Charles not only felt much pleasure at the fact, but expressed it, whenever he looked back and saw the men in the same attitude, and at precisely the same distance, marching like windmills with their arms lifted.

Thus they reached Chivy. The Russians, so probably were they ordered, halted at the entrance of the village, faced about as they had done, and retraced their steps in the same order and attitude to Etonvelles.

Chivy is a little village of about seventy houses, and that of Mother Sabot was almost at the other end of it, towards the city of Laon.

The old woman had gone frequently to the door, to see if the ass was coming back, for a trip her husband had to make early the next morning, rendered the want pressing.

Mariette therefore partook of the animal's welcome: accompanied and recommended by Round Charles too, all progressed as well as possible.

He told Mariette's story, which always made a deep

impression on women, and supper and lodging were offered cheerfully, both by Mother Sabot and her husband.

Charles delighted at his good action, with active legs and merry heart, as he had promised Javotte, fairly ran home.

As he passed through Etonvelles, however, he saw before a house which doubtless was that of the officer, the three Grenadiers, still motionless, with their hands fixed to their positions on the seams of their pantaloons and on their caps.

In all probability the young officer had not yet returned.

Mariette slept little. How could she? being so near Conscience. The first ray of the sun found her up— and when Father Sabot was about to set out and tapped at her door expecting to awaken her, she met him, all dressed.

He went with her to the heights of Clacy, that is, a full league from Laon, where he left the high, and took a cross road.

Mariette went on; she had now nothing to fear— Laon was before her, rising on the height, crowning that table land which in his despair the Titan had sought to scale, and on which he had left in vain four thousand dead and three thousand wounded.

She found a Russian guard at the gate of the city— but it did not even ask the young and graceful girl for her Pass. She entered, and was soon on the square where the old Merovingian tower of Louis Outremer once stood.

Not knowing the city, she had to ask her way, and approached a sentinel who walked up and down doubtless before, the quarters of some officer of rank, and asked where was the hospital.

The sentinel shook his head to express that he did not understand.

Mariette showed her Pass.

The sentinel could not read, but when he saw the impression of the seal, he knew at once that the paper was an order or a requisition, and called to a non-commissioned officer to approach.

Mariette saluted him with more politeness than she had the soldier, and showed him the Pass.

The non-commissioned officer thought the matter grave enough to be referred to an officer, and having respectfully returned the paper to Mariette, went for one.

The latter soon came, stroking his moustache. Mariette's appearance produced its usual effect, for he advanced with a smile, and said in French, with a strong German accent,

"Good morning, my pretty girl! How can I serve you?"

"Sir, can you," said Mariette, "show me the way to the hospital?"

"There are two. Which would you go to?"

"The one in which Conscience is, sir."

"Who is he, Mademoiselle?"

"Conscience is a poor French soldier, who during the battle lost his eyes."

"Was he a horseman or a footman?"

"He was in the Artillery, and drove a caisson."

"Ah, I understand—he was a Hussar, *a garde roue*, as we say. Then he is in the Cavalry Hospital."

Turning to a soldier, he spoke a few words in Ger-

man, which the latter heard respectfully with his hand
to his cap.

He then said to Mariette,

"Follow this man—he will show you the way."

Mariette made a courtesy at the officer, who in return waved his hand kindly to her and said,

"DER TEUFEL ! SEHR SCHONE ! SEHR SCHONE !"

Mariette would have blushed had she known what
the compliment was

Light as a gazelle, she was at some distance following the soldier, who it seemed to her walked very
slowly indeed.

After about five minutes, the Prussian soldier pointed out a great door surmounted by a stone cross, before which walked, with his left arm in a scarf and his
sabre on his right shoulder, a sentinel who by the fragments of his uniform was recognised as having belonged to the Cuirassiers.

The sentinel looked at the Prussian.

"HIER !" said the latter.

"Hier ?" repeated Mariette.

"JA, HIER !" said the Prussian.

Mariette understood.

"That means," said she, "that he is here—that we
are come."

"JA," said the Prussian.

"Thank you," said Mariette, and she hurried towards the great door which was surmounted by the
cross, the entrance of which the cuirassier barred.

"No admission," said he frowning, and in an angry
tone.

"What ! no admission ?" said she, shrinking.

"None. Do you not understand French ?"

"Yes—and because I do speak French and address a countryman, I hoped I could enter."

"You are wrong; there is no admission."

"My God! Why?"

"Orders."

"Sir, for heaven's sake let me beg—"

"Back!" said the cuirassier.

"But I am come so far," said the young girl.

He made a gesture of brutal menace to her.

"Sir," said Mariette trembling, "I have a Pass."

"From whom?"

'From the Russian General-in-chief."

"Do not know the Russian General-in-chief," said the cuirassier, with increased agitation.

"My God," said Mariette, lifting her hands to heaven, "what shall I do, and what will become of me?"

"Do what you please, become anything you please, provided you clear out at once."

"It seems to me, comrade," said a voice behind Mariette, "that you treat the poor girl rather sternly."

"I know no girls that come escorted by Prussians, and with a Pass from Russians."

"The fact is, my child," said the third speaker, "that the Pass is perfectly good for a Prussian or a Russian, but to a Frenchman it would be better to come empty-handed, and say, 'I have business with,' or 'wish to see such a one; let me pass.'"

Mariette had turned around, and recognized a uniform which was not unfamiliar to her. Then amid the bandages across the soldier's brow, which covered an eye, and a part of the cheek, she recognised a face she knew.

"My God!" said Mariette, "am I not mistaken? am I so fortunate as to have met you?"

" Mariette !" said the Hussar.

" Bastien !" said Mariette; " my friend, my protector, I am come from Haramont to see Conscience, who,
perhaps will never see me. I shall die; Bastien, you
understand, I shall die if I do not see him."

She had nearly knelt with arms outstretched towards
the Hussar.

" Be easy, Mariette, you shall see him," said Bastien; " I promise you, or I will lose my name."

Approaching the cuirassier, he said,

" Comrade, this is a country-woman from the same
village with me, who has come to see her lover, poor
Conscience, the one, you know, who had his eyes
burned."

" Yes," said the cuirassier. " I know all that."

" Well."

" Well, the orders say no admission : and she shall
not pass."

" Ah yes," said Mariette. " It shall not be told that
I came from home to see Conscience, that I promised
Madeleine to bring him back, and that having undergone so many dangers, I returned as I came. If I
have to force the doors I will try it, even though the
sabre of that wicked soldier pierce me."

She moved forward, but Bastien checked her.

Placing himself between her and the cuirassier, he
said,

" You heard, did you not ?"

" What ?"

" What the poor girl said, that she would pass the
door, if your sabre pierced her heart."

" Ah, I know all those farces."

" It is no farce," said Bastien, who began to bite his
moustache, (a very bad sign with him,) " but true grief

and real tears, a brave soldier like you, comrade, should be able to see man's blood flow, but not women's tears."

The cuirassier saw a slight accent of menace in the words of the Hussar, and winked his eye. It was his method of expressing dissatisfaction : he said,

" And do you think for your peasant girl's tears, I am going to violate orders, and run the risk of twenty-four hours under guard ? Thank you."

" Since when would a soldier refuse to run that risk to serve a comrade."

" For another I willingly would, provided that other asked me in a suitable manner."

" Why for another, and not for this girl ?"

" Because she is too intimate with Russians and Prussians to be French at heart."

" Cuirassier, my friend, you should know that she is French at heart, being the betrothed of Conscience, and the friend of Bastien."

" It matters not, I am not sure enough to run the risk of the guard-house."

Bastien's upper lip was almost hidden by the lower one.

" Cuirassier, my friend, when I tell you a thing you should be sure of it."

The cuirassier winked so as almost to seem one eyed.

" And if your word did not suffice, what then ?"

" That as I told Mariette she should go in the hospital, or I would lose my name, she must go in, will or will you not, inasmuch as I do not mean to lose my name."

" Your name ? tell it me, so that at five this evening, I may call it aloud somewhere beneath the rampart."

"Very well," said Bastien. "Do so at five o'clock, on the side towards Saint Marcel. You need not shout very loud, for I will be there, though both my legs and sabre are shorter than yours."

"My God," said Mariette trembling. "Bastien Bastien, I understand you. On my account you have engaged in a duel."

"What of it, Mariette? Many a man has fought for an uglier face than yours."

"I will not have it, Bastien. I will ask pardon of that ugly cuirassier, and beg him so that he will suffer me to pass."

"Bah, Mariette. That soils one's sleeves, as we Hussars say. The affair is begun, and must be ended."

"But if aught befell you on my account, Bastien, I never would forgive myself."

"Ah; do not be uneasy, Mariette. No, this is mere sport, for the heavies are not as ill-natured as they seem, and all may be ended yet by a bottle to the health of the father of all, who is below there, and whom the fools call Nicholas. Well, let Jean Camp-kettle march and counter-march before the door of the hospital, and come with me."

"Why? Must I then go away?"

"Certainly, for the present."

"But Bastien, I cannot without seeing Conscience; you told me just now I should."

"Yes; I say so again."

He looked at the church clock.

"Well?" asked Mariette.

"Well! it will be in less than a half an hour."

"Before I see him?"

"Yes."

"Bastien, dear Bastien."

"But you must go away, sit down on that stone bench and chat awhile."

"Ah! as long as you please. You say I am to see Conscience in a half an hour?"

"Now you will see him in twenty-five minutes, as five minutes have passed since I made the promise."

"I will see him in spite of the cuirassier?"

"In spite of the cuirassier."

"How, Bastien?"

"Easily. He will not be forever in front of that door."

"Ah! I see, at nine, in twenty minutes, another will replace him."

"Exactly, Mariette, and as the next probably will not be a hound like him, what this one refused, will be granted us."

"But if he too refuses."

"I have contrived a way, so that he will not."

"What?"

"You will see what."

"Soon?"

"In a quarter of an hour." Bastien looked at the clock.

"My God! how long a quarter of an hour is!"

"True, when one neither drinks nor smokes, it is fifteen minutes."

"Bastien, you put me in mind, that perhaps you have taken nothing?"

"Twice or thrice, that is all."

"Yes, Mariette, as for two days, I shall perhaps be locked up, I will not refuse."

"Well, be quick!" said Mariette, hurrying him towards a cabaret, "for we have but ten minutes."

"Ten minutes! Bah! in ten minutes, one does much."

Bastien entered the cabaret, and said, " Waiter, a bottle, a loaf and two glasses."

" Ah! Bastien, I never drink."

" I know how to make you."

" No, no."

" You will see."

Taking the bottle, he poured a few drops in Mariette's glass, but filled his full.

" Those few drops."

" Not them even, I drink but water."

" To the health of Conscience," said Bastien, as he lifted up his glass.

" Ah," said Mariette, " if that be it, I will not refuse. I would fear misfortune if I did."

" May you see him in five minutes!" said Bastien.

She repeated Bastien's words, and drank.

" Ah, I knew you would drink," said the hussar, boldly attacking the bread, and the greater part of the first, and the whole of the latter disappearing before five minutes had passed.

The clock struck nine.

X.

How Mariette took the last fifteen Difficult Steps.

———

MARIETTE heard every stroke of the bell as if the hammer had fallen on her heart. When the last had finished, Bastien said,

"Come."

"Ah! the five minutes are over."

Bastien took Mariette to the door of the cabaret, where they paused and looked towards the door of the hospital.

A dragoon escorted by another dragoon and an hussar, relieved the cuirassier, who received the orders and prepared to keep his post for two hours.

The wounded men did not wish to have foreign sentinels at their door, and had obtained a guard of their own, or rather of the most advanced of the convalescents. Thence came the succession of arms and uniforms.

The cuirassier and Bastien exchanged glances, which meant on the cuirassier's side—

"At five o'clock."

And on Bastien's, implied assent.

The cuirassier left, and disappeared at an angle of the street.

"Now," said Bastien, "wait here a minute, Mariette, and when the dragoon shall have yielded me his place and left, come—"

"Have you yet hopes?" said Mariette with a quivering heart.

"More than ever—but attention to the command."

He advanced towards the Dragoon with the dandified air all soldiers, particularly Hussars, affect, and which was one of Bastien's peculiar graces.

Though not intimate with the Dragoon, Bastien knew him, and among all these fragments of the Napoleonic glory, there was a religious community of thought —the fraternity of misfortune.

The cuirassier had been so rude and so tenacious to Mariette only because she came with a Prussian escort and Russian Pass.

He had treated the young girl with a purely national opposition. But for that, his heart, used as it was to its covering, would certainly have yielded to the prayers of Mariette and persuasion of Bastien.

Bastien had nothing of the sword to apprehend from the Dragoon, but he resolved not to risk a refusal.

He therefore adopted another manœuvre with the new sentinel, and approaching him said,

"Good day, Dragoon."

"Good day, Hussar."

There was a pause.

"Tell me, Dragoon, if you would be disposed to do a favor to a comrade."

"Certainly, provided it did not affront my regiment, and was not contrary to orders."

"Well," said the Hussar, "did you notice that great chap you relieved?"

" The cuirassier ?"

" Yes."

" Well !"

" Well, we had some words together."

" About what ?"

" A girl who is at the door of the cabaret, at the corner of the street with a dog at her feet."

" A pretty girl, and a fine dog," said the Dragoon, looking up and stroking his moustache.

" Yes, we had some words five minutes ago, and at five o'clock are, below St. Marcel's bastion, to give each other a few gashes."

" You want me as your second ?"

" No—because if you do me the favor I ask, you will be here while we are there."

" What ! I here ? Do you think I am posted for twenty-four hours ?"

" Wait till I explain."

" Well, I hear," said the Dragoon gravely.

" Well, the cuirassier had a fancy of which I could not rid him."

" What ?"

" Not to fight before nor after five o'clock."

" Odd," said the Dragoon, who could not see why a man should not fight all the day.

" Now," said Bastien, "I had to do exactly as he pleased, since I had called him out."

" Well—"

" That is rather inconvenient, as at five I mount post, and am on till seven."

" You should have told him."

" I did, but he would not hear me."

" He must be particularly fond of five o'clock."

" It is a mere whim, though, for he offered to stay

four hours, two for him and two for me on post, so as to fight at five o'clock. One might think he was only brave at that hour."

"The French soldier is brave at every hour," said the Dragoon sententiously.

"True," said the Hussar, who did not wish to oppose a man of whom he was about to ask a favor.— "You see, though, Dragoon, I refused the offer."

"You were wrong, Hussar."

"No—because I said, ' The Devil ! between this and five o'clock, I will find some comrade, whose tour of duty I will take on condition that he does mine.' When I saw you take your place for the contra-dance, I said, ' There is my man.' Do you understand ?"

"No."

"You do not understand that you will do me a favor by turning over the special orders—I know the others —and give me your place in consideration of a bottle of Clamecy, to be drunken after relief, and a clasp of the hand to men—' Dragoon, yours for life or death.' "

"Yes, I am to mount guard at five o'clock, while you are down there ? Good."

"Exactly."

"That will do," said the Dragoon, "but you will owe me ten minutes by the clock—"

"Very well, I will pay that over a second bottle."

"So be it The orders are—' Carry arms to all Prussian, Russian, or French officers if they wear epaulettes—to suffer no women but the Sisters of Charity to enter the hospital without leave, and permit none of the invalids to leave it without a surgeon's *Exeat*."

"All right. The same for a change—"

"Yes."

"Thank you—then at five?"

"I will be faithful."

"Now, Dragoon, as every service is worth its price, go to the cabaret and say to that young girl who is looking at us, as politely as you can, 'Mlle. Mariette, Bastien the Hussar wishes to speak to you and your dog.' She will say, 'Thank you, Dragoon,' and that will repay you for your trouble."

"Do not be uneasy, Dragoons have always been famous for civility to the fair sex."

"Then," said Bastien, "as Dragoons know the infantry as well as the cavalry drill, *Left* HALF FACE— *Forward* MARCH!"

The Dragoon obeyed the command, and advanced, cap in hand, towards Mariette, and spoke to her.

As soon as she heard him, she sprang from the wall against which she leaned, and hurried to Bastien.

"Shall I see Conscience?"

"Certainly," said Bastien.

"You have permission?"

"No, but I give you—"

"What! give me permission?"

"Certainly. I am on post."

"But the orders—"

"There are no orders for you."

"Then I may go in?"

"Yes; but if asked for your Pass, say you left it with the sentinel, who was to restore it when you left."

"Thank you, Bastien. What can I do for you?"

Bastien took hold of the young girl's arm and drew her towards him.

"Mariette, tell me of Catharine, to give me something to think of during the two hours I am on post."

He added in a lower tone—

"And the twenty-four, I shall be in the guard house."

"Oh!" cried Mariette, who heard only the first portion of his remark, "can love make us so selfish?"

"Selfish!" said Bastien.

"I speak of myself, Bastien. I mean, make me so selfish as not to remember Catharine."

"Well," said the Hussar, prepared for the tenderest of catastrophes.

"Well! she loves you, dear Bastien, and weeps for you all day, for she thinks you killed."

"Ah!" said Bastien, much moved. "Catherine weeps for me. What will she say when she sees me with the patch over my eye?"

"That you are welcome, Bastien, for the day she sees you, will be the happiest of your life."

"Then I can write to her without fearing that another will open the letter?"

"Write to her with no fear but that tears of joy may blind her, and prevent her reading your letter."

"Good girl!" said the Hussar, wiping away a tear which hung in the corner of his own eye.

"Well," said Mariette, "are you satisfied?"

"Name of Names, I should be hard to please if I were not—but now it is your turn to be satisfied. Go in."

"Which way?" asked Mariette, delighted."

"Straight before you. That is all."

"But which of those doors must I open?"

"Look, the one before which Bernard is lying."

"Poor Bernard!" said Mariette, "I had forgotten him."

Thanking Bastien again, she entered the yard light

as one of the deer which crossed the forest of Villers-Cotterets.

Bastien saw her leave, and said in a low tone,

"I will probably be rewarded for the service I have done her, by a sabre-cut, and twenty-four hours under guard. What of that though—she is worthy my bearing more than that."

He added in a kind of peroration,

"Name of names; in the Regiment that was a pleasure."

XI.

THE BLIND WARD.

THE hospital of Laon had a ward devoted not only
to blind soldiers, but to persons in the city, afflicted with ophthalmic affections, who the Senior Surgeon of the hospital, celebrated in such cases, attended.

This room intended for patients deprived of sight, in
danger of losing, or likely to recover it, had a strange appearance, the only characteristic of which was profound
sadness. This was enhanced by the fact that the windows, covered with green paper, shut out every ray of
the sun, and prevented the entrance of clear light. To
strangers admitted by the authorities of the hospital, it
was a sad place, the feeble light of which was more unpleasant than darkness itself. It seemed a kind of
limbo, neither night nor day, through which dark
phantoms walked with silent steps and extended arms,
or where they leaned for hours against the wall without speaking.

Every heart felt a secret anxiety at the entrance of
this dark realm of blindness. It had been said that in
the descent to the dark regions of the world of mystery,
all halt half way between life and the tomb, in a
funereal state, which was neither existence nor sepul-

ture. Before anything was distinct, the eye had to grow used to this tint of green paper over the glass, the effect of which was, that those of the patients who began to see, were almost as much distressed at this factitious light restored to them, as at the darkness from which they had emerged—all, whatever might be the degree of their convalescence, had to wear a green visor over the face, so that the very surgeon who treated them, had to call them by name, to distinguish the spectors from each other, and to apply the remedy demanded by the severity or the amelioration of the disease.

At the moment we write of, the immense ward, thirty feet square almost, had but eight or ten patients.

Conscience was one of the eight or ten.

In spite of his misfortune, the young man had lost neither his faith nor his calmness. The invisible world amid which Conscience once had lived, had not failed him : since he had been deprived of his outward sight, he had, so to say, plunged more deeply in the interior world which the dreams of fools and extatics, two classes of invalids for the physicians, the majority of whom are materialists, class together."

This was not, however, the case with the poor blind companions of Conscience's obscurity and darkness. To them, the lad was a great consoler, and replaced the material world from which they were exiled, by revelation of another, visible perhaps only to the eyes of death, and into which, by a special privilege, Conscience had always penetrated with the eyes of the soul, and in which, as we have said, he saw more distinctly still, since the eyes of his body were closed.

They then as usual, sat grouped around Conscience, who, seeing that consolation dropped from his lips

sometimes loosed the wonderful visions which illumin-
ated his brain. When Conscience spoke of the soft
light of another world, which was an eternal day, of
which God was the sun, and the angels the stars, where
all good hearts, all pure souls, were united to receive
their reward for the good deeds they had done in
the flesh in this perishable world; as he called this new
world, for even in his dreams, man cannot invent, made
like ours, but adorned with all the charms of a youthful imagination, this world of faith, with its shaded
forests, flower bordered gardens, its vast peaceful lakes,
its murmuring streams, its thousand colored birds,
speaking the languages of man, all listened to him, and
as they did, heard so well that for a moment the poor blind
regretted nothing. Conscience by a dream had restored
to them what they had lost, and all sighed not for what
was really gone, but for the future world revealed to
them.

A time, however, came, when the lips of the young
man were sealed, as the burning weather of July dries
up a spring which has been too much used. Then the
light kindled in their imaginations by the burning dis-
course of the revealer, gradually became darkened, and
went out one by one, as the tapers which illumine a
church and make glittering the white cloth and golden
ornaments of the altar. Then the blind patients relapsed not merely into their simple night, but in the double physical and moral obscurity, in which the absence
both of light and of his conversation plunged them. Then
each one silently felt his way to his accustomed place,
bearing a portion of that flame, that light of day, last
kindled at the tabernacle, which he nursed in his
mind with a worship similar to that of the vestal of an-

tiquity, the life or death of which was her own existence or destruction.

Conscience, on the contrary, while his companions followed the fluttering light of their dreams, as lost travellers pursue the will-o-the-wisps, they see bounding over the meadows, relapsed into reality, and saw the cottages on the two sides of the way, the one with its crown of vine tendrils, the other with its robe of moss, and in these two cottages having a common life, made sad by his own absence, his grandfather on the bed of pain, Madeleine, Dame Marie and Mariette weeping, while the child, in the carelessness of his age, ran in the bright May sun, he was himself never to see, after the emerald flies and the painted Iris.

He sate in the most remote angle of the door, plunged in all of these sombre reflections, when all at once he trembled; it seemed to him, that an imperceptible noise, to which he had grown unused, was heard on the steps, and that he heard his name pronounced by a female voice. He had perceived the low, plaintive sound a dog utters, when after long absence, his master returns, he felt in his heart so accessible to this intuition, that something mild, gentle and consoling as the breath of an angel approached. Instinctively he advanced and walked panting with outstretched hands, directly towards the door, as if he had regained his sight. The door opened, at that moment something like a magnetic current was established between him and the person who appeared at the threshold. From each bosom there escaped one exclamation, Conscience, Mariette. Before this was completed the two young people were locked in the arms of each other.

To this cry of joy, however, followed one of pain. Taking her head from Conscience's bosom, Mariette regained her sight. She saw the dark ward, the spectres seated against the wall slowly rising and approaching, and then again she threw herself into the young man's arms and gave vent to that painful accent, which contained at once love, pity and pain—

" Conscience, my poor Conscience !"

Her arms fell inert, as if her strength had deserted her, and maintained her erect position only in consequence of the support his shoulder afforded her.

Conscience understood so perfectly what was passing in her mind, that he did not even attempt to console her. He folded her in his arms, and did but utter the murmur of her name, twenty times, as if the echo came from his heart, while Bernard, who seemed aware that his time was not yet come, stood removed, nntil these outbreaks of joy and agony were satisfied.

The humble animal, aware of his superiority in the scale of existences, waited until Conscience's hand should descend to the position Nature had assigned him.

Joy however soon triumphed over grief. A painful sigh escaped from Mariette's lips : her glance at the young man became less painful, and in a tone already full of gratefulness if not of happiness, she again repeated—

" Conscience, my poor Conscience !"

During this time the poor blind men whom Mariette saw move at her appearance, had slowly approached and formed a half circle around her. They touched her hands as if they would become acquainted with the good, kind Mariette, of whom Conscience had so often spoken to them, and who had penetrated their hell if not like Christ to rescue all, at least to ransom one of them. The touch of these kind but curious

12*

hands terrified Mariette, and roused her from the stupor in which she had fallen.

She clasped Conscience more closely, and drawing him to her, said,

"Beg them not to touch me thus, for I do not know their meaning, nor what they wish with me."

"Fear not, Mariette, they are all my friends—and consequently all love you. Alas! you do not know that the poor blind see with their fingers, and touch your dress to know something of you. If they dared, they would touch your face to know you entirely. Let them do so, Mariette, for they have not the least evil intention."

"Ah, then, I pardon them most willingly; but, Conscience, as it seems to me this should not be, sit with me on this bench, and bid them leave us for a moment alone. I have much to tell, so much . . ."

She led Conscience to a bench, and sate by him, clasping his hands in hers.

We will not seek to accompany them in their first interview after so long a separation.

Only a being gifted with sight lost among the blind, could see the face of the young girl express all the sentiments of the heart, and pass from joy to grief—from tears to enthusiasm.

At intervals she pressed Conscience's hands most energetically. Then her love poured the balm of hope into the young man's heart; the scarcely perceptible sounds of her voice, for she spoke for her beloved alone, were at that time sweet and touching as a love song.

Conscience had lifted up the visor over his eyes, as if to increase his chance of seeing Mariette. His sightless pupils, covered with a white film, were lifted to heaven, and his head slightly thrown back against the wall, exhibited his face marked with a dreamy attention.

The other blind formed a wide circle around him, and at a distance listened as if they could hear what the two lovers said, and looking as if they could see the young man and young woman with interlocked arms, with their heads together and with the dog at their feet—a charming group, which might seem to have been arranged by the merciful eye of God.

XII.

The Chief Nurse.

WHILE this sweet and tender conversation was going on between the young couple, the door opened, the head-nurse entered the room.

Mariette and Conscience were so well masked by the blind, that at first he did not see them.

Yet at the sound of the opening door all had faced about, and though the blind could not see, they guessed at his anger.

"Where is the young girl who came in this room without a permit?"

Mariette trembled, and arising, leaned against the wall. She could not speak.

"Well," said the nurse, "are all blind here? Can none neither speak nor see?" said he, pushing aside two or three of the patients, and coming within the circle.

"What is the matter, nurse?" asked Conscience.

"This young girl has entered this room, saying that she had given her permission to the sentinel. I went myself to ask for it, and he searched in vain all his pockets, saying that he had lost it, after ten minutes time. My report however is made, and the Hussar when he is relieved will have his forty-eight hours under guard.

"Monsieur," said Mariette in her gentle voice, and clasping her hands, "take pity, I beg you, on the Hussar, who is from our country—on Bastien. He knows how I love Conscience, how anxious I was to see him—and as I wept when the cuirassier drove me away, he sacrificed himself for me. Monsieur, do not punish him for his companion."

"Then what I suspected is true?"

"Excuse me, but what did you suspect?" said Mariette.

"That you had no permission."

"No, sir."

"How? No?"

"I have no permission, but merely a Pass."

She timidly took General Sacken's Pass from her bosom.

"What is this? What are these words and this seal? It is a Pass for the high roads, and not to enable one to glide into hospital wards. I know nothing of it. Come out of this as soon as possible, my beautiful—"

"Monsieur," said Mariette, "if you please—"

"Heh?" said the nurse, amazed at his wishes being opposed, even by a prayer.

"One half hour, only a half hour longer. I will pray God for you, and in gratitude will kiss your hands."

"Have done with this child's play," said the nurse, like a man who has made up his mind and is resolved not to change it.

"Oh! I see half an hour is too long—just a quarter?"

" Not an instant—not a second—not a minute."

" For heaven's sake, sir. I am come from the other end in the department. In one day I travelled, thanks to the kind hearts of those I met, fifteen leagues to see Conscience. Already I have caused a duel and the punishment of poor Bastien on my account. At last I see Conscience, who is unable to see me again, and have scarcely been able to commence to console him, when you drive me away. Oh! if you knew how much remains to be said, I am sure you would pity us."

" Will you go or not ?" said the nurse, stamping, " or must I push you out by the shoulders ?"

" Monsieur, Monsieur, do not kill me," said the young girl. " Hush, Bernard, do not growl so—Monsieur is good, and will permit me to remain yet a few minutes longer : he will have pity on the poor blind man, and will not tear out his heart. Monsieur, you too are a man, and a similar misfortune may befal you ! Well, were you without sight, and did your sister, your mother, or she you loved, come to see you, would you not be in despair, if any one wished to turn them away ? You will not turn me away, sir ? You will suffer me to remain here to take care of Conscience— not for an hour, a half, a quarter, or for a few minutes, but until he can leave the hospital and return to Haramont. Sir, for the love of God, I beg you . . . "

Mariette fell on her knees, controlling Bernard with her little white hand, for the dog's eyes glared, his breath was panting, and lion-like he lashed his sides with his tail in anxiety to spring on the man.

The patients murmured, for this cruelty seemed in Conscience's cruelty to wound them all.

Conscience stood erect and silent, but with clenched

hands. The good young man evidently needed all the patience with which he was endowed to sustain him.

The nurse seized Mariette's arm.

" Hush !" said he to the invalids who murmured around him. " Hush and obey, or I will kill the dog and send the girl to the hospital."

He had not finished this double threat which he began while Mariette was kneeling and trying to restrain the dog which was ready to strangle him, when he felt, as it were, an iron ring closing around his neck. It was, in fact, only Conscience, who had joined his hands, and thus, for the first time in his life, united menace and action.

" Ah !" said the young man, growing pale, and fixing on him those eyes, to which the loss of sight gave a terrible expression. " Wretch! bad man! false Christian! You will kill Bernard and send Mariette to the hospital. It is well for you that this ward is so silent and dark that perhaps even God has not heard you."

The nurse uttered a stifled cry, and the poor invalids who gathered around, seemed a storm ready to overwhelm him.

" Conscience," said Mariette, restraining Bernard with one hand, while with the other she took hold of the young man. " Conscience, for heaven's sake release that man, and he will doubtless repent of the evil he has done us."

" You are right Mariette," said Conscience, letting his hands fall to his sides, let us not make ourselves more unhappy than we are. Come, Mariette, let me kiss you for the last time."

Perceiving the efforts of Mariette to restrain Bernard, he said :

"Here, Bernard, my friend, here, I was so happy that I had forgotten you."

Bernard, delighted at these words, the first his master had spoken to him, for a moment forgot the nurse, and rising erect before his master with a plaintive growl, passed his tongue over Conscience's dimmed eyes.

Mariette, however, saw that a man was there whom it was necessary to disarm.

She let go Conscience, and with a calmer dignity than might have been expected in her age and condition, advanced towards the nurse. She was, apparently, self-controlled, but could not restrain two great tears, which fell in silence on her cheeks.

"Sir," said she, "I go, forgive me, forgive Bastien, and above all, forgive Conscience, and I promise you that God, who has set us the example of mercy, will reward this good action in you. You too, have a heart, and to it I appeal. You will be good enough to forget, and I will remember you in my prayers to God."

Whether the nurse did not wish to expose himself a second time to Conscience's prayers, or to Bernard's teeth, he was disarmed by this submission.

"Very well," said he, "go, and if the violation of orders be not known, for your sake I will be silent."

Mariette kissed his hand.

"Ah, you are a kind man," said she. "I knew it. Yes sir, I will go at once, after one last embrace."

Again she threw herself into the arms of the poor invalid, to whom she gave a long tender kiss, murmuring in his ear words of consolation.

"Be calm, Conscience, before the day is gone, I will have a permission to see you again."

Unable any longer to restrain her grief, she advanced towards the door of the room. When there, she looked back, and after uttering a piercing cry, turned to re-enter the room. She met the nurse, however, who barred her progress, and she was forced to go, leaving Conscience weak and feeble, sunken on his seat and unable to restrain Bernard, who stood ready to fly at once to Mariette's aid.

Mariette returned, and found Bastien still on post at the gate surmounted by the stone cross.

There exhausted, trembling, and with a lacerated heart and distressed soul, she cast one look around her, as if to ssek before she left that asylum of grief, some one whose protection she could invoke to enable her to keep the promise she had made to Conscience, or rather to herself.

A woman, elegantly dressed, was at a window of the first floor which seemed to be occupied by the employes of the civil hospital, which during the invasion was also become a military one.

Mariette saw this woman between her tears, and thought that hope might come from her, she wiped away her tears to see more distinctly, and thinking she read an expression of pity on her face, rushed towards the window, and lifting her hands as if to a Madonna, exclaimed,

"Madame, for the sake of heaven, of your husband, your mother, of all dear to you in this and the other world, hear me."

The lady looked at Mariette like one who did not understand what was said to her, or like one who was hesitating between emotion and the fear of ridicule.

She half drew back.

Seeing this, and divining the cause, Mariettte uttered a cry, which was so sad, so plaintive, and so poignant that the lady paused, and looked with surprise at the young girl who called to her, and in the face of whom might be read fear of repulse, and gratitude for an anticipated favor.

Pity triumphed over fear, and she said,

"Come up, my child, and tell me how I can serve you."

Then with the smile with which women accompany good deeds, she said, "If I can do what you wish, I will with all my heart."

Mariette did not hesitate, but rushed up stairs.

XIII.

The Surgeon's Wife.

———

THE lady awaited Mariette at the threshold of her open door, and taking hold of both the young girl's hands, she drew her into the room.

"Tell me, my poor child," said she, "the cause of your great distress."

She made Mariette take a seat.

Mariette obeyed. Before speaking, however, she pointed to an officer, who sate before a desk in the same room, writing, the gold embroidery, like that of a general, on the collar of whose coat, intimidated her much.

By the intuition peculiar to women, the lady understood her at once.

"Ah!" said she, "do not be in the least afraid of that gentleman. He is fully engrossed by business and does not pay the least attention to us."

"Then, Madame, let me tell you all," said Mariette.

"Do so, my dear child."

There was such tenderness in the voice which thus addressed her, that Mariette no longer hesitated, and said :

"This, Madame, is all our story. We are poor peasants of Haramont, at the other extremity of the department, sixteen or eighteen leagues hence. My mother, myself, my young brother, Father Cadet, Conscience and Madeleine lived in two cottages, situated opposite to each other. We never left, or lost sight of each other, and loved one another as if we had belonged to the same family, with the exception that Conscience was more than a brother. But the conscription took Conscience from us, and he left us. We received many letters from him, full of hope, which at first sustained our hearts, until at last, Madame, one came, that his eyes were bad, and that he was afraid he would lose his sight. It, however, enclosed one for me, which told me all, that he was blind incurably . . . Oh! Madame, this almost killed me. I fainted on the ground, and saw neither the sun, nor the trees around us. Fortunately, God saw me and took pity on me. He restored me to life, and in doing so, inspired me with the idea of joining Conscience, who, for twenty years, had with him two mothers, and one who loved him and who now has nothing. I then received the price of a calf we had sold, and left, resolved to walk hither in three days. Kind persons, however, had mercy on me, so that I came more comfortably and without expense in one day. This morning I sought to see Conscience, but was told no one could enter the hospital, and especially the blind ward, without a permit. To whom was I to go? I knew no one and had not seen you. I implored a poor lad of our village, Bastien, an Hussar, who on my account, will probably fight a duel to-day, a thing that adds to my trouble. Bastien took the duty of one of his comrades, and let me pass, in spite of the orders, saying, that for a friend like me, he would risk twenty-four hours under guard. I then, Madame, glided into the blind ward. Have you ever been there? It is very sad.

I saw Conscience, and was at once both very happy and miserable, when the head nurse came in, and forced me to leave, having almost insulted me and beaten me."

The man with the embroidered collar made a movement.

"Oh," exclaimed Mariette, who saw that without wishing to do so, she had informed on the man, "he told me it was not his fault, that he was forced to act thus, so that I forgive him . . . sincerely and especially since I have seen you. I then left as if I were mad, having promised Conscience, that I would find some one to protect us, to unite us and to prevent our being again separated. Having left him, I lifted my hands and eyes to heaven, and saw you—and to me, I do not know why, Madame, it seemed that you would be the guardian angel I sought for. For that reason I lifted up my hands and came to; for that reason, I am at your feet."

Mariette had really fallen at the lady's feet, and the face of the latter, while our heroine spake, was become covered with tears, nor could she restrain Mariette from kissing her feet, as if they had been those of a Madonna

The lady did not speak, but looked inquiringly at the officer with the embroidered collar, who having turned around caught her glance, and after a gesture to bid her wait, said to Mariette,

"I did not, my child, hear the beginning of your story, for I was writing. You say the young man, Conscience, is blind ?"

"Yes, sir," said Mariette, who as soon as the officer spake had arisen.

"Is he not an Artillery soldier, whose eyes were burned by the explosion of a caisson ?"

"Yes. sir."

" Is this soldier, my child, your brother ?"

" I have already told Madame," said Mariette, abashed.

" True, but I too told you I did not hear."

Mariette lifted up her chaste and limpid eyes, and fixing them on the officer, said,

" No, sir, I am not his sister—but from childhood we lived near each other, and almost under one roof.— One of our mothers, mine, nourished us both ; his relations are mine ; since we knew what toil, joy, grief, and pain were, we shared them—so that I believed for a long time he was my brother."

" But you do not now ?"

" Since his misfortune, I felt he was not my brother."

The officer left the desk and approached Mariette.

Mariette trembled, but the lady took her hand, and gave her confidence.

" Poor child !" said the lady.

" Then you love him ?" asked the officer.

" Yes, sir," said Mariette warmly, " with all my heart !"

" But if you be not rich . . ."

The officer paused.

" Have you any property ?"

" Sir, Conscience's grandfather had land that he cultivated himself with an ox and an ass, but he has been attacked by paralysis. Besides he yet owes something for his land, which it may be, he will not be able to pay, for the Kossacks have bivouacked in our plains, and their horses have crushed down every thing, so that I fear Conscience will not be richer than I am."

"Well, my child, if not richer than you, it would not be reasonable for you to become the wife of a poor blind man."

"Sir!" said Mariette, who had not understood him.

"I say, my child, you must console yourself for what has befallen Conscience, and love another."

Mariette trembled in every limb.

"I, sir," said she, "forget myself and abandon Conscience, because, poor fellow! he can no longer walk? Cease to love my betrothed because he is unfortunate? Sir, do not say such things to me, for they pierce my heart like a knife, and make me shiver all over my frame."

The young girl stepped back and seemed about to fall, as if she had really been stabbed.

The lady arose and sustained her.

"Ah, you have hurt the poor girl."

"I did not mean to do so," said the officer, "and I will prove it to you."

Turning to Mariette, he said, "My child, would you be satisfied if Conscience could return with you to your village?"

Mariette looked anxiously at the officer, as if she feared she had misunderstood him.

"Excuse me?" said she.

"I ask, my child, if you would wish to return with him to your village?"

Mariette uttered a cry of joy, surprise and doubt—an expression which was indescribable passed over her face; her blue eyes, limpid as the azure of heaven, were fixed anxiously on the officer, whom they seemed to question.

"Satisfied—happy?" murmured she. "Oh sir, such a question almost deprives me of consciousness. I beg you, sir, not to deceive me, for after what I have suffered it would be my death. Is that possible? May I hope for it?"

She reached forth her hands towards the officer.

"One must always hope, my child, and though those who wish us well should fail, be not the less grateful to them."

"Ah!" said Mariette, "then you will try?"

The officer smiled and nodded—

"I will do my best," said he.

"Oh Madame, how can I prove my gratitude to your husband, Madame?"

"Kiss me, my child."

"Madame, I must kiss your hus—"

The lady folded her in her arms, and touched her brow with her lips.

The officer, who was the Surgeon-in-chief, girded on his sword, which was on a chair, took his chapeau, bowed at his wife, smiled at Mariette, and left.

Mariette had not strength to thank the officer. A few unintelligible words escaped from her mouth, and seemed to follow her protector as he hurried down the stairway.

"Now," said the lady, who was alone with Mariette, "that you are somewhat calmer, let us think of the more material cares of life. It is nearly noon, and I am sure that you have eaten nothing."

"True, Madame, I have only swallowed a few drops of wine to the health of Conscience."

"And you have eaten nothing?"

"I could not—my heart was too full."

"Well," said the lady, "now that hope has somewhat relieved your heart, you must breakfast."

"Mon Dieu, Madame," she replied, confused at so much kindness.

"Who knows, if Conscience be restored to you . . ."

"Well, Madame—"

"You will probably set out at once?"

"On the spot."

"Then you see you will need strength for your journey."

She rang the bell, and a servant came.

"Get breakfast for Mademoiselle. Get especially a good *bouillon*—she needs that more than any thing else."

"Ah, Madame," said Mariette, "God only can reward you for so much goodness."

Mariette's heart was overflowing. Far from being able to utter an adequate expression of her thanks, she could scarcely speak. She could but clasp and kiss the hands of her benefactress.

In about five minutes the servant returned and said that breakfast was ready.

The lady took Mariette by the arm and led her into the *salle-a-manger*.

Mariette at first was rather bashful, but soon grew bolder. Her healthful and vigorous constitution, though her form was very slight, needed sustenance. Besides her kind and generous hostess pressed and almost forced her to eat.

When breakfast was over, a sound like that of the feet of several persons, was heard on the stairway.

Among them, Mariette, whom anxiety made listen to every sound, fancied she could discover one step that seemed uncertain and to hesitate.

My God!" murmured she.

With deep emotion, she turned towards the door,

13

which was opened, and Conscience entered, followed
by the Surgeon-in-chief.   Conscience had his knapsack
on his shoulders, and had a staff in his hand. He said,

"Mariette, Mariette, are you not here? I am no
longer a soldier. I have my discharge, and a letter of
route, and I can return with you to Haramont."

"Is this so? Is this the case, Monsieur?" said Mariette, who as yet dared not believe him.

"I tell you it is," said Conscience. "The Surgeon-
in-chief has done all this for us."

He entered the room, with outstretched hands, feeling for Mariette.

The latter however was unable, or rather was too
grateful to meet him. She turned to the lady, and
falling at her knees, said,

"Ah Madame, my benefactress, if you be not saved,
if heaven be not open to you, for whom is happiness
reserved?"

Powerless, she folded her arms around the Surgeon's wife, as much to keep herself from sinking on
the ground, and to adore and thank her hostess: she
said,

"Thanks, thanks, for my heart is bursting with joy.
I shall die of happiness.   Thanks, thanks to you! . . ."

XIV.

The Pilgrimage

———◆———

MARIETTE was right: the Lord had suffered as much joy as she was capable of bearing to rest on her. Her arms were loosened, her eyes closed, and she fainted.

Fainting caused however by an excess of happiness, is neither long nor dangerous. Mariette soon recovered, and found her hands in Conscience's.

The union of these two loving beings who had fancied themselves separated, was a moment of joy, in which all the spectators who had contributed to their re-union participated.

When she had once recovered her presence of mind and thanked the worthy Surgeon-in-chief and his wife, Mariette had but one wish, to leave as soon as possible the place in which she had suffered so much.

The desire was too natural to need explanation to be understood. The surgeon advised the patient to bathe his eyes with emollients when he had them, and when without them to make a substitute of cold water.

It was especially necessary that his eyes should remain covered, if not with a bandage which would completely intercept day, at least with a green veil.

As for the rest of the treatment, the physician of the place he chanced to be in, would prescribe.

The Surgeon wished Conscience and Mariette to take the Paris coach, which would have left them at Villers-Cotterets. They both, however, declined, saying that they preferred to return on foot, and alone, than again be separated if not by distance by the presence of others.

The Surgeon and his wife accompanied them to the street door, where they found Bastien.

The joy of Bastien was great, for the appearance of the surgeon and his wife had told him all that had passed. Mariette was not undisturbed about the quarrel which had taken place on her account, and which was to be decided at five o'clock.

Bastien, however, re-assured her. He had studied out an infallible blow, which was to terminate matters with the cuirassier by a gash over the latter's head.

Mariette could not refrain from participating in Bastien's conviction, and bade adieu to the Hussar with calmness.

Bastien was anxious to accompany his two friends to without the city. As they, however, would leave by the Soissons gate, and he was to meet the cuirassier by that of Saint Quintin, which was in precisely the other direction, he did not insist on the matter.

Bastien, therefore, bade adieu to, and promised to rejoin them as soon as possible at Haramont.

Mariette led Conscience as far as the corner of the first street, where she paused, and said :

" Conscience, had you not another reason than that you gave the Surgeon-in-chief, for wishing to return on foot to our village ?"

"Had not you, Mariette?" said Conscience, who understood that both he and she agreed in their hearts.

"I remembered," said she, "that I had made a vow . . . ."

"Of a pilgrimage to Notre-Dame de Liesse?"

"Exactly, and as in the last but one of your letters, dated from Chalons, you expressed a similar wish, it occurred to me to propose to you to accomplish it together."

"Strange," said Conscience, "I was about to ask you to do so."

"Well, you see, our hearts, now as they ever have been, and will be, are alike. Let us set out for Notre Dame de Liesse."

It was only necessary to ask in what direction lay Notre-Dame de Liesse, and by what road they were to proceed thither.

The first paper satisfied them, and Conscience and Mariette set out for the miraculous shrine.

They had, however, to pass nearly all the city.

A strange sight to the inhabitants who were at-tracted to their doors, was that young and beautiful girl in her holyday garb leading the poor blind soldier through the streets. Laon, too, is not a large city, and the story of Mariette's devotion had already tran-spired. Every spectator, therefore, was touched to see Conscience walking by her side, with his knapsack on his shoulders, and the green shade over his eyes. The pride and joy which shone on Mariette's face, dif-fused something eminently noble and beautiful over her whole bearing.

Even the dog, the modest Bernard, participated in the triumph.

Mariette was so proud of this triumph that she

walked with her radiant brow erect, without shrinking from the attention their appearance excited.

Mariette was anxious to quit the city, the victory she had won had been so warmly disputed that she yet was surprised at, and thought it strange. The consequence of this feeling of doubt, was, that she scarcely believed in it, and constantly feared to be the victim of some accident, and shudderings passed over her whole frame at the idea that any chance or the whim of an individual might wrest from her, him whom she had regained with such trouble, resistance, tears and love.

At last she reached the gates of the city, and saw extending before her the long row of trees, the vast horison of the country, and breathed freely for the first time.

Then, only, a frank, free, and joyous exclamation burst from her breast, for only then did she really think herself safe.

"Ah!" said she, lifting her eyes to heaven, and making the sign of the cross. "Conscience, Conscience, now we are free, for nothing intervenes between us and the sight of the Lord."

Conscience did not need stimulation, as long as he was in the city; he had, if not seen, divined the curiosity of the crowd. Once in the fields, he also felt free, satisfied and happy as a poor blind creature who presses the woman he loves to his heart can be when doomed to see her only with the eyes of memory.

What Conscience saw, however, almost as distinctly as with the real sight, was the green and flower strewn plain, the leafy wood echoing with the songs of birds, the azure May sky, with its thin white clouds slowly sailing across the blue firmament.

Rapidly however as they walked, on that day they could accomplish but five leagues, having left Laon after three o'clock. They slept therefore at Gizy in the usual inn of the Pilgrims.

Mariette began her almost mother's part. She saw that Conscience needed nothing, bathed with spring water, his lustreless eyes, for the pellicle of the cornea which had been burned was about to exfoliate. After a meal, which modest as it was, was far more luxurious than what the lad for two months had been used to, she took him herself to a room prepared for him, and then delightedly sought her own.

To do so was to leave him, but she was satisfied that her absence was but momentary, that nothing really separated them, and that at dawn on the next day she would find him where she had left him.

And the next day, as the rising sun, penetrating the small windows of the inn, it was warm, though as yet wrapped in the morning clouds, as the early birds chirped on the branches of the trees of the garden, arranging the while their feathery toilette, Mariette rapped gently at the door of the room occupied by Conscience, whom she found already dressed and ready to set out.

A dozen pilgrims had passed the night in the same inn with Conscience and Mariette, and all stood prepared in the yard.

Among them were some who journeyed for themselves, and who hoped divine intercession would relieve incurable maladies which physicians had abandoned.—Others had come in simple devotion, as representatives of invalids doomed to inactivity. Each of these pilgrims, whether for his own sake or in behalf of another, seemed to feel the necessity of telling others his trouble and—as in this sad world doubt is the lot of all—of sustaining his own faith by that of a stouter heart than his own.

In a quarter of an hour Conscience and Mariette were acquainted with the sorrows and hopes of all who surrounded them   It then became necessary for them, to avoid the imputation of wanting that confidence, the unfortunate have in each other, of telling not only that Conscience was blind, but how he became so.

The story of Mariette, for she spoke while Conscience caressed by the sweet sound in her voice, smiled and listened, aroused sympathy in all, which was translated by hopes and encouragements.

Each one had the story of some blind man to tell.— All had known some one cured by the intercession of our Lady of Liesse. Some of those favored by her had even been blind from their birth, and one the victim of an accident had yet greater chances.

What however made all these chances more real, was the ardent faith of the two young people.

They continued to advance, and from the top of a hill saw the village of Liesse with a wood in the back ground, and amid the humble houses the tower of the miraculous church.

Each fell on his knees, and one of the pilgrims utter-ed a chant, which all followed, if not with words, at least mentally.

When the chant was over, they made the sign of the cross and arose, and at the sight of the holy oasis, for-getful of all the fatigue of that and of the preceding days, doubled their pace, to reach the sooner the end of the journey.

Our young couple with the deepest devotion entered the church, still perfumed by the odor of the incense and lighted with tapers. Every where on the walls hung the *ex voto* of grateful pilgrims, and a huge circle of the faithful prayed around the principal altar, where in a rich robe, with the holy babe in her arms, stood the venerated Madonna.

Mariette and Conscience knelt as near the altar as they could get, and the first emotion of each was to plunge as deeply as possible in silent prayer, which while apparently separating, in fact united them, for each praying for the other seemed endowed with another more devoted and more exalted soul than the first.

Certainly the Saviour from the height of heaven saw these two souls thus linked at his mother's feet, and smiled on their prayers.

When the two prayers were finished, and it was almost at the same moment, their hands were clasped again, for they were so satisfied of the chastity of their love, that this was almost a continuation of the prayer.

" Now," said Conscience, slightly clasping her hand and smiling, for he was afraid that his words would distress her—" now Mariette, as I must accustom myself to see by your eyes, tell me who Our Lady before whom we kneel is, that I may see her glitter like a star amid the night that surrounds me."

" Oh," said Mariette, "she is very beautiful, and glitters so that I scarcely dare look at her."

" She stands on an altar covered with lace, in a marble niche. She wears a diamond crown, a collar of pearls, and a robe of gold, with golden and silver lilies, which seem natural. Our Saviour is in her arms, which are covered with golden bracelets, He wears a robe like hers, and smiles on us. All is lighted by such a number of tapers that I dare not even attempt

13*

to count them. Oh my poor Conscience, could you but see!"

Conscience closed his eyes, crossed his hands on his breast, and made in his mind a kind of luminous picture of all Mariette had said.

"Thanks," said he, "I see her with the eyes of the soul."

"Holy Lady of Liesse, grant that my Conscience, who kneels before you, and for whom I would give my life, having seen you with the eyes of the soul, some day may see you with those of the body."

Suddenly inspired, she advanced to one of the vases of holy water by the side of the water, dipped his handkerchief in it, and moistened Conscience's eyelids.

"My God, Mariette!"—he guessed what she had done—" is not this sacrilege?"

"Sacrilege," said she, "is in the heart, and God who knows my wish will judge."

"Mariette," murmured Conscience, "I think you are right, for the water seems fresher even than that of the spring, and may do me good."

Mariette lifted her hands to heaven, and with an indescribable expression of faith, exclaimed, "God grant it may be so."

XV.

Conscience's Dream.

———————

IT was ten o'clock in the afternoon, and though it was early in May, as is sometimes the case, the heat exceeded that of the warmest days of the year. A burning vapor had in the morning arisen in the form of a cloud from the earth, and now seemed to descend in flame. Not a breath of air moved the trees, and the birds were mute. The lizards alone, those fire-worshippers, for whom the rays of the sun are never too warm, glided rapidly amid the grass, while the busy bees sailed through the air bearing to their hives or trees the harvest of wax which man contrives to turn to his profit.

Apart from these noises, which were rather motions than sounds, all the voices of nature were silent. Far as sight could extend, not a living soul was visible. All creation seemed to slumber.

A hundred paces from the pool of Salmoncy, on the edge of a little wood of the same name, Conscience slept with his head on his knapsack. The branches of two young oaks cast a leafy roof over him, while Mariette watched by his side with a compassion full of love, driving away with a bough covered with rosy flowers, the flies which persisted in alighting on his face.

And all around him, not in the wind, for we have said there was none, but in the slight motion of the air effected by Mariette, the blue gentian bowed its cup, and the companella bowed as it shook its thousand cups.

It was the day after the one when they had prayed together in the Church of our Lady of Liesse. Thence they had gone to the Inn of the Pilgrims, a poor inn used by poor guests, for in general the rich of this world have heither faith to undertake, nor courage to accomplish such pilgrimages.

They had returned with those bouquets of gold and silver the Pilgrims buy at the church door, and with which at home they deck their mantel-pieces and head-boards of their beds, to prove to their descendants that they have accomplished a pilgrimage.

The next day, having heard mass, they set out. It was, consequently, nine o'clock.

They had left the high road on being told that by doing so, they would save two leagues, and by follow-ing a by-path, at noon had reached the pool of Sal-mouey, where they sate down to rest, and where Conscience, yet enfeebled by the hospital diet, and from fatigue had softly glided from conversation into slumber. He had slept thus for two hours, and Mari-ette, who was unwilling to awaken him, began as she computed the distance to the village of Prasles, where they had been advised to halt, to be uneasy about the duration of his sleep.

Another thing, also, made her uneasy. It was that the sun, as it moved to the west, for, to Mariette the sun moved, was about to fall on Conscience's eyes.

Laying her rosy bough by his side, Mariette went into the wood, cut two green boughs which she placed between Conscience and the sun, and hanging her apron over them, made a kind of tent over the eyes of the sleeper.

She then took up her bush again, and resumed her place by her friend so as to be also in the shade.

Thus she continued for half an hour longer, listening to the respiration of Conscience, and so to say, counting the pulsations of his heart.

From time to time, Bernard, who lay at the young man's feet, opened his eyes, lifted up his head, looked at his master, and seeing that he did not awake, again replaced his head on the grass and sank to sleep.

Mariette, who never moved her eyes from his face, fancied that she saw some nervous contractions of his cheeks, and that by his quickening respiration, some painful dream agitated him.   She was about to arouse him when all at once he opened his sightless eyes, and tossing his arms, cried :

" Mariette, where are you ? Mariette ?"

The young girl took his hands.

" Ah !" said Conscience with a sigh.

His head sank back on his knapsack.

" My God, Conscience, what is the matter with you ?"

She put her arms under his neck, and tried to lift him up.

" Nothing," murmured Conscience.

" But you tremble in every limb."

" I had a terrible dream.   That during my sleep you had left me, and on my awaking, strange dream, for in my sleep I saw—that you were gone."

Resting his head in his two hands :

" My God," murmured he, " never did I suffer so much."

"Poor lad," said Mariette, "who abandon yourself even in a dream to the idea that I can leave you. You are ungrateful."

In a gentler and kinder voice, she said, "God will punish you, Conscience, if you yield to such fancies."

"Mariette," Conscience said, "dreams come from God, and sometimes if not a presage, are a warning."

"A warning! . . . what mean you, Conscience?"

"Nothing, my dear Mariette. I did but talk to myself as I often do. Help me up, Mariette, it must be late, I do not know how I came to sink into this heavy sleep."

With a sigh he added, "it was God's will."

Mariette looked at him with surprise, and said:

"My God, Conscience, what are you murmuring there? Can a dream so overcome you? You dreamed that I left you? Well, dreams must always be taken by contraries. You dream that I had left you; it is a proof that I am bound to you for life."

Conscience felt for Mariette's hands.

He soon found them, for Mariette placed them in his.

Clasping them, he fixed his dull eye on hers, as if he wished to tell her the secret that oppressed him. All at once, however, his muscles threw off their contraction, he shook his head, and said in a broken voice:

"Mariette, give me my knapsack, and let us go on."

"Yes," said Mariette, "I will go on, but I will carry your knapsack."

"You, a woman? impossible!"

"Conscience, you know I am strong. Besides, when fatigued I will buckle it on Bernard, who, I hope, is large enough to be able to carry it."

She laughed, hoping that Conscience would join in her mirth.

On the contrary, Conscience, seeing the efforts the young girl made to amuse and console him, became more and more distressed.

"Very well. Put me in the middle of the road, give me my stick, and let us resume our journey."

Mariette did so, and having given him her arm, said :

"Listen, Conscience, if I walk too quickly check me, for I must regulate my steps by yours ; yet Conscience, I confess to you," continued she, seeing that his head sank on his breast "that I wished we had not feet, but wings like the birds, which fly so rapidly, and come, they say, from so far. Ah, could we at once fly to our homes."

Conscience sighed.

"Be easy, however," said Mariette, with an apparent feeling of joy she was far from entertaining, "for if we lack wings, we have resolution and courage, and by means of them to-morrow evening or the next morning we will be there. Think of our return, dear Conscience, of your mother's joy, of the satisfaction of mine, of the delight of Father Cadet, and of little Pierre. Do you see, Conscience? she fancies you in a hospital, on a miserable pallet, within four walls, and does not fancy that you have just risen from sleeping beneath the blue canopy of heaven, free as that lark which sings as it soars to heaven. Hear, Conscience, hear it. Oh, could you, like it soar to heaven. I scarce see it, so far it is."

"Yes," said Conscience, "I see, but alas, unlike you, I cannot see it. I shall never see again, for, alas, I am blind."

"Do I not see for you? Am I not here to guide you, to tell you the form and color of things? Did you not see the Madonna yesterday, when I described her to you? Well, Conscience, I will ever be by your side to do thus. Is not that misfortune made a blessing, which says, 'Conscience never again shall be separated from Mariette, nor she from Conscience.'"

"Yes, Mariette, I know. There is supreme bliss in the idea. Yes, by your eyes I see better than I do by means of my hands; when you speak, your voice makes me tremble with emotion, and when I hear you, I see. Listen, at this moment as you walk before me, and as I follow you, a heavenly lustre seems to penetrate my dimmed eyes. I feel as a man would, who, with closed eyes, followed an angel of light. There are moments, Mariette, when I think God restores my sight, to show you to me in this world, as you will appear in the other, when you shall have received from his hands, the eternal recompense you will so well have merited. But—"

Conscience sighed and shook his head sadly.

"But what?" asked Mariette pausing.

The blind man divined that Mariette had paused. He reached out his left hand and placed it under Mariette's right arm.

"But, my beloved, my dream just now has made me think."

"What?".

"That God, Mariette, who made you at once, both brilliant and tender, náturally made devotion one of your virtues. This devotion, Mariette, you offer me; with all your heart you do so. While, though you should offer, I should not accept it."

"My God, Conscience, have you ceased to love me? What have I done to deserve this?"

The young girl looked at Conscience with clasped hands, and was ready to sob aloud.

"Nothing, Mariette, and so far from not loving, I adore you; the adoration of a poor blind one like me, can never pay for your devotion to me."

"Pay! who spoke of pay?"

Conscience smiled sadly.

"Let me continue, Mariette, and let us talk calmly . . You are young, and beautiful. You have a strong heart, and a great soul. You are used to toil, and inactivity, instead of being repose to you, is fatigue. Well, I cannot—understand me—I cannot, blind as I am, rob you of youth, beauty and life, because you love me and pity me. What will become of you, when you are old, and when I shall have made you poor? What will become of you when our relations shall sleep beneath the grass of the cemetery? You will be deserted, in want, sad, and why? Because you obstinately persisted in loving me."

"My God and Savior, do you hear him? Thus he rewards me."

"Be quiet, Mariette. For what you would have done in this, and in the next world, I will be as grateful as if you had done it. You, poor child, offered, and I refused. If God granted, do you see? not that my poor eyes were restored to me—that would be too much—but to grant me sufficient sight to be able to work a little, to lead Father Cadet's ox and ass in the furrow, to go into the forest for wood, if by toiling twice as much as others, I would earn half what they do. If I were sure only of the daily bread for which we pray to God, I would here, where we stand, fall on my knees before you, and say, ' Thanks, Mariette, for being so beautiful and good, and merciful enough withal to love me.' Alas, though," continued Conscience, shaking his head, "that may never be."

"For heaven's sake, Conscience," said Mariette, "hush. Do you not know that you are breaking my heart, and that I am weeping bitter tears, that in despair I wring my hands ?"

" I see nothing," said Conscience, "nothing but night."

He added in so low a tone, that all Mariette's attention was required to catch the sound,

" Nothing but death."

"Death ? You think of death !" said Mariette, "and for that you would separate yourself from me. You were right, for while I was by your side, you could not die. Conscience, this is not all, you distress me so that I cannot go on. No, I will not go a step towards the village, unless you explain yourself here. Come, Conscience, let us sit by the side of the road, for I have lost my strength and cannot continue."

Conscience let himself be led to the road-side and sate down.

"Now," said she, "explain yourself, and tell me all that is in your heart."

"What, Mariette, is in my heart, is, that you must promise not to neglect your youth for me, that you will not sacrifice your existence, and that henceforth you will be to me but a sister. Mariette, you are but nineteen, and there still are festivals at Longpre, at Talle-Fontaine, and at Vivieres, and handsome lads to escort you."

"Ah ! that is what you sought to get at ?" replied Mariette sobbing. " Thus you thank me for my kindness—no, I mistake, for my love. Do you not see that

you torture me more than the executioner could?—
' There are festivals and handsome lads,' and he says
there are such things yet in store for me! My God!
tell me, for you know if I have deserved this!" she
sobbed.

Now though Conscience could not see her tears, he
could hear her sobs.

" Mariette," said he, seizing her hand, " understand
my idea, and read my heart. Had I ten eyes, I would
suffer them to be burned out one after the other, if I
might thus ruin the right of preventing your loving another. But an accident has blinded me for life. You
see, Mariette, blindness is a suffering no human being
with two eyes can conceive of. God would punish me
if I linked you to such misfortune."

" Then," said Mariette, somewhat consoled by the
grief Conscience expressed, " if I followed the advice
you give me—if I went to the festivals with the handsome lads you speak of, you would forget Mariette as
she would forget you."

" Forget you, the only human being that has remained
visible to me? How can I forget you, of whom my
whole life will be one dream and memory? Of what
else but you can I think?"

" Then if I were to cease to love you, yet you would
love me."

" I, Mariette? until death."

" Then all is said. As I love you, and as you love me,
there is no use talking . . . . Conscience, truly as there
is a God, who made the sun that shines on us, before
Martinmas of next year, I will be your wife, or if you
refuse me, I will be a grey sister at the hospital of Villers-Cotterets, and will nurse the poor blind, who are
nothing to me, because the one I love refuses me."

"Oh!" cried Conscience, "You would marry me, Mariette."

"Yes, I would marry the man, who would have ten eyes burned out, to have the right to love me, and prevent me from loving another."

"Mariette, this is grand, beautiful and sublime, but—"

"Be silent," said Mariette, putting her hand over his mouth, "just now, I heard you out without opposing you, or interupting you, though every word made my heart bleed. Well! now I wish to speak without being interrupted."

"Go on, Mariette—it is pleasant to hear you."

"Well! If Mariette were blind, would you have deserted her? Would you have deserted the poor girl, left her wandering at hazard? Tell me, would you have done so? If, in her misery she still persisted in loving you, would you have crushed her heart by deserting her, to dance with some beautiful girl at some festival? Conscience, answer me."

"Mariette, I dare not . . . "

"I know you dare not. Well! I will answer for you. Had you done so, you would have been a wretch. Conscience, let there be no discussion, no reply. There is my hand. May God bless you."

Then, pressing her lips on those of the soldier before he could think or move, she said, "Conscience, I am your wife."

Conscience uttered a cry of mingled pleasure and pain, in which his strength passed away.

"Mariette," said he, "you will have it so . . . . "

"Yes, I will," said Mariette. "Yes, I will take you to church, to repeat aloud, and with head erect, the oath I take here. Yes, I will do so."

Conscience could not reply, he kissed the hands of Mariette, weeping and sobbing.

"Oh !" murmured Conscience, " if there were any hope."

Mariette seemed ready to answer. Her lips were half open, but a burning sigh escaped from them, and she passed her hand over her brow, as if to wipe away a vertigo.

" No," murmured she, " it would be too cruel if the kind Surgeon-in-chief were mistaken."

" What do you murmur there in so low a tone ?" said Conscience.

" I am praying God to take care of the handsome young lad with whom I hope some day, to go to the village festivals."

They resumed their journey. Conscience sadly shaking his head, and Mariette looking with her bright eyes to heaven, as if she sought the star of hope which guided the shepherds of yore to the Cradle of Bethlehem.

XVI.

MARIETTE'S DREAM.

A T dawn the next day, having slept at Prasles, a
little village of five hundred souls, on the cross-
roads, three leagues from Laon, and five from Soissons,
they resumed their journey through woods and fields,
according to the directions of the peasants in the villages and in the fields.

The weather had continued unchanged and fine.
The sun was still bright and enlivening, but tempered
by the morning breeze, which might, perhaps, at a
later hour be swallowed up by the increasing heat of
the day, as would be the transparent diamond drops,
which fell from the leaves and branches of the trees.
The song of the birds, who had been silent on the day
before was re-awakened, and seemed like a dew of har-
mony to penetrate the sonorous air. The grasshoppers
chirped, the butterflies hovered, and the bees hummed,
each contributing his cry to the universal concert,
which the awakening earth sent like a hymn of gratitude to its creator.

Mariette revived, and consoled, refreshed, by her
morning toilette, like the plants by their bath of dew,
seemed to have wings like the butterflies, song like the

birds, which she strewed along the path of her blind companion to render it shorter and more easy.

Conscience smiled. The perpetual song and joy of Mariette re-opened his heart. He walked some time in silence, and then paused.

"Mariette," said he, "how gay you are this morning!"

"Because I am happy this morning."

"Happy to see the bright sun, are you not? To hear the welcome of the birds, and the hum of the laborious bees? That makes you happy!"

"Yes, and more than that too."

"Then, my good, kind Mariette, you do not repent of your promise yesterday.

"No; for God has already rewarded me for it."

"Rewarded?"

"Yes—I too have dreamed, not such a sad dream, Conscience, as your's was, but a bright and sparkling dream."

"Tell it me."

"Take my arm, walk slowly, and I will."

"Let us walk slowly. We have time enough, have we not The journey, Mariette, is so pleasant with you—now for your dream!"

"Listen. Yesterday evening, after I had bathed your eyes with the good fresh water I got from the spring myself, and which did you so much good, I left you in your room, and asked our hostess to show me mine. The blessing of good God certainly rests on you, Conscience; all who see, seem at once to pity and to love me. While pitying you, and caressing me, and asking if I needed nothing, our hostess took me to a little room, very clean and nice, such a one as would do for both of us, Conscience . . . In this room was a little bed, white as possible, but the woman made an excuse for the absence of curtains. 'Bah! though,' said she, 'it is all the better to-night, for the moon will light you like a lamp, and to-morrow, as you wish to leave by daylight, the first ray of morning will awaken you.' She kissed me, and told me that her daughter was in service at Fismes, and that before she went to sleep, she would pray for her and for me. In half an hour, I was in bed, my candle was out, and I had said my prayer before my bouquet from our Lady of Liesse's. It was in vain, however, that I was in bed, and my candle out, I do not know why, but I could not sleep. Happy thoughts, doubtless, kept me awake, for I have been so delighted, Conscience, since our explanation, and if you knew . ."

She kissed his brow.

"Dear Mariette," murmured Conscience.

"What, though, contributed most to keep me awake, was a bright moon, which seemed to look gently on me through my window, so that both myself and my bed were illumined by its rays."

"Mariette," said Conscience, "how well you describe and how distinctly I see all you speak of. You are right, Mariette. With you, I shall be able to do without my eyes."

"I do not know when I went to sleep, so gentle was my passage into slumber. It seemed, however, that whether open or shut, my eyes saw the moon, which seemed in all its lustre to look at me. Gradually, those spots which make it a kind of face, seemed to become regular, and smiled on me, gradually assuming not only the form of a head, but of a body. It grew like our Lady of Liesse, with the child Jesus in her arms. She wore her diamond crown, and her robe decked with natural flowers and with golden lilies, but besides the diamonds she had around her brow a coronet of light.

Understanding that this was the true Madonna, for she was in heaven, I glided from my knees, saying—'Hail, Mary! full of grace, the Lord is with you!' I saw a ray of gold fall from her feet to my chamber, down which she glided, filling the window like the niche in the church. I turned to look for you, feeling so delighted that I wished you to share my happiness: and there you were kneeling with me. I do not know how and when you entered, but you with your blind eyes looked with me at the Virgin, to whom we lifted our hands and prayed. She then came into the room, still holding the infant Jesus in her arms, and approaching the foot of my bed, took thence the holy bouquet, and placed them in the hand of Jesus, and having said a few words passed by me, as she did so replying to my sign of the cross, by a smile, to you. Jesus too smiled, and reaching forth his hand, touched your eyes with the blessed bouquet, when you too, in a tone of joy so deep that it almost seemed pain, exclaimed, 'I see, blessed Virgin, I see!' At this sound I opened my eyes. Alas! it was but a dream. All had disappeared, but the moon still shone, though somewhat paler, and was descending. This much of reality, however, remained, Conscience, 'Faith, calmness, and almost confidence.' Therefore am I so happy to-day ... Well, Conscience, why do you not reply?" said Mariette.

"Because, beloved, I hear you yet. While you spake, Mariette, my heart overflowed with joy, for I saw all the bright and tranquil moon growing to be the Virgin with the coronet of diamonds and glory of light, her golden robe and purple roses—and silver lilies—all was so vivid, that when you told me the infant Jesus

14

had touched me, I felt the tickling of the blessed bouquet, and I seemed to see countless sparkles of light."

"You saw—you felt that," said Mariette,—"joy!
joy! joy!"

"Mariette," said Conscience sadly, "you should not
nurse a foolish hope. What I saw and felt was the
effect of imagination, excited by your words. Let us
thank God for this consolation sent us during our journey, but ask no more. I do not say what he can not,
but what he will not grant."

"It matters not," said Mariette, "for believe me,
Conscience, there is a presage beneath all this. I love
and venerate the Mother of God since our pilgrimage
to the chapel, even more than before. Now let us walk
faster before the sun becomes high, and at noon we
will sit down to rest beneath some tree, or if we come
to a village, we will pause until the heat grows less."

They continued their journey in silence,—for each
was immersed in thought—Mariette about her dream,
and Conscience about her account of it.

The result of this abstraction was, that Mariette, who
was the guide, did not attend to the direction as she
should have done, in an unknown district and in a cross
road.

The path of the two young people became gradually
narrower and less distinct, and ended in a meadow
with little groups of trees.

Mariette looked around her, and seeing no traces of
the path, stopped.

"Mariette, what is the matter?" asked Conscience.

"My dear Conscience, I have done prettily!"

"What?"

"I have walked, walked, walked on, thinking of
other matters, and have left the road. We are now by

the banks of a stream which divides the meadow, and I can see no way to cross over it."

"That is bad. You have no idea, Mariette, how fatiguing it is to walk without seeing clearly, and to stumble at every inequality, even when one has so excellent a guide as you are. Is the water deep?"

"No—it is broad, but one can see the bottom. Bernard has crossed it without swimming, and awaits us on the other side."

"Then what is there to prevent our doing so likewise?"

"Nothing—except that we will wet ourselves to the knees."

"Ah! that will be no great difficulty on so hot a day as this."

"Besides, we will thus avoid a long detour, which probably would take us farther out of our way."

"Come on," said Conscience.

"Very well—hold fast to my neck."

"Why?"

"Because the bank is steep on both sides. Fortunately on the other side, the branches of a willow hang almost to the water, and if you cling to them they will assist you."

Conscience descended to the water, and sustained by Mariette, reached the other bank, where, as the young girl had told him, he easily climbed up by means of the green willows.

He sate down and said, "Ah, it is well that you were mistaken in the road. This water is very refreshing. Is this a good place to make a little halt?"

"Very—and if you please, we will breakfast."

"Willingly," said Conscience, "for I am hungry,

and it has been long since I felt an appetite The fresh air causes it."

Mariette took a loaf and a piece of cold veal from the double paper in which they were wrapped, cut the bread, and divided the meat into a number of little pieces, of which she gave Conscience a portion as if he had been a child.

" Mariette," said he, " you are the personification of devotion and goodness, and I do not see how I can reward you for so much love and pity."

" Good !" said Mariette. Let us talk of all my goodness—because by my assistance you crossed a stream, and because I wet myself to the knees, because I cut you a piece of bread you do not know how you will ever be able to reward my pity and love. Indeed Conscience, you estimate too highly, the little services which I expect to make the happiness of my life."

" Good, kind Mariette !" said Conscieuce. After a moment, he continued—

"'. Is the water of this stream clear ?"

" Like crystal."

" Let me drink then."

Mariette had bought a wooden bucket, which she used both to drink from and to carry water, in which from time to time she bathed Conscience's eyes. Mariette went to the stream, and returned with it full.

Conscience took the bucket, and having drunken, said—

" How good it is !"

" But," said Mariette with the gayety which had not left her since their explanation on the previous day— " it is but water after all. "

" True. Perhaps it is good only because you give it to me."

" Ah !" said Mariette, " that is polite." She made a courtesy which poor blind Conscience could not see.

" But do you now eat and drink."

" I would willingly drink, but you have emptied the bucket."

" True. When you have finished you shall bathe my eyes, for it seems to me it will do me more good than any other has done."

" Why wait ? If, dear Conscience, it will do you any good, the sooner I bathe them the better."

" The fact is, Mariette, my eyes smart, and that is doubtless the effect of the heat of the sun."

Mariette had however already gone to the stream, and returned with the bucket full of fresh water, in which she dipped her handkerchief and began to moisten his eyes.

" Ah," said he, " what a pleasant sensation. One might almost think it a second baptism, it is so reviving. Your hand is so light."

" How you reward me by these thanks. That, however, will do, for I remember the prescription of the Sugeon-in-chief."

" Whither are you going, Mariette ?"

" Whither am I going ?"

" Yes, it seems to me you move."

" To hang my handkerchief in the sun, so that I may dry it and put it in my pocket again, Mr. Curious."

" Go, Mariette, go."

Guided by the sound of the steps of the young girl, and by the song with which she accompanied her steps, Conscience directed his sightless eyes towards a place covered with grass and flowers, on which she spread her handkerchief.

All at once, Conscience uttered a cry.

Mariette turned around, and saw him with his eyes fixed, and his mouth half open.

"My God," said she, "dear Conscience, what has happened?"

"Mariette," said he, trembling, and gently pushing her away.

"What means this?"

Conscience, by muscular effort arose without the aid of his hands, which he reached forth towards Mariette, saying, "there, there."

The young girl, without knowing why, placed herself in the place he indicated in the sunlight, which shone on her like a mantle of flame.

"Mariette," said Conscience, "I see you, my eyes are not entirely gone."

The young girl trembled as if she had been attacked by vertigo.

"Conscience, dear Conscience, do not kill me with joy."

"I tell you I see you; like a dark shadow it is true, but yet I see you. I repeat to you, Mariette, my poor eyes are not altogether dead. Your dream is fulfilled."

Mariette fell on her knees, and thanked the Virgin in fervent prayer.

Conscience saw this as one sees in the obscurity of a mist.

"I see," said he, "and the proof is, that now you kneel. Mariette, you see that I see."

"Holy Mother of God," said the young girl, "you have worked this miracle. Holy mother of God, we never will forget you, and swear, that, before we die, we will make another pilgrimage to your Holy Chapel, not to invoke, but to thank you for this mercy."

After this invocation, by a great effort she sprang from the ground into the young man's arms.

"Conscience," said she, "is it true that you have seen me?"

"I saw you," said he.

"Ah!" murmured they, as they stood locked in each others' arms, with their eyes lifted to the heaven. "Glory to God, who has suffered his heavenly glance to rest on us!"

XVII.

God continues to Guide Them.

——◆——

THE cry of joy and gratitude was deep as that
which rises from the abyss to heaven in the prayer
of the dead.

Conscience saw again the light of the sun, and all
the magnificent creation which glows in that light.
Conscience emerged from the hell of darkness into the
paradise of day.

Then a future of happiness and love was unfolded to
his eyes, life again returned to him, not supportable as
Mariette's devotion promised, but bright and joyous as
the will of God had made it.

Mariette first recovered consciousness, she was recalled to it by a fear.

One thing the Surgeon-in-chief had said, was never
to leave Conscience's eyes exposed to the light for
more than five minutes, and the visor of Conscience
had been off for nearly a quarter of an hour. He now
saw as if all the air were filled with flame, and as
if the horizon were an ocean of fire.

He did not tell Mariette what he felt, but he willingly consented to her replacing the visor and veil.

Mariette gladly did so.

"Oh," said she, fastening on the visor, and tying the strings of the veil, "how glad I am. I not only do not feel the fatigue of my feet, but it seems to me that I have wings."

"Dear Mariette!"

"Yes, were your sight restored, what a joy and gratification it would be. When I think of it I stifle, for I am not yet used to it. But you see, Conscience, you see."

"That is to say, I had a glimpse of you, Mariette," Conscience gravely observed.

"Yes. That is what the Surgeon kindly told me yesterday, and what I refused to let you know yesterday, when you said, 'My kind Mariette, what are you murmuring there?' 'My child, I can promise nothing, but it is possible his sight is not entirely gone, and that one, and perhaps both eyes may recover their transparency, for God himself has prepared the chief remedy for your friend's misfortune, in the perpetual closing of his eyelids, which gradually may restore them their primitive polish.' These, Conscience, were his very words, I made him repeat them three times, that I might retain them in my memory, so as to be able to repeat them to you, if a good opportunity ever presented itself."

"Mariette," said Conscience, clasping the young girl's hand, "if things prove so, I see how happy we shall be. Then I will accept gladly and with all my heart what you have proposed—for only just now, I saw that I did nothing there but dream—which in itself is not bad. But then as I told you, I would toil from morning till night, and you, Mariette, would dream or work only to amuse yourself."

14*

"And our kindred, dear Conscience, how glad they would be, how they would rejoice as long as they lived. What a paradise of joy does God promise us. Even the animals Pierrot, Tardif, and the black cow, would rejoice as Bernard does when he licks your hand unnoticed by you. But why do you look down and weep?"

"Mariette," said the young man, "for heaven's sake be silent. Talk not of all the joy which may escape from us. Oh! Mariette, it would madden me if, after having had a glimpse of you even in a dream, all this should escape from me."

"Conscience, the Madonna of Liesse has miraculous power, and God is great."

"Come," said Conscience, rousing himself, "enough for to-day. As yet I am not sufficiently strong, either in body or mind, to bear such emotions. Let us go and get over as much ground as possible, for it seems to me we are forgetful of our parents. Go on, and if there be any eminence take it as a starting point to discover our way."

"Yes," said Mariette, wiping her eyes with her apron, "I will see."

She got on a little mound and looked around her.

"Well?" asked Conscience, who guessed at her occupation.

"About three quarters of a league, I see a church tower. We will go to it and ask our way."

Almost sad, she went to Conscience, who having lifted up his visor sought to see, and who had replaced it, saying with a sigh,

"Lord God who gave me breath, grant that I may never despair."

They went directly to the tower Mariette had seen, and in about three quarters of an hour entered the village of Bray-en-Laonnais.

They there learned where they were. Since leaving our Lady of Liesse, they had come about ten leagues, which proved that they had either travelled very slowly amid their alternations of joy and sorrow, or that the road was longer.

Be that as it may, Conscience was wearied, and they were forced to rest awhile in a little inn. They learned that they had inclined too much to the left, and that they were five leagues from Soissons and three from Villers-Cotterets. That to regain the road they had to go by Vailly, to cross the Aisne at Celles, and sleep at Sermoise.

Then they would have to go but seven leagues the next day.

They reached Sermoise with difficulty, and halted there.

Emotion seemed to have exhausted Conscience. Every ten minutes he lifted up his visor, sought to distinguish objects, and seeing the uselessness of his efforts, sadly let it fall.

Mariette even dared not speak to him of the moment of hope which they looked on as an illusion.

They slept at Sermoise, not having courage to go farther. Conscience's feet, though he had refreshed them by dipping them in every spring, were bruised by constant contact with the pebbles; but what most fatigued them was weariness of mind from the perpetual recurrence of one idea and of one hope.

Strange indeed was it, that one day which had seen the dawn of so much hope, should witness its extinction in such dark doubts.

Thus, the heart of man is formed. To sorrow it is a rock of granite, to joy a mass of snow.

Faithful to their resolution they passed through Acy, Rosieres, and Busancy, which they reached about eleven in the morning, and halted for a time. Weary however as Conscience was, he wished to set out again.

Since morning, Mariette had not passed a brook or streamlet without trying the virtues of the water on Conscience's eyes. It was an unlucky day, however, for darkness shrouded the eyes of the young man apparently more closely than ever.

The matter was still worse. Beyond a doubt the efforts Conscience had made to see on the burning day when his sight burned as often as he took off his visor, had doubled the intensity of the inflammation, and subjected him to severe pain when water touched them, or when by design or accident the visor which sheltered them was removed.

They advanced thus for three quarters of an hour without speaking, so downcast they were. As, however, they passed the little village of Vierzy, they asked some questions. The great green curtain before them was the forest of Villers-Cotterets, and they were but three leagues from Haramont.

This revived Conscience's courage if not his strength.

" Come, Mariette," said he, " let us remember that our mothers expect us, and that in three hours we will be with them."

" Oh, I ask nothing better than to continue our journey. I am not fatigued—lean on me, Conscience."

" No, Mariette, walking in that way I fatigue you with my false steps. No, walk on. Give me the end of your handkerchief, and I will follow you."

Mariette did not object, and walked before him.

Bernard seemed to partake their sadness. He was fatigued as they were, and walked by their sides.

From time to time Mariette looked back. Conscience with his head on his breast followed her in silence, or rather dragged himself behind her. What wearied his body was his crushed soul—the fading away of every hope, the loss of a beautiful and glowing future—of that ineffable joy, unheard-of happiness he had caught a glimpse of, on the day when, by some incomprehensible accident, light had penetrated his eyes, and which had faded away with that light.

Alas, the poor fellow had reached that state he so trembled at. He was on the borders of doubt. He had nearly passed into despair.

Mariette, who saw how much Conscience suffered, because she suffered herself, had not courage enough to speak to him, lest he should detect that she wept.

All at once, however, she was forced to speak—for Conscience stopped, and seemed about to fall.

" My God !" said she, " what is the matter ?"

"Mariette," said Conscience, " let us stop, I beg you. I can go no farther. My strength is gone."

" Take courage, my friend," said she, sustaining him in her arms. " We are near a hedge which closes a pretty house, and go but twenty paces farther and you will be able to rest in its shade. If this house be inhabited by Christians, you will be aided."

"I need only repose. It is not the road but grief that overcomes me. It matters not ; let us go on."

Rousing himself, Conscience advanced to the hedge. When, however, he reached the bank on which it grew, he sank on the ground, like a man whose head and legs each give way at once.

Mariette, when she saw this, uttered a feeble cry, and fell on her knees by his side.

A slight noise, to which Mariette paid no attention, was heard from the other side of the hedge.

As Conscience's eyes closed and as his head fell back, she murmured:

"My God! after all we have suffered, can it be that you will not have mercy on us?"

XVIII.

ANOTHER DOCTOR.

THE noise on the other side of the hedge, which had not distracted Mariette from her painful impression, was caused by the attention paid to what was passing, by one of those episodical personages, whom the peregrinations of Mariette and Conscience so frequently brought them in contact with.

This personage was an old man of sixty or sixty-five years of age, with white hair, and a grave and gentle face. He wore pantaloons of white cassimere and a dressing gown of grey felt.

His dark black eye shone beneath grey brows, and a grey moustache shaded his upper lip.

There was about him that military air which betokens one used to battle-fields.

When Mariette and Conscience paused beneath the hedge, he sate on a barrel, having a cup of coffee before him, and held a paper in his hand, which as he read it, made him from time to time gnash his teeth, as if he had bitten an unripe apple.

This paper was the old *Journal de l'Empire*, then the *Journal des Debats*.

There is a Belgian proverb, which says, "the Maca-ron, bitter and sweet together, is the emblem of mar-riage."

The paper, to the man of the military air, was both bitter and sweet, for after having thrown it down again and again, he had as often taken it up, to gnash his teeth over it.

It was, therefore, only necessary for him to hear the noise made by Conscience as he sank on the ground, to hear the exclamation Mariette uttered as she knelt beside him, to pass from the Journal to man, from *le Journal des Debats* to Conscience.

He therefore looked through the hedge, the upper portion of which was less dense than the base or cen-tre, and saw the touching picture we have described.

"Oh !" murmured he, "who, and what is that group of a young man, girl and dog ?"

He listened.

"Conscience, Conscience," said Mariette, with clasp-ed hands, "answer me, Conscience. Do so, I beg, or I shall think you are about to die."

Whether because he did not hear, or had not strength enough to reply, the young man shook his head and sighed.

"Conscience," continued Mariette, "can it be that your courage fails at the end of your journey. We are scarcely two hundred paces from the edge of the forest of Villers-Cotterets ; we are near Haramont. We may be there this evening, not on foot, for I know your feet are all bleeding, but in a carriage which we will hire at the next village, for nineteen of my thirty francs are yet left, all having been so kind to us. I say we may this evening be with our mothers, and once at

home, you will have no fatigue, and will have only to
to pass from one cottage to another with me for a guide."

" Yes," said Conscience, " I know that in two hours
we might be at home . . those two cottages, however,
which are so dear to us, I shall never see, nor mothers
Madeleine and Marie. I shall never see Father Cadet,
nor Pierre, nor the ox, nor the ass, nor the black cow."

Mariette gradually recovered strength at this complaint—she saw that he had to contend with immense
despair.

" But Conscience," said she, " it is certain that you
have seen ?—caught a glimpse—it matters not, but for
a moment your eyes recovered transparency. Well believe me, this light is not extinct, the pain you feel is inflammation. Be patient, Doctor Lacosse is very wise,
and will undertake the care of your poor eyes. He will
succeed. Instead, though, of consoling, I distress you.
You weep again."

" Mariette, I do not know why, but my heart is
breaking, I think I shall die."

Conscience's hand fell on the turf, and his head escaped from Mariette's arms. He had fainted.

" Help ! help !" said Mariette, " Water, water !"

Rising as if beside herself, and leaving the young man
in charge of Bernard, who gently licked his face, she
ran to the first door, which was that of the house of the
old man.

Just as she was about to touch the knocker, the door
opened, and the old man appeared accompanied by a
servant, whose costume more clearly betokened his old
profession, for he wore a soldier's fatigue cap and other
portions of uniform.

The latter held in his hand a vial and a little coffee-
spoon.

"Ah, sir; twenty steps from you a poor young man is dying. Come, sir, come, I beg you."

"I am coming, my child," said old the man. "Be not uneasy, however, for I saw all through the hedge, and there is no danger. It is but weakness."

"Then, sir, you will cure him?" said Mariette

"Yes, my child—come, Baptiste."

They went to Conscience. Mariette followed them so excited that she could scarcely walk.

Bernard saw aid was being brought to his master and bounded joyfully to meet the old man.

Baptiste looked one after the other at each of the group, and said, "On my word, Doctor, this must be a good fellow to be loved by both such a pretty girl and such a fine dog."

Of all the phrase, Mariette only heard the word "Doctor."

"Ah," cried she, "are you a physician, sir?"

"Yes," said Baptiste, "and a famous one, who has seen much more than ever happened to this lad."

"Then, sir, good God has again blessed us by sending you to our aid."

In the meantime the two men had reached Conscience, and while the servant held up his head, the old man placed a spoon-full of the liquid in the vial, in Conscience's lips.

Mariette, with her eyes fixed on Conscience, uttered a few broken words, half a prayer to God, half thanks to the stranger.

"Be easy, my child," said he, "this is mere faintness, and in a minute, the poor lad will have recovered his senses."

"Is it so, sir?" said Mariette. "Do you not say so because I will die if he does? He will not die, sir?"

"Do not fear. You love this soldier?"

"Oh, sir!"

"Whence come you with him?"

"From the hospital of Laon, whither I went for him.
You do not know, sir, that he is blind, having lost his
eyes by the explosion of a caisson."

"Ah! that is more serious. Let us, however, first attend to his fainting, and then look after the other matter."

"Monsieur," said Mariette, "see he opens his eyes.
You are right—he breathes."

"Mariette," said Conscience, who had regained his
senses.

"Conscience," said Mariette, "I am kneeling by
your side. With me is a doctor, who promises to take
charge of, and cure you. Do you not, sir?"

The old man looked carefully at Conscience's inflamed
eyes.

"Since you met with this accident," said he, "have
you never felt better?"

Conscience tried to speak. He was, however, so de-
bilitated, that his words were unintelligible.

Mariette replied for him.

"Yes, sir. But yesterday, it seemed to him that his
eyes cleared up. Yesterday, he thought he saw me."

"I did see you," murmured he.

"You hear, sir," said Mariette; "he says so himself.
Well! since then, there has been no amelioration in his
eyes, and he has as you see become hopeless. Despair
has brought him to this condition more than fatigue."

"He is wrong. It may be, that the membrane is only bruised, and will regenerate itself."

"Who ever you be, sir, thanks for the hope you give,

whether it be realized or not. Unfortunately, though," said she, shaking her head, "God has made falsehood a virtue to physicians."

"Know, young man," said Baptiste, "that my master is an old officer, who, as surgeon-in-chief of the Consular and Imperial Guard, served through the revolution and Empire. Consequently, my master tells no falsehoods."

Then in an angry tone, he said to his master,

"Who is that white face who talks so to you? Do you hear what he says?"

"Hush, Baptiste, what he says is right enough," said the old man, with a smile.

"What, you hear him talk so, and say it is right enough? Had any one told you so fifteen years ago, you would have cut his throat on the spot."

Then shrugging his shoulders, and sighing, he said,

"Old age—how rusty one becomes."

"Come, my friend," to Conscience,—"you are now recovered. Make an effort to walk to the house, where you will be more comfortable than you are here, and we will try to do something for your eyes."

"Oh, sir. Do not take so much trouble; after a brief repose, I shall be able to go on. The liquid you gave me has restored my strength. Mariette join with me in thanking Monsieur, and let us go."

"Wait a bit," said the old man. "You became sick at my door, and you must come into my house. You are good folks, and I do not wish you to exhaust your strength. You shall not go until you have rested, and refreshed yourselves with a glass of good wine. Perhaps by examining those eyes closely, some remedy may occur to me."

"Come, come, then," said Mariette. "It would be

tempting God to refuse. Monsieur, we are but poor peasants, and never can pay you for your care, but my prayers, sir, shall be inexhaustible as my love, and as long as I live, I will pray for you and those dear to you. Do what you will, sir, and may God grant you many and happy days in this world, and in the world to come eternal love."

Mariette having thus determined, Conscience could not object. Supported on one side by her, and on the other by the Doctor, he entered the house, Baptiste hastening before to open the doors for them.

XIX.

HOPE REVIVES.

WHEN they entered the house, Baptiste received his orders, which he transmitted to a second servant, who at once disappeared.

He then went into the sitting-room, where he found the Doctor and Mariette rolling up an arm-chair for Conscience to sit in.

All three entered the room. Bernard was afraid of the well-waxed floor, and stood respectfully at the door.

The Doctor led Conscience to the chair and turned his back to the light.

When Conscience sate down, Baptiste left.

A few minutes after, he returned with a bottle and three glasses on a waiter.

"Come here," said the Doctor.

"Here I am, Major."

The Doctor took the bottle by the neck with the care which those fond of old wine always show for age, and filled three glasses.

He gave one to Conscience.

334

" Drink it slowly," said he, " in large mouthfuls, and I promise that it will do you no harm."

Conscience took the glass.

" Excuse me, sir. It is wine," said he, " and I never drink it."

" So much the better," said he, " the effect will be greater. Drink, my friend, drink. It is a medicine."

Conscience prepared to obey him.

The Doctor gave Mariette the second glass.

" You, too, must be fatigued," said he, " and the wine will revive you."

" I think," said Baptiste, who looked at the three glasses of liquid topaz, " that this wine would rouse the dead."

" Well," said the Doctor, taking the third glass, " to the recovery of your friend."

" Oh, sir," said Mariette, " with all my heart."

The three, at the same moment, placed the glasses at their lips. Baptiste had no glass, but smacked his lips, like a man who in imagination tastes an absent liquid.

The old Doctor emptied his glass at a single swallow, and uttered a *Hem* of satisfaction.

Conscience carried his slowly to his lips, and tasted it with the distrust always exhibited by the blind. Then, overcoming his repugnance, he swallowed his wine.

As soon as Mariette had touched it with her lips, she put it aside as if it had been fire.

" Monsieur," said she, " I ask you pardon, but it is impossible for me to drink this."

Baptiste took the glass respectfully from the hands of Mariette, who hastened to wipe her hands with her handkerchief. One might have thought the wine a corrosive, every trace of which she wished to efface.

" Good !" said the Doctor, " it is well Baptiste is not offended with you, for you have lost a glass of the veriest nectar ever ripened by the sun of Andalusia. You are not offended with her, Baptiste ?"

" No, she is too pretty ; your health, Major, and the company."

He at once swallowed the glass of wine, and having done so, like his master uttered a " Hem" of satisfaction.

He swallowed the wine, however, more quickly, and his " *Hem*" was more sonorous.

The effect the Doctor anticipated was produced. The warmth of the generous fluid entered into Conscience's circulation. He felt its vivifying influence; the color returned to his cheeks, and a smile came to his lips.

" Monsieur," said Mariette, from whom none of the sensations of the young man escaped, " what you gave me seemed unpleasant as a drink, but appears excellent as a remedy. See how he revives. Are you not better, dear Conscience ?"

" Yes, much better, gayer and stronger. Strange, Mariette, but hope returns, and I am hungry."

" Oh, ho ! a moment," said the Doctor. How we are getting on. You must first have a bath, my friend. You must remain twenty minutes in the water. See to that, Baptiste ; exactly twenty minutes. In that time the patient must bathe his eyes with emollients, and then take him out and bring him hither. You hear, Mr. Soldier ? Be obedient as if you were with your Regiment. Those are my orders."

" You are very kind, sir, and give your orders in too benevolent a manner for them to be disobeyed."

Rising, he said :

" I am ready, M. Baptiste, will you lead me ?"

Conscience reached forth his hands, one of which Baptiste took, Mariette seized the other.

"My child," said the Doctor to Mariette, "I have something to say to you."

"I will but take him to the door, and will return at once."

"Go, then," said the Doctor.

Mariette did so, and at once returned.

The Doctor had detained the young girl to question her about the accident, and what she knew of the treatment, and about the return of sight, she had referred to, which had delighted them so.

Mariette told all she knew with the charming naivety we are familiar with, but which the Doctor was ignorant of, and which changed almost into paternal kindness the philanthropic interest which he had exhibited since he first saw them.

During this time, the Doctor listened with attention, and both approved and improved the treatment. In fact, Mariette, had fancied that she remarked that approbation and hope triumphed over fear.

"Very well," said he, when Mariette was done, "we will test the matter."

He rang for Baptiste, who soon came.

"Well, did you give him a bath?"

"Yes, Major. I had some difficulty in keeping the dog from emptying the bathing tub. The animal was very thirsty."

"Did you bathe his eyes in Guimanse?"

"Yes, Major."

"Take him out of the bath and bring him hither, after you put a bandage on his eye."

Baptiste faced about with military precision, and dis-appeared.

15

The Major lowered the blinds, so as to change the burning light into a demi-tint.

Mariette saw the old man make these preparations with shudders of anguish and anxiety. Had he not said, his experiment would be decisive?

At every external sound she turned towards the door.

At last she recognised the hesitating step of Conscience. The door opened, and the young man appeared leaning on Baptiste's arm.

The Doctor beckoned to Baptiste to take him into the centre of the room.

When there, Conscience and Baptiste had reached the spot he indicated. The Doctor placed Mariette on the right of Conscience, and stood himself on the left—both being within the circle of vision. Then telling Mariette by a gesture to be silent, the old man told Bastien to take off the bandage.

This being done, he said—

"Now open your eyes, and tell me if you see any thing in mass or in detail."

For an instant Conscience winked his eyes: then his sight seemed to grow stronger, and his dull pupils wandered around the circle before him, pausing on Mariette.

All at once he uttered a cry, and advanced rapidly with open arms to Mariette.

She wished to hurry to Conscience, but a gesture from the Doctor checked her.

She stood motionless and panting, shivering as if in an ague.

Conscience had advanced to her. When on the point of touching her, he paused and put forth his trembling hand.

"Mariette, is it you I see, or is it but a shadow—an error of the imagination? Oh, if it be you, for mercy touch me."

"Conscience, dear Couscience," said Mariette, seizing his hand.

"Then I see—I will not be blind, Mariette—I see."

"If you see, tell me the color of Mariette's shawl," said the Doctor.

"She has her red shawl, Doctor."

"True," said Mariette. "Oh what happiness! This is not a mistake. Yes, Conscience, I have my red shawl on."

The Doctor seemed surprised.

"She has her red shawl? Are you not mistaken in that, my friend?"

"No, Doctor."

"And you see red?"

"No, I see only something greyish. But one day at his house, Doctor Lacosse told me, that when it was dark red was deeper than the other colors. Mariette's shawl seems dark grey, and consequently is red."

"True," said the Doctor. "Embrace, my children, and be of good hope."

Turning to the servant, while they were locked in each other's arms, he said,

"Baptiste, replace the bandage over those blind eyes, which will in a few months, I hope, see clearly enough. Take him to his room to rest, so that he may set out again early to-morrow. Mlle. Mariette will either dine with me or with Conscience, as she wishes"

"Oh with Conscience, Doctor. I am so happy that I really must see him to be convinced of my happiness!"

"So be it. You hear, Baptiste?"

"How, Doctor, can I thank you?" said Conscience, who seemed overburdened with joy.

"Be calm," said the Doctor. "Calmness above all things is necessary. With it, alum and rose-water, and some soothing salve, we will cure you yet."

"And you will not be the first," said Baptiste. "Oh young man, your falling into our hands was no misfortune."

"Well, my child," said the Doctor, "you do not follow your friend."

"Oh sir," said Mariette, falling on her knees, "let me first thank you."

"Are you mad?" asked the Doctor, seeking to lift her up.

"Mariette seized his hands, and keeping her humble posture, said, "No, I am not mad, and I will not rise until I shall have told you that I trust you will be better rewarded for this than if you had cured a king's son. God discharges the debts of the poor, and is rich in mercy and in blessings. My God! will you not bless our preserver as we do ourselves?"

"Yes, my child," said the old man, " God will hear you, or rather has heard you, for I already feel myself rewarded beyond my deserts. Kiss me, my child, and rejoin your friend."

He kissed Mariette paternally on the forehead, and said as she ran after Conscience,

"Who will tell me, mankind are naturally bad?"

The next morning at seven o'clock, his pretty country carriage, drawn by a dapple-grey horse, was at the door of the house to which Mariette had gone so anxiously.

A peasant boy held the horse.

Baptiste had a whip in his hand, and plaited the lash with especial care.

Bernard was gamboling about, and evidently waited for some one to come.

The Doctor came first; he was followed by Mariette and Conscience, the latter of whom had his visor over his face, but was calm, serene, and smiling.

He leaned on Mariette's arm and held the old man's hand to his breast.

When at the steps of the carriage he hesitated a moment, and then opening his arms, said,

"Doctor, I would embrace you."

The Doctor asked nothing better, and clasped him in his arms.

Then he said, "Go, Conscience, you forget that your mother awaits you."

"Yes, Doctor, you are right. Baptiste, help me into the carriage. Mariette, thank the Doctor, and tell him we will ever love him."

"Yes," said Mariette, "God knows we will."

"Come, Mademoiselle, get in. We only wait for you."

Mariette got in and sate on the back seat by the side of Conscience.

"Now," said Baptiste, "what road?"

"The shortest" said Conscience.

"Then we will go by Fleury, leave Villers-Cotterets on our left, go behind Saint Remy, and through the Chataigneni directly to Haramont. Do you think so?"

"Yes, that makes our road a league shorter."

"Then up, Marengo," and he laid his whip on the horse's side with such zest, that he set out on a long

trot on the track of Bernard, who seemed to know the
way.

"Au revoir," said Conscience and Mariette; "A
pleasant journey," said the old man—and five hours afterwards, they were at the two cottages, where stood
grouped together, unable to realize the unexpected return, on one side Dame Marie, Pierre, and Catharine,
and on the other, Madeleine supporting Father Cadet,
who was beginning to get about.

The barking of Bernard was answered by the lowing
of Tardif, the cow, and the braying of the ass, who
knew in their stables what had happened.

XX.

In which it is almost proven that Conscience had better have continued Blind.

———

WE will not attempt to describe the effect produced on the inhabitants of the two cottages by the return of Conscience and Mariette.

Instead of weeping for one child, the mothers had begun to weep for two. Mariette had not been heard from, and though the six days had not passed, her absence seemed to have lasted six centuries.

Conscience was first welcomed. He was the true traveller, having been absent six months.

Then came the turn of Mariette, the devoted heroine —and last, Bernard.

Mariette was the poet of this new Odyssy. Like Francesca di Rimini she told the story of Conscience as Paolo did, listening with his head on his mother's shoulder.

Many sighs and tears interrupted this simple story. Many blessings were heaped on the charitable souls whom God had brought in contact with the two pilgrims.

The two bouquets of gold and silver flowers brought

from our Lady of Liesse, were hung one in each cottage in the most conspicuous place over the chimney.

About two o'clock in the afternoon, when the dapple grey horse had made the acquaintance of Tardif and Pierrot, having been well fed and rested, as Baptiste had been by the cottagers, he was taken from the stable and burdened with countless thanks, for the old Doctor and the driver having left the cottage on the left, bade adieu to those he had made so happy.

Whipping up his horse he retraced his steps to Longpont, where he arrived in two hours after he left Haramont, his arrival at which had produced such an impression.

A greater sensation was produced on no one than on Catharine, whom chance had taken to Dame Marie's house, and who, having had no news from Bastien, did not know whether he was dead or alive. She loved the hussar with all her soul, and therefore was delighted to hear from Mariette's lips details which assured her of his life.

True, when Bastien left Mariette it was to take a walk with the cuirassier towards the Saint Quentin gate, but he seemed to calculate so certainly on giving his adversary a cut over the face, that the fact had left a feeling of gratitude on Mariette's heart, but none of uneasiness. She did not therefore mention it to Catharine.

All the rest of the day, the villagers stood in the road between the cottages.

Conscience had to tell all the details of the terrible battle of Laon, until the moment of the explosion which had blinded him. Mariette also described her journey, the pilgrimage, and the intervention of our Lady of Liesse.

Night recalled each to his fireside, and all the village that evening talked of Mariette and Conscience. They spoke of their marriage, which no longer was a mystery, Conscience having repeated the promises of devotion Mariette had made, when despairing of ever regaining his sight, he looked on the rest of life as an anticipation of the hours awaiting him in the vestibules of death.

In all the village, none envied the future happiness of the young people; on the contrary, all who knew the state of Father Cadet's affairs pitied them, for the old man was much involved by the triple derangement produced by the attack of apoplexy, of which he began to recover, of Conscience's departure, and of the return of the Bourbons.

Let us explain all this, and unfold to the reader Father Cadet's real situation. Having for a moment fancied himself rich as Crœsus, he was on the point of discovering that he was poor as Job.

The apoplexy with which he had been attacked had, as we have said, prevented him from attending to the working and seeding of his ground, but in that respect he was fortunately aided by neighbor Mathieu. The field had however been deprived of that daily visit, to which it had been used, and the jealous ground on that account, or on account of the badness of the year, promised, if not sterility, a poor yield.

Now had Conscience been there to watch over its wants.

But alas, Conscience was absent. He was measuring out powder at Brienne, Montereau, Mergan-Bac, at Laon. Conscience, who would not have pulled a feather from a thrush, was in his humble sphere of action the conqueror of the Pyramids, of Marengo and Aus-

15 *

terlitz; an occupation for which he had very little taste
and admiration as his friend Bastien entertained.

We have seen how Conscience, doubly excusable in
his various homicides, by the necessity of the defence
of the territory, and his obvious unwillingness to obey
the law of recruiting, had been checked in his career, in
which, little as it was to his taste, he had discovered
such sang froid as to attract the attention even of the
Emperor, who had said to him, " The first time we
meet again under fire, remind me that I owe you the
cross"—words the fruit of which he was probably
about to gather, when the explosion of his caisson
made him disappear like Romulus in a blaze.

Then came the complete occupation of the territory,
the entrance of the allies into Paris, and the restoration
of the throne of the Bourbons, additional causes of the
ruin of Father Cadet and of the families in the cottages
also.

Alas, amid these great catastrophes and events, the
historian attends only to the rising and falling fortune
of the great of this world.   He pities the overturned
throne, the neglected genius, the revulsions of fate, the
hazard of fortune, and rarely fails to find a complaint,
a look or sigh, for the humble existences crushed by
the wheels of those who ride in the car of fate.

Now this is the triple ruin brought on the inhabitants
of the two cottages by the great events which changed
the aspect of Europe.

The occupation of France first brought a Russian
force of thirty or forty thousand men to Villers-Cotterets.   It would have been difficult to lodge this force in
the five hundred houses which compose the city and in
the adjacent villages.

This force made a bivouac which covered three square leagues.

Father Cadet's eight or nine acres were included in these square leagues, and were covered by a camp of Kossacks, whose horses had trampled on the grain just beginning to come up.

The yield of that year, therefore, was not to be thought of. Tnue, the straw which covered it, would naturally be converted into manure, and the ground, though unproductive in 1814, would, no doubt, be admirably prepared in 1815. But before that time eighteen months would pass, and on Martinmas, one hundred louis were to be paid to Master Niguet the notary.

Nothing at first seemed so easy as to borrow eight hundred francs, on the security of eight acres of ground which ten years of constant toil had made of the best quality, and which were only liable to a mortgage of sixteen hundred francs.

We will however return to this. We have spoken of three causes of ruin, and having explained the first, which was the Kossack devastation, will omit the second, and speak of the third, the question of payment, which was the gravest of all.

The second cause of ruin was, that in consequence of the foreign occupation, Mariette's daily trips to Villers-Cotterets had been interrupted. A young girl without a safe conduct, beautiful as Mariette was, could not even think of passing a bivouac of so many men.

Besides, what could she sell? There were no cows at Longpre, and consequently, no milk. The milch cows there had been killed, and the black cow had escaped in consequence of the special protection of the officer in command at Haramont. The great age of Tardif and Pierrot made them respectable, even in the eyes of the half-famished Kossacks.

In a bivouac of fifty thousand Kossacks, there was no milk, no commerce, and, consequently, the resources of the cottage on the right were all dried up, while, as we have said, a third disaster awaited that on the left.

The Bourbons were restored, and the old servitors who had followed them into exile had returned with them. Nobles and Priests on their return, all had claims : there was not one who had not been despoiled, and who did not demand justice against *robbery*.

Thus was entitled that great act of justice, which in 1792 enriched the French people with the property of those who conspired and fought against it.

Now the nine acres of Father Cadet were but a shred detached from the lands formerly held in Haramont, Bonneuil, and Largny, by the Convent of Longpre.

Those holding from the Convent had reappeared in the neighborhood, and said they hoped that restitution would be made to them as well as to others.

We need not say they did not even talk of indemnifying the new holders.

This was, then, the precarious situation of Father Cadet, and of the two families.

It will now be understood how necessary it was that the kind of miracle which had begun to restore sight to Conscience should be accomplished at once, as on him depended the prosperity of all.

The first thing to be done was to attend to his convalescence. On the next day Conscience went to Villers-Cotterets with Mariette and Bernard. It was their usual walk, but the bivouac had made the birds, squirrels, and deer wild.

The soldiers stared at the beautiful girl, but were restrained by two sentinels, the respect they owed to their officers, and by the interest inspired by respect to misfortune. The remains of Conscience's uniform, also enabled them to see that he was a soldier, suffering the consequence of some accident, and the brotherhood of the field of battle, now that the contest was over, was established even among enemies, and they protected the blind and his guide.

Both, or rather including Bernard, the three reached Villers-Cotterets, in which for six months they had not been seen.

Amid the great events which had taken place in their absence, as may be imagined, they had not been remarked. Their re appearance, however, had.

All looked with sympathy at the strange group.

They went directly to the house of Doctor Lacosse.

The Doctor already knew of Conscience's return, of his terrible accident, and of the improvement which began to manifest itself.

He, therefore, received him most kindly.

"Ah, it is you, my lad? Come hither, and tell me all about the accident."

For the tenth, twentieth, and the fiftieth time, Conscience had to tell him all about it.

The Doctor listened attentively, and then having taken Conscience to a window, opened the lid by force, and examined it.

"This is well," said he "the outer pellicle of the cornea has been touched, and its transparency has been injured. The membrane, however, gradually exfoliates and regenerates itself. The winking of the lids will restore its polish, and then, my lad, you will see as well as you ever did."

"Indeed, sir?" said both he and Mariette.

"I promise you," said the Doctor.

"What must be done now?" asked Mariette.

"A very simple thing; I will give you a simple prescription, in obedience to which the apothecary will prepare you an ointment, and Conscience must put it on his eyelids every morning and evening. In a fortnight or three weeks he will be well enough to come alone for another prescription."

While the Doctor wrote this prescription for M. Pacquenot, the Apothecary, Conscience and Mariette were locked in each others' arms, and shed tears of joy.

They had now nothing to fear, for the first Doctor had hoped, the second promised, and the third affirmed.

They returned rapidly as possible, to bear the joyful news to Haramont.

XXI.

The Horizon Darkens.

———

NOTHING less than this news would have sufficed to lessen the anxiety of another kind which began to take possession of the two families.

With his nine acres of ground, as we have said, Father Cadet was on the point of being reduced to misery. Doctor Lacosse, had, it is true, charged nothing for attending to him during his illness, but the druggist had not been so liberal, and before he recovered, Father Cadet had to expend at least fifty crowns.

We have seen that when Mariette was about to go to Laon for Conscience, the old man had offered her his last gold piece. It had been replaced in the leather sack, not to remain there any long time, but had gone with five others, saved by Dame Marie and Madeleine, to pay for M. Pacquenot's remedies.

To make up the fifty crowns, it had been necessary, also, to add some change.

This was the state of things when Conscience returned, to the great delight of the hearts of all, but not to the relief of their purses.

Father Cadet, during the rest of his life, would remain powerless, Conscience, while convalescing, would be unable to work, and no reliance could be placed on little Pierre for four or five years.

Thus of the two families composed of three males and three females, the natural supporters were disabled and the women had to provide for all.

We know what is the value of the product of the needle and wheel of a village woman.

True, peasant life costs little, but the two invalids increased the expense.

In spite of the failure of the harvest, Father Cadet easily found resources, but we have mentioned the terrible reports current, about the property of the Emigres, which made his situation more complicated.

It was known, that Father Cadet owed sixteen hundred francs on the nine acres of land, which was nothing when they were worth twelve or fourteen thousand francs, but which was an enormous sum when they would not sell even for sixteen hundred francs.

No one offered to serve him: not even neighbor Mathieu, who, being somewhat similarly situated, would have been unable to serve him, had he offered to do so.

He determined to do all that was possible under existing circumstances.

Political events did not aid him.

On the 30th of May, the guns of Paris announced the treaty between France and the allied powers.

The hostile troops were to evacuate France.

On the 15th of June, the Russians broke up their bivouac, and bade adieu to the people of Haramont, Largny and Villers-Cotterets, to the great delight of the latter.

For a moment, France forgot in the free air she breathed, that she was restricted to the boundaries of 1792, that she had lost her universal supremacy, and lost in the Mediterranean, in the gulf of Mexico, in the Indian Ocean, Malta, Tobago, Saint Lucia, the isle of France, Rodrigua and the Sechelles.

She regained her soil, she again became mistress of herself, and collected her children, who were dispersed in the provinces of the North, in the armies beyond the Loire, and in the hospitals.

On the day after the departure of the Kossacks, Father Cadet said that he wished to see his land. A long time had passed in making this effort. At first, he walked a few steps by means of the aid of Madeleine's arm. But as long as the Kossacks were there, he had carefully avoided looking at, and thinking of it. He felt as Collatins would have felt towards Lucretia, had she survived Tarquin's outrage.

Madeleine, as usual, offered the old man her arm. He, however, refused it. He wished that no one might witness the emotion he was aware he was about to undergo.

She exhibited some anxiety about his being able to walk so far, it was nearly a quarter of a league, but he made an effort, stood up, and crossed almost the whole floor without limping, and asked them only to help him down the bank. The rest would not trouble him.

Madeleine looked anxiously after him, but seeing that he had come to the turn of the road, she relied on his energetic will.

He went on, and came in sight of the vast devastated plain.

For more than a league, he could see nothing but ground trampled by the horses and men, half-broken barrels and great black spots, which showed where the fires had been kindled.

He shook his head sadly and went on, but when he came to where his field should be, he looked in vain for it.

Every landmark had disappeared. There was neither enclosure nor ditch to tell the proprietor, "This is your own, and does not belong to your neighbor."

Father Cadet tried to lift his hands to heaven, but his left hand could not accomplish the movement, and fell heavily to his side.

Two tears rolled from his eyes : one of his hands was powerless, but both eyes wept.

" Lord God," murmured the poor old man, " must I at the end of my life see such calamities ?"

Then as his memory told him he must be near his land, he stooped to see if beneath that heap of mud and straw he could find his landmarks.

A little wood which belonged to Mathieu might have aided him in the search, but the wood had been cut down.

In his heart Father Cadet was not sorry for this, for the wood, which had been full of briars, was a shelter for a colony of hares, which were hidden by day, but at night ate down Cadet's grain and clover.

A few stumps of what had been trees indicated the situation of the wood, and by means of it he was enabled to approximate to one of his landmarks.

He was trying to establish the other, when a hand was placed lightly on his shoulder.

He turned around and saw the man who had sold

him the two last acres of land, and to whom he owed the sixteen hundred francs.

The seller, unlike Father Cadet, seemed joyous and happy.

" Good day, Cousin Maniquet and the *company*," according to his usual phraseology, although Maniquet was alone, said Father Cadet.

" Very well—and how are you, Father Cadet ?" said Maniquet.

" Badly,—very badly." Cadet shook his head sadly.

" Bah ! you will live thirty years yet."

Father Cadet shook his head more sadly still.

" Cousin Maniquet, the ass alone knows where the saddle presses."

" Yes, I see. You spake of your paralysis. Will not your left arm and leg get strong ?"

" Thank God, that is not what I complain of, for my lame leg, as you see, has brought me thus far. My land, though, Cousin Maniquet, my land—"

" Ah ! I see. Your land—"

" I have come to look for the landmarks, and though I once could find them with my eyes shut, I cannot now."

" Do not let that disturb you We will find them again."

" Find them again ? It will be very difficult to do so, changed as every thing is."

" Yes. You know I border on Vaumoise—"

" Yes."

" I sold you these two acres because I wished to purchase more in that direction, and also because I had no confidence in this land which had belonged to a convent."

Father Cadet sighed, for Cousin Maniquet had touched one of his wounds, and certainly not that which was nearest being cured.

"Ah! I think," said he, "you were right to get rid of them."

"I think so too. You remember I told you I bordered on Vaumoise, and the consequence was, as soon as I had security from the officers, I came to the bivouac to sell my vegetables."

"Ah!" said Father Cadet.

"Yes—a wagon load every day, and as Louis XVIII. paid them well for the services they did him, those Kossack robbers paid good prices."

"Then you lost nothing by the invasion?"

"On the contrary, I gained, and I am only sorry it did not last three years instead of three months."

"There are others to whom it would have been a great misfortune. '

"Yes, Father Cadet, but you know that one man's misfortune is another's gain. All is but good and bad luck. This time I was lucky, and on another occasion it may be different."

"But," said Father Cadet, who was not very much pleased with Maniquet's conversation, "how will all this enable me to find my landmarks?"

"Easy enough. I came hither every day, as I told you, and as I foresaw what would happen, one day I brought a dozen stakes ready sharpened in my wagon, and I said to the Kossacks, 'Do not mind me, for you are encamped on my ground, and while the limits are visible I wish to mark them.' They said that was right, and let me drive in my stakes—so that thanks to this precaution *we* will find *our* limits."

This plural possessive pronoun made Cadet uneasy, and he looked anxiously at Maniquet. To satisfy himself, he said,

"It was really very kind in you, Cousin, to take such interest in my affairs."

"Ah—you see, Father Cadet, your interests are become mine."

"How so?" said the old man with flushed cheeks.

"Certainly, you still have two payments to make?"

"Yes."

"Of eight hundred francs each."

"True."

"At Martinmas of the current and of the next year."

"You are right about dates."

"Ah! I am a systematic man."

"But now I owe you nothing."

"Wait. I said—Bad luck has befallen Father Cadet. He is paralytic. His grand-son Conscience is blind—the Kossacks are on his land and have half-ruined it."

"And then, Cousin?"

"Then?"

"Yes."

"I said, it may be at pay-day he will be in trouble." Father Cadet stifled a sigh.

"Eight hundred francs is not found every day in the road, especially under a Kossack's horse's hoof. Well, he will be troubled about payment. That though may be arranged."

"Ah," said Father Cadet, "as the security is good, you will allow me time, will you not?"

"No, Father Cadet, do not trust to that. I too have purchased, and have payments to make precisely when yours become due. Now, Father Cadet, you have always been prompt, and I have relied on you as you have on me. Now this concerns you much."

" True," said Cadet, stifled almost.

" I then reflected—Father Cadet cannot rely on the harvest of this year, for it is destroyed, and may be unable to pay. Then as mortgager, you know I have a first mortgage, Father Cadet ?"

" Yes, I know."

" Well, if he do not pay, it will be painful, and I will be forced to sell his land."

Father Cadet closed his eyes, and gaped like a man who has a rope around his neck. Maniquet continued,

" Now as the land is depreciated in value, these fools, thinking the nobles and priests will get back their estates, I will buy it for a trifle, for a loaf of bread, and then no harm will come of my having marked out the limits. That is why I drove the stakes."

The old man made grimaces as hideous as if these stakes had been in his own bowels.

Maniquet continued—" You may therefore be easy, Father Cadet, for your land will not be confounded with that of your neighbors, and in the year we will find it better than ever, for I need not tell you that hay ashes and offal will make famous manure. Oh ! the land needed a year's rest, for you will confess you over-cropped it. What is the matter ? Are you sick ?"

The old man trembled, and Maniquet offered him his arm, which Cadet refused.

" Very well, Cousin Maniquet. I am glad you told me this, for a man fore-warned is fore-armed."

" Then you will pay me at Martinmas ?"

" I do not say so."

" You will not pay me ?"

" I do not say so."

" What then ?"

" We will see."   This was a by-word of Father Cadet.

" Adieu, Cousin *and company*," said Cadet.

With death in his heart, he returned towards the village, dragging his paralytic leg behind him.

" Lord God," said Cadet, " it lacked but this.   That field cost me four hundred louis d'or, and that beggar will buy it for a morsel of bread."

In a yet lower tone he added,

" It shall not be.   I will sooner strangle him with my good hand."

XXII.

All but Conscience.

<hr/>

ON his return, Cadet found the space between the cottages filled by the population of the village.

It was grouped around Bastien, who had re-appeared in the village, with his face adorned with two sabre-cuts, so that he was not to be recognised. They did not, however, prevent Catharine from uttering cries of joy as soon as she saw him.

One of these cuts he had when Mariette left him at the door of the hospital; the other he had gotten from the cuirassier.

We have seen that Bastien had left Mariette asking her to be perfectly easy on his account, he having studied out a perfectly infallible cut at the face.

Unfortunately, the same idea sometimes occurs to two people, and the cuirassier entertained at the same moment, the idea he did, and Bastien received the blow instead of the cuirassier, the latter exhibiting greater quickness.

His first visit had been to Conscience, and he therefore came to see his comrade, and to ask how his eyes were, followed by all the village.

360

We know that Conscience's eyes were doing as well as possible. Unfortunately, what took place between Father Cadet and Maniquet proved that all was not going on well in other respects.

Father Cadet had but one hope, that Master Niguet, who had many moneyed men among his patrons, would find some one ready on a second mortgage, to advance the sum due the person from whom Father Cadet had purchased.

The thing became the more feasible, as when Maniquet was paid, the second would be the first mortgage.

As the next day, Mariette taking advantage of the absence of the Russians, purposed to resume her trips to Villers Cotterets, and reap as much advantage as ever, from the milk the black cow gave in abundance, it was arranged that Cadet should be placed on Pierrot, and being supported there by Conscience, should call on Master Niguet to attempt to effect the negociation.

On the next day the old man and the two young people set out. Bernard, as usual, drew his car, and Pierrot bore Father Cadet.

Mariette would have regained all her old customers, and would even have had new ones, if she had milk enough. The black cow, however, gave but two measures of milk, that is, sixteen sous worth, an enormous quantity for one cow. Mariette had therefore to serve but a few, and gave offence thereby.

While she was going her round, Father Cadet was taken by Conscience to Master Niguet's house.

He found the notary in the same place, in the same chair, and surrounded by the same clerks. A throne had fallen, an invasion had taken place, a dynasty had

16

been restored, without removing a grain of dust from the cushions of the venerable notary.

Conscience waited in the ante-room, where he found Madame Niguet, to whom he had to tell his adventures, at the end of which the old lady saw a marriage contract to be drawn up by her husband. She suggested it to Conscience, who received the proposition sadly enough. Of Mariette and himself, he would in a few months, probably, be the poorest, for if his sight, according to Doctor Lacosse's anticipations was restored, he would bring to Mariette a husband, if not blind, maimed.

While Conscience was speaking to Mlle. Niguet, and while she, who had remedies for everything, was disapproving the prescription, Father Cadet, after a troublesome preamble, told the notary why he was come.

M. Niguet listened with the greatest attention, but shook his head from time to time.

Father Cadet remarked these silent refusals.

"Is what I ask impossible, M. Niguet?" said he.

"Not impossible, but difficult. You have no idea how valuable money is, and people talk much of the plans of Louis XVIII. in relation to the property of the emigres, and especially of that of the church."

"You then think I cannot borrow?"

"I do not say so. I will try, but I can promise nothing."

Father Cadet sighed, and shaking his head, said sadly, "Ah! *the other* took away our children, and restored them to us without eyes, legs, or arms . . . Sometimes he did not return them to us at all, but he left us our lands."

"Father Cadet," said Master Niguet, "is it possible that you are a Buonapartist? If so, I beg you, highly as I prize your patronage, to give it to M. Menesson, or to M. Lebigue. I wish to have only the business of His Majesty's faithful subjects."

"Oh. M. Niguet excuse me if I said anything wrong about either this one or *the other*. I go for the land, and he who gives it me will be not only my king, but my God, for he will give me and my family bread."

Father Cadet arose, and trembling almost as much as when he had last been in the room, went to the door muttering,

"Not able to borrow sixteen hundred francs on a field worth twelve thousand, if it be worth a *hard*. Oh, such things do not happen under the other. Adieu, M. Niguet and *the* company, Come, Conscience."

Conscience could not see Father Cadet, but by the sound of his voice, which was more tremulous, and his tongue more indistinct than usual, he saw that the old man had an unsatisfactory interview with the notary.

Mariette and Bernard awaited them on the green lawn of the park. Mariette had been fortunate, and had not a drop of milk left.

It was a great thing that this resource was left, but with only sixteen sous a day to provide food for herself and her mother, it was not probable, that economical as she might be, she would be able to lay aside the eight hundred francs which Father Cadet needed on Martinmas next.

At any other time they would have gone to Mathieu, who under a rude exterior was very kind. Half however of Mathieu's land had also belonged to the nobles and to the church and had like Cadet's been encamped on by the Kossacks. Nothing could be expected from him, for during the sad year 1814 no thing grew on his eighty acres, and if he had any ready money, as charity begins at home, it was probable that he would keep it.

There was no doubt about the matter, though, for only a few days before Mathieu had gone for the same purpose to M. Niguet, and had met with no better success than Cadet had.

At any other time, too, Bastien would have offered some resource. They might rely on his devotion to Conscience, for the Hussar, like all kind hearts, as soon as he knew the young man better, had passed from one extremity to the other. A small resource might, therefore, have been expected from Bastien, who drank no white wine in the morning, nor played checkers in the evening, and who from the two hundred and fifty francs of his cross, and his pension of four hundred livres could easily have saved a hundred francs a month, since having again taken the charge of Mathieu's horses, he was fed by him. Unfortunately, Bastien was in as bad repute as Cadet and Mathieu's land, for since the return of the Bourbons, Bastien was become a Brigand, a Buonapartist, a companion of the Ogre. Consequently, the Government has ceased to look on him as its creditor, and Bastien was much pressed— never having during his economy saved anything.

We know Julienne's farm-house had been burned, and that the Kossacks had eaten up her cows. Far from being able to help those who had saved her stock and child, she had been reduced to such want, as to be forced to enter the service of the farmer of Bonneuil herself as a manager.

At first they thought of selling Pierrot and Tardif,

but Pierrot was very old, and his obstinacy being known for twelve leagues around, lessened his value. Tardif, though yet able to draw the plough, was not fit for the butcher. Kossack teeth alone could have masticated him, and the gentlemen from the Don and Volga, who were in the habit of eating their horses, when too old for service, were all gone.

Besides, Conscience, he and Mariette alone, with the hopefulness of young hearts, did not despair, were opposed to selling Pierrot and Tardif. He had on his re.turn, a long conversation with them, and in their names made ample promise of services they were yet able to render.

Conscience was a sublime image of the faith that animated him. Father Cadet, completely discouraged, never left his bed, except for his chair, and his chair but for his bed. To all objections he replied only by shrugs.

Though the land was in danger of gliding into Maniquet's hands from Father Cadet's, Conscience would not nelgect it, and consequently having harnessed Tardif and Pierrot to the plough, thanks to his voice, was able to revive all their strength and ploughed the land.

On the second day he told Father Cadet so.

" Well," said the old man, " but where shall we get seed from ?"

" God will provide it," said Conscience, calmly.

" Yes," said Cadet, with a sad smile, " but suppose he gives us seed in October, in November we owe eight hundred francs to Maniquet, and who will give that ? Will God ?"

" Why not ?" said Conscience, with sublime naivety.

Father Cadet was incredulous, and shook his head.

In October, Conscience harnessed the animals to the

wagon, and went to the farmers in the neighborhood, with his sweet, sad smile, and said to them,

"If you have more corn than you need for seed, give me some to sow Father Cadet's land. God will restore to you what you give me, by averting the storm from your fields, and the birds from the ripened grain."

All gave to Conscience, not only of their superfluity, but a portion of what they needed. Country people refuse each other money but not corn.

One who would not give a beggar a hard, will share with him his loaf.

Conscience returned at night with three sacks of grain, a little more than he needed to sow Cadet's land.

The old man was surprised, and lifted up his hands to heaven in thankfulness, as six months before he had done in despair.

That evening Conscience felt his strength much greater, and without saying any thing, took the prayer-book of Madeleine, opened it, and to the great surprise of the three women, who shed tears of joy, read aloud:

"What shall I render to the Lord for all that I have received from him? He has loved me, and has rescued me from death, for love of me. He has covered me with grace in this world, and prepared me for eternal life. Oh, my soul, bless the Lord! Let all that is in me bless his holy name!"

On the next day, Conscience sowed Father Cadet's land as if the old man had only eight days after, that is to say, on the 11th of November, to pay the terrible sum of eight hundred livres, which, like Damocle's sword, hung above his head, and that of all his family.

While Conscience was seeding, he received several

visits from Cousin Maniquet, who encouraged him in his praiseworthy efforts, with a voice which betrayed both anxiety and irony, as the calmness of the young man terrified the usurer, or as the known destitution of the family encouraged him.

XXIII.

Official Documents.

—◆—

THE fatal 11th of November came, and M. Niguet had sent no message, either verbal or otherwise.

The emotion of debtor and creditor were equally great. The debtor was pained at being unable to pay, the creditor feared he might be paid.

The 11th of November passed without a word from Cadet. He was satisfied that all effort to procure the frightful sum was vain.

The other members of the family were equally silent.

Night came, and none slept except Conscience, who slumbered calmly as usual.

On the next day, at dawn, he set out to harrow.

At the end of the village he met Maniquet.

" Good morning, my lad. Whither so early ?"

" Good morning, Cousin," said Conscience—" and you ?—"

" Oh, I have business in the city."

" I am going to the field."

" By the by, the field, you know, my lad . . ."

" What ?"

"It is not paid. Strange, in so exact a man."

"If he did not pay, Cousin Maniquet, you may be sure it is because he could not."

"Yes, but will he pay to-day or to-morrow?" asked he with the anxiety naturally inspired by Conscience's very great calmness.

"I do not think he can."

"How? You don't think he can?"

"No."

"But you know I warned him."

"What about?"

"That if he did not pay at the appointed time I would enforce my rights."

"Do so, Cousin Maniquet," said Conscience with the same tranquility.

During this conversation, Tardif and Pierrot had stopped, but at Conscience's voice they resumed their route.

"And you are not going to harrow?" asked Maniquet.

"Why not?"

"Why not? I told you—"

"Not at all. The land will yield a crop to some one—to you perhaps, if it does not remain in Father Cadet's possession. Whoever though has it for the time being, should keep it in good order."

"Good lad. Continue to act so, for you are in the right road."

"And do you, Cousin, pause, for I fear you are not—"

"Do not trouble yourself—that is my business," and Maniquet continued on to Villers-Cotterets.

There was this difference however between them.— Maniquet frequently looked silently back on Conscience

16*

and passed his hand over his sweaty brow, while the other walked quietly on without looking back, with a calm brow.

On the third day, at two in the evening, Cadet saw M. Chaix, a huissier from Villers-Cotterets, a descendant of Moliere M. Loyal, enter, and with a forced politeness hand him a little piece of stamped paper.

" Put it on the table," said Cadet with anger in his heart and a frown on his brow, for it was the first time an officer of the law had ever crossed his door.

" Very well," said M. Chaix. " If you know what it is, I have nothing to say. Good morning, M. Cadet."

" Good morning, M. Chaix *and company*. This is probably the last stamped paper you will bring me, and we will not be apt to meet again."

Madeleine sate in the corner, and M. Chaix did not see her. She wiped away the tears with her apron.

Father Cadet took the paper, and turned it over and over again.

Just then Conscience came in He had put Pierrot and Tardif in the stable after having harrowed the ground

" Look at this paper M. Chaix has just brought," said Cadet. " Can you tell what it says ?"

Conscience said—" Yes, grandpapa—it is a summons to pay interest and capital."

" Well, what is to be done ?"

" Wait for a second summons."

" Will there be a second ?"

" There will be."

" When ?"

" On the day after to-morrow, probably."

" Who told you so ?"

" I enquired."

" Of whom ?"

" Of a good man, whom Maniquet spoke to, before the term expired, to prosecute you, and who refused."

" Who is he ?" asked Cadet, amazed that any huissier should refuse to prosecute a debtor.

" M. Demay."

" Ah !" said Cadet. " *He* was a friend of poor William. Then we must wait."

" Yes—we must wait."

They did so.

Nothing is so exact as law papers, and what they expected, came on the next day but one.

It was an iterative, under the penalty of a seizure of immovables, to pay within twenty-four hours, &c. &c.

" Do you hear, my lad ?" said Cadet.

" Yes," said Conscience with his usual placidity.— " You should not be afraid : it is a form of law. A delay of thirty-four days is allowed *in part* .   "

" How learned you are, Conscience," said Cadet, surprised.

" Yes," said Conscience with a smile—" thanks to M. Demay."

" And what shall we do when the thirty-four days are gone ?"

" M. Demay will tell us."

They waited until the 15th of December, when M. Dechaix came with two attendants to draw up a *proces-verbal* of the seizure, and went on the spot to describe it. Father Cadet refused, but Conscience offered to accompany them.

" There is no use," said Cadet. " He will find somebody."

" Who ?"

" Maniquet, to be sure."

M. Chaix was obliged to hunt for the field alone.—
Having however satisfied himself that neither Conscience nor Cadet had gone, Cousin Maniquet came
himself.

When the huissiers were gone, Bastien glided into
the cottage.

" Conscience," said he, " come here. I have something to say."

Conscience smiled and gave him his hand.

" I have an idea," said Bastien.

" What is it ?"

" That we take our sabres. You have yours, I
hope ?"

" Yes."

" And hide ourselves in the wood."

" What for ?"

" To wait for them."

" For whom ?"

" The huissiers, and give them such a drubbing that
the devil would not know them. That would be pleasant, as we said in the Regiment."

" Hush, Bastien," said Conscience, "do not think
of such a thing, which would ruin us entirely, if we be
not lost already."

" Name of names—to think those beggars suppressed
my cross and pension !"

He made a gesture, which recalled Ajax blaspheming
the Gods.

" Ah ! if an opportunity comes to send them back
again, will it not be pleasant ? If you need me, Conscience, remember I am yours for life or death."

Bastien left murmuring, " Curse the Huissiers and
the Bourbons, what on earth are they for, except to
incense honest people ?"

Two days after, M. Chaix, passing through Haramont, left a copy of the seizure, which fixed the day of sale at six weeks, that is, towards the end of Jan. 1815.

Conscience, at the old man's request, read the paper from beginning to end.

"Well! do you see?" said he, when Conscience was done.

"Yes," said the young man, "it is true that a sale is ordered in six weeks."

"Then in six weeks they will sell?"

"No, grand-papa."

"But the stamped paper says so."

"Bah! Grand-papa, if one believed all the stamped paper said, one would be perpetually afraid of being broken on the wheel."

"Jest away."

"I do not jest," said Conscience gravely.

"You hope the land will not be sold?"

"I am sure it will not be sold."

"How will you help it."

"I will go to Soissons, and employ an advocate, who will make an *incident* . . . . "

"What is that?"

"We will ask a delay of three, and six months, in consideration of the circumstances."

"But that will cost fifty francs, at least."

"It will cost an hundred."

"Where am I get them?"

"I will try to find them."

"And if you do, if the lawyer makes the incident, and obtains a delay of three, of six months, what then?"

"What then?"

"Yes."

"Grand-father, one should not always doubt as you do."

"Why not? I look around me, and see nothing."

"Look, grand-father, at that little piece of blue sky. Do you see nothing there?"

Father Cadet put his hand over his eyes, and looked attentively. He said,

"I see nothing."

"Well, I see God," said Conscience.

"Grand-father," said Madeleine, "confide in this boy. He is, I tell you, a blessing to the house."

XXIV.

In which an incident not produced by the Soissons Lawyer occurs.

————◆————

THE reader, perhaps, is surprised that for some time we have not spoken of Dame Marie and Mariette. Why should we? Their lives were so mingled with those of their neighbors that to tell one was to tell the other. To say that Madeleine wept, is to say that Dame Marie was unhappy, to say that Conscience did not despair, was to say that Mariette hoped.

The young people seemed to love the more as their misery increased. They leaned on each other for mutual support.

It will be remembered that the sale had been fixed for the latter part of December. Conscience waited until the 15th without any apparent anxiety, and on the 16th set out.

He returned the same night, having travelled the fourteen leagues in one day, but as the road was good and frozen hard he returned fresh as if from a mere stroll in the forest.

He was anxiously waited for.

Bernard, who had accompanied him, announced his return by appearing first at the door.

All hurried to meet him.

He approached with a cheerful smile.

"Well!" cried they all, when they were in sound of his voice.

"God has blessed my voyage, I could not pass Longpont, without seeing the old Doctor. You remember him, Mariette."

"Yes and then——"

"I told him the object of my journey: he gave me a letter to one of his friends, a lawyer, who not only undertook the case *gratis*, but promised to make any advance necessary if we take the matter into the *Cour* Royale.

Dame Marie clasped her hands, and Mariette said: "I knew it."

Father Cadet shook his head, for he could not see how Huissiers refused to prosecute, and lawyers acted *gratis*, and even made advances.

Conscience alone, could work such miracles.

Cadet would not believe it at first. He had to do so, soon, for one day on her return from the city, Mariette brought a letter.

It was from M. Grevin, a lawyer at Soissons, and said that a delay until the 15th of March had been granted.

M. Grevin could obtain nothing more. His letter was post paid.

There was a respite for two months. Conscience was right, for they could now trust in God, and even Father Cadet hoped.

The lawyer said that, having obtained the first delay, he would ask for another. True, the Court rarely granted the second delay, but sometimes it did.

Time rolled on, and the ruin of Cadet was become the village theme, and we must say of the three hundred people in Haramont, two hundred were deeply grieved at Cousin Maniquet, whose conduct was much censured.

Cousin Maniquet therefore, instead of repenting, did as base minds are wont to, and instead, by repentance, of regaining his popularity by offering Cadet time, went himself to Soissons, where he employed a lawyer to press matters, who promised that the Court would not grant a second delay.

Thus it is with lawyers and Huissiers, among whom are both good and bad, though unfortunately the latter are the most numerous.

About the 1st of March, a letter from M. Grevin came. He wrote to the family to collect all its resources, and appeal to all its friends. He had seen several of the judges of the court, who had been surrounded by agents of the adverse party, and who fearing they would be accused of protecting a detainer or the property of the nation, would grant no additional delay.

When this sad letter arrived, Cadet, who had begun to feel his hopes revive, was leaning on Madeleine's arm, after a visit to his land.

He found his field looking well, and apparently grateful for the care he took of it. The Kossack's manure had done wonders, and everywhere it looked like a green carpet. It was now high enough to wave in the breeze, half winter, half spring of March.

He would now be very obstinate if he hoped, and tears came into his eyes.

To abandon the field won with such toil, and from which he hoped so much, when the next harvest would have paid what was due; even with the costs! To abandon it because a man, a Christian, would not allow him a little time, which all men except the executioner grants his fellows.

There was now no help.

Bastien, who shared all their counsels, offered to go and cut throats with Maniquet, if the latter would consent.

That was a bad idea, for Maniquet would not consent.

Mariette proposed a new pilgrimage to Liesse, to which Conscience objected, "Our Lady of Liesse knows all things. She is aware of our trouble, and of our faith, and knows our wishes will come to us."

Father Cadet did but sigh, and go from his chamber to his bed, and back again. The old man in his excitement almost forgot the terrible attack of apoplexy, which had stricken him a year before.

The fatal moment drew nearer and nearer, and the danger of the unfortunate family was more imminent. Thus passed the 2nd, 3rd, 4th, 5th, and 6th of March. The sale was to take place on the 15th.

On the morning of the 7th, while the two families breakfasted at the round table, which was poorly enough supplied, Bernard seemed uneasy, and went to the door. Suddenly Bastien rushed in pale, with wild eyes, and dripping with sweat, appeared at the door with a printed paper in his hand.

All arose, for they saw he bore great and important news.

"Landed," said Bastien "landed."

"Who?" asked Conscience.

"He, I tell you, he !"

"But who ?"

"The Emperor."

"The Emperor," cried all.

"The Emperor landed ?" asked Conscience. — "Where ?"

"I do not know. But he has landed."

"You are mad, Bastien."

"Not so. The paper says he has landed."

The news was really so great that all forgot their private sorrows.

Conscience took the paper from Bastien's hand, and read—

"ORDERS.

"On the information of our beloved and faithful Chevalier, the Sieur Dambray, Chancellor of France, commander of our orders, we have ordered and decreed as follows :

"ARTICLE I.

"Napoleon Bonaparte is declared a traitor and rebel, having invaded the Department of Var with an armed force.

"Consequently it is enjoined on all Governors, commanders of armed forces, National Guards, civil authorities, and individuals, to oppose, arrest, and take him at once before a council of war, which having identified, shall subject him to the penalties assigned by law.

"Given at the Chateau of the Tuilleries, March 6, 1815, in the twentieth year of our reign.

"LOUIS."

"What !" said Bastien, "twentieth year of our reign—that cannot be."

"It is printed as is the rest."

"Well, I like that. But what the Journal says

about Louis XVIII. having reigned twenty years, is not true."

"Who knows?" said Conscience, "so many strange things have happened—"

"What! did I serve Louis XVIII.? Did he gain the battles of Austerlitz, Jena and Wagram? Did I lose these fingers and get this cut for Louis XVIII.? and did he give me this cross? This is pleasant, as we said in the Regiment."

Bastien would have been more diffuse, but the village was roused, and hearing the noise on the *Place*, he could not concentrate his energy in Father Cadet's cottage.

He took the paper from Conscience, and left shouting, "Bah! in the twentieth of our reign!"

The inhabitants of the cottage in the first place were stunned, but did not see how it could affect their fate.

It did, however, in the highest degree. The gigantic star had almost invisible planets.

On the 1st of March Napoleon disembarked at the gulf of Juan.

A courier from Marseilles took the news to Lyons on the night of the 4th and 5th.

On the 5th it was sent to Paris by telegraph.

The Monitor of the 6th contained the orders just read.

On the 7th the journals conveyed the news to the provinces.

When the provinces heard of the debarcation Napoleon was at Grenoble. On the 12th he was at Lyons. On the 14th he marched on Paris.

On the 15th, it will be remembered, Cadet's sale was to take place.

On the 12th, however, M. Grevin requested the Court in consideration of the circumstances, to postpone the sale. As the circumstances were grave, the sale was postponed until the 15th of June following.

This was the incident which prevented Cadet's land from being sold March 15.

M. Grevin had not foreseen, but took advantage of this incident.

XXV.

Peus ex Machina.

———

AT eight o'clock on the evening of the 20th of March, Napoleon entered the Tuilleries.

He set to work at once to organize every thing. Cambaceres was made Minister of Justice, the Duke of Vicenza appointed to Foreign Affairs, Davoust to War, the Duke of Gaeta to Finance, Decres to the Navy, Fouche to Police, and Carnot to the Interior.

On the 26th of March all the *corps* of the Empire were convoked to express to Napoleon the wishes of France.

On the 27th one might have fancied the Bourbons had never existed.

"Mon Dieu!" said Bastien, "I wonder if he yet dates his decrees 'in the twentieth year of our reign.'"

In all this Father Cadet had seen but one thing; that the nobles and priests were not to be feared, that his land had recovered its original value, and that he might be able to borrow on it not only the eight hundred livres he owed Cousin Maniquet, but the three or four hundred francs costs for the two orders of sale, delays, &c.

Consequently he had himself placed again on Pierrot, and as he was now better, accompanied by Mariette alone, early in April he went to the house of M. Niguet on the Soissons road in Villers-Cotterets.

He came to ask if a loan was not more feasible under the Empire than under the Monarchy.

M. Niguet, none knew why, was a great royalist, and received his old client very coldly, telling him the Government of July 20 had no stability, and that he knew certainly that the allies were eagerly arming, and that the return on which Cadet relied was but the prelude of a second invasion.

Father Cadet returned to Haramont more downcast than ever. M. Niguet was his oracle, not only in law, but in politics.

What most terrified Cadet was, that Maniquet, who like Niguet, had doubtless his agents abroad, telling him what the allied sovereigns intended to do, was not at all uneasy, and went about rubbing his hands, and saying,

" Ah ! we will see what incident M. Grevin will raise now.'

About the beginning of May, M. Grevin wrote a letter to Cadet, advising him to take advantage of the circumstances and collect all his resources, as there was no means of preventing or even delaying the sale any longer.

Time rolled by with a rapidity which events seemed to double. All Napoleon's efforts to obtain peace failed. He had written a circular to the *kings his brothers*, to which some had replied *No*, and others had made no answer.

He had announced the speedy arrival of the Empress

and the King of Rome, but at the end of May they had not come.

His circular had found the kings his brothers busy with important matters.

They were dividing Europe at the Congress of Vienna.

There was at the capital of Austria a great drawing of blanks, a public adjudication of souls.

Alexander the Lion first put forth his paw, and took the Grand-Dutchy of Warsaw.

The Emperor Francis, who had a great moral advantage over other sovereigns, in having dethroned his daughter and grand-son, claimed Italy as it was before the treaty of Campio Formio. He wished to collect again what his two-headed eagle had let fall after the various treaties of Luneville, Presbourg and Vienna.

Prussia devoured parts of Saxony, Poland, Westphalia and Franconia, and unrolled itself like a huge snake, with its tail on the Memel and its head at Thronville on the Rhine.

The Statholder of Holland, elevated to the grade of king, asked that the addition to his hereditary states of Belgium, Liege, and Luxembourg might be confirmed.

The King of Sardinia asked that Genoa might be added to his continental states, from which he had been absent fifteen years.

Each great power, like the marble lions sculptors used to put at the gates of gardens, wished to keep some little kingdom like a ball under its claw. Russia wanted Poland, Prussia Saxony, Austria Piedmont, Spain Portugal, and England, which had paid the expense of five coalitions, wanted two kingdoms, Holland and Hanover, instead of one.

It will be seen that these details kept Napoleon's

brothers, the kings, too busy for them to be able to reply to him.

He had then to appeal to the diplomacy of the cannon, which we must after all say, the Conqueror of the Pyramids and of Marengo and Austerlitz was most familiar with.

This diplomacy frightened Madeleine very much, for she was afraid her son would be called out again; the sight of Conscience, however, was yet very weak.

Catharine was equally afraid on Bastien's account. Bastien had twice returned from that fine thing called war, once minus a portion of his hand, and a second time, plus two sabre cuts. She was afraid that the third time he would not come back at all.

They were not thought of, for without them, the Emperor had collected an army of one hundred and eighty thousand men.

Having long hesitated whether with this force he would await the coalition in France, or venture to march against it, he determined to bear the war into Belgium, to surprise the enemy by one of those bold movements he only had the secret of. Had God seconded him, he would have crushed and annihilated Wellington and Blucher when they thought him *hors de combat.*

Early in June, thirty or forty thousand men passed by Villers-Cotterets to Soissons, Laon and to Mezieres. The heart of Bastien bounded with delight at the sound of the trumpets and drums and the cries of *Vive l'Empereur.*

Bastien would have been happy during the first fortnight of June, had not the recollection of Conscience distressed him, and if he had not known that on the 15th of the month which presented to him so magnificent a spectacle, a whole family would be ruined.

17

He shook his head, knit his brows, and said in a tone half of sorrow, half anger,

" Name of names."

But all Bastien's oaths brought no remedy. On the 8th of June, the last troops passed, and there being nothing to see at Villers-Cotterets, Bastien returned to Haramont.

The whole village pitied Cadet, but either from self-ishness or inability, no one prepared to aid him. We know that unaided, the old man could not but be ruined.

He went from his bed to his door, and laid down only when his strength was exhausted. This excitement, however, did him much good, and made him use the paralyzed leg almost as well as the other, and when he thought of Cousin Maniquet, he used the left arm almost as well as the right.

He never, however, went to his land.

Instead of clinging together, the women avoided each other, for they could exchange no consolation. Sometimes, they met unintentionally at church, whither each had gone to utter the same prayer.

Even Conscience was less calm. It was in vain he said to Mariette, " Be easy, for nothing shall separate us."

She heard this promise with all the sympathies of her soul, but wept as she said,

"Then you mean, Conscience, that nothing shall separate us."

Conscience had been to see Mathieu, who had discharged his first ploughman, to whom he gave five hundred francs a year and his board, and asked employment in his place.

Mathieu engaged him at once, and said if Mariette

wished employment as dairy-maid, she too would be employed, and could sell the milk at the city.

Mathieu knew that by confiding this to Mariette every drop would be sold, Mariette would make one hundred and fifty francs a year, and would also like Conscience be fed.

This double promise was a great security for the future, and Conscience on his return to the cottage communicated it to the rest of the family. Lodged and fed at the farm, Conscience and Mariette, by keeping two hundred and fifty francs for themselves, could put four hundred in the common chest of the two families, that is, enough to feed the two families.

This, though, far from consoling Father Cadet, increased his sadness.

"Ah!" murmured he, "to plough the land of others instead of one's own, is hard."

To Conscience it presented one advantage. It hastened his marriage with Mariette, for it was almost impossible for them to leave home for Mathieu's house without being married.

It was determined then to accept Mathieu's offer, and to publish at once the banns of Conscience and Mariette.

This being resolved on, the two young people determined on no longer delay. On the 12th of June Conscience and Mariette went together to register their names at the Maire's of Villers-Cotterets, the principal place of their canton.

God granted them at least the consolation of being unhappy together. They were received with great sympathy, and all were ready to pity them, to pity Father Cadet, and to throw a stone at Maniquet.

Sympathy however was not strong enough to induce

any one to offer them the twelve or fourteen hundred francs they needed.

It happened that at nine o'clock A. M., Conscience and Mariette were waiting for the Maire's to open— ten was the hour, an important piece of intelligence, substituted curiosity for the sympathy they excited.

The carrier was distributing the newspapers, in the official part of which was read :

" JUNE 11.—His Majesty the Emperor will leave Paris for the army at nine to-morrow.   He will pass by Soissons, Laon, and by Mezieres."

He must then go through Villers-Cotterets.

He was to leave on the 12th, for the paper which said " to-morrow " was dated on the 11th of June.   If he set out at nine, he would pass Villers-Cotterets at noon.

The passage of Napoleon was a sufficiently great event to make the people of Villers-Cotterets forget the misfortunes of Cadet, and the sympathy excited by the inauspicious marriage of Conscience and Mariette.

All the people therefore went into the streets, running in groups hither and thither.

Conscience and Mariette had not been insensible to this news, and the latter had asked Conscience to remain at Villers-Cotterets, to enable her to see the man of whom from him and Bastien she had heard so much.

Conscience consented, and they resolved after having made the double declaration at the Mairie and at the church, to wait at the post-house, where the Imperial cortege must stop.

At noon they did so.   The rumor of the Emperor's coming had spread to the neighboring village, and all hurried to see the man of destiny.

About one, Bastien came, having heard the news

twenty minutes before. He took five minutes to put
on his uniform and sabre, and came a league in fifteen
minutes.

"Name of names!" said he, "I am in time."

Looking around, he said, "Ah, Conscience, I hoped
to find you and Mariette here."

"Did you look for us?—did you wish to see us?"

"Yes."

"Why?"

"You will know. I have my ideas—"

"Are they good?"

"Ah! if they succeed, it will be pleasant, as we said at
the Regiment. But ch. I hear wheels. It may be
the Little Corporal."

"But," said a citizen, "he cannot be here so soon."

"Eighteen leagues at four leagues and a half an
hour. He left at nine, and it has struck one. He cannot be far. Eh, postillion?"

He spoke to one of twenty or thirty postillions, who,
decked with tri-colored ribands, awaited Napoleon.

"Certainly. He left Paris at nine, and cannot be
far from Vauciennes now."

"Oh," said Bastien.

All conversation stopped. Every eye and ear was
on the alert, and the sound of wheels was heard.

Then arose in the distance, the cry "*Vive l'Empereur.*"

Just then, as if under the influence of electricity, the
crowd trembled, and the cry "Vive l'Empereur" arose
from every heart. Napoleon was, at this time the impersonation of nationality, for in their brief passage, the
Bourbons had seemed anything else.

Amid all this the carriages drew near.

All at once the shouts were reiterated, mingled with "there! there!"

The crowd opened, and three carriages drawn by horses white with foam, and driven by postillions covered with dust, dashed down the streets of Soissons.

The first was drawn by six horses, and held three persons; two on the back, and one on the front seat.

On the back seat were Napoleon, and Jerome on his left hand.

The other occupant was General Letort.

The cries of " *Vive l'Empereur*" were perfectly phrenetic.

The Emperor lifted up his head, bowed with thought, and asked:

"Where are we?"

A firm voice replied, "At Villers-Cotterets, my Emperor."

Napoleon looked kindly at the speaker, who was Bastien.

Two paces from the carriage door, and exactly opposite it, stood the Hussar, erect and motionless, with one hand on his colbach, and with the little finger of the other on the seam of his pantaloons.

The Emperor saw the cross on his uniform, the sabre cuts on his face, and his mutilated hand.

" Ah! one of my *braves?*"

" Who dates from Marengo, sire."

" And the sabre cut?"

" From Austerlitz."

" And the cross?"

" From Wagram, sire."

" Come hither."

" I am here, sire."

" Can I do any thing for you?"

"Thanks, your Majesty. I ask only your esteem, but if you would do something for my comrade I would thank you."

"Where is he?"

"There. Conscience, do you not hear His Majesty call you?"

The Emperor had not done so, and Conscience stood motionless.

"Come hither," said the Emperor.

Conscience drew near, and Mariette clinging to him like the ivy to the oak, hung panting on his arm.

"Well!" said the Emperor, "what do you ask for your comrade?"

"Sire, this fellow, Conscience, here, goes into fire coolly as his dog does into his water. You can see his dog there behind him. He too, was a Hussar, but belonged to those with four wheels; so that one day, it was at Laon, Sire, you may remember it, for you and I were both there, his caisson blew up. Fortunately, it was a trifle, for he was only blind six months, and now is delighted to see you. But that is not it."

"Well, what is it then?" said the Emperor with the brusquerie, and good nature which made him the idol of his soldiers. "Go on; I am in haste."

"The Kossacks trampled on Father Cadet's fields to such a purpose, that last year they produced nothing—and the old man could not pay eight hundred francs, he owed an old usurer named Maniquet, who had a mortgage on his land, which the men with spectacles fixed so that all will be sold in three days, and the family, with Mariette, there, is she not pretty, my Emperor? are obliged to go as hirelings to old Mathieu, a very good man, by-the-by. But as Father Cadet says, 'It is hard to plough another man's land, instead of one's own.' "

" And what does this lad want ?"

" Oh ! in three days he will want a large sum, fifteen hundred francs at least."

" Jerome," said the Emperor, smiling, " where is the purse ?"

" Sire," said the ex-king of Wesphalia, " under the seat, but I must have a few hundred Napoleons in my travelling-desk."

" Give them to me."

Jerome poured into the Emperor's hands all the gold he had.

" Come hither my lass," said the Emperor, " and hold out your apron."

Mariette obeyed in silence. Her bosom, however, panted, and her eyes were filled with tears.

The Emperor let the golden shower fall into her apron.

Turning to Conscience, and fixing his eagle eye on him, he said :

" Did I not tell you, when we met again to ask me for something ?"

" Yes, Sire. Your Majesty bade me ask for the cross."

" Why did you not ? It is well my memory is better than yours."

Taking off the cross, which he was in the habit of fastening to his coat by a pin, that when the opportunity afforded, he might give it away, he presented it to Conscience, who received it with a cry of joy, and first kised the Imperial hand, and then the cross.

" Your name is Conscience, is it not ?"

" Yes Sire."

"Letort, write it in your *agenda*. You, my man," said he to Bastien, "I thank. Having served me as you have in war, you cannot serve me better in peace. Let us hurry, Jerome. We have lost a quarter of an hour."

"Not so, Sire," said the King of Westphalia. "In that quarter of an hour you have made three people happy."

"True. Adieu my friends. Pray for me, and for France."

His head fell again on his chest.

Cries of "Vive l'Empereur" arose from every lip, and the carriage was dragged by six horses rapidly away, making sparks fly from the pavements. Horses, coaches, drivers, all vanished like a vision full of light, which appeared for an instant, but impressed itself forever in the mind of those who had seen it.

Alas, all this hurried to Waterloo, that is, to ruin.

17*

XXVI.

Conclusion.

CONSCIENCE stood motionless, with his cross in his hand, and Mariette with the gold in her apron. Bastien danced and tore his hair with joy.

"Name of names," said the Hussar, "this is a pleasure, as we said in the Regiment."

The whole population saw this scene, some laughing, some weeping.

Conscience felt a hand on his shoulder. Startled, as if from a dream, he looked around, and saw the Huissier Demay, who had acted so kindly about Cadet, and who had given him such good advice.

"Come," said he, "lose no time. Since God has worked a miracle, let us use it. There are but three days before the sale, and we must make an offer to Maniquet. Give me twelve hundred francs, and I will answer for everything, interest and capital. Hurry with the good news to Father Cadet."

"Yes, yes, but Bastien first. Where are you, Bastien?"

He reached forth his hands, like a drunken man, scarce able to stand.

"Here I am," said the Hussar, throwing himself on his friend's bosom.

They clung together.

Then Mariette came and said, "And Bastien, will you not kiss me?"

"What, not do so when you ask me? I will do it twice."

He gave the young girl a burning sonorous kiss on each cheek.

This first expansion of joy having been indulged in, they thought of M. Demay's proposition.

They went into the post-house, and counted out sixty Napoleons to the Huissier, who had taken charge of the arrangement. There yet remained two hundred and fifty Napoleons or five thousand francs.

This was a fortune.

"Come," said Bastien, "let us go to Haramont, at a gallop. There are people there who weep, while we are rejoicing."

"Dear Bastien thinks of all," said Conscience.

"Yes," said Mariette. "He is so kind, that I intend to ask a favor of him."

"Of me? Mariette, I promise to grant it before you ask. Name of names! it will be pleasant, as we said in the Regiment."

"Very well—I will hold you to your word, Bastien," said Mariette. "Now for Haramont, for Haramont."

They hurried joyfully through the park, followed by Bastien, who shouted after them, "Wait, wait; you forget me."

Bastien had come in a quarter of an hour, but in consequence of waiting for Mariette, was twenty minutes in returning to Haramont.

When they saw the cottages, Mariette paused, stifled with emotion.

She wished to give Conscience the gold.

"You," said Conscience, "are the angel of the house and should bear the good tidings."

"Thanks," said Mariette.

They looked around them, but Bastien had disappeared. The young man, under a rough exterior, hid much delicacy, and did not wish to be present when Conscience and Mariette reached the cottage. It would look like claiming thanks.

They smiled, and each murmured,

"Kind Bastien."

Bernard, less delicate than Bastien, had preceded them, and by his joyous bearing, seemingly proclaimed himself the messenger of good news.

This joy of Bernard, whose intelligence was well known, caused some surprise in the house. Madeleine closed the book of prayers, from which she was reading to Father Cadet, who, to avoid talking, pretended to sleep, and who opened his eyes with amazement at the joyous group which followed Bernard.

Conscience threw his arms around his mother's neck. Mariette went to the old man.

"Hold out your hands, grandfather," said she.

"Why," said the old man incredulously, and morosely.

"Hold them out."

Father Cadet, like a pouting child obeyed.

Mariette emptied a handful of gold into Cadet's two hands. The old fellow uttered a cry of joy.

Then came a second, and a third handful.

All this was to the great surprise of Madeleine, who looked on, and of Dame Marie, who seemed stupified at the sound of this gold, which had attracted her from her cottage to the door.

"But," said the old man, "who gave you this gold? Can it be that I dream?"

"No, grandfather, no. It is real gold—hear it ring."

"But who gave it you?"

"Ask Conscience." She wished to leave him something to say.

"The Emperor, grandfather. The Emperor himself."

"The Emperor!" exclaimed all.

"And this cross which he took from his breast, and which I now can wear on mine."

"Ah!" said Cadet. "I am dizzy."

"Grandfather."

"Ah, there is no danger, for now it is produced by joy. We shall be able to pay Cousin Maniquet."

"He is paid."

"But the land?"

"Will not be sold,"

"This money?"

"Is yours to buy more, and to secure yourself a calm old age."

The old man clasped the gold towards his bosom and advanced to place it in his casket, but he paused, and shook his head, saying:

"No. This gold is your portion, and the land is your inheritance. They say, that man makes the land, but it is not so. 'Land makes the man.' But," added Cadet, "you must let me see it every day, and when I cannot walk thither, you must carry me, my children."

"Yes, grandfather," said at once Conscience and Mariette.

Then kneeling they said,

"Bless your children, for henceforth they are bound forever; betrothed in sorrow they will marry in joy."

Cadet lifted up both hands, the left as well as the right, and placed the latter on the head of Conscience, and the first on that of Mariette.

"Name of names," said Bastien, who just then came in. "How you bless, Father Cadet. It makes water come into one's mouth."

"Good day, M. Bastien, *and company*," said the old man, nodding to the Hussar. "Ah, you see us very happy."

"And to Bastien we owe all."

"How so," said the old man.

While Consscience told the story, Mariette took Bastien's arm.

When Conscience had done looking at Bastien in a supplicating way, Mariette said,

"Bastien, you remember, I have a favor to ask."

"What is it," said Bastien, wiping the tears from his eyes.

"Bastien," said Mariette, in her softest voice, and with her sweetest smile, "will you not marry Catharine?"

"Bastien evidently did not expect this; he stared, bit his moustache, reflected, and seemed to make up his mind.

"Well, Mlle. Mariette, as it will please you, I will consent to do so."

"Oh," said Mariette, delighted.

"On one condition—that you put on the wreath of orange flowers."

"I will, Bastien, but I do not understand . . ."

"Ah! then I will tell you—but perhaps I had best not—when, though, you shall have put on her wreath, if there be one joker in the village, who dares to make an allusion to the past, thousand names of names, it will be pleasant, as we said in the Regiment . . ."

That evening, Father Cadet went alone to visit his field, and brought back a head of wheat, which had seventy grains.

He found one yet more heavily laden, but as on his return, he met Cousin Maniquet, and told him the money was now being paid to M. Niguet, and gave him the second sheaf as a token of what the yield would be.

Exactly one month after, two couples were married at the church of Haramont—Conscience and Mariette, and Bastien and Catharine.

Madeleine insisted on the mass being said at the altar, above which hung the picture of Christ calling little children to him.

The whole village witnessed the ceremony, and took the brides and grooms to Cadet's cottage, where the wedding-feast was served. Tardif, Pierrot and the black cow had their racks full of fresh grass, and Bernard the fragments from the table.

When they came from the church, and were passing the threshold of the cottage, Conscience smiled, and placed his hand on his grandfather's shoulder, and in a gentle, but somewhat inspired voice, said,

"You see, grandfather that in that far off corner of

the sky, in which you saw nothing, there was something.''

"You are right, my son," said Father Cadet; "God was there.''

THE END.